Way Past Cool

Jess Mowry

Blue Works
Port Orchard + Seattle + Tahuya

Way Past Cool
copyright 1992, 2005, 2006 by Jess Mowry
published by Blue Works

ISBN 1-59092-172-0
9 8 7 6 5 4 3 2
First trade edition April 2007

Design by Buster Blue of Blue Artisans Design.
Cover image by Todd Marna.
Blue Card™ concept by Grace M. Garcia.
Ratings Block™ concept by Grace M. Garcia.

For information about reprint or other subsidiary rights, please contact Mari Garcia at mgarcia@windstormcreative.com.

Blue Works is an imprint of Windstorm Creative, a multi-division, international organization involved in publishing books in all genres, including electronic publications; producing games, toys, videos and audio cassettes as well as producing theatre, film and visual arts events. The wind with the gear center was designed by Buster Blue or Blue Artisans Design and is a trademark of Blue Works.

Blue Works
c/o Windstorm Creative
7419 Ebbert Dr SE
Port Orchard, WA 98367
www.windstormcreative.com
360-769-7174 ph

Blue Works is a member of the Orchard Creative Group, Ltd.

Library of Congress Cataloging in Publication Data available.

To Jeff
for believing in the heart thing.

Thank you to everyone at Windstorm Creative
for making this edition of *Way Past Cool* possible.

Way Past Cool

Jess Mowry

"Gordon! GUN!" screamed Curtis, diving off his skateboard onto trash-covered concrete.

Gordon dove from his board too, all one-hundred-eighty pounds rolling and skidding then scrambling warp-seven behind a dumpster as a full-auto fired from a battered black van. Velcro ripped and his backpack burst open. Books and a binder tumbled out. Another gun joined the first, a rhythmic steely stutter of Uzis in chorus. Bullets pocked brick, sending chips whizzing and spattering to a whine of ricochets that sounded just like the movies. The dumpster rang dully as silver dents stitched its rusty sides.

Gordon was a born leader, first to risk his butt, with a natural balance of brains and balls tempered by a healthy helping of fear. As with all good leaders, his decisions came fast under fire; if they happened to be the right ones, so much the better. But there were times when a gang leader had to do stupid things—like jumping to his feet and offering his head and shoulders as an easy target while he cupped his hands to his mouth and bawled, "DOWN, suckers!"

The warning wasn't needed: the other boys had already

scattered among garbage cans, their boards abandoned and darting away as if seeking cover too. Gordon's stupidity would be remembered later as cool, though he never considered that. In another sort of war he might have won a medal.

The auto-fire cut off: thirty-two-round magazines emptied fast at 550 rounds per minute, as most kids in West Oakland knew. It was as if somebody had switched on silence. Gordon jerked the old .22 pistol from the back of his jeans and got off three quick shots in the van's general direction before the worn-out little gun jammed. Its popping sounded weak and wimpy after the 9mm Uzi snarls.

But the van peeled away, rubber screeching and blue smoke blasting from rusty chrome side pipes. Gordon cursed and beat the gun's butt on the dumpster lid. It fired again, once, defiant now in the sudden morning stillness. Brick dust puffed from a building across the street, and a window nearby slammed shut. The van's engine roar faded up the block. Tires squealed as the van got sideways around the corner.

"Motherfuckin piece of SHIT!" raged Gordon. He almost whacked the gun again, but caught himself in time and looked around instead while wiping a skinned and bloody elbow on his jeans. "Yo! Anybody hit?"

Four heads poked up from behind a ragged row of garbage cans: Ric and Rac, the twins, identically flat-topped and wide-eyed, Curtis with his long, ratty dreadlocks, and Lyon's fluffy bush, like an Afro gone wild.

"Hey!" squeaked Curtis, his expression amazed. "I got myself shot in the back!"

Beside him, Lyon lifted Curtis' tattered T-shirt, plain and faded black like the other boys'. . . gang colors. "Yeah? Well, you for sure be takin it cool, man. Let's check it out."

Curtis squirmed, trying to look over his shoulder. "Well, how the fuck I sposed to take it?"

The twins squeezed close too, their mouths open in duplicate wonder and tawny eyes bright with curiosity.

Gordon walked over, carrying the gun muzzle-down.

Lyon glanced at the fat boy over Curtis' head. "That thing gonna go off again, Gordon?"

Gordon spat on the garbage-slimed concrete, holding the pistol like a snapping rat by its tail. "Now how the fuck I know, man? Piece of shit jam up just when you needin it, an then go off when you don't! How many goddamn times I say we gotta save back for some kinda better gun?"

He scowled at the other boys, and pointed. "An how many motherfuckin times I gotta tell you dudes *not* to hide a'hind stupid ole garbage cans in a firefight?" He aimed a finger at one can bleeding yellow goo. "Dumpster steel mostly stop bullets. *Them* don't!" His eyes, obsidian hard in a coffee-colored face, softened slightly and his voice gentled down. "So, how Curtis?"

Lyon dabbed at Curtis' shoulder blade with the tail of his own tee. "Stop that silly wigglin, sucker!" Spitting on his fingers, Lyon wiped more blood. The scent of it was coppery, like new pennies. Finally, he smiled and patted Curtis' arm. "It be only a cut. Like from a chunk of flyin brick or somethin. Nowhere near his heart. That be all what matter."

Curtis tried to reach around to his back, but couldn't. "Well, it for sure *feel* like I been shotted!"

Gordon wedged his bulk between the cans and peered at the wet ruby slice across the smaller boy's honey-bronze skin. He snorted. "Shit. Don't signify nuthin, man. You ever get yourself shot for real, you fuckin well know it! We all check out how way past cool you handle it, then!"

The twins exchanged identical glances and snickered in stereo. "Best believe, sucker!" said Ric. "Gordy been shot! He give it a name! Word, you, Curtis!"

"Yeah!" giggled Rac. "In the butt, he shot! Yo, Gordy, show us again!"

Lyon had a funny V-shaped smile that looked mostly smart-ass even when it wasn't. "Bein shot sposed to mean you way past bad." He turned his smile on Gordon. "Course, gettin butt-shot just don't tell the same, huh?"

Gordon chewed his lip a moment, then growled. "Pend a lot on whose butt you talkin, don't it?" He jabbed Rac in the chest with a finger. "An stop callin me Gordy, goddamnit!" Squatting with a grunt, he started picking up his garbage-stained papers.

"Well," said Ric, "I get myself shot, I want it be in the arm, Gor-DEN!"

"Word!" agreed Rac. "Wear a tank top all the time. Look way past cool, believe!"

Gordon spat again, barely missing Rac's Nikes. "Yo, raisin-brain! Gettin shot more like to make you way past DEAD! Ever hear of somebody actual shot in the arm real-time? That ain't nuthin but TV dogshit, sucker!" He glared at the gun, then looked up at Lyon. "I feel like dustin this goddamn thing, man. Prob'ly end by killin one of us someday stead of doin any good."

"So?" asked Ric. "What you spect for twenty dollars, dude?"

"Word!" added Rac. "Kmart blue-light-special kinda gun, all that is! Deek even say."

Gordon's nostrils suddenly flared. "Deek, huh? Listen up, suckers! Deek talk a fly out shit, he wanna! Only a motherfuckin fool figure he gots somethin to say worth the ghost of a dog! Next time he come by curb-preachin you, tell him to fuck off!"

"Well," said Rac, "spose he get pissed an tell his bodyguard to shoot me?"

Lyon grinned. "Then ask him if he do you in the arm."

"Just shut up, Ric," said Gordon. "For once."

"I'm Rac," said Rac. "He's Ric."

Gordon sighed. "Whatever." He stood and shoved the pistol at Lyon. "Here, man, see if you can fix this piece of shit again."

Lyon looked closely at the gun. "Mmm. I see what happen. Rimfire bullets be most like to jam. That cause the primer stuff be in the rim, an with cheapo bullets like these it don't all the time go clear around. Then the fire pin hit a empty spot an you end up with jack."

"Or a dirt nap," growled Gordon. "Shit! I don't wanna hear all that stuff, man! Like we gonna be pop-quizzed on gun fixin in school or somethin! It the onliest goddamn gun we got, an the onliest goddamn gun we 'ford right now, so's just make it shoot again an stop rattlin my goddamn chain, huh!"

Gordon heaved another sigh and stared around the alley mouth at the wreckage; scattered skateboards, books and binders, and more sheets of somebody's homework fluttering in the gentle morning breeze. He scowled when he recognized them as his own. "Shit an goddamnit to hell! Ain't this a motherfuckin BITCH!"

Lyon watched as Gordon snatched up the papers and tried to wipe them clean, then gave up and stuffed them into his pack. "Yo, Gordon, tell the teacher you got em all dirty gettin drive-byed."

"Too fuckin funny, man! Ain't one of them stupid teachers gotta live around here. Not know from nuthin what is. Shit, this my goddamn English story too. . . how I gonna spend my motherfuckin summer vacation! Been bustin my goddamn ass over it all cocksuckin week, an now ole Crabzilla gonna kill me for sure!" Gordon scowled at the twins' grins. "You two! Get your asses busy pickin up your own goddamn shit! We gonna be late an get tardies out the wazoo!"

Ric and Rac moved as one. They were wiry, hard-muscled, Hershey-brown boys of thirteen, wearing tight black tees faded to gray, ragged 501s with ripped knees, and big battered Nikes. Their eager, snub-nosed faces made them look like African imps. Their mother had named them from some old book about kids who made fools out of grownups. A desperate teacher had once pleaded with them to dress differently so she could tell them apart. They'd shown up next day with their initials Magic Markered on the front of their shirts.

Curtis was still trying to touch his own back. He was the smallest of the gang, twelve and childlike, with the prominent tummy and smooth-lined body of a little boy. A lot of kids figured him for the mascot. His dad was white, and Curtis could gleam like polished bronze when clean. His parents were trying to save enough money to move to Jamaica someday.

Lyon laid the gun on a dumpster lid and wiped Curtis' cut a final time, then dangled his long bloody fingers in Curtis' face. Curtis winced. Lyon grinned. Everything about Lyon was long; narrow, lean-jawed face with high cheekbones, and tall slender body more delicate than skinny. His teeth looked too large for his mouth. His ebony eyes were tilted up at the corners and, like his V smile, always seemed a little sly. He had a funny loose way of holding or moving his hands that made them look like paws. He read books because he wanted to, and could fascinate or terrify with magic tricks or spooky stories. Lyon appeared fragile but most kids left him be.

Lyon licked his fingers. "Mmm. Way cool blood, homey. Maybe I take me some more. Tonight. When the moon be full."

Curtis went very still. His voice broke. "Not funny! Maaaan, don't be sayin them kinda things!"

Rac snickered. "Yo! That time of month already, Lyon-o? Hey, what you call a used Kotex?"

"Vampire tea bag!" answered Ric.

Curtis glared. "Eat shit an die, suckers! So there!"

"You two your very own HBO, ain't ya?" said Lyon.

"Everybody just shut the fuck up!" roared Gordon. "Goddamn honky show here!"

"Donkey show," said Lyon.

"Whatever." Gordon tugged at his pack straps, then faced Curtis. "An you stop actin like a goddamn puss! Spose you wanna go to 'mergency, now?"

Curtis considered that.

"Way past fun," Lyon told him. "Get to sit on your butt an wait for hours, aside all kinda cool people what been shot an stabbed, ODin an pukin all over the place. Yo, they prob'ly give you stitches. Leave a hot scar. Like Frankenstein."

"Um... naw, I don't wanna," murmured Curtis.

Lyon's eyes lost some of their slyness. "Well, it gonna be bleedin some, open like that. Better take off your shirt so's it don't stick."

Gordon nodded. "Good idea." He peered at the cheap digital watch on his wrist. "Shit! Now we for sure late!" He studied the watch, frowning and flicking it with a finger. "Shit, I think it busted."

"Yo," said Ric. "Hold it up to your ear, man."

"To check if it still tickin," added Rac.

Gordon did, and the twins burst into laughter. Gordon, a month shy of fourteen, was the oldest. He was a big, heavy-breasted boy with a belly that hung over his jeans and bobbed whenever he moved. For all his jiggly softness there was muscle buried beneath the fat, like a small tank wrapped in foam rubber. His T-shirts never covered his middle, and his jeans sagged so low that his bullet scar usually showed. His hair was a natural bush, and his flat-nosed, heavy-lipped face made him look dense unless you paid attention to his eyes. He kicked the squatting Ric in the butt with the toe of his ancient Airwalk, sending both brothers sprawling. "Shove it in *your* ear, asshole! There! Now you know what time it is, fool!"

"Well," said Curtis, coming out from behind the cans and stripping off his shirt. "Don't feel up for sittin in class bleedin all goddamn day. Mom an Dad both at work. Maybe I just bail myself on home an watch TV or somethin."

The twins got up and examined his back again. "Um, yo," asked Rac. "What that shiny white shit way down inside there?"

"Bone!" said Lyon, slapping Rac's hand away. "An keep your goddamn dirty finger outa it!"

"Mondo gross!" said Ric. He shook a finger at his brother. "Can't touch that!"

Curtis turned to Lyon, his eyes widening. "No shit? You mean my skelenton showin?"

Lyon laid a paw on his shoulder. "It be okay, man. Leave a cool scar for later on. Better'n just a pussy ole shot in the arm, any day."

Curtis looked thoughtful, then puffed his little chest almost as far out as his tummy and made a face at the twins. He strutted to the alley mouth and peered cautiously up the deserted street. "Wonder if them motherfuckin gang-bangers still motorin round here?"

Lyon glided up beside him and gazed toward the corner where the van had gone. Oily smoke mixed with streamers of gray-white gunpowder still drifted in the cool air. The sun was spilling over the roofline and down the buildings, turning grimy orange brick into gold. The faint breeze was still stirring in from the Bay, as yet untainted by garbage stink and exhaust fumes, smelling of salt and hinting of faraway places. Lyon's long delicate hand clasped Curtis' shoulder again. "I come home with ya, homey. Patch you up good as new. Gots any peroxide at your place?"

"Nuh-uh. Gots Bactine, I think."

"That do. Keep them ole maggots from hatchin." Lyon flipped a finger at the empty street, then glanced at the rusty little .22 he'd brought with him. "Showtimes! There be them big dudes with their full-auto Uzis, an go bailin warp-seven cause Gordy gots the balls to shoot back with *this!*"

Ric moved close to Gordon. "Yo! Gordy gots 'dustrial strength balls! Word!"

Rac stepped to Gordon's other side. "Believe! That why he lead!"

Gordon shrugged. "Don't call me Gordy." He jerked his jeans up a little and eyed his watch again with a frown. "Well, I don't figure it cool for us to scatter right now. Three blocks back to Curtis' place, or bout the same to school. We better decide which one we goin for, an keep together. Yo, Lyon! Maybe you should oughta fix that gun right now, man. Ain't a good idea to be skatin round with a bullet stuck in the chamber." He stared at his watch once more, then whacked it.

"So, what in hell you spect for two ninety-eight at Kmart, man?" asked Ric. "A goddamn Seiko or somethin?"

Rac poked his brother. "Shut up, doofus! His mom give him that for his goddamn birthday! It a *heart thing* like Lyon always talkin bout. Yo, sucker, what *your* mom ever give you from the heart?"

Ric snickered. "YOU, sucker! I the first, 'member?"

"BFD! By one stupid little minute! So, shoot bullets through me, why don't ya!"

Lyon fingered the gun. "Well, what I sposed to fix this with, my dick? I need me somethin like a screwdriver for poppin out the bullet."

Gordon tore the watch from his wrist and flung it into a

garbage can. "Mmm, s'prised you can't magic it fixed, man." He pulled a switchblade from his pocket and thumbed the button. Nothing happened. "Shit!" Gordon pried it open with his fingernail. "Try this. An please don't bust it."

Handing the knife to Lyon, he dropped his hands to the roll of fat where another boy's hips would have been and scanned the street. "Shit, we so goddamn late now them school doors is prob'ly locked! Best we all just bail on back to Curtis' place an hang."

Curtis looked happy, until the twins faced him and demanded, "Yo! Gots any food?"

"Um, well, it gettin kinda close to the end of the month. Gots bread... an this big new bottle of ketchup."

The twins made identical faces and turned on Gordon. "Yo! We don't score school lunch... " Ric began.

"We don't get nuthin all goddamn day!" Rac finished.

Gordon sighed once more. "I gots enough food for everybody. Mom workin steady again. Best we go my place, stead of Curtis'... I spose."

"Better," said Rac.

"Word," added Ric. "You ain't sposed to leave your dudes go hungry."

Rac nodded. "Word up! By rules!"

Muscle hardened somewhere in Gordon's chest. He clenched big fists. "Shut up! Don't need me no 'minders bout the rules from you two suckers! Curtis! Quit fuckin with your goddamn back! Get busy an snag all our boards fore some car come by an run 'em into street pizza! Yo, Lyon! Get that gun fixed so's we can bail the hell outa here!"

Gordon faced the street again. His forehead creased. "Goddamn if that dint look like the selfsame ole van what done a drive-by on us a couple days ago." He glanced at Lyon. "Same sorta big dudes. . . least sixteen. But why in hell they tryin to do us?"

Lyon returned to the nearest dumpster and laid the gun on the lid. He eyed it a moment, then poked the knife point into the ejection port. "They pass some sorta new law say you gotta have a reason for shootin black kids?"

Curtis returned with his arms full of boards and started standing them upright against the dumpster. "Oughta be a rule bout it, anyways."

"Word!" said Ric. "Give it a name!"

"Straight up!" added Rac. "Law say black kids eat shit an die!"

Gordon snorted. "Yeah, next you be tellin me there salt in the goddamn sea! Swear you two gots one little brain between ya, an trade it off." He ran a finger across Curtis' back, then drew bloody zeros on the twins' foreheads. "Yo! That there all what the world figure you worth, suckers! Shit, it say all the time on TV how people like otters an little white rats better'n you. Leave them nuthins on till I say you take em off. Make you 'member what is an what ain't."

Lyon rapped while he worked on the gun. "You ain't furry an cute, so's you way cool to shoot, be a whale or a seal, then you got some appeal." He pried out the misfire round, tossed it away, then worked the gun's action a few times, slapped the clip back in, and handed it to Gordon. "Should be workin now, man. You be figurin the Crew got somethin up with these drive-bys?"

Gordon scratched his head, which made him look like a stupid fat boy. "Cross my mind, man, but goddamn I figure how... or why.

Ain't none of em ole enough for drivin', an even they rousted that van, for sure weren't them in it. Nor the time last neither. An, hey, you tell me how they ever score the buck for *one* Uzi, never mind deuce. Shit, all they gots be that ole snub .38, an it ain't much better'n this!" He flipped the little pistol in his palm.

"Well," suggested Curtis. "Maybe they pay some big dudes to do us?"

Gordon snorted again. "Uh-huh. With what, man, Wesley's looks?" He paused a moment. "Less they done cut some sorta deal with Deek... " He shook his head. "Naw. Don't figure, man. We most never fight with em no more. Not since we all little ole kids. Shit, why should we? Hood they got no better'n ours."

Gordon snagged his board, a street-scarred Steadham full-size, and decked easily despite his mass. But then a siren sounded in the near distance, and he froze. His eyes shifted to Lyon.

The slender boy's head came up. His face turned skyward and his hands dangled loose in their pawlike way. The other boys waited, watching him. At times like these his ears almost looked pointy. "Two blocks up an three over," he murmured. "Comin this way, warp-seven. Ain't no ambulance nor fire truck neither."

Gordon's eyes calculated. "Most nobody call the cops over some shootin." He glanced in the siren's direction and fingered his jaw. "Course, if they come, it with their screamer full-on, just like now. That give whoever gots the full-auto plenty of time to bail. Best we chill our own fire." He buried the pistol under a sackful of sodden garbage in the dumpster, then wiped his hands on the tail of Rac's tee.

"Shit, man!" squeaked Rac. "Shoot bullets through me, why

don't ya!"

Gordon grinned. "I know. It ain't fair. Shut up." He jerked his jaw toward the street. "Let's motor. Be cool."

The boys grabbed their boards, decking and following Gordon out of the alley and down the sidewalk. They rolled fast in file, Lyon second on his pug-nosed Chris Miller, then the twins on identical Hammerheads. Curtis brought up the rear on his ancient flat-deck Variflex. The siren's yelping came closer, beating between the buildings and echoing through the canyons of brick and concrete. The boys had almost reached the lower corner when the cop car skidded around the intersection behind them, fishtailed, recovered sloppily with screeching rubber, and blasted down the block. The boys neither looked nor altered their pace.

The car braked suddenly at the alley mouth, its nose diving as if scenting the gun smoke, but then the boys were spotted and it dropped ass and squeaked off after them, slewing sideways into the intersection just as Gordon reached the curb, tires smoking as it slid to a stop. Its engine almost strangled, shaking the whole car, but struggled back to a loping idle that slowly smoothed out. Its siren blipped silent on a rising squeal but the rooftop strobes kept firing. Inside, the radio spat catfight sounds.

The boys tailed their boards and bunched together behind Gordon, waiting. Their faces switched on expressions of stupid, dull-eyed sullenness while their hands hung loose and open at their sides. The car doors burst simultaneously wide, one cop, white, on the passenger side, crouching behind, shotgun leveled at Gordon's chest through the open window. The other, black, gripped his gun double-handed over the car's roof. Strobe fire glinted ruby and indigo off his chrome-silver sunglasses.

Gordon yawned and hitched up his sagging jeans.

It was a long half second. The cops poised, tense. They were bulky, big-bellied men in gunmetal-blue uniforms. Their shirts were stretched tight over bulletproof vests, and they were belted by black leather that creaked with the weight of cuffs and clubs, walkie-talkies, and strangely shaped pouches packed with state-of-the-art stuff for survival in a hostile environment. Helmeted in stark white, they looked like intergalactic mercenaries grounded on a planet whose native inhabitants hated their guts. The strobe lights fought a losing battle against the gold of the climbing sun. The scents of hot rubber and steel, of leather and plastic, polyester and polish, radiated out from the car. The engine settled into an indifferent idle, its exhaust ghosting steam in the cool morning air. The radio hissed and spat its alien language.

On the sidewalk stood small black, brown, and bronze figurines that a moment before had been living and laughing. Now, the only hint of humanness was the blood seeping down Curtis' back. A big fat fly lazily circled his shoulder, sparking metallic iridescence in the sun like a tiny high-tech toy.

The cops' faces could have come from the same sort of action-figure mold as an old HeMan, Master of the Universe. It was even hard to tell them apart. "Against the wall!" ordered the black, a dusty line from any movie. "Spread!" he added, never doubting these kids wouldn't know the script by heart.

The figurines moved, little androids now, automatically obeying alien orders. Backpacks, books, and binders hit the sidewalk like so many weapons. Skateboards were left where they stood. The cops' eyes shifted uneasily behind their chrome mirrors, studying roof lines and blank windows above for an ambush. Finally, the cops moved after the boys, who were lined against grimy brick, their backs and balls vulnerable. The scene—the kids, the two big men, the shotgun wary while the black cop holstered his pistol but left the snap undone—would have looked bogus on network TV, like a parody of something from a long time ago. The black cop considered the row of little sculptures, then squatted with a grunt and creak of leather and tore into the backpacks like a gorilla who smelled a banana. He seemed about as disappointed when he didn't find one.

Finally he stood with another grunt and rubbed his back. A shiny black boot freed homework to the breeze and sent Lyon's board skittering into the street. A smile crossed the white cop's mouth as a garbage packer swung ponderously around the corner and bore down on the board. The driver, black and tired-looking, took the scene at a glance and didn't seem to find it a parody of anything. His heavy-gloved hands moved gently on the big wheel, guiding twenty tons and ten huge tires in a delicate dance around the skateboard. The truck rumbled away. The cop's smile clicked off.

The black one began searching the boys, slapping where he should have patted, and jerking arms back to check out their undersides like junk-shop merchandise that nobody could make you buy if you broke. For some reason he passed over Lyon and started with the twins, looking slightly confused as if he hadn't counted right. "You two. Turn around. Well, ain't that cute."

Four tawny eyes stared through the man.

"What're those marks on their foreheads?" asked the white cop. His eyes narrowed. "Looks like blood."

"Is," muttered the black one. "Initiation rite. Back against the wall."

The twins exchanged glances and secret smiles nobody else could see before turning and spreading again.

Moving to Gordon, the cop found the blade and yanked it out, raised it and an eyebrow to his partner with an I-told-you-so smirk, then thumbed the button. Nothing happened. He frowned. "Cheap shit from Taiwan." He shoved it in his pocket.

Reaching Curtis, he fingered the small boy's dreadlocks, then wiped his fingers on Curtis' jeans and studied his back. "Got us a little Rasta mon here. Peace, love, an ganja. So what happened to you, Ziggy?"

Curtis' voice carried all the emotion of an ATM terminal. "I fall down." He thought a moment. "In busted glass."

"Uh-huh," said the cop. "Say somethin for me in Rasta, mon." The fly had settled and was busy sucking blood. The cop smacked it flat with his palm.

"Pussy clot!" hissed Curtis.

"Welcome to a kinder, gentler America, boy." The cop turned to face the row of backs, dropping his hands to his belt. The white cop lowered the shotgun slightly. "Anybody hear some shootin a few minutes ago?"

"No," said Gordon.

The black cop gave the white another smirk and stepped back to Gordon, nudging the boy's feet farther apart with his boot. "Uh-huh. Figured you did the talkin, fat boy. Only kids packin that much lard around here are the ones makin a profit. So what's your gang dealin, fat boy? Rock? Ice? Or you the kind sell hospital garbage to little kids?"

Gordon said nothing.

"Uh-huh. So what you call yourselves, fat boy?"

"Friends," said Gordon.

"Uuuuh-huuuuh." The man thunked the back of Gordon's head with his knuckles. "C'mon, fat boy. We seen you dudes always hangin out together. Gangs always got baaaad names, like the Crew. So what's yours, fat boy?"

Gordon sighed, tensing for what would come next. "I just tell you."

Knuckles made a watermelon sound on Gordon's skull. "Uh-huh. More like smart-mouth little niggerboys. So who shot your Rasta 'friend,' lard-ass?"

"He fall down. In busted glass."

"Uh-huh. Maybe you can't take no name cause the Crew come an smoke your butts? Word say they some real bad-ass dudes."

"Uh-huh," Gordon murmured.

The cop whacked Gordon's head against the wall. "You gonna go far with that mouth of yours, niggerboy! How come you ain't in school?"

Gordon took a breath. The shotgun's muzzle lifted a little. "We takin our Friend home. Cause he fall down. In busted glass."

The cop snapped his holster strap. "Yeah. Right. You oughta get a medal! Ain't gonna catch me cryin when the Crew come down an show you what time it is!" He scattered skateboards with his boot.

Lyon murmured something, so softly that only Curtis next to him heard. There was a small metallic click.

"GODDAMMIT!" bawled the black cop, grabbing at his pants pocket where the point of Gordon's blade poked through. Startled, the white brought the shotgun up, ready.

Cursing, the black cop carefully pulled out the knife, ripping his pants a little more, then laid it angle-wise in the gutter against the curb and broke it with his boot heel. There wasn't a sound from the kids, but quivering shoulders revealed silent snickers. Chrome eyes watchful, the cops slid back into their car. The white racked the shotgun, then the car clunked into gear and squeaked away. "Get a life, suckers!" the white spat back.

"I take mine over yours any day, motherfucker!" Gordon muttered. He turned from the wall, rubbing his brick-bruised forehead, and hesitated because the car was only halfway down the block. But he felt the other boys' eyes on him and flipped the finger anyhow.

Like a broken spell, the hard little sculptures softened and became kids once more. The twins sidled up to Gordon with grins. Rac squeezed the fat boy's biceps. "Yo! There the rock!"

Ric giggled and draped his arm over Gordon's broad shoulder. "An ice! Maaaan, Gordon total cool like it under fire! Way cool. Way past cool!"

Gordon smiled a little. "Uh-huh. You can go an rub them zeros off now. Cops gots a way of turnin everbody into nuthin."

"Give it a name," said Rac, dabbing at the tail of his tee with his tongue and wiping his brother's forehead with it.

"Word!" agreed Ric, doing the same to Rac's forehead. "Like the ghost of a dog!"

Curtis moved close to Lyon and gazed up into the slender boy's face. "Um, you done that knife thing, huh, man?"

"Done what?" the twins demanded.

Lyon shrugged, his narrow eyes siy as usual. "Just a coincidence, homey."

"Did Lyon make a curse?" asked Rac. "How he do that anyways?"

"Who know," said Ric. "Fuck that. What's a 'incidence?"

Gordon's eyes shifted between Lyon and the broken knife, but he said nothing, just nudging the twins and pointing to the mess on the sidewalk.

Curtis searched Lyon's face again, then smiled and darted into the street to rescue Lyon's board as a car rounded the corner. It honked at Curtis, and all the boys fingered it and bawled curses. The car laid a patch and warped away. Maybe its driver would spread the word he'd been attacked by a youth gang. Curtis returned, grinning and panting, and gave Lyon his board. Lyon turned him around to wipe blood and smashed fly from his back. Gordon and the twins gathered up their school stuff and repacked their packs.

Curtis knelt down beside Gordon. "Um, you figure what them asshole cops say is true? Bout the Crew gonna smoke us?"

Gordon shuffled his wrinkled papers. "Naw, that just dogshit, man. Cops always sayin stuff like that. They like seein us fight. Hope we kill each other."

"Why?"

"Save them the trouble," said Lyon. "One time I read this book. Tell where back in the olden days some of them KKK dogfuckers liked to get us fightin so's they could watch an laugh over it."

Curtis rose and came back beside Lyon. "Well, shit. Seem like we be pretty fuckin stupid to go puttin on showtime for them assholes!"

Lyon nodded. "Mmm. You say it, homeboy."

The morning breeze had given up, beaten back to the Bay by the reek of overflowing dumpsters, alleys slimed by the walking dead, fumes and smoke from worn-out engines, leaking drainpipes, stopped-up sewers, and the sour sweat of too many people backed into too few corners. There were other smells, homey ones, of breakfasts cooking, bathroom steam, and the soapy-clean scent of new-washed laundry. But, like the antiseptic of hospital halls or the heavy perfume of funeral flowers, they were never enough to cover the stink of something sick or something forgotten that crumbled and rotted with its bones poking through.

The blue of the sky was yellowing as a black Trans-Am swung into a Burger King lot and cruised around to the drive-up window. It was ten years old, big and sleek, muscle sheathed in sheet metal. Its glistening polish, blood-crimson striping, and mirror-chrome Centerlines told of regular care by a megabuck detailer. Panther-footed on fresh low-pro Goodyears, arrogant as hell and expensive to feed, it was the kind of car most kids dreamed of but could never afford if they lived to be ninety.

But the driver was just six years older than the dream, and looked one less behind the wheel. Still, he handled the power with casual cool, always aware of the envy eyeing him from the sidewalks. A lot of white dudes in the better parts of town might wonder how Deek lived the dream. Most black kids knew, but more than a few envied him anyway. Engine rumbling a deep bass beat, CD deck pumping a Too Short rap, Deek idled his 'Am up to the order window. The slim, dark girl in her lame-looking uniform felt the big muscle-car's jungle-cat purr as it circled the building and glided to a stop, and pretended she didn't give a shit.

Markita was the same age as Deek, but had a two-year-old son at home in her mother's small apartment, and her weekly wage wouldn't have paid for one of Deek's tires. She remembered a crack dealer back in school, a dude she *could* have gone with if doing the right thing hadn't seemed so important, and imagined for a moment how she'd look now beside this boy in that way bad machine.

Deek himself didn't look particularly bad. He was main-framed for something small, quick, and lean, so what would have been beef on a bigger-boned boy quivered on him like chocolate pudding. Markita didn't see him that often; maybe once or twice a month and never this early in the day, but each time he showed up his designer jeans strained tighter on his butt while his soft boy-breasts got floppier and his belly hung farther out of his T-shirts. She doubted if he could have run a full block or lifted anything heavier than a sixer of beer, but then the game's name was survival and Deek seemed to be fully equipped for that.

His clothes were always fresh, like they'd never been sweated in, and his top-line L.A.s never seemed to see sidewalk. He wore enough gold around neck, wrists, and fingers to pay a month's wages to a whole Burger King crew. Markita had to admit that if she had only one word to describe his chubby-checked, double-chinned face she'd have to go with "cute"—like the Beaver might have looked at sixteen if he'd been black and pigging for years on junk food—though his golden eyes glinted as hard as the real thing. His hair was sheened and sparkly, and long in the old Michael Jackson style, like he could care about being hip or trendy.

Sunlight struck fire from Deek's pudgy hand as he leaned from the car window. Markita blinked behind bulletproof glass. Her own slender fingers were bare of even that single signifying band. The shine of her short curls had already been dulled by the frying-fat fumes, and just the thought of another long day made her feet ache. Her voice came out knife-edged and bitchy, surprising her. "May I take your order, please?"

Her eyes shifted to the shadowy figure beside Deek, half hidden by the car's low roof line and camouflaged by the black-on-black interior. She wondered who rode shotgun with the chubby little street prince: some ebony airhead, or maybe a blond bubble-brain to show the poor niggers that drug bucks could buy what you couldn't score with a high school diploma or a hard-muscled bod. Deek without money would still have been cute, like something that squeaked when you squeezed it. But Markita had stopped sleeping with that sort of stuff a long time ago. She bent for a better look, pretending to straighten a napkin stack.

It was another boy: the bodyguard, and a necessary accessory. He was gunmetal black, and built so wiry and hard that Markita doubted there was an ounce of fat on him anywhere. He was tall and long-limbed with what some old people called "African" features, like Markita's, though his hair was razored crisp and flat. He had big buck teeth behind loose lips that probably never quite closed, eyes like warm obsidian that some might call soulful, and the sort of long-backed build where T-shirts made in Taiwan for "normal" kids would always leave his belly button bare. Even in new 501s and black satin tank top he seemed out of place in the high-tech machine, reminding Markita of a *National Enquirer* photo showing a Kenyan jet pilot posed in his cockpit clad in just a loincloth. This dude would have looked way past cool in a loincloth. Fact was, he would have been righteous with a bone in his nose. Next to him, Deek should have been wearing a beanie with a propeller on top. The boy was slumped bonelessly in the seat with a beer bottle clasped upright in his crotch. He looked either half drunk or all the way bored. Markita felt her heart warming toward him for some reason.

Deek thumbed down the CD and gave Markita a cute smile. "I have me a big breakfast an a extra order of Tater Tenders, girl." He glanced at the other boy. "Yo! Ty!"

Ty seemed to come back from somewhere else. "Huh? Oh. A egg-a-muffin, I spose."

"This ain't McDonald's, stupid!"

The tall boy bent over the console and peered up at the order window. Seeing Markita, he gave her a smile that looked low-tech and harmless and infinitely patient. Markita didn't think that the short snap of "Ty" fit him at all. She couldn't imagine those thick homely lips ever being self-programmed to say it. They'd more likely mumble a shy "Tyler" or "Tyrone" and then relax back into a good-natured goofy grin once more. She pictured his walk, planting one huge Nike flat on the pavement at a time in no particular hurry to get anywhere. He probably couldn't rap to save his life, or give a particular shit about it. He wore no gold that Markita could see, though there was a fine silver chain around his neck and some sort of small, quarter-sized medallion hanging from it under his shirt between the starkly defined plates of his chest.

"Um?" he asked. "Where the menu?"

Markita felt warmth again. She made a little movie in her mind. Ty was the kind of boy who, had he stayed in school, would have plodded to graduation on a solid C-average and gone with an "African" sort of girl like, well, like herself. She would probably have to teach him the mechanics of love, but he would have always known the meaning. He would marry the girl and go to work for a scrap yard, confident at the iron controls of a 1930s-technology crane but uneasy with a pocket calculator and intimidated by an ATM. Markita's eyes strayed to the small, tight nipples on his chest, like tiny buds beneath the black satin. They'd be the same color as the rest of him: hardly noticeable. He'd be a gentle savage in bed, patient and caring to his family, and in a few years they'd be able to afford a house with a yard in a good East Side neighborhood. Eventually their children, maybe Markita's own son, whom Ty would be just as proud of as the others he'd father, would teach him Nintendo games and how to program the VCR. Markita couldn't have explained why she seemed to know all this, she just felt as if she did—now that it was too late.

"The fuckin menu was back there on the goddamn post, stupid!" Deek rolled his golden eyes at Markita and added a hopeless shrug. "Give him the same's me, girl."

Markita watched as Ty slumped back in the seat and took a gulp from his bottle. The beer was Heineken dark, she noted. Only prime shit for Deek. She turned away from the window to a skinny, slope-shouldered boy who lounged at the grill and stared into space. His name was Leroy, and he looked like one. Bib overalls would have fit him just fine. He was finishing high school at night, after dropping out for about a year to deal on corners. He'd made pretty good buck for a while, until he'd tried to collect a credit from a cracked-out sixth-grader who'd opened him up with an old Denny's steak knife. He was taking a computer course too, hard to believe as that was. He'd asked Markita out a few times but she hadn't accepted... yet. She hoped he would ask her once more. "Two breakfasts, Leroy." She lowered her voice, though the window glass was a full inch thick. "Make one a special."

Leroy giggled—Markita was getting used to that—and snagged his spatula. "One mega-size booger comin up! So who givin the lady some shit this early in the mornin?" He glanced out the window, then whistled and turned back to the grill. "Mmm, MMM! You really playin with power there, homegirl!"

Markita moved to the hot racks and took down two boxes of Tater Tenders. "Just do it, Leroy. Or I will. An you make sure I know which's which so the fat little showtime get what comin to him." She added gently, "An don't be callin me homegirl."

Leroy giggled again. "That one a lot more'n showtime, girl. Show you first, maybe, but then he *tell* you what time it is, best believe!" He grabbed his crotch. "Yo, gimme a second an I add some secret sauce."

Markita made a face. "Leroy, you so gross!" Then she noticed a fly flat-backing it on the floor. She smiled and knelt to pick it up. "I hope it usually take you longer'n a second."

Leroy turned, momentarily confused, then smiled too. He had nice eyes.

A few minutes later the Trans-Am nosed into a parking space at the back of the Burger King lot, easing up to a fence whose battered boards seemed held together only by the layers of spray-painted words and symbols and gang marks. Deek revved the engine once, then cut the ignition and it died with a snarl. The rap thumped softly on, its bass beat a feeling more than a sound. Deek yawned and stretched. "Feel like shit, gettin up so early, man." He glanced at the big gold watch on his wrist. "You *believe* it only ten fuckin o'clock?"

Ty was gazing out the window, watching as a mother led her two small children across the street. They sucked on Popsicles. Ty tried to remember the last time he'd had one. Grape was his favorite. "Seem funny, don't it... seein other dudes goin to school?"

Deek coughed up something and spat it out the window. "Naw, it don't. What the fuck they learnin there anyways?" He jerked a thumb toward the restaurant building. "Just enough to be spendin the rest of they goddamn lifes workin in one of them grease-bomb factories, that what!" He gave Ty a smirk. "Stop watchin em, stupid. Hell, I seen you standin there at the window some mornins. It like pickin a goddamn scab. Leave it be an it heal."

Ty said nothing. He opened the sack and passed a boxed breakfast to Deek. Deek had his own apartment in an ancient three-story building where the owner didn't give a shit what happened as long as the rents were paid. The city had wanted to knock what was left of it down after the earthquake, but the owner had written a letter to the Oakland *Tribune,* pleading that his poor people would have nowhere to go, and their "plight" caught the ass end of a brief burst of black unity. He'd gotten by with bolting a few four-by-fours over the biggest cracks, and the structure was now officially quakeproof. Deek had one room, top floor front, but it had its own bath... sort of. Mostly it was in the same kind of nuke-attack mess as any other sixteen-year-old boy's.

For Ty and Deek the days usually ended long past midnight, often after spending the last hours watching the VCR or old TV movies, with pizza and beer or ribs and beer, or beer all by itself. Deek smoked a little dope sometimes, but it only gave Ty headaches. Deek would zone out on the ratty old sofa and Ty would finally drag him to bed and strip off his clothes. Deek slept till at least noon and treated everybody like shit until about five or six in the evening. Ty was used to that. Deek did three things well: eating, sleeping, and dealing. Ty covered most everything else.

Midmornings, Ty weighed and measured and chopped and packed. It was mostly rock, though ice was becoming a volume seller, and there was a little coarse coke for the rich kids... dogshit grade, nothing near the quality of what went up the noses of whites across town. It was simple, mindless work, like digging a ditch or boxing burgers or punching a keyboard. Deek bought from a good supplier, didn't cut any more than it already was, and sold full weights—or at least never bitched that Ty packed full weights. Ty supposed it was pretty good shit, considering, and tried not to think about who it was for.

Sometimes Ty mopped party puke from the floor, unstopped the greenish-orange thing in the bathroom that passed for a toilet, or swabbed out the rusty shower stall with Pine Sol. Once in a while he changed the sweaty gray bedsheets and did the laundry when there were no more clean socks. Since he didn't have a license, he rode his skateboard to run messages and check on or collect money from the street-corner dealers. Most were boys younger than himself, and not all carried guns or were good with their blades, so it wasn't too much of a prob when some got greedy or tried the same old shit each thought was original and Ty had to beat them up. He did it with cool efficiency and no particular anger. He had a big .45 Army pistol and generally just flashing it kept the kids chilled and shit to a minimum. Deek had once told him that the dudes who managed paper boys probably got more trouble. Ty had had to shoot a few times, but never hit anyone he knew of.

He also brought back the takeout food and cigarettes and scored the beer from the store where Deek had an account.

The oldest of five brothers and sisters, with a mother who worked long days and sometimes into the night, and a father who was kind in his way but who never came home anymore, Ty knew how to cook and often did on the apartment's crusty old three-burner range. He also shopped for groceries. Other kids just figured he rode beside Deek all the time and smoked butt. Ty didn't care what anybody thought; he knew this was the best job he'd ever get, and it depended on keeping Deek alive.

Once in a while he went home, sometimes for dinner but really for love. His mom had finally started accepting the money he brought, mostly because the younger kids needed stuff, and life wasn't getting any cheaper. If there were points of light beaming out like the TV talk said, none seemed to be shining in Oakland. His mom could have gotten more from welfare than her job—most mothers could—but pride had a way of backing you into funny corners sometimes. Ty suspected she prayed for him; at least there were moments late at night when he felt as if somebody was, and who else would? Ty supposed there was a God, somewhere, but He didn't seem to like kids very much, and black ones not at all. If Ty ever wondered why he still wore the little silver St. Christopher medal, he figured it was because his mother had given it to him when he was about three.

Ty never stayed long on his visits; he hated lying about what he did to the younger kids as much as the gleam of knowing pride in his twelve-year-old brother's eyes. The boy knew what is, and it wouldn't be long. Going home made Ty sad. It was funny that, no matter how drunk he got every night, he'd still wake up early like he had to be in school. Often he'd stand at the window and watch the other kids on the sidewalk below. If there was a future, Ty had figured out that it wasn't something he wanted to think much more about than who those little bottles and packets were for.

"Naw," said Deek, shoving back the box. "The other one, man. With the X on it. Girl say it made fresh. This one been on the racks for a hour."

Ty shrugged and switched boxes. "She, um... she kinda nice, huh?"

Deek flipped back the lid and ripped open a packet of plastic silverware with his teeth. "Stupid tramp, man! She just like I tellin you, be workin in there time she forty same's all them other suckers shaggin off to school ever goddamn mornin. Pitcher yourself washin cars or bussin tables, man. That all they gonna let a stupid Buckwheat-lookin niggerboy like you do, don't matter you got a fuckin diploma or not!"

Deek started to shovel pale scrambled eggs into his mouth, alternating with gulps of beer. He frowned as Ty clicked the door handle. "Where in hell you goin?"

"Gotta piss."

Deek glanced back at the restaurant and smirked again. "Shit, maaaan! Don't go wastin your time on *her!* Last I seen a face like that was on a goddamn clock, an a fuckin cuckoo come outa it! You feelin the need, we score us somethin nice tonight. Jesus, ain't you learned nuthin yet cept how to slide on a rubber?"

Ty's lips clamped over his teeth, something that seldom happened, as if it cost him too much to make his harmless face hard. Deek had girls up all the time... minks that would never have looked twice at Ty in school or on the street. Some were older than Ty or Deek, a few were younger, but they all seemed practiced at doing anything to, with, and for a dude except talking to him. Ty had learned a lot about sex in the past few months but little more about love than he already knew. Sex was something that felt so good for a few minutes you could die happy right there inside the silky wet lips of a cunt. But when it was over, you had nothing left but a fast-fading memory maybe a lot like crack. You panted and sweated, searching for something right up until that last intense second, but then there was only emptiness and the same sort of something-wasted feeling he'd had when he was his little brother's age and beat off in the bathroom. He'd been surprised at first to feel like that after "real" fucking; thinking that maybe he just didn't know enough. But now he'd had all the variations he wanted— including one night alone with Deek when just for the hell of it they'd checked that stuff out—and fucking was just something he did when he needed to; better than beating off but nothing at all like he'd imagined love would be.

He'd thought about that a lot, mornings packing bottles, and decided that love was what you gave and got from your family. Sex didn't seem to have much to do with it. The real mystery was how you could start a family of your own to love and be loved by when all you got from the world was hate or indifference.

Lately, Deek bought only one girl at a time. Ty got sloppy seconds. It didn't matter; he'd sit out on the fire escape and smoke Kools until it was his turn. Sometimes Deek liked to watch. Ty didn't give a shit about that either... it was only fucking, after all. Sometimes the girl would stay all night, and Ty would make her breakfast while Deek slept. A few seemed to think that was funny as hell. Those who talked then, and actually said something, just told the same stories of drugs or unwanted babies or busted-up families and running away that Ty had already heard a million times before. But most just figured they could score something extra, probably because Ty looked so stupidly dense at the stove in just his jeans, or padding his big bare feet across the worn-out linoleum to put plates on the table. The last girl to spend the night was one of Deek's bargains, picked up at the bus station. She seemed to have dropped three years off her "fifteen" in the slanting gold sunlight of morning. She'd run from Mississippi to the fabled "City of the Black," and Ty pictured her with her hair full of little bows in a gingham dress... whatever the hell that was. He'd given her the bus fare home and fifty dollars more. He often wondered if she'd gone.

Deek preferred to sleep alone. That meant with Ty beside him. Ty didn't mind that either. It was no different from sleeping with his brothers except for the gun beneath the pillow. After that one night when they'd tried boy stuff together, both had decided it wasn't worth the effort. But, more than once, Ty had wakened to find Deek holding tight to him in sleep.

Ty pushed open the door. "I not talking to nobody, man. Just tellin you I gotta piss, that all."

Deek shook his head. "Yo! Them dudes gonna show anytime now. You stay. You my goddamn bodyguard, ain't ya? How it look?"

"You askin me, look goddamn stupid, your bodyguard wettin his pants. *That* how it look!"

"So? Stupid your thing, an you do it good. Piss here, you can't hold it. Ain't nobody around wanna see your black dick anyways."

Ty let out a sigh. He stood and pissed on the car's front tire. If Deek noticed, he pretended not to. Ty got back in and quietly forked scrambled eggs.

"Stop drinkin so goddamn much an you wouldn't gotta be pissin ever motherfuckin time you turn around," Deek advised. He studied the tall boy a moment and his golden eyes warmed a little. "Maybe you drinkin too much, Ty?"

Ty's lips had relaxed so his teeth showed again, but his own eyes stayed cool. "Gots a prob with that too?"

"No." Deek's tone hardened. "Long's you don't stay so drunk you can't do your job. Had me another bodyguard... "

Ty sighed again. "I hear part of that story a'fore. So what happen to him?"

Deek glanced at his clean pink fingernails. "Sucker got into shootin up. Stuff I don't sell. Guess he got hold of some bad shit one night. Cold stone dead on my goddamn floor. I drug his ass downstairs, load him in my trunk, drove out by the Bay, an dump him in the mud. Whole paragraph bout him three days later. Page six of the *Trib,* man."

"I do my job. Do it good. Just like you say."

Deek nodded. "Course you do, man." He smiled and slapped Ty's thin shoulder. "Fact is, I don't know what I do without ya."

The morning sun beat on the midnight-black car. Heat ghosts shimmered up from its sheet metal. Deek pulled off his shirt and went back to eating. Ty glanced at him, thinking of half-melted chocolate Easter bunnies, then poked at his own breakfast. Suddenly, Deek stiffened. "FUCK!"

Ty turned. "Now what I done?"

Deek shoved a Tater Tender under Ty's nose. "Check *this* shit!"

Ty had to cross his eyes to see. Then he grinned. "So? Ain't you never seen no little ole fly a'fore? Can't hurt you none. Already dead. Be thankful it ain't no rat turd. What my mom always say."

"Yeah, right! Musta been nuthin but nonstop terminal tee-hees growin up in your family! Like Little House in the Ghetto!"

Ty shrugged. "There some good times, spite all. Guess it don't take much for makin you happy when you little."

"Or stupid!" Deek flung the potato patty out the window, then carefully checked out the rest of the box before stuffing another in his mouth and muttering around it. "Least your folks *wanted* you." He swallowed, and added. "Even if you was a retard." He eyed the tall boy like he had the Tater Tenders. "You stink when you sweat, know that? An you sweat all the fuckin time, like now. An, if I been born with a face like yours, I shoot my ownself. Stop that goddamn smilin, asshole! Why you gotta go smilin all the goddamn time?"

Ty went on eating. "Easier'n not, I spose."

"My ass!" Deek glared at his food, then toward the restaurant. "You figure that dribble-lip cunt done it on purpose?"

"I think there a law 'gainst givin people unnatural stuff."

"Too funny, asshole!"

Ty munched a Tater Tender. "Naw, she not do that to you. Be a scared."

"What *that* sposed to mean, stupid?"

Ty shrugged again. "Mean what I mean it to mean, that all."

A dented Dodge van, over twenty years old and painted a streaky charcoal black with spray cans, humped into the lot and rattled to a stop beside the Trans-Am. Its brakes squealed and its engine dieseled on a few moments after the ignition cut, farting blue smoke before it finally died. Heat wavered out of the snaggle-toothed grille along with greenish wisps of antifreeze steam. Ty slipped his .45 out from under the Heineken sixer at his feet, flicked off the safety, and laid it on his leg. "Check me out. I doin my job.

See?"

Deek scowled. "Oh, shut up, stupid!"

The van's driver was a muscle-bulked boy of about seventeen. Wrenching the outside handle, he shouldered open the door and slid out. He wore heavy old work boots, one torn toe showing bright steel, dirty Levi's, and a ragged T-shirt that used to be white and clung to the solid slabs of his chest and washboard belly like a coat of paint. He wore a satin black bandana around his head. Another boy, slimmer, but not much, clad the same but minus his shirt, stayed in the van and watched Ty watching him as the driver walked to Deek's side of the car. Both boys had Ty's gunmetal tone, though theirs seemed dusty and dull with the half-wild scruffiness of junkyard dogs. The driver stopped at Deek's window and offered a cautious grin: a guard dog in daylight who suspected a petting. He sniffed the air. "Breakfas time, huh? Lotta hungry folks these days." His voice was as solid as his body and seemed just as hard to keep leashed.

Deek's mouth was full, and he casually chewed and swallowed before snagging a box of Sherman browns off the dash. He fired one, then held out the box to the big dude. "TV say everthing only gettin better all the time."

The big boy carefully took a thin cigarette in his thick callused fingers. His forehead furrowed a little as he leaned in for the flame. "Cain't trus' nuthin they say, brother. We come up the coas', through this rich little town call Sanna Cruz. Seen people on the street holdin signs sayin they work jus fo food. WHITE people! Shit, you *know* thangs gotta be some bad when white folks start livin like niggers!" His eyes ran over Deek's rolly body with a curious kind of envy. "Course, you be doin all right fo yo'self, brother. *That* I seein wit my own eyes!"

Deek blew smoke. "Word. Well, now you dudes afford a Burger King breakfast too. Maybe."

The big boy stiffened slightly. His frown deepened. "What you sayin, 'maybe?'"

Ty held the .45 in his lap, his finger on the trigger. His eyes stayed steady on the other boy in the van. He could smell the dude at Deek's window, a rough mix of oil and leather and sweat that made him think of his dad for some reason. Except for the Night Train fumes. "Yo, brother," Ty called softly. "I like to see your hands, man. Both em, okay?"

The big boys exchanged glances over the car's roof, then the one in the van shrugged and kicked back in the seat, hands clasped comfortably behind his head. There might have been a hint of respect in his eyes.

Deek smiled. "Did you do one?"

Smoke snorted from the big boy's wide nostrils. He straightened, chest expanding. "Hey, man! You never say nuthin bout doin one! You... you never even say nuthin bout *hittin* one! Now, what you tellin me?"

Deek grinned, cute enough to cuddle. "Aw, chill out, big brother. It cool. You totally right. All I say was to give em another major-nasty full-auto drive-by. But, hell, I gotta make sure, don't I?" He spread his pink palms and his golden eyes scanned the big boy's smoldering ebony. "An you done it. . . didn't ya?"

The big boy dropped his hands to his hips. His deep voice went high. "Well, COURSE we done it, man! It like like I give you my *word!* Bof clips this time! We *earn* our money!"

Deek looked hurt. "Did I say you didn't, man?"

The big boy looked confused. His hands slid to his sides. "No... no you dint." He searched the asphalt at his feet. "Folks jus talk dif'rent here, that all it is. Half time you never know if they sayin what they meanin."

Deek grinned again. His chubby brown hand touched the hard black of the big boy's forearm. "Yo, it all cool, brother. Word." He took two Heinekens from between Ty's feet and pressed them into the big boy's hand. "Here, man. An for your homey too."

Ty watched the other boy, who was looking as confused as the first one had sounded. Ty had the picture in his mind; the first dude would be standing with the bottles in one hand and the cigarette in the other. Ty heard the rip of Velcro as Deek pulled a roll of bills from his belt pouch. Deek would hand the big boy a fifty. Holding money out in the open usually freaked anybody a little, and the dude would have to stick the Sherman in his mouth to pocket the half-buck. The smoke would probably water his eyes. Deek was MC Control in these situations, though why he was bothering to run the whole number on these dudes, Ty couldn't figure... unless it was just to keep in practice. Ty almost felt sorry for the big boys.

Deek had spotted them a few days before, about sundown, standing by their van, which was dead in the street with a flat front tire. Both boys had worn helpless expressions, saying they knew their spare was flat and there was no one to call. Deek had offered them a ride to a gas station. Their faces had lit with stunned hope and wonder at the glistening ebony dream coming to their rescue.

Ty had casually checked out the van while the dudes were getting in each other's way in their rush to take off the wheel. The tangled blankets in back, scattered work clothes, soup cans, and the smell of unwashed males and dirty socks said it all. Eager as puppies in the Trans-Am's back seat, they'd started bragging about their new Uzis before a block had rolled by. Deek had scored them a room and gotten them flat puking drunk that night while Ty had gone through all their things and confirmed the Uzis. They were semis converted with mail-order parts: the select-fire switches had three positions but only the letters S and F. The clips were the standard 32s, though Ty was surprised that these sort of dudes coming to the "big city" wouldn't have brought along the bigger 50s. But then they were probably low on cash after scoring the guns.

"Uh," said the big boy, pulling the cigarette from his lips and wiping his eyes. "Thanks, brother. I, uh, spose you ain't gonna be needin us no more?"

Deek killed his bottle, slipped it back into the sixer, and patted his belly with a satisfied sigh. "Mmm. You brothers gonna be hangin town a while?"

The big boy nodded hard. "Sho. This kinda work what we come fo."

Deek twisted a finger in his neck chain, the gold clicking softly. "Mmm. Well, I might gots another job you could do. Same thing, dif'rent kids."

The big boy grinned, again nodding hard. "Sho, man! Sho! We do it, best believe!" He suddenly looked shy. "We wuz lookin at some cars a while ago. Cool ones. Course, nuthin in this here class." His grin widened. "Maaaan, you sho nuff got some foxes in this here town!"

"They cost."

"I hear that, brother! Course, what don't?"

Deek snickered. "An I hear that." He reached to the console and picked up a Polaroid picture. It was a trifle fuzzy, but showed five boys practicing curb moves on skateboards. He handed it to the big dude. "Them. Today. Same street, but about four blocks east. They get outa school round three-thirty an always ride together. Pick your own place, you wanna, but they usually cut behind one block that mostly truck shops an stuff an fuck around for a while like they doin in the pitcher."

The big boy studied the snapshot. "Sho!" He walked quickly back to the van and handed the picture and bottles to the other boy, then bent down and looked past Ty to Deek. "Uh... you be wantin us to *do* one?"

Deek sighed out smoke with a patient sound. "Accidents happen. But no more'n one, hear me? Bunch of dead kids no good to nobody. I get the money to you back in your room tonight." He grinned. "Course, you trust me, man?"

"Sho we do, brother! Hell, you been nuthin but good to us!" The big boy hesitated, his forehead creasing again. "Jus... well, we jus figure this kinda stuff pay mo better, y'know? Special when *this* happen." He pointed to a little hole just behind the doorframe. "What I sayin is, you never tole us them little ole kids got guns! You spect these here little shits got em too? I mean... well, like I sayin, you coulda tole us... "

Deek choked on Sherman smoke. His voice broke. *"Told* ya!"

he squeaked. "TOLD ya!" He kicked open the door and stomped around to the big boy, his belly bobbing. He jammed a chubby finger against a chest like armor plate. The big dude stepped back a pace. The top of Deek's head came about level with the big boy's chin. Deek leaned back and glared upward. "Where the fuck you comin from, nigger?"

"Uh... Bakersfield."

Deek looked blank for a second, then laughed. "Shit! Well, what they do down there anyways, grow motherfuckin *cotton* or somethin? Jesus Christ, boy, listen up! MOST little shits in this town got guns, so don't you come bitchin to me bout some snot-nose seventh-grader poppin your ass with a wimpy .22! Shit! I could get this done for half what I payin you. . . for a goddamn dime bag of rock if I want some other little snot to do it! Get real or die, sucker!"

Deek spun on his heel and stalked back to the car. "I get the buck to your room tonight," he shot over his shoulder, then added a grin across the car's roof. "Twenty fuckin dollars do *both* you dudes. Little kids work cheap. 'Member that!

"Bakers-fuckin-field!" snorted Deek, watching in the mirror as the van pulled into the street and chugged away, trailing smoke.

Ty thumbed on the .45's safety and took another swallow of beer. "Mmm. Matter of fact my mom tell me one time they do grow cotton down there."

Deek shrugged, firing the engine with a roar. "Times I figure *you* be happy in a cotton field, stupid."

"Yo! Touch my tee an die!" squalled Ric, dancing away from Gordon.

"Can't touch this neither!" snickered Rac, in step with his brother.

Gordon gave the garbage-glopped gun and the twins a pair of equally disgusted glances, then crooked a finger at Curtis. "Gimme yours, man. You ain't wearin it anyways."

"Hey!" squeaked Curtis, sidling behind Lyon. "Not fair! All kinda shit already happen to me this goddamn mornin!"

Gordon flicked slime from his hands. "Sure it fair, sucker. Wasn't for you an your goddamn back them cops wouldn't of slapped us around so much. Now, give!"

Curtis clung to Lyon's hand, peering hopefully up at the slender boy. "Yo, do I gotta, man?"

Lyon slipped an arm around Curtis in a quick hug. "Well, it gonna need washin anyhow. Then your mom gots to sew it." He grinned. "Sides, callin that sucker a pussy clot not be helpin us one helluva lot. Make for Gordon takin your heat, what it is."

"But it was a cool thing to say anyways," said Rac.

"Word!" added Ric. "Way cool! One to ten, that be a eight. Believe!"

"An takin heat be Gordon's job," finished Rac. "Word by rules!"

Lyon squeezed Curtis' shoulder. "Seem like all dogshit takin be poor Gordon's job sometimes. Aw, let him use it, Curtis. We just might be needin our gun again pretty soon. Never know."

Curtis untied the T-shirt from around his waist and tossed it to Gordon. "Pussy clot," he whispered, twining his fingers in Lyon's.

Gordon sighed. "I heard that." He wiped off the pistol and spat. "Life ain't nuthin but a goddamn Popsicle course."

"Obstacle course," said Lyon.

"Whatever."

Meantime, the twins were ranging farther up the alley, poking into dumpsters and cans like a mongoose team on *Wild Kingdom.* They weren't so much looking for something as just not able to stand the thought of missing anything. Suddenly Rac stiffened, rising on tiptoes and peering intently over a dumpster toward the alley's far end. Ric instantly joined him, then both turned and beckoned to the other boys. "Yo, Gordy!" hissed Rac, finger to his lips.

Carrying their boards, Gordon, Curtis, and Lyon ran to the twins, all taking cover behind the dumpster. Ric pointed. "Yo! Check this out!"

Morning shade still filled the alleyway, but silhouetted against the sunlit street at the opposite end were the figures of two boys. The smaller was backed against the wall while the other, bigger, made jabbing motions at him with a gun. The smaller boy squatted. It looked like he was untying his shoes.

Lyon leaned across the dumpster lid, straining forward, his eyes narrowed to bright black slits. "The little dude be Marcus Tibbet. Third-grader. Live in my buildin. Never seen the other, but he not wearin Crew colors, nor nobody else's look like, neither."

"I can see that much!" growled Gordon. "An I don't give a shit if he *was* somebody! He in our ground now. By rules, his ass ours! So, what kinda gun? An I already check it chrome-plated."

"Prob'ly nickel."

"Whatever."

"Um?" whispered Ric. "You mean, like money nickel?"

Rac poked him. "Shut the fuck up, doofus!"

"*Both* you shut the fuck up, goddamnit!" hissed Gordon.

"Mmm," murmured Lyon. "Some kind small 'volver. Like the pawnshop man be callin a lady's gun."

Gordon gave a short nod. "Yeah? Well, bullets still come outa them little holes fast enough for dirt-nap time."

"Dude look nervous as a bitch cat havin a litter," said Lyon. "Check how he keep on lookin out at the street."

Curtis pressed against Lyon. "Yo, maybe he gots him a watcher out there?"

"Naw," said Gordon. "Then he not need to keep checkin for himself." Gordon considered a moment, then shed his backpack. "Okay! We gonna take him! Leave all your boards an shit here. Spread wide. Get busy!"

With Gordon leading, gun up and ready, the boys fanned out

among the rows of cans and dumpsters. They darted silently up the alley, each checking for places to hide as they ran. As Lyon had said, the bigger boy with the gun was splitting his attention between the smaller kid and the street entrance. It was the little boy, Marcus, who first noticed the Friends coming. Instead of staying cool, he just stared stupidly.

The big boy, tall and lean but no older than Gordon, saw where Marcus was looking. He spun around, his eyes first widening in surprise, then slitting as he tried to aim at all five running shadows at once. By then Gordon was only about a hundred feet away, and dove behind a dumpster, then leaped up and aimed his own gun two-handed the way cops did. The other boys scattered for cover. Orange flame spat from the muzzle of the tall boy's gun. An instant later came the sound, a flat crack echoing between the alley walls and the thunk of the bullet denting the dumpster. Gordon's .22 popped no louder than a cherry bomb. Twice. One shot flew wild into the street beyond, barely missing a beer truck and pocking a building on the far side. The second tore into the tall boy's thigh.

He screamed and crumpled to the pavement as if he'd been hit in the heart. His gun clattered on the concrete as he cried and clutched at his leg with both hands while curling into a ball. The Friends were on him in seconds, the twins grabbing his arms, Lyon and Curtis a leg each. The boy screamed again as he was jerked flat on his back. He howled and twisted until Gordon jammed the .22's muzzle against his forehead. "Shut up, sucker! Or you dead! Word!"

The boy's eyes crossed for a second as he stared at the gun.

Then he went limp as laundry. The twins began dragging him into the shadow of a doorway. He only whimpered now. Tears ran down his cheeks. A ruby stain spread slowly on his faded jeans over the bullet hole. Lyon picked up the small shiny revolver and checked it out carefully. Curtis danced here and there, trying to help the twins but mostly getting in the way. Gordon finally grabbed his arm.

"Watch the street!" Curtis darted for the alley mouth.

Ric and Rac had the tall boy pinned against a steel-plated door, his legs sprawled out on the pavement while they held his arms. The bloodstain was still spreading, but not very fast. Gordon yanked up his jeans, which were slipping low from the run, then walked over and put the pistol to the boy's head again. "You keep shut up, sucker! I get back to you!" He handed the gun to Rac, who immediately stuck the muzzle into the boy's ear.

Gordon went across to Marcus, who still squatted wide-eyed, crying harder than the boy who'd been shot. His fingers seemed frozen to his shoelaces. He wore an old Hammertime tee, purple shorts, and brand-new Cons. He started to blubber as Gordon and Lyon stared down at him. His voice came out high and squeaky. "Fucker tryin to steal my goddamn SHOES, Gordon! Say he gonna kill me if I not give em him!"

Gordon was still panting from the run. He yanked at his jeans again and wiped sweat from his face. Across the alley the tall boy started to moan. Marcus slumped against the wall, pulled up his knees, buried his head between, and choked and sobbed. Lyon broke open the revolver and flashed it to Gordon: there were only three cartridges in the cylinder counting the one already fired, and all were green with age. Gordon shrugged, then half turned to the tall boy. "I tellin you to shut up, sucker!"

"Jesus, man, it fuckin HURTS! I gonna bleed to death here!"

Gordon scowled. "You hear me, asshole? Second warnin's for good cops an bad movies! Lyon! Go an check him out."

Lyon went to the boy and crouched beside him. He snapped the gun shut, spun the cylinder to a live round, and gave it to Ric. Ric poked the muzzle into the boy's other ear. The dude went still, clenching his teeth and squeezing his eyes tight shut. Lyon bent close and studied his thigh. Long delicate fingers probed. The boy whimpered again but kept his eyes closed. Then Lyon rocked back on his heels, wiped his fingers on the cuff of the boy's jeans, and crossed his arms on his knees. He studied the tall kid, then asked, "Yo. Gots a name, man?"

The boy's eyes opened, narrowly. "Keeja."

Lyon's smile flickered. "We all be just regular niggers here, man. Your slave name be cool."

The boy studied Lyon, then closed his eyes once more. "Justin."

"Mmm. Well, Justin, fact is, I seen dudes hurt worse eatin shit off their boards. Shit, I prob'ly pick that little ole bullet out with my fingers, cept you scream an scare everbody. You live, whatever that worth... longs you stay shut up. Word."

Gordon was just standing and staring down at the little boy, looking partly pissed but mostly confused. Lyon returned to kneel beside the crying kid and lay a gentle hand on a small quivering shoulder. "Yo. Marcus-homey. Chill it, man. You be okay, so stop all that baby-ass shit. Nobody got no time for it."

Gordon squatted with a grunt and lifted the little boy's chin. "Hear Lyon-o, man? Chill out. *Now.* What the fuck good cryin gonna do ya? Wipe your goddamn face an get your ass up out that garbage. You a *man* goddammit, act like one!" He glanced at the boy's new shoes, big as moon boots. "Cocksuckin eighty-dollar Cons! What in hell you spect to happen? That sucker run em past some used clothes place an score him enough for a bag an a half."

Lyon helped Marcus to his feet, sniffling and choking, snot shiny on his lip. "My mom just give em me yesterday. My goddamn *birthday,* Gordy!"

"Don't call... Oh shit! What the fuck *that* got to do with nuthin?" Gordon roared. "Figure the world give a shit cause your mom love you an it your motherfuckin birthday? Yo! Maybe your mom don't know what is... but you goddamn well do!" Grabbing the little boy's shoulders, Gordon shook him like a flour bag full of chicken parts. "NOW STOP THAT CRYIN OR I WHACK YOU UPSIDE THE HEAD!"

Marcus quieted. He stared up at Gordon and wiped his eyes with savage swipes. He puffed his little chest. "I cool, man!"

Lyon smiled and high-lived the boy. "Course you be, man. Way past cool."

Gordon crossed his arms over his chest and nodded. "Mmm. That more better. Ain't no boys in this hood. Spose you know it gonna cost ya? Rules don't come for free."

Marcus sniffled a few more times, but dug in his pocket. "Gots... um... " He counted in his little palm. "Two dollars an... um... forty-seven cents. That enough, man? I can sco' some more tomorrow."

Gordon took the money and shoved it in his jeans. "Yeah. You covered, man." He glanced over his shoulder. "We runnin a special on assholes today."

Marcus followed Gordon's eyes. "Yo! You gonna do that sucker, Gordy? Shit, I pay extra to see that, man. Word! I seen a dead kid once, but I never seen nobody get iced!"

Gordon frowned. "Ain't nuthin cool bout killin somebody, stupid. An don't call me Gordy! You pay for rules, rules 'tect ya. Nuff said! Anyways, why ain't you in school?"

"Oh, I wuz just goin. What it is, my mom take me to the doctor this mornin. Got me a ear affection. Wanna see my excuse?"

"No. Get cruisin. An keep your mouth shut, hear me?"

The little boy nodded hard. "Word up, Gordon! Straight! I cool!"

Lyon led the kid to the alley entrance. "Yo, Marcus-man. Rub some dirt over them shoes. Soon's you can."

"Oh, shit, Lyon! My mom have a total cow!"

Lyon nudged Marcus up the sidewalk, exchanging glances with Curtis, who stood at a corner wall. "Listen up! You be figurin your mom wanna see you wearin a little dirt, or nappin in a whole lot? Cool dudes use their minds, man. Stay alive. Now get your butt off to school."

Marcus hunched his shoulders and started up the street. "Okay, Lyon. But I *still* hope you waste that motherfucker!"

Lyon gave Curtis a shrug, then returned to the alley. Gordon was squatting in front of Justin, between his sprawled legs. There was blood smell in the air, but the stain on Justin's jeans wasn't much bigger. Flies circled hopefully. Justin's long-muscled body had that hollowed gauntness of never having enough to eat. His plain white tee, jeans, and Nikes were ragged and dirty, and his untended hair was matted. He was sweating even though the morning was still cool, and his scent was strong and sour. His teeth were still clenched and he breathed through them in shallow sips. His half-open eyes were dull and hopeless.

Gordon checked the boy's earlobes; the left was pierced but hadn't had a ring in it for a long time. There were no holes in his arms, but Gordon spread his unresisting fingers and found burns. In Justin's pockets were only a pipe and a switchblade and eighty cents. Gordon shoved the coins in his own pocket, and checked out the knife, which was better than his own had been.

Justin's voice sounded the way his eyes looked. "Please don't kill me. I dint know this was anybody's ground. Swear to God. Let me go. I never come back here. Please."

Gordon snorted. "Shit! You sayin you never seen our marks?"

Justin's eyes lifted slightly to search Gordon's face. "Swear to God I dint, man! I only seen where the Crew's ground end. That all!"

"He lyin," said Ric in a cheerful tone. He twisted the gun a little.

"Like a motherfuckin doggie," added Rac, poking his gun deeper into Justin's ear.

Justin winced, and his eyes dropped to stare at nothing.

"Keeja."

Justin looked up at Lyon.

"One time you had pride, man," the slender boy said. "An a heart." Then he shrugged. "Don't tell me the story. I hear it all a'fore."

Gordon bent forward and slipped the knife blade into Justin's left nostril. "Member what I say bout second warnins? Real time mostly give you none. This here your first, last, an onliest!" He flicked the blade, slicing a quarter-inch slit in the boy's nose. Justin's body went steel-hard for an instant but he stayed quiet. Blood trickled over his lips to spatter his chest.

"That mind you we gots us rules here," said Gordon. He rose and turned to Lyon. "Figure he walk?"

"Hurt like hell, your bullet in there, but he walk he be wantin to bad enough."

Gordon studied the knife again, then sighed and dropped it between Justin's legs. "You hear? You walk! You get your crack-ass the fuck out our hood!"

Gordon stepped back. The twins hauled Justin to his feet. He yelped and clutched his thigh as weight came on his leg, and would have fallen but for Gordon grabbing him. "Ahhhuuuggg!" he squalled. "I can FEEL it in there! I CAN'T walk, man!"

The twins moved back, their guns still pointed. Justin's face seemed to melt into that of a lost little kid. He slumped against Gordon, tears and blood dripping down Gordon's shirt. "What I do, man?" he sobbed. "Got no home. Nobody give a shit! Now I shot! I don't wanna die, man!" He buried his face on Gordon's broad shoulder.

Gordon's forehead creased. His hand drifted to Justin's back and made a few pats. The twins looked uncertain as they held their guns, flicking tawny glances at Lyon. Curtis peered around the corner. Lyon picked up the knife and slipped it into Justin's pocket. "You shoot us first, 'member?"

Justin kept his face hidden on Gordon's shoulder. "But it
hurts!" Then he jerked up his head and stared at Lyon. "Make it
stop, man! Take it out! Please! I hear you say you could."

The twins' eyes widened and locked on Lyon. Their guns now
pointed at the pavement. Gordon shifted uneasily, his hand still
wanting to pat Justin's back. "Um, can you, Lyon? I mean, if that
what he really want?"

Lyon scanned Justin's eyes. "It gonna hurt, man. More'n you
ever dream. Listen up. There be a kid-center place three blocks
over an bout four east. They not no Boys'an Girls' Club or nuthin.
Not ask no stupid questions, nor tell no cops neither. They fix you.
Feed you. Help you get clean, but only if you really want."

"But I can't *walk,* man!" Justin's eyes hardened. "What your
motherfuckin rules say over *that,* sucker? Say, leave me here to
die? Say call the cops to kick me, put their dogs to bite me, then
lock me up cause I got no home? Nobody *want* black kids, man! I
been there! The places they put you, even you ain't done nuthin, be
just like prison, man! You locked in! Gimmie a chance, man! Take
it out. PLEASE!"

Lyon looked into Justin's eyes a moment more, then nodded.
He pulled the blade from Justin's pocket, flipped it open, and
tested the edge on his thumb. "Kay, man. But I warn ya." He
pointed. "Ric, Rac! Take him back in the doorway. Hold him like
you was. Curtis-homey! Yo! Come take a leg here. Gordon, you
take the other one. Hold him tight."

Quickly, the boys took their positions, pinning Justin against
the rusty steel door again. Lyon was moves, wasting no time.
Kneeling, he sliced Justin's jeans open over the wound. Justin

watched, his thin chest heaving, but there were no more tears. Lyon nodded to himself, then wiped the blade and his fingers on his shirttail. His eyes lifted to Justin's. "You sure, brother?"

Justin squeezed his eyes shut. "Just do it!"

"Um?" asked Curtis. "Maybe we should give him a bullet to bite on?"

"Don't be a goddamn fool!" muttered Lyon. He sucked a breath, then his long slender fingers moved fast. The blade flashed. Justin screamed once, but the other boys held him down. Lyon's quiet voice cut the silence that followed. "Game over."

Justin's eyes fluttered open. He stared at Lyon's bloody fingers and the little chunk of ruby-dripping lead they held.

"Want it, man?" asked Lyon.

Justin's eyes closed. "No."

Lyon shrugged and flipped the bullet toward the alley mouth. Rac patted Justin's shoulder. "You got balls, man. That musta hurt." Ric nodded. "Yeah, Justin, you musta been a pretty cool dude one time."

"You gots a good heart, man," said Lyon. "Be listenin to it more." Stripping off his shirt, Lyon tied it tight around Justin's thigh. Ric and Rac helped the boy to his feet. He tried his leg, winced, but nodded to Lyon. "Um, thanks, man. Three blocks back an four east, you was sayin?"

"Word... Keeja." Lyon folded the knife and handed it to the boy.

Justin limped toward the alley entrance. He stopped, bent painfully down and picked up the bloody little bullet, then slipped it into his pocket before going on.

Gordon gripped Lyon's shin shoulder as if it were something fragile and easily broken. "What he callin himself, that African name? It don't change nuthin."

Lyon shook his head. "No. It don't. Sometimes bad be sad."

Gordon sighed. "Times I don't unnerstand you at all, Lyon."

Curtis moved to Lyon and shyly slipped an arm around his slender waist. "That cause he magic. Ain't sposed to unnerstand magic shit, just believe an get your ass out the way an let it work!"

Rac made smacking sounds with his lips. "Aw, kiss him, why doncha, Curtis!"

"Word!" added Ric. "We all *know* you wanna!"

"Assholes!" bawled Gordon. "Shut the fuck up an gimme them goddamn guns fore you go and shoot yourselfs in *the* brain!" He snatched both guns from the twins.

Ric shrugged. "Well, leastways we score ourselfs a new bang-bang, huh?"

"Yeah," said Rac. "So what kind is it, Lyon-o?"

Lyon took the revolver from Gordon and peered closely at the tiny letters. "Iver Johnson. What ole people call a Sat'day-night special. Top catch, see? Obsolete. Can't say how big... maybe a .34 or 37.50 or somethin else they ain't made in a million years. Prob'ly be a pain in the butt findin bullets for it... why Justin only packin three." He glanced at Gordon. "Maybe the pawnshop man tell us more when we go by for scorin them .22 bullets."

Gordon frowned and shoved the automatic back in his jeans. "Ain't s'prised. If that sucker had him a decent gun he'd prob'ly sold it to buy more rock." He considered. "Well, we gots but two shots left in the .22, an deuce more in that Ivy-Jackson thing. Maybe we better go by an see the pawn man fore we take Curtis home. Case more shit happen. Shit come in piles, y'know? Might be a cool idea to re-up our marks too. I gots some paint, home."

"But we hungry, goddamnit!" squalled the twins.

"An Curtis here still be bleedin some," added Lyon.

Shaking his head, Gordon started back down the alley. Lyon moved to follow but the twins barred his way.

"Yo! So who get to carry the nickel gun now?" demanded Rac. "The Ivory-Jason?"

"Yeah," said Ric. "You gots your magic, don't need no gun. Give it me!"

"No, ME," yelled Rac, shoving his brother. "I say so first!"

Lyon smiled his V and handed the revolver to Curtis. The small boy made a face at the twins and slipped the gun carefully into his jeans, like Gordon. "It a Iver-Johnson. An both you be pussy clots. So *there!*" He and Lyon walked together after Gordon, Curtis with his little chest puffed, and strutting. Ric and Rac stomped along behind; they didn't weigh much and it was hard for them to stomp loud enough to be noticed.

"Dint want the motherfuckin thing anyways!" muttered Rac. "Goddamn wienie-dude gun, all that is!"

"Yeah!" agreed his brother. "Bozo-leted Ichy-whatsis!"

"Um?" Curtis murmured to Lyon. "Gordon way past cool shot, huh? For to just hit the dude in the leg like that. Just like a movie, huh, Lyon?"

Lyon let out a soft snicker. "Gordon be lucky he hit him anywheres. Almost do a beer truck, case you didn't see."

"Oh yeah. But what if he accident'ly kill the dude?"

Lyon shrugged. "Justin be tryin to do Gordon, weren't he? Sides, what is, is. What ain't, ain't worth nuthin. Magic always do the right thing. Believe."

Back at the other end of the alley the boys picked up their school things, shouldered packs, and decked their boards, then rolled in file down the block once more. There were more cars moving in the street now, and people on the sidewalks. As always, a siren sounded somewhere in the distance, and the faint jangle of a burglar-alarm bell carried from blocks away. The Friends skated casually, weaving around people, dodging the legs of wineheads and zoners sticking from doorways, eyed occasionally by other kids but generally ignored by adults as if they didn't exist at all. They reached Gordon's block and were almost to the steps of his building when the fat boy cut suddenly into the deep-set doorway of a burned-out storefront. The other boys followed instantly, tailing and peering with Gordon down the street. A gleaming black Trans-Am was curbed on the opposite side. A cop cruiser was double-parked behind it, strobes firing.

Gordon laughed. "Yo! Them's the same two cocksuckers slapped us around! Let's check how Deek sucker like bein treated niggerboy style! Maaan, he always got shit in that car... everbody know! Maybe them cops do some actual good... bust his ass fore he kill somebody else!"

"Mmm," murmured Lyon. "Maybe, one time, we see the law work."

"Wish I had me a camera," said Curtis.

Ty was thinking about going home for supper; he could stop at a market and buy as many groceries as he could carry... maybe a pack of Popsicles for the kids. His brother Danny wanted a new pair of Nikes, the major-buck kind. Ty wondered what his size was now... the little dude was growing so fast. Then Ty saw Deek's eyes flick up to the mirror.

"Shit!" Deek muttered.

Ty glanced in the outside mirror in time to see the cruiser light its strobes, remembering Danny calling it "popping cherries." The .45 was in Ty's lap, along with a half-empty Heineken. He slipped the bottle back into the sixer, laid the gun on top, and covered all with Deek's T-shirt. Deek's face had paled slightly as he swung the car to the curb and stopped. Ty noticed that he cut the front wheels back out again and left the engine running with his foot on the clutch. Maybe it was the beer, but Ty felt cool, even though the Trans-Am's trunk packed mega trouble. Deek was a good driver, and the 'Am had twice the acceleration, cornering grip, and top speed of any city cop car. It was also registered to a blind post-box number. Ty knew Deek wouldn't hesitate a second to abandon it if he had to. The chase might even be fun... like an Eddie Murphy movie. The picture of Deek bailing his jiggly lard across some trash-choked vacant lot almost brought a smile to Ty's lips. But then Deek gave a snort of disgust.

"It just *them* suckers! Shit! Hard to believe it been a week already, huh?"

Ty shrugged. "Time warp fast when you havin fun, I spose." He glanced in the mirror again, seeing the white cop waiting in the car. The man's face behind his chrome gasses wore the same sly, shit-eating expression that Danny had put on the day Ty had caught him shoplifting in Pay Less Drugs... a goddamn Speak 'N Spell, of all the stupid things to steal! Ty had bought it for him anyway.

The black cop ambled up to Deek's window. Deek ripped open his belt pouch and dug out five hundred-dollar bills. A few people on the sidewalk had slowed their pace as they passed, watching the scene with eyes that were curious, hopeful, or hostile. But Deek's chubby fingers moved fast, hidden between his legs, as he folded the bills and sandwiched them into the Trans-Am's papers.

The big cop leaned casually against the car, his voice pitched to sound routinely bored, but loud enough for the people on the curb to hear. "License, registration, and proof of insurance, please."

The sidewalk people moved on, one or two looking disappointed. A bag lady with a cartful of cans and crap stayed, but she hardly counted as human. Wordlessly, Deek handed the stuff to the man.

Ty's gaze drifted across the street to the burned-out building. He'd seen the skate kids cut in to the doorway, and watched them now as they peered from the shadows behind broken window glass. Ty didn't know much about them... just another young dogshit hood gang. The big fat boy was the leader, though he didn't look too bright and it was a miracle he could ride at all. The twins were born followers, hyper to the max and probably a bitch to keep under control, but they'd be fearless and loyal to whoever they respected. There was the small kid with his childlike potbelly and long, tangled dreads: maybe half white, judging by his features and the yellow-brown tones in his hair, and no doubt the mascot who took all the shit and got the dirtiest jobs. Both he and the tall, slender boy were shirtless, and all were cutting school. Ty couldn't blame them much; it had probably been one hell of a morning. Ty tried to get a better look at the slim graceful boy with the big puppy feet and the loose, pawlike hands. For some reason Ty had always been curious about him; it was strange how hard it seemed to see him clearly. Like a ghost in a movie, he never appeared as solid and real as the other boys. Ty sometimes wondered if his pure blackness could somehow shimmer the air around him like heat waves from asphalt. He couldn't really be called girlish, yet was almost more pretty than handsome, and, without a shirt, looked too delicate and fragile to survive in this neighborhood. Of course, the other gang members would protect him. Ty frowned slightly: some boys that age would use a pretty dude until they got the facts of life straight. But Ty didn't think that was happening here. The fat kid might lead, but the slender boy hovered ever at his elbow, and

Ty suspected he was the one really in control.

Ty smiled a little, recalling how blown-away those two big boys had been that these kids had shot back. He could guess the gang's thoughts as they peered from behind glass fangs; they would be figuring that the cop had gone back to his car to run Deek's license. They'd be hoping that the 'Am would get searched, found full of rock, and that he and Deek would be slapped around, maybe whacked a few times with the cops' clubs, then handcuffed and hauled away forever. Ty knew this because when he was their age he'd have prayed for the same. He suddenly wanted another beer, but fired one of Deek's Shermans instead and ignored the wistful look the bag lady gave him. One hand strayed to the little medallion on his chest.

Ty closed his eyes, sucking smoke deep and holding it. He remembered back to when Deek was first scheming him out as a bodyguard. They'd been cruising in the 'Am, just sipping beer and listening to some old Rick James on the CD, when these cops had pulled them over. Till then, Ty wasn't sure about taking the job, as if some small part of him, only half real like a ghost, still stood on the sidewalk clutching his scarred old skateboard and watching the gleaming car pass him by. But seeing Deek casually slip money to the cop, Ty had felt something crumble inside him, and the hungry young ghost on the curb had faded forever.

Now he gazed over at the other young boys and felt only a worn-out sort of sorrow... like finding a favorite T-shirt after losing it for months only to discover it just wouldn't fit anymore. In a way those kids were a kind of last defense. Ty felt sympathy, knowing that what they were fighting was so huge and powerful and so far beyond their understanding that they might as well have been trying to stop a tank with BB guns.

Ty himself didn't understand much more, except that there *was* something, and he figured whatever that something was for sure didn't want to be understood. He'd seen a TV special once about the Great Pyramids, and that's how he visualized it: he and Deek were just a couple of bricks on the bottom. On the next level up was the older black dude with the Mercedes and Afro-yuppie suit who Deek scored from about once a week. Above that was only a rumor of a white man uptown. And beyond that the pyramid towered into the clouds and Ty could only imagine what might be hidden up there. Lying awake at night, Ty tried to forget what the pyramid was built on—enough to know what it was made from; power and money and greed. Its cement was probably hate and fear and hopelessness. Ty always pictured the bottom bricks as black.

To Ty, these cops were on no higher a level than his own — more likely one row down. Under them were the kids who sold for Deek in the parks and streets and schools. There were about thirty at any time, though the exact number changed almost daily as new ones came in and others got out. Some were busted... usually the new ones and often in their first week. Others just quit, and a few just stopped... or, as that old anti-smoking commercial on TV went, *actually, technically, they died.* Below them were the kids who dealt only to use. Math had never been easy for Ty, but he figured a conservative estimate of 30 x 5 for them. They just *stopped* a lot, more often at the hands of their own burned customers than what they put into their own bodies. And the foundation for the whole structure was the kids who crouched in doorways or stairwells with their pipes and papers and points, begging on the streets for money to "get something to eat," fucking it for the kids who were really starving and *had* to beg, and breaking into cars and apartments and preying on all those younger or weaker... or alone.

Without friends.

Ty smoked and watched the boys, thinking how funny it was that everybody outside places like this should be so stupidly amazed that kids wanted guns and banded together in gangs. What in hell else were they supposed to do, go it alone and get picked off one by one? Trouble was, gangs, like individuals, could be bought and used by those smarter and more powerful.

Ty frowned and idly fingered his medallion. Like now. Like those kids over there had no idea how Deek was fitting them into the pyramid... the one that was black on the bottom but white on the top.

Ty flipped his half-smoked cigarette out the window, watching as the bag lady scrambled for it. Hell, he thought, didn't those kids watch anything on TV but cartoons? For sure, the facts and figures on the news were mostly lies, but after a while you could *see* them! If you paid attention. If you didn't fuck up your mind. It was plain as dogshit on the sidewalk that if you were rich and white and got caught doing drugs you had a *dependency problem.* You went on TV and told everybody how sorry you were and checked into a place for rich fuckups. A poor black kid with burns on his fingers got dragged into an alley by the cops and beat to a pulp before being hauled off to jail. When are you ever gonna get real, little brothers!

The cop came back to Ty's window and handed him the papers without a word. His face was expressionless behind his chrome mirrors. Ty could see Deek's reflection in silver. It was funny how a dead expression was also a childlike one. Deek said nothing; there was nothing to say that wouldn't have been an even bigger joke. Deek let out the clutch and swung the car away from the curb, not bothering to signal because the cop car stood guard for him.

Ty studied the gang boys as the Trans-Am purred past. Four faces showed sullen hatred for what they couldn't understand. Ty knew the feeling well. It was what would eventually cement them into the pyramid after they were beaten down by banging their heads against it for a few more years. Ty had seen that look in so many eyes for the last few months that he hardly noticed it anymore, even though he knew that, given half a chance, those kids wouldn't waste a second killing Deek and himself on the spot. But there was something different in the fifth face: the fragile features of the slender boy. Maybe it was the shadows, or the way he always seemed so hard to see. It made Ty uneasy.

Deek saw where Ty was looking. His foot came off the gas and his eyes flicked to the mirror as the cruiser made a squeaky U-turn and dwindled down the block.

"Yo, stupid! How come you never say nuthin? Shit, this's *perfect!*"

Ty shrugged. He picked up his beer and chugged it while Deek cut the car across the street and pulled to the curb, facing the wrong way, directly in front of the gang. Ty could feel the tenseness of the younger boys, trapped as they were in the doorway. He snagged the .45 and flicked off the safety as the fat one reached behind his half-bare butt and the others automatically spread out as wide as they could between the walls. The hate was still there, maybe tempered a little by fear, but the fat boy's jaw was set and the twins' tawny eyes like frozen gold. Only the smallest kid looked uncertain. He pressed against the slender boy, who just seemed to watch with no expression at all. Ty caught a flash of something silver passed from the small kid to the older one, whose long, loose paw closed over it. Ty gave the block a quick checkout; traffic was light, and the cops wouldn't be back. Most people on the sidewalk, at least those under forty who had more than Jell-O for brains, seemed to have found some excuse to cross over to the other side of the street. Only an old lady with a grocery bag walked obliviously between the car and the doorway. Ty slipped out fast and stood, his door left half open while he leaned against the car. His big hands were clasped casually on the roof, cradling the pistol so the boys could see what is.

He didn't exactly point it at them, just close enough to signify. Ty knew about their .22, but the silver glint in the slender boy's paw bothered him. He wished that Deek had given him time to snag the short-barreled Uzi carbine from the back seat. Even drunk or stoned Deek was no fool, and he hadn't lived to sixteen by taking these kinds of stupid chances. Ty supposed, as always, he had a reason.

Despite the Heinekens, Ty's senses were sharp, aware of the street life around him. The sparse traffic, both ways, would slow momentarily until the drivers read the word, then speed up to get past. On the opposite sidewalk people were doing the same.

Nobody wanted to witness. Even the crazy bag lady moved on, her shopping cart's wheels squealing rustily.

Deek leaned from his window. "Yo, Gordy! What's up, dude?"

Ty saw uncertainty creep into the fat boy's eyes: he might have been ready to die but Deek's cheerfulness took him off guard. The hand hovering back by his butt came slowly to his side. For a moment he hesitated, then took a breath and stepped from the shadows. Even sheathed in rolls of fat his chest was impressive. He came halfway across the sidewalk, warily, like a rat in the open. "So, what you want, Deek? An don't call me Gordy, I hate that!"

Deek put hurt in his voice. "Hey, I'm sorry, Gordon. Didn't know. Just cool to see all you dudes okay."

Ty watched the fat boy's eyes narrow in suspicion. "Why not we be okay, Deek?"

Deek shrugged. "Shitty world, man. That all." Back in the doorway, Ty noted the twins easing closer to the sunlight, curious now. Only the slender boy remained deep in shadow, his half-naked body blending into the background, hard to see. He seemed to be studying Deek. He'd slipped one arm around the smaller kid, keeping him back too. His other paw half concealed what Ty now saw was a little silver gun. It was aimed from the hip full at Deek. Ty wondered how good a shot he was. Though small, the gun was bigger than a .22. Ty gave a mental shrug; he'd done the best he could to cover Deek's ass. The rest was in God's hands. That thought caught him by surprise... funny thing to think.

As always in these situations Ty felt as if time had slowed. Little details stood out sharp. The sun creeping down the storefront had warmed the broken window glass and a tiny triangle dropped from the frame and hit the concrete with a musical note that seemed loud. The fat boy tensed again. The twins' eyes shifted for an instant. Only the slender dude's gaze never wavered.

There was stubbornness in the fat boy's tone. The words came out like they tasted bad. "This *our* ground, Deek! Why you come schemin round here?"

Ty watched the fat boy. There was a hollow triangle in his T-shirt where the twin rolls of chest fat overlapped his belly. That would be a good target, close to the heart, but he'd have to shoot the slender kid first. That wouldn't be easy. Then, to Ty's amazement, Deek popped the door and got out, stretching casually and wiping at the wet under his armpits just like any other kid. Gordon was probably heavier than Deek, and Deek was a good head taller, but Gordon probably had bigger bones. Some kids seemed meant to be fat and looked almost cool that way. Deek wasn't one of them.

Deek's voice was soothing. "Yo, Gordon, I fucked up, okay? Jeez, shoot bullets through me!" He made a vague wave down the street. "What I sayin is, I was just motorin through. How the hell I know them cocksuckin cops gonna curb me? I *sorry,* man. Shit, you *know* I wouldn't try sellin round here without your permission an a righteous cut besides."

Gordon's forehead creased slightly. Two vertical lines appeared over his nose. Ty recalled his mother saying once that those kinds of lines meant a person spent a lot of time trying to figure things out. Somehow you never imagined a fat kid doing much thinking.

Gordon seemed to search for words. He hitched up his

sagging jeans. "Well... "

Behind him, their toes over the sunlit line, the twins edged forward, eyebrows up, breathing through their mouths. The slender boy stayed where he was. His grip tightened on the small kid. The gang's scent came to Ty's nostrils: dirty jeans, old sport shoes, oily hair, and the bittersweet tang of kid sweat. For a second Ty thought he caught a trace of blood smell, but couldn't be sure.

Gordon finished with a lame, "Gots no goddamn right bein here at all, man."

Deek spread chubby pink palms and moved closer to Gordon. "Hey, I hear you, man. An I promise it ain't gonna happen again. Swear to God."

Father of lies, thought Ty. That's what the Bible called the devil.

Gordon seemed to feel the eyes of his gang. His back, curved by the weight of his belly, straightened a little. "Yeah, well... "

"Listen up, dude," Deek went on. "Word. I just had to make a little ole detour. What it is, Wesley wanna talk to me."

Gordon was instantly alert. "Bout what?"

Deek's palms spread wider. His own jeans were slipping. Compared to Gordon's big boy butt Deek had an ass like a girl's, Ty thought.

"Hey, Gordon, you a leader too. You know I can't say. Be breakin the rules, what it is." Deek seemed to think a moment, then stepped even closer to Gordon and laid a big-brother hand on his shoulder. Ty barely heard him whisper. "The Crew maybe havin some drive-by probs, man. Seem Wesley needin some major bucks for scorin himself a decent gun."

Even the twins, closest to Gordon, couldn't have heard. But Ty saw the slender boy's eyes narrow to slits. Gordon looked uncertain for a few seconds, then demanded. "So, what you callin a decent gun, man?"

Ty stiffened as Deek turned with a smile, stepped to the car, and snagged the Uzi from the back seat. All the gang boys tensed. Gordon's hand darted behind his back. The little silver gun gleamed in the slender dude's dark, delicate fingers.

But Deek only held the carbine up sideways for a second or two. "Somethin like this decent enough for ya?"

The twins' eyes went wide as surprised panther cubs. "WAY cool!" breathed one. "PAST," sighed the other. "Word!"

Deek grinned, then casually tossed the gun back into the car. "Word up, you dudes *never* need worry bout nuthin no more, packin one of them! Yo, Gordon, I could make it happen for ya. Straight."

Gordon's mouth had opened slightly. Now it shut with a snap. He snorted. "Uh-huh. Cept how we 'ford bullets for the goddamn thing?"

Deek shrugged. "Aw, there's always ways, man. But what can I say? You just seen the future." He snickered. "State of the art. Believe. Just think on it, that all." He smiled again and took the keys from the ignition. "Anyways, like I sayin, I sorry as hell bout crossin your ground out askin first." He walked back and keyed the trunk lid. "Yo! I pay you dudes for me fuckin up."

Gordon came slowly to the rear of the car. The twins crowded close behind him, all caution gone, expecting more wonders. As if on display against the soft black carpet in the Trans-Am's trunk, next to the grocery boxes holding the real merchandise, were two cases of Heineken.

Deek waved a gold-ringed hand as though performing a magic trick. "Hell, they even still cool, Gordon. Shit, I know you an your dudes don't do nuthin else. They both yours, just for lettin me motor through. Deal?"

Ty watched. Street pride was a funny thing; you never knew what rule it would follow, but it was based a lot on practical logic. He caught the flick of the fat boy's eyes to the slim kid's, and saw a slight nod in the shadows. That confirmed what Ty had always suspected about who did a lot of the gang's real thinking, though Ty's respect for the fat boy's brain had risen a point or two. The twins were trembling like eager puppies.

Gordon stepped back and crossed his arms over his chest. "Okay, Deek. One time, *this* time. An that all it for, hear?"

Grinning, Deek moved aside as the twins scrambled for the beer. "Oh, for sure, Gordon. But I just sayin that my offer always open to ya. Course, that just business, you understand?"

"Mm. Spect I unnerstand a lotta shit, man. We let you know, but don't go holdin your breath or nuthin."

The twins carried the cases back to the sidewalk. Still grinning, Deek slammed the trunk lid. "Word. I think hard, I was you, man. Specially if the Crew go an score some major fire." Deek paused a moment, then bent close to Gordon. "Word up, there some big dudes schemin your hood, man. WAY bad dudes! We talkin Gorilla an Cripps class, little brother! Hope you got mega bullets for them two pop toys of yours, man!"

"Shit," muttered Gordon. "Four third-graders kick *anybody's* ass! Little bullet go through big dude easy as small dude! Save your preachin for somebody who give a shit!"

Deek shrugged and twirled his key ring. "Yo! That was for free, Gordon. Everbody gots to have friends!"

"Mmm. I could say somethin, but I won't."

Ty waited until Deek was back in the car before sliding in himself. He watched the slender boy all the while. Their eyes met again for an instant. Ty picked up another beer and popped it as Deek swung the 'Am into the street and squeaked away.

Deek's beeper sounded as they reached the next block. He pulled up to a corner phone booth smothered in spray paint and surrounded by a glittering pool of its own shattered glass. It was still working, though, because Deek talked for a few minutes, then returned to the car looking almost happy for so early in the day.

"Gots a new one wantin a job," he snickered, sliding back into the seat. "Told him to meet us tonight at the Burger King. Always helps to pig em out first, specially the hungry ones." He released the parking brake and shifted into gear, then glanced at Ty. "You figure that black-ass bitch gonna be there?"

Ty frowned and shrugged. "Naw. Too many hours. Child-labor law. Even if she black as sin." He took a swallow of beer, then added, "Like me."

Deek snickered again and shook his head. "Maaaan, it just too fuckin bad there ain't no more Panthers around. You be a natural. Yo! Black pride an brotherhood be a long time dead, stupid, case you ain't figured it out yet. Only black asses you got to worry over is mine an yours!"

Early evening was hotter than hell in Gordon's apartment as the sinking sun beat on the building's back side. The small front room was dim, lit ruddy red through the single window's pulled-down shade like the sullen glow from a furnace door's glass. That wall was bare brick, graced only by a faded wood-framed picture of Martin Luther King and John F. Kennedy that had once belonged to Gordon's grandmother. There was also a new glossy eight-by-ten of a young Huey Newton in sixties Panther battle gear, and a pair of African spears crossed over a shield, cheap imitations that only looked real from a distance and the sole reminder that Gordon had a father somewhere. Mortar crumbled constantly from between the bricks and dusted the worn-out carpet. From afternoon to sunset the wall radiated heat like a barbecue pit. The window itself was painted solidly shut, and the transom above the triple-locked hallway door was nailed over with plywood. Now the trapped air was a steamy soup of sweating kids, cigarette smoke, and the sharp winey scent of Heineken dark. A ratty old couch sat in the center of the room. It faced the hall door and a TV on a card table.

The TV's screen flickered blue-white with a *Little Rascals* episode. The soundtrack sputtered, chunks of it missing, and the background music was ancient beyond understanding. But the boys sat on the floor with their backs to the couch and watched with more interest than they usually showed for cartoons.

Gordon, Curtis, and Lyon wore only their jeans, their shoes and socks scattered wherever they'd been kicked. The twins were naked and drunk. Gordon had his 501 buttons mostly popped open so his belly spilled free into his lap. A beer bottle stuck up between his wide-spread legs. A Kool dangled from his lips as he carefully copied his English composition onto fresh binder paper with ponderous strokes of a first-grader's huge pencil in between glances at the TV. He frowned as he tried to ignore the twins' constant chatter. Ric and Rac had killed almost a case by themselves and their normally flat stomachs bulged drum-tight and awkward like pictures of wild jungle boys. Gordon flicked ashes into a tuna can and looked over at Lyon, who was sitting beside him. Lyon was blowing smoke rings and sipping his sixth beer. Nobody had ever seen him drunk.

Gordon rolled his eyes toward the twins. "Maybe they pass out soon. I hope."

Lyon smiled his smile and puffed another perfect smoke ring. "When it come by beer, they be like the rats on that ole anti-coke commercial."

"Word. Hell, they be like that with everthing. Gotta have it all *now.* 'Member that time we find the dumpster unlocked 'hind KFC, an them two stuff down chicken till they can't even skate?"

Lyon sent a small smoke ring chasing a larger and piercing it.

"Tigers burn bright. But I think panthers brighter."

"Huh? That some kinda magic talk, man?"

"Naw. Forget it."

Gordon leaned forward and thumbed up the TV as the twins chattered on in their own special language of mostly half-finished sentences. Then Gordon turned to Lyon once more. "Figure that pussy little sucker gonna smoke Miss Crabtree into marryin him? Shit, she way too fine a lady for that schemin prick, anybody see! She a way cool teacher too, best believe. Wish we had somebody like that in our school, huh?" He took a gulp of beer. "Spose she long dead anyways, huh? Or maybe recycled into somebody else."

"Reincarnated, man."

"Whatever." Gordon blew smoke and straightened his homework papers. "Yo, Lyon, do white folks ever get carnationed into black?"

"Mmm. Only the good ones. What it is, being black a major 'sponsibility. It way hard to do right. That why so many fuck it up an forget why they here. Yo. 'Member back when the paper tell bout M. C. Hammer scorin himself a six-million-dollar house an bail Oakland? That sorta what I sayin. I mean, who in hell *need* a six-million-dollar house? You say what you want, man, but way I see it, ain't nobody gonna be happy nowheres till everbody happy everwheres, no matter what color they be."

Rac swung around to face Lyon. "Yo! So what happen to *bad* white people?"

"They come back as dogs nobody want, so they end up street-pizza or gettin put to sleep."

"Oh. Guess that why a dog's ghost signify less'n nuthin, huh?"

"Give it a name."

"Well," said Ric, aiming his Kool at the screen. "Black or white, Gordy right, I for sure wish we had us Miss Crabtree 'stead of ole Crabzilla! But I think she needin somebody, know what I mean?"

"For poppin her cherry," added Rac.

"Shut up," said Gordon. "An stop makin ever goddamn thing dirty all the time!"

"Well," said Lyon. "Don't be worryin over her. Best believe Spanky an his gang be seein right through that slimy little sucker like glass. Him an Buckwheat be smokin his butt anytime now. Word."

Gordon frowned slightly. "Spose you seen this one a'fore too?"

"Course. Wanna know what happen?"

"No."

Curtis had been busy back at the kitchen counter and now came padding over to the couch. He carried a beer in one hand, and his own tummy was puffed like a balloon from trying to pace the bigger boys. He concentrated on keeping to a straight line, and carried a plate balanced carefully in his other hand. "Yo! Ketchup sandwiches comin up!"

Ric and Rac, slumped shoulder to shoulder on the other side of Gordon, their chins and chests glistening with spilled beer, snickered out Kool smoke. "Don't ya gotta eat em first for that to happen?" asked Rac.

"Shit!" said Ric. "You mean that all what left we can eat here?"

"Well," sniffed Curtis. "You both be pussys so why don't you go an eat yourselfs?"

The twins exchanged glances. "That pretty cool," giggled Ric.

Rac considered. "For Curtis." Both snagged two of the drippy red-and-white things and chewed messily. "No goddamn napkins?" demanded Rac.

"SHUT UP!" roared Gordon.

Putting the plate on the couch, Curtis sat clumsily down next to Lyon. The gash on his back had been covered by gauze stuck to him by Big Bird Band-Aids. His hand shyly found the slender boy's.

Ric gulped beer and giggled. "Yo, Curtis! Ask if Gordon let ya use his crib!"

"Word!" snickered Rac. "Give it a name! Kiss him now, why don't ya?"

Gordon clenched a big fist in front of Rac's nose. The twins exchanged glances of innocence. Suddenly, Ric grabbed his brother and wrestled him flat on his back, scrambling on top and pressing him down. "Oooooh, Lyyyyon! You make me go all squishy inside like ketchup sandwiches!"

Rac squirmed and wiggled, both boys gleaming and slippery as seals. "You can tear off all my clothes but you can't make me pant!"

"Hey!" giggled Ric. "My mom say that!"

"No shit? Mine do too! Ain't that a 'incidence!"

"Stop that!" bawled Gordon. "It dirty an gross! An this here my mom's goddamn 'partment!"

Snickering, the twins staggered to their feet, their arms going over each other's shoulders. Snagging their bottles, they stumbled, laughing, for the bathroom.

Curtis scowled. "Prob'ly gonna go an beat-off!"

Gordon spun around and glared after them. "You do, you

goddamn well gonna clean it up! Ain't gonna have my mom thinkin I done it!"

Lyon grinned. "They prob'ly couldn't even find their dicks now with all four hands an a flashlight."

Gordon set his homework pages on the couch, flipped his pencil across the room, and turned back to the TV. "Well, I like how Buckwheat an Spanky always workin together like brothers. An that was a long time ago when black an white kids wasn't sposed to hang together. They was a way cool gang, huh?"

Lyon nodded. "That the way gangs oughta be, man, good, but not takin no shit off nobody neither." A shadow crossed his face. "So, what you be thinkin bout Deek, man? You be figurin it worth a couple cases now an again for lettin him motor our hood?"

Gordon stared at the TV and shrugged. "Not now, man. I mean, we sposed to be kicked-back an partyin, ain't we? Just forget the goddamn street a while."

Lyon blew a last smoke ring before crushing out his Kool. "Mmm. That be the one thing most hard to forget. There time for partyin, an frontin, an maxin, an time for fightin. Seem like we don't got much time for thinkin."

"School time sposed to be for thinkin, man."

"Well, there thinkin, an then there *thinkin* with your own mind."

A commercial came on for the Ninja Turtles' new pizza machine gun, the colors starkly bright in the room's sullen shadows. Gordon sighed and took another gulp of beer. "Mmm. Well, you figure Deek talkin anywheres close to straight bout Wesley an his dudes workin for him to score themselves a good gun? I mean, the Crew always up for keepin their ground clean. Same's us."

Lyon combed long fingers gently through Curtis' dreads to take out the tangles. "Could be... *if* Deek talkin straight, specially bout them big dudes schemin. After all, man, guns be the only way we got a chance with somebody twice our size. I ain't sayin Deek don't lie like a dog most times, but if the same kinda shit what happen to us this mornin come down on the Crew, just might be they gettin scared enough to try goin for some of Deek's dirty bucks." Lyon gazed into space for a while, his fingers moving slow and careful. Curtis lay with his head on Lyon's leg, his eyes closed and a smile on his bronze little-boy face. Lyon looked back at Gordon. "Main prob to my mind be, if the Crew score themselves a Uzi, it turn out just like the TV always sayin bout that Middle East shit. Balance of power gonna get fucked up. Word."

Gordon frowned and glanced over to his narrow bed near the kitchen counter where the two small guns lay atop the gray USN blanket. "Well, the pawnshop man tell us he can still special order bullets for that ole Michael Jackson."

"Iver-Johnson. But what good that gonna do us up against a Uzi, man?"

"Yeah. Shit." Gordon fingered his jaw. "But why Wesley even wanna put moves on our hood, Lyon? Word come to me say he gots enough probs in his own."

Lyon shrugged a slender shoulder. "Uzi change things. Same's why Deek always be schemin round here when he already gots more money than God." Untangling his fingers from Curtis' hair, Lyon jerked a thumb toward the bathroom doorway. "It be the same sorta reason them twins go an drink they fool selfs to death, you let em. Gettin more shit always make you *want* more shit, man. Don't know why, but that what it is." Curtis was asleep. Lyon gazed down at the small boy's peaceful face. "There be this too, Gordon. We start lettin Deek cruise round here, little kids gonna see him. Some gonna start creamin their jeans over that goddamn car. Others gonna want to buy what he sellin. That make us workin for Deek any way you figure it, man. Hell, you see that."

Gordon pulled up his knees and dropped his chin into his hands. "Yeah. Spose I do. Maybe I just waitin to hear you say it in that real-time way you got. Well, all what I know is, if the Crew come by a better gun than us, we gonna have probs. An ain't no way we ever gonna score our ownselfs some major fire without we find us some mega money." He met Lyon's eyes. "So, magic-boy, you tell me where we gonna score that kinda buck, cept by some sucker like Deek? An, even Wesley stay cool, what about them big dudes, man? Bet your ass *they* got Uzis or Tens or somethin else way past bad. Like you say, how small dudes like us gonna keep equal?"

Gordon sighed again and nodded toward the TV. "Musta been way past cool, bein a kid back in them olden days. Even if we did gotta ride the butt end of buses." His eyes narrowed as he turned back to Lyon. "Yo. Y'all thinkin somethin again. I can always tell cause you get that magic look."

Lyon smiled and drained his bottle. "Ghost of a dog, man. Just thinkin I wish we knowed more bout Deek. Anyways, let it chill. Tomorrow another day."

Gordon nodded. "Yeah. But I totally outa ideas, man. Course, I could do me some schemin on Wesley at school. Times he talk free when his dudes ain't around."

Lyon grinned. "Special when he be sweatin to copy somebody's homework." He glanced at the binder sheets on the couch. "That story of yours all done over, man?"

"Close enough for Crabzilla. Times I get to wishin I knew me more big words, like you. But then I gots more on my mind than goddamn homework right now, best believe. Like keepin us all alive. THAT how I gonna be spendin my motherfuckin summer vacation! Word!" Gordon killed his beer and reached for another. "Lyon? Was things always this shitty for kids?"

Once more Lyon shrugged. "It the way things be *now* what matter."

The Little Rascals ended by saving the day, and the news came on. There were two million homeless people in the United States and eight million predicted by the year 2000. The President was giving ten million dollars to Czechoslovakia, and aid to the kinder, gentler U.S.S.R. was being considered in Congress. Gordon leaned forward and turned off the TV. The sun was gone, and the room went dark as the screen dwindled to a single tiny point of light. Gordon got to his feet, his unbuttoned jeans slipping low, and switched on a dim, yellow-shaded floor lamp by the couch. He stood for a moment looking down at Lyon and Curtis. "Um... you can use my crib, y'know? Anytime."

"Huh? Oh, thanks, Gordon, but I ain't sleepy."

"Um..." Gordon pointed to Curtis. "I mean... well, y'know? You an him?"

"Mmm? Curtis gonna be spendin the night with me again. I call his mom so's she don't worry. His parents don't like seein him drunk."

Gordon flushed. "I mean, for you *an* him."

Lyon laughed. "Oooo." He looked down at the small sleeping boy, then grinned up at Gordon. "Now shit, here I figure you know me better'n anybody, man. But, what it is, I spose me an Curtis love each other, but not *that* way."

Gordon plopped down on the couch, crinkling his homework sheets. "Oh. Um... well... shit. Course I never ask, but this last couple years I just figured you was... " He swallowed. "Um... gay."

Lyon grinned. "Mean, Christmas mornin an all that shit, man?"

Gordon grabbed a bottle and took several big gulps. "Well, times you mind me of Michael Jackson."

Lyon looked thoughtful. "What it is, Michael Jackson's a werewolf, man. That why he be lonely an nobody understand him. Word!"

Gordon took another swallow of beer. "Well, it just that you all the time so... gentle, man. What I sayin is, somebody dint know you, figure you maybe for a puss."

"Mmm. So, what you really sayin is, black dudes ain't spose to be gentle?" Grinning again, Lyon stood and puffed his slender chest, making the fine muscles stand out. He pumped a biceps and posed. "Maaaan, I gonna smoke me some butt tonight! Jo mama!"

Gordon snickered. "That look just plain stupid, man. Somethin Wesley do."

"Well, what I sayin is, everbody be half boy an half girl."

"WHAT?"

"Figure. You gots a mom an a dad, don't ya?"

Gordon considered that a long time. Finally, he nodded. "Mmm. So, what you tellin me is everbody gots a gentle part an a hard part, an the girl part's the gentle one?"

Lyon grinned again. "Not always, man. Ever hear of Lucrezia Borgia or Lizzie Borden?"

"They do stuff like Madonna?"

"Times I think Madonna want to do stuff like them. Anyways, ain't no rule say a dude got to be bad. . . least when there no reason to be. Yo. Even a bad-ass ole panther take time out to be gentle to its cubs, huh. Now you see what I sayin?"

"Maybe after I think on it some more." Gordon rolled the bottle between his palms and looked at the floor. "But I never seen you schemin a girl, man."

"Well, I never seen you neither."

"Um... you ever figure I get a girl to like me, Lyon?"

"Course! Yo! Lisa Thompson in fifth period all the time peekin you out, man! Mean to tell me you never even notice? An she ain't the only one, best believe. Thing is, girls come at you sorta sideways most times. You gotta pay attention. It like lookin for magic signs."

Gordon reached for the last sandwich. "Sound more like some kinda game to me."

"Mmm. That be givin it another name, man. Take up a lot of your time, you start in playin it, best believe."

"So how come you ain't playin it? For sure you gots the looks."

"Don't gots the time."

Gordon glanced down at himself. "Shit. Check me out. I just a stupid-lookin fat boy, man."

"You ain't stupid. An bein fat in this hood show you some kinda survivor. Lotta hungry kids give they left nuts to be your size. Word."

Gordon was quiet while he finished the sandwich, then he looked up at Lyon again. "What it is, man, I never even kiss nobody a'fore. I mean, cept my mom, course, but that a different thing."

Lyon smiled. "It come natural."

"You mean, *you* been kissin girls, man?"

"Done me a lot more'n kiss, best believe. Rubbers I carry in *my* wallet never get all dry an crackly."

"Well, how come you never say?"

"Nobody never ask. Sides, ain't nobody keepin score, an whose business it be but my own?"

"Yeah. That right, huh, man? Well, um, how you do it a'zactly... I mean just the kissin stuff with your tongue an all?"

"Same's you skate. Or do anythin else. Your own personal style."

"Mmm. Spose that mean gentle work for you?"

"Lotta girls *like* gentle. You be s'prised, man."

"Well, guess you fuck all the time then, huh?"

Lyon shrugged and waved a careless paw. "Tell you a secret of the universe, Gordon. Word. *Any* doofus can fuck. It real lovin what seem to come so hard." He frowned. "It most like, well, if you ain't loved when you little, it major hard to learn lovin at all."

Gordon nodded slowly. "Yeah. I think I hear that, man." Still looking thoughtful, he glanced at the clock atop the TV. "Mmm. Seven-thirty. My mom be home in bout a hour an a half."

Lyon snagged an empty bottle from the floor. "Well, I help you clean up all this shit. What you wanna do bout them twins? They prob'ly zoned in the bathtub or something."

"Aw, I drag em out by my bed and throw a blanket over em. Go down an call their mom to say they spending the night again." Gordon frowned and looked back over his shoulder. "SHIT! Them suckers in my MOM'S room!" Stumbling to his feet, jerking up his jeans and almost tripping over Curtis, Gorden roared, "What the fuck you doin in there?"

Rac's grinning face appeared around the doorframe. "Tryin on cheap jewelry. Yo, check it out! We gonna be *gentle* niggerboys!"

He and Ric staggered into the room wearing necklaces, bracelets, and earrings. Curtis sat up, stared, and rubbed his eyes. Lyon hid a grin behind a long paw. Gordon's face turned purple. "You motherfuckin... PERVERTS!"

There was a knock on the hallway door.

For a second, all the boys froze. Then, jewelry jingling, bellies jutting, the twins dashed to Gordon's bed and grabbed the guns. Even drunk they still moved like an attack team, flanking the hail door with their guns up and ready. Gordon eased to the peephole, keeping his big body clear of the door panel. Lyon glided silently to the kitchen. He slipped two long knives from a drawer and passed one to Curtis, then both boys took up positions beside the twins.

"It Tunk," whispered Gordon, his eye to the peephole. "One of Wesley's dudes. He packin his board. Don't see nobody else." He turned to Lyon. "What you figure, man?"

"You sure he alone?"

"How in hell I know? Could be the whole goddamn Crew all up an down the hall and I couldn't see em through this motherfuckin thing!"

"Oh, shit," Curtis whispered, clutching his butcher knife, its blade dripping crimson ketchup. "What if they already score emselfs that Uzi an come for to do us?"

"Shush!" hissed Gordon. "Don't borrow trouble!" He thought a moment, then peered back out through the peephole. "Yo, Tunk! You alone?"

The voice from the hallway was high and punctuated by squeaks. "Word, Gordy. Wes send me, man. 'Bassador. Rules!"

Gordon glanced at the twins; both were breathing hard and deep, shiny with sweat and swaying a little on their feet. But their tawny eyes burned bright. Ric had the safety off on the .22, and Rac held the revolver's hammer back with a thumb. Both gripped their guns double-handed, and their teeth gleamed in their dusky faces.

"Okay," called Gordon. "Rules, man. But I gonna open this door fast, an I want you fly your ass in here warp seven! Get by the TV, an then you CHILL! We gots TWO guns, man! Leave your board outside."

Tunk's voice got even squeakier. "Nuh-uh! No WAY, José! Not my goddamn board! Ain't no rules bout boards, Gordy! There a fuckin ole junkie cruisin your second floor, if ya wanna know. Ain't losin my board to some stinkin ole needle sticker!"

Gordon gritted his teeth and eyed the twins again. "You two better chill! Same's the cops sposed to do, till you actual SEE somethin in his hand! You go an blow him away by accident we gonna have World War III all over the hood! Word!"

Rac snorted. "We cool, Gordy!"

"Yeah!" said Ric. "Go for it, man!"

"Okay," called Gordon. "Board cool, Tunk. But you *move* your ass!"

Gordon unsnapped the locks and yanked back the door. A small boy burst like a blur into the room. He landed solidly in his oversize Nikes near the TV, then spun around as Gordon slammed the door and shot the bolts. But Ric and Rac jammed a gun muzzle in each of Tunk's ears and he froze, clutching his skateboard over his balls.

"Rules, Gordy, rules!" Tunk squeaked. "'Bassador! No goddamn guns in my ears!"

Tunk was no bigger than Curtis, with the same childlike body, but soft velvet black like a moonless midnight. He was loose-lipped and pug-nosed with eyes big and bright under long silky lashes. He wore old 501s with one knee ripped open, a huge gold earring and wrist chain that had to be fake, and a camouflage Army shirt, sleeves rolled up and so big that he looked like a caricature of a street kid in a *Little Rascals* episode. His board was a battered old Tony Hawk, and his big eyes got even bigger when he saw Curtis' knife dripping red.

"Oh, shut up, man," growled Gordon. "Nobody even touch you!" He checked the peephole once more, then pressed an ear to the door panel and listened. Finally, he sighed. "An don't call me Gordy, goddamnit!"

Tunk puffed a little. "How bout just Gordy?"

His V smile flickering, Lyon stepped over to Tunk. Curtis hovered near with the knife. Unbuttoning Tunk's shirt, Lyon ran his hands up the small boy's ribs, patted his pockets, and checked the tops of his shoes. "He be clean, Gordon." Lyon jerked his thumbs in opposite directions and the twins moved back and lowered their guns.

Tunk dropped his board on the floor and flapped his huge shirt like a caped crusader to reveal the rest of him. *"Course* I clean, suckers! Rules!" He puffed his chest again, sniffed, then buttoned his shirt's top button, which came about to the height of his tummy.

Gordon yanked up his jeans and brushed sweat from his forehead. "Yeah, yeah. You safe, man. Prob'ly a lot safer than in that hall. Chill out. Wanna beer?"

Tunk's face brightened. "For sure!" He strutted to the couch and plopped down on top of Gordon's homework. Curtis handed him a bottle. Ric and Rac stayed close by, still watchful. Tunk tilted back the bottle, expertly chugged almost half, then burped, wiped his mouth, and grinned. *"Kickin!* You score this from the Deeker, huh?"

"Rules," muttered Gordon.

"Oh, yeah." Tunk snagged a Kool pack off the couch's arm. "Yo! These anybody's?"

Gordon waved a palm.

"Thanks! My brand!" Tunk popped a cigarette into his mouth. Curtis fired it with his Bic. Tunk sucked smoke, then blew out a satisfied cloud and studied the twins. "Way cool look, bros. Like MTV."

Ric and Rac dropped the guns to their sides, looked at each other, and giggled.

Tunk chugged more beer, smacked his lips, and eyed Curtis' knife. "Shit, dude, you do somebody tonight?"

Curtis looked shy. Lyon took the knife and licked the blade. "In the shower."

Tunk snickered and made stabbing motions. "I get it! Eee, eee, eee!" He watched as the twins sat down on the carpet and reached for fresh beers, then pointed. "Yo! So where y'all score that way cool chrome gun?"

"Nickel," said Curtis.

"Rules," said Gordon. He frowned. "So, I spose you here to tell us the Crew gonna start workin for Deek sucker soon?"

Tunk made a face. "Gimme a break, man. Rules." He killed the bottle and burped again. "But it's 'portant, Gordon. Word up!" He eyed the last sixer on the floor.

"Go for it," said Gordon.

"Way cool!" Tunk popped another bottle and again chugged half. "Shit! That taste megalicious! No lie! Oh, an if you wanna know, we gots a test tomorrow in Crabzilla's class. Maaan, she EVER on the rag today! Believe, believe!"

Lyon smiled. "She been like that ever since Toto 'scape out her bike basket."

"Huh? Oh." Tunk giggled. "Word! So how come you dudes wasn't in school? Cop come round talkin the big-buddy program. Got to kick back a whole half hour for that."

Gordon snorted. "We already been big-buddied. Anyways, maybe we just not feel up for goin today. So why you here, Tunk?" He pointed to the clock. "My mom be home soon, an we gots a junkie to clear out the buildin... less you lie?"

Tunk lay back and gulped more beer, then lazily waved a hand. "No lie. Word. Wes wanna meet. Neutral ground."

Gordon's eyes flicked to Lyon's. "Yeah? This bout Deek?"

Tunk killed the second bottle, burped again, and sighed happily. "Rules. But you gettin warm. Wesley askin, so's you get to pick the place. Long's it neutral, y'know."

Gordon snorted again. "I know by rules, man."

Tunk felt beneath him, pulled out Gordon's homework composition, and studied the first page a moment. "Yeah? Too bad you don't know there ain't no K in vacation."

Gordon turned surprised eyes to Lyon. The slender boy shrugged. "You dint ask."

Lyon sat down close to Tunk. "Yo. 'Bassador be 'portant job, man. Look like you get yourself major thirsty warpin all the way down here too." He popped another bottle and handed it to the small boy.

Tunk grinned and slumped deeper into the couch. "Gotta say, this here shit's my weakness, man. My mom tell it be the death of me!" He giggled. "Least I go happy, huh? Course, I can't get too wasted... gotta skate all the way home, an your hood turn mega-mean this time of night. Couldn't pack my blade on account of this 'bassador stuff, y'know."

Lyon cocked an eyebrow at Gordon. "That be cool, Tunker man. Me an Curtis 'scort you back to your marks after the talkin done. Be your very own bodyguards. Here, this last Heinie got your name all over it."

Tunk gulped again. "Maaan, you dudes way past cool! Know how to treat your bros. One up the rules even. Ain't no wonder we don't fight. Um, gots another smoke too?"

Lyon shook another Kool from the pack, fired Curtis' lighter for Tunk, and handed him the last bottle. Ric and Rac had slumped together, their backs against the couch. They were nodding, the guns loose in their hands.

"Rules be mostly for street time," said Lyon. "Here, we all be like regular homeys." He took Curtis' shoulder and turned him around. "Yo. Check this out, Tunker. Here why we not be in school today. Drive-by. Full-autos in deuce. This for free, man."

Tunk carefully checked out Curtis' back. "Mmm. There some word on that."

Gordon's eyes shifted to Lyon, then back to Tunk. "What word?"

Tunk looked uneasy before shrugging. "Rules, Gordon. Sides, lots of word go round don't mean dogshit." He finished the third bottle, set it aside, then picked at the label of the fourth for a few seconds. "But I tell you this, man. For free. Same a'zact thing happen to us today. After school. This ole black van come rippin by an spray us! Two full-autos, uh-huh, uh-huh! Just like you say!" He jammed a thumb to his chest. *"I* say they Uzis. Tell by the sound, if you wanna know. Wes not so sure, but he shoot back an that motherfuckin van bail its butt, best believe!"

Gordon sat down on the arm of the couch, picked up his homework, frowned at the pages a moment, then set them carefully aside. "Any your dudes get hit?"

Tunk considered, taking a gulp from the bottle. "Mmm. I don't figure I should oughta say, man. Rules again. But all our dudes actin like dogs gone hyper an bout to piss on the floor, uh-huh. Word up, there some big gang schemin out both our hoods."

"Mmm," said Lyon. "Word up, by Deek, what you really tellin

us, huh?"

Tunk nodded, then frowned and studied the bottle. "Shit! Now I so fuckin wasted I just now gone an told you stuff I shouldn't, huh?"

Lyon smiled and gripped the smaller boy's shoulder. "Yo, brother, we cool. We not be sayin nuthin to nobody. Sides, we just went an told you some free stuff by us, 'member?"

"Did ya?" Tunk thought hard, then solemnly nodded. "Oh yeah. You did." He slumped deep in the cushions, unbuttoned his shirt and slapped his belly. "Aw, what the fuck, dudes. I drunk. I happy. Shoot bullets through me. So, Gordon, where ya wanna meet?"

"How bout that ole car wash? The one what been closed since way back in the earthquake? After school tomorrow. Say, bout four?"

Tunk tilted up his bottle and chugged the whole thing, then giggled and wiped his mouth. "Gonna do it, do it good, I say! For sure Gordon. Fact is, we was hopin you pick that place...." He held up his palms. "I mean, don't go gettin paranoid or nuthin... you can pick another one. It just bout the best place around for a meet, that all."

Gordon glanced at Lyon, who nodded. "Sure, man," said Gordon. "The car wash."

Tunk let out a big burp, then struggled to his feet, making it on the second try. He gave Gordon a clumsy high-five. "Done deal, dude."

Curtis handed Tunk his board. "Yo. Hot ole Hawk, Tunk! How's it cruise on them Rat Bones?"

"Aw, nuthin nuclear, man, but it get me there. Y'all still skatin that ole Varifiex, huh? Always wanted to check me out one of them antique flat-deckers."

Curtis picked up his own board. "Well, you prob'ly miss the kicktail at first. Most dudes do. But it a way cool street cruiser. Word up, I gonna score me a Steve Steadham full-size in Jamaica! Yo, wanna trade for the ride back tonight?"

"Shit yeah, dude! Let's do it!" Tunk grinned. "If I can still ride at all with my tank fulla Heinie." He swapped boards with Curtis as Lyon sat down and started putting on his socks and shoes. Curtis went searching for his own. Gordon handed Lyon his T-shirt. "Here, man, Curtis can wear Ric's."

"That be Rac's."

"Whatever. Ain't neither of 'em goin nowhere more tonight, believe." Squatting beside the sleeping twins, Gordon began taking off the jewelry.

Lyon shrugged into Gordon's tee, so big it draped him like a poncho, then knelt and slipped the revolver from Rac's limp fingers. "We run that junkie off on the way out so's he don't be hasslin your mom comm home." Tucking the gun into the back of his jeans, he faced Tunk. "You dudes gonna be packin all your fire to the meet?"

Tunk snickered. "Gimmie a break, man! 'All' our fire! Meanin that puss-pop .38?" He slapped his forehead. "Aw, shit! I just went an done it again, huh?"

Lyon patted his shoulder. "Yo. That just be your heart talkin, brother. We cool. Sides, you could score yourself some points by Wesley, tellin him we gots two guns now."

"Mmm. Figure I should, man? Wes hyper to the max already."

Gordon glanced up. "Might scare him into callin off the meet. An best believe we need to talk bout this shit."

Tunk considered. "Well, I don't know. Seem I gots 'sponsibility by my homeys, man. For sure Wes ain't gonna be stoked over hearin you dudes one gun up on us." Tunk's eyes shifted between the fat boy and Lyon. "Maybe. Maybe I just won't tell him less I figure it need to be said." Tunk searched Gordon's face. "It... like a trust thing, y'know? I stickin out my ass here. You could hurt us bad with that other gun, we dint know you gots it."

Lyon patted the small boy's shoulder once more. "Yo. What it is, we leave the tellin or not tellin up to you, man. Like you say, it be a trust thing. More, it be a heart thing."

Tunk nodded. "You dudes way past cool. Make me wish I live a block closer so's I be in your hood."

"Well," said Curtis, straightening from his shoes. "You can still come over an hang...." He looked at Gordon. "I mean, to trade moves an stuff... " He turned to Lyon. "Y'know? Just like a regular kid?" Spreading his palms, he faced Gordon again. "Can't he?"

Gordon slid the bracelets off Ric's wrist and shook his head. "Rules, man."

Tunk nodded slowly. "Yeah." He fingered Curtis' board. "What it is, first thing happen, you dudes start figurin I schemin on ya. Or Wesley think I schemin for ya. Just can't work, man. Rules make things hard sometimes."

Lyon touched Curtis' arm. "We ain't, none of us, regular kids, man."

Curtis stared at the floor. "Yeah. I think I just now figure what that really mean." He looked up at Lyon. "Things be all cool in Jamaica, huh?"

Lyon smiled. "Believe."

Curtis slipped into Rac's tee, then went to the door. He stood on tiptoes to peer through the peephole. He stiffened. "Yo, Tunk! That there the junkie you was tellin us about?"

Tunk came over by Curtis, stumbling a little, and stood on his toes too. "Word! That the ole rag bag, for sure!" He looked over his shoulder to Gordon. "Yo! Anybody home cross the hall, man? Sucker checkin out the door, if ya wanna know. Listenin for people inside."

"Shit!" spat Gordon. He dropped the double handful of jewelry on the couch. "That ole Mrs. Washington's 'partment. She cook nights at some hospital. Way cool lady. Sometimes bring home cookies an shit for us. Hell, she gots nuthin in there but a goddamn ancient Sony! Black an white!"

Tunk had his eye to the peephole again. "Yeah? Well, that sucker just pull a little crowbar, if ya wanna know. Nice lady gonna lose her Sony, best believe, ya don't get busy, man."

"Shit! What a motherfuckin day!" Gordon grabbed Ric by the shoulders and shook him hard. The boy stayed limp as laundry. Shaking Rac brought only a mumbled curse.

"Shit!" Gordon snatched the pistol from Ric's hand and flicked off the safety. "Wanna help us, Tunk? Nuthin in the rules say you gotta."

Tunk grinned. "Bet your ass I help, man! Be fun! But I tellin ya, that sucker out there gots the terminal twitchies. Never know what they gonna do like that. Maybe gots a blade sides that bar. Ya gonna shoot him?"

Gordon moved to the door and stared through the hole. "Not if we don't gotta. Somebody might go an call the cops an then there be some great big huge donkey show right when my mom come home all tired. Shit. There enough of us here to take that sucker even with them twins drunk on their goddamn asses!"

Curtis snagged the two knives off the TV and offered the bigger to Tunk. Tunk tried the edge on his finger, then grinned and shoved his shirt sleeves higher. "Word up, man! Course we take that cocksucker! Shit, I turn him into deli slices with this! Extra thin! See if I don't!"

"Well," said Gordon. "Try not an hurt him any more'n you gotta, man. We don't want no goddamn blood all over the fuckin place, if there any way other. Special not *his* kind. Prob'ly all fulla AIDS."

Lyon suddenly snapped his fingers. "Yo, Gordon! You mom gots any sheen? In a spray-can?"

"Huh? Yeah. In the bathroom."

Lyon nudged Curtis. "Toast time, homey!"

"Word! Just like Michael Jackson!"

"Huh?" said Tunk.

Lyon shoved the revolver into Tunk's hands and darted for the bathroom. Tunk put down the knife and checked out the gun. "Whoah! Way cool fire, Gordy! Yo! What kinda gun is it anyways?"

"Pull the trigger, bullets come out. But there only two, so don't waste 'em. An don't call—"

"Sorry. I forgot. Um, look like you trust me, huh, man?"

"Mmm. Guess we do." Gordon turned to Curtis, who had

pulled out his Bic lighter and was turning up the valve. "You know what the fuck you doin, man?"

Curtis' little-boy face beamed. "For sure, Gordon! Me an Lyon done this lotsa times!"

Tunk broke open the revolver and checked the two bullets. "Shit, man, these things all green an yucky! Figure they even go off?"

"Dude try an do me with one this mornin. Shoot just fine for him... 'cept he miss."

"Oh." Tunk snapped the gun shut again.

Lyon came running back with the can of hair sheen. "Yo, Curtis! Get busy!"

Across the hall, a tall, thin dude in dirty jeans, sweatshirt, and ragged old-style Cons levered at the doorframe above the dead bolt with a small shiny crowbar. He was probably twenty but looked twice that, with his gaunt face, gray-toned skin, and the bruise-like smudges under his eyes. His movements were stiff and jerky like those of an animated movie-corpse and he shook all over like something wound too tight and ready to snap its spring. He let out a screech and whirled around as Gordon's door burst open, whipping up the crowbar and taking a wild swing at the two small shadows that sprang at him.

Lyon ducked the bar, twisted on his toes, and aimed the spray can. His delicate finger jammed down the button and held it, shooting sheen all over the dude's face. The dude cursed and clapped one hand over his eyes as he stumbled back, the other slicing the air with the sharp steel bar. In the next instant Curtis landed crouching beside Lyon. He jerked up the Bic with both hands and fired it into the spray stream.

There was a muffled FOOM. Yellow-blue flame exploded around the dude's head, blinding bright in the dim-lit hallway. The can recoiled in Lyon's hands but he kept his finger pressed tight on the button. Fire hissed like a blowtorch from the nozzle. The dude's hair crackled.

The dude screamed. The crowbar clattered on the bare board floor as he clawed and beat at his flaming face and hair. He twisted frantically to get out of the fire stream. He staggered back, slammed into a wall, tried to run, and crashed face-first into the other. He stumbled in circles for a few moments, then finally broke into a blind lope for the stairwell. Blood gushed out of his nose from hitting the wall. His screams echoed down the narrow hall. Lyon followed him, cutting off the spray, but pale yellow flames still flickered and crackled in the dude's matted hair. The smell was sickening. Lyon kept the can aimed, urging the dude on with curses and yells as loud as the screams. Curtis trotted at his side, the lighter clutched ready. Gordon and Tunk trailed behind, adding their own bawling and shouts to the noise, guns held up in case the dude tried to fight.

Other doors creaked cautiously open on chains for a second or two, then slammed shut again. Peepholes darkened as eyes watched. The big dude lurched to the head of the stairs. The flames were dying out, but his hair still smoked and stank. He ground his fists into his eyes, blinking hard, lashes charred, trying to see his attackers. Suddenly, Gordon drove between Curtis and Lyon in a football block, slamming his loose bulk into the big dude's body. Another scream echoed in the hall as the dude went over backward down the steel-edged steps in a tangle of arms and legs, animal cries, and fleshy thuds. He hit the landing below with a crash that seemed to shake the whole building. Then there was silence except for the panting of the boys.

They crowded together at the top of the staircase, teeth gleaming and eyes glittering in the dimness. The bulb was gone in the stairwell, and they could see only a black smoking bundle on the landing below.

"Fuuuuuck!" came Curtis' awed whisper. "Maybe we done him anyways?"

Then there were low moans, whimpers, and a curse. The still-smoking shape struggled to its hands and knees and started to crawl away.

Tunk snickered and puffed his chest. "Stick him with a fork, dudes, he DONE!"

Gordon hitched up his jeans, cupped his hands to his mouth, and roared down the stairwell, "An don't come back, sucker! This FRIENDS ground! Next time, you DEAD!"

Behind the boys, another door opened. They turned to see a tired-looking man in dusty work clothes. He asked, "You get the bastard, Gordon?"

"Yo, Mr. Franklin. Spect we did."

The man nodded. "Your mother home yet, son?"

"No sir. Bout another fifteen minutes, I 'spect. But my friends here just now leavin. They make sure that sucker gone fore my mom come in."

The man smiled a little. "How you doin in school, boy?"

Gordon kicked a toe at the banister. "Um, mostly C's. Gots me one B, though. In English. Mostly cause Lyon here help me."

The man looked where Gordon pointed, seeming puzzled for a moment. He blinked, then smiled again. "Hard to see him in the dark. Well, keep them grades up, son. Onliest way you gonna get sornewheres. You boys be careful now." The door closed.

The boys walked back up the hall. A stink like burned chicken feathers still hung heavy in the air. Lyon, Tunk, and Curtis got their boards. Tunk gave the revolver back to Lyon. "Maaaan, you dudes way past BAD! Word up! Yo, gots any more hot moves like that?"

Lyon grinned. "Rules." He turned to Gordon. "Sorry I can't stay an help you clean up some of this shit."

Gordon put the pistol on top of the TV and began gathering bottles. "Aw, no prob. Um, but how you spell vacation, man?"

Lyon spelled it for him, then added. "An best you get that story done right, or Crabzilla kill ya for sure."

Gordon stood in his doorway as the other kids walked back to the stairs. "You boys be careful now," he called.

"What it is," said Deek, flipping away his Sherman as he locked the 'Am and armed the alarm. "Black kids just keep on gettin stupider an stupider!" He turned to Ty and counted on chubby fingers. "What juvie most full of? Black kids! What jail an prison most full of? Black kids! An, that ain't enough for ya, what color the kids cuttin an shootin each other in the streets?" He snickered. "Gonna deny some more, stupid? It just like that ole sayin... battle of brains an you gots no ammunition!"

Ty tugged on the tail of his brown leather bomber jacket to make sure it covered the .45 in the back of his jeans. The Trans-Am was parked prominently beneath the brightest light in the Burger King lot like a showpiece on display. Which it was, thought Ty. He checked his watch: 8:17. The new kid they'd been supposed to meet at eight would probably be sweating bullets; thinking he'd blown it somehow and Deek didn't want him after all. That was part of the plan. While there was no shortage of kids creaming their jeans to work for Deek, even Ty had to admit that the majority were too stupid—though "stupid," like "funny," could mean a lot of things that had nothing to do with intelligence.

Deek was careful in choosing his kids. Some, especially those who already had guns and were way past streetwise, came on so showtime bad that they blew their chances in the first minute no matter how smart they really might be. It totally disgusted Ty to see some ten- or eleven-year-old with wax in his ears and snot on his lip bragging over his piece or how many times he'd used it. Most were lying, desperately begging recognition from anybody that they lived and breathed, or at least adding one zero to the number of times they figured they'd done something way bad or cool. But none of that shit got by Deek or impressed him. The trouble with showtimes was that they wanted to *look* like dealers, dressing the part like pint-sized pimps till they flashed on the street like neon. Besides, showtimes always had the biggest mouths and the tiniest balls, and broke like glass if busted. Deek preferred the quiet kids: the lean and ragged and hungry ones. It was funny to Ty how those always seemed the darkest too, like himself. They blended into the background, hard to see, but that had little to do with their color. They were more like small and sad-eyed ebony ghosts, haunting the sidewalks or hovering half invisible in doorways or drifting past bars late at night, sighing a soft, almost shy chant of rock, rock, rock, no louder than a breeze stirring trash in the gutter. And no one but the buyers seemed to see them, or hear. Ty also thought it funny how loyal most of them were, like they'd finally found something to believe in after a long, lonely search through a rotting world of hunger and lies, where everything good and everything beautiful was guarded by bars and glass. Sometimes it was hard to tell if the bars locked you in or out. And then there was that magic kingdom sealed inside a TV screen.

Many of the kids dealt for "good" reasons: to feed smaller brothers or sisters, or to support unemployed or unemployable parents. A few were even sent to Deek by mothers or fathers or foster-home people, though those were usually rejected on sight because they were fucked up or unwilling anyway. There were no solid rules, but Deek's instincts were generally right. That was good, because handling them later was mostly Ty's job.

Deek pocketed the keys and started for the building. The evening air was chill with a taste of fog to come, and he wore a black leather jacket with the cuffs roiled back to show his gold wrist chains. The jacket was almost new with a lot of zippers, and expensive as hell, but cut for a slim body—and already too tight for Deek to zip up. Ty figured to score it soon for his brother. Sometimes Ty tried to picture Deek as a thin hungry kid. He couldn't, though he often suspected that Deek had been one, once.

Maybe because Deek had had to get up earlier than usual that morning, he was a little loose from drinking all day. Ty kept careful watch on the shadows as he followed Deek across the lot. Ty's own stomach felt heavy with beer, but the alcohol seemed to fire his senses and heighten his wariness. Deek hadn't let him go home like he'd wanted, and the combo of beer and the cops on top of confronting the gang of young boys had stretched even his patience thin. More, the vision of that strange slender boy in the shadows, his eyes meeting Ty's twice in what might have been sympathy, kept scratching at the back of Ty's mind. Ty's mom sometimes went to see an old lady who did weird things with bones and claimed to tell fortunes. Ty mostly figured that was ten dollars down the toilet. He didn't believe much more in magic than in God... at least he wasn't sure, but it was easy to see that the slim kid believed in *something,* and it probably had more to do with bones than the Bible. Ty fingered his medallion once again.

"Black kids hungry, man!" Ty suddenly blurted to Deek's back. "An it ain't only for food!"

Deek stepped up on the sidewalk that surrounded the restaurant building. This brought his face almost level with Ty's. Ty figured Deek was going to be pissed now; there had been a few times when Deek had hit him, though he always apologized soon after. But Deek only laughed and tapped a finger against Ty's chest, rattling the medallion on its cheap silver chain. "Oh, get real, stupid. Shit, you been there, so stop tryin to smoke yourself. You know same as me that to them little fucks bein BAAAAD is the only thing in the world what matter... all the time braggin bout their blade scars or bullet holes, strippin off their shirts to show 'em. Black kids got nuthin else on their tiny little brains. An all the time the real world is laughin at em cause they locked up in places like this where all they can do is be 'bad' to each other!"

Deek laughed again and patted the top of Ty's head. "What your prob is, you born bout thirty years too late. Ain't no more Panthers, my man. Ain't nobody fightin to make nuthin better. An all them little suckers think it so way fuckin past cool to be endin up dead or spendin their lives in cages like animals cause they figure it the badge of bein black. Yo. See the joke, man? Them little shits stuck behind the bars of whitey's cage an thinkin *that* make em bad!"

Deek swung around and aimed a finger through the window.

"That there was our new boy, man. Wanna bet me it ain't? He make you proud? He give you hope? Shit! Check him out, stupid... just one more little black sucker!"

Ty looked through the glass. At this hour on a weekday night the restaurant was almost empty, just two high school couples laughing and talking together at one table and, at another near the door, an old dude in dusty coveralls who might have been a janitor. The rest of the business was mostly drive-throughs. A velvet black boy, black as Ty and maybe twelve, tall for his age so he seemed even thinner, sat alone in a corner booth. His elbows were on the table and his face buried in his hands, so Ty couldn't see him too well, just an uncut fluff of hair and a puppyish body about twenty pounds lighter than it should have been. Though worn and faded, his clothes were clean, signifying he still had somebody who cared. His jeans were a year too tight, and his Nikes were banded with electric tape to hold them together. There was a pattern to the banding, like how he'd tried turning it into a decoration, too. Pride was a funny thing. There was a scarred old skateboard under the table: the reason his toes were so heavily taped, and his shirt was only a black satin tank top despite the evening cold. It was too big, probably a castoff, and one strap had slid from his shoulder and dangled at his elbow. The boy's posture said the rest. A small cup of coffee, the shadow line showing it was still half full, though no steam rose, sat in front of him. Smoke curled from a cigarette in a tinfoil ashtray that held another three butts. The boy looked like he could have been crying... could've been in love for the first time and torn up about it, or could have had an overdue homework assignment. But Ty knew what that lost and lonely look really signified.

He'd be perfect, thought Ty. One more brick for the bottom of the pyramid, and so right for the job that he even looked familiar. In his mind Ty compared him to the fighting stances and defiance of the gang boys that morning. Once, maybe this kid had been a fighter too. But twelve years of fighting had worn out his heart.

Deek snickered and draped an arm over Ty's shoulder. "Yo. That YOU, man! Prob'ly just how you look four, five years ago. Come to think on it, that still sorta how you look sometimes, when you figure nobody watchin. I ain't always asleep when you stand by that goddamn window in the mornin's." Suddenly Deek stiffened. "SHIT! You *believe* it that selfsame dribble-lip cunt!"

Behind the counter's bulletproof glass Ty saw the same dark girl who had served them that morning. Though long-limbed and slim, and draped in the baggy fast-food uniform, her body showed pride in breasts carried high, and a soft curve of hips in perfect proportion to the slenderness of her waist. Her hair was cut short in tight, natural curls, accenting what some old people would call the Africanness of her features... nose wide but small-bridged, fierce cheekbones, and full-lipped mouth. She wore the lame little cap shoved far back from her smooth forehead as if in contempt, the way a cheetah might treat a circus costume. She was the kind of pure black girl who would never appear in any McDonald's or Burger King commercial or be pictured playing with Barbie dolls beside some blond child on TV. Ty wondered if she, like himself, had ever envied the Arnolds and Websters and Cosby kids of the world. But there was a sort of defiance in her very blackness—the way she wore her hair and the way her sleeves were rolled high past her elbows to bare strong, slim arms—that made Ty suddenly regret his own razored head. He pictured himself in that Afro-ish bush of the boy's, recalling his mom saying once that the style had been called a natural way back in the sixties. Ty noted the grace of the girl's moves, and the cool caution with which she kept watch on the customers. She might hate this city as much as he did, but she'd learned to survive in it.

Ty saw the slight softening of her long-lashed black eyes as they lit on the solitary boy. She seemed to hesitate a moment, then drew a small cup of coffee from the machine, scooped a handful of cream and sugar packets from a tray, picked up a cloth, then disappeared around the racks. She came into the customer area a few seconds later through a steel door back by the bathrooms. The cup and packets she carried in one hand, the cloth in the other. Ty watched as she went to the boy's booth and set the coffee near his elbow, then spread the packets with a fan of her fingers like a magic trick to please a small child. She smiled, her teeth large and white against skin as velvety midnight as the boy's. Her hand hovered near the boy's shoulder as if wanting to lift the strap of his shirt back up to where it belonged. It was something a mother would do, a little automatic gesture of love. Ty knew because he'd seen his own mom do those things. She murmured something, and the boy looked up, suspicion changing to surprise that anyone would be nice without a reason.

"DAMN!" Ty's long frame jerked rigid. Blood seemed to burn in his veins like battery acid. Fists clenched, teeth bared, he tore away from Deek and ran to the restaurant door. The old dude in coveralls looked up as the spring closer screamed under the force of Ty's

shoulder, waited until Ty stalked past his table, then got quietly up
and left. The high school couples went silent, the girls clutching
their bright nylon totes while the boys eyed Ty with cautious
hostility.

Ty's Nikes were noiseless as panther paws crossing the
polished tile. Automatically, he noted the high school boys,
probably seniors, one average-sized and uncertain, the other
muscle-bulked with his big jaw set in suspicion. Ahead, the dark
girl glided away from the boy's booth, graceful and wary as a slim
cat herself, her hand clenching the wet cloth like a weapon. Ty
figured she would dart to the kitchen to tell the manager or call the
cops. He didn't care. She didn't seem afraid of him—and even
furious as he was, he found he didn't want her to be—but he gave
her only a glance before his eyes locked with the boy's.

The boy had turned when Ty slammed through the door,
searching Ty's face first with hope, and then his expression had
hardened into the narrow-eyed sullen look little kids wore when
they were scared shitless but trying to be cool. The boy swallowed
once, like a cartoon character, then squeaked, "Yo, Ty." It came
out half question.

Ty's lips curled back from his big teeth. "You stupid little
NIGGER!" He grabbed his brother's arm.

In the kitchen, Leroy looked up from scraping the grill as
Markita slipped through the door and slammed it behind her. The
room was hot despite the rumbling vent fan; the building's original
design probably hadn't considered bulletproof glass at the counter.
Leroy was stripped to a wide-mesh black tee, his uniform shirt and
the hat he righteously hated flung in a ball in a corner. The long

knife slash shone pale down his body. The manager wouldn't be back until nine, when Leroy would leave for his night school, and the chances of a field inspector showing up in that neighborhood after dark were pretty slim. The manager was white, but trusted Markita and Leroy completely. Besides, they worked every hour they could get without him having to show overtime on the books.

Like Markita, Leroy was bone-weary but snapped alert when he saw Markita's face. "What up, girl? We gettin hit again?"

Markita ran up front to the racks and peered around them into the customer area. "That dealer, from this mornin He outside! His bodyguard just now come bustin in an grabbed some little boy! Maybe I better call the cops!"

Leroy flung down his scraper and ran up beside Markita. He squinted between the burger slides, seeing Ty yank a smaller boy out of a booth. The kid was cussing up a storm, twisting and squirming in Ty's grip, and stubbornly bracing his Nikes on the floor. They squeaked as Ty tried to drag him away.

Markita made a move toward the wall phone, but Leroy took her arm. "Best you keep yourself clear, girl! It be way past game over, time the cops even get here. Then they be pissed at us for callin 'em! Manager ain't gonna be too stoked neither. You know it for a fact!"

Markita shook her arm free. "Goddamnit, Leroy! Nobody NEVER does nuthin! That why this stuff always happenin!"

Leroy gripped Markita's arm again as she turned for the phone, holding her back. "Wait, girl! Chill a minute! Check it! There the dude lettin the little kid snag his skateboard."

"So?"

Leroy held on to her arm. "Listen up! If the dude was gonna do the kid, he sure as hell wouldn't be lettin him bring his board along! LOOK! How them two actin 'mind me more of tryin to get my little brother in the bathtub on a Sat'day night. Damn if it don't!"

Markita stopped trying to pull away. She had to admit that's exactly what the scene looked like. It would have almost been funny if she hadn't known what Ty was and who he worked for. She watched the tall homely boy drag the smaller one toward the door in a series of squeaky jerks. The kid was still struggling wildly, and tears glittered on his cheeks, but he seemed a lot more pissed off than scared he was going to be murdered. Markita saw the big high school dude stand as Ty skidded the kid past the table, but Ty muttered something, swinging around for just a second and flipping up the tail of his jacket. The big dude paled and sat down fast. Ty kicked the door partway open, shouldered it wider, then flung the young boy into the night. Markita felt Leroy's hand gentle on her arm.

"Leave it go, girl," Leroy murmured. "Whatever it is, be a black thing, an ain't nuthin nobody can do."

Deek was waiting outside near the doorway, Sherman in his lips, jacket collar up against the chill. Fog was creeping thick from the distant Bay, oozing through the gap-toothed board fence at the back of the lot like spirits on *Ghostbusters*. Deek raised his eyebrows, his expression more curious than anything else as Ty flung the kid out the door. The small boy stumbled, almost falling, and dropped his board. It rolled toward Deek. Deek put out a toe and stopped it, then leaned against the wall, arms crossed over his chest, to watch.

The kid recovered at the edge where the concrete dropped off to the asphalt of the drive-through lane. He spun around, his Nike sole squealing, and straight-legged a kick at his big brother's crotch. Ty had half expected that; he knew all the moves that boys his little brother's age would make. Those he hadn't done himself at twelve he'd learned of fast in the months of handling Deek's dealers. Dodging, Ty grabbed the boy's outfiung foot and yanked. The kid crashed flat on his back, his breath wuffing out. "Fucker!" he gasped. He jerked back his leg and tore free of Ty's grip, then scrambled up, eyes squinted with tears and face twisted in rage. "I fuckin KILL ya!" he hissed, going for Ty with small fists swinging.

Almost casually, Ty flipped out a long arm and whacked the kid across the mouth with his open hand. The boy staggered backward, slipping off the edge of the sidewalk, arms windmilling, feet scrabbling for balance. He recovered, shaking his head in wonder while spitting blood from a split lip. But he leaped for Ty again, eyes slitted in little-kid fury, teeth bared behind curled-back lips, and sobbing out sounds from deep in his throat.

Deek flicked ashes from his Sherman. "What IS this shit?" he demanded.

Ty snagged a fistful of the kid's huge tank top, big and loose because it was an old one of his. He held the boy at arm's length, beyond the range of furious kicks and small flailing fists. "It a family thing. Nuthin to do with you. I want the night off, Deek."

"*What?*" Deek scowled and flipped his cigarette away. "*Yo!* You know goddamn well we gotta meet them Bakersfield suckers at ten!"

"Goddamnit, Deek, this Danny! My BROTHER!"

Deek's eyebrows shot up. *"That's* Furball?"

Ty's patient eyes narrowed. Danny's street name came from the scrawny little cat on the *Tiny Toons* TV show, the one with the rag bandage around his tail and a notch in his ear and the perpetual bad luck. Danny's left ear had been nicked in a knife fight when he was eight.

"Yo!" Deek yelled. "He gots a—"

Distracted, Ty heard the snick of the switchblade too late. It was Taiwanese junk, but Danny kept the cheap steel sharp. There wasn't much pain as the blade slashed through Ty's leather sleeve, just a sort of burning drag across his forearm and the sudden wet warmth of welling blood.

"DAMN!" Ty cursed himself. He'd known that Danny always carried the knife, just as he knew the boy was now fighting on instinct. None of Deek's dealers could have pulled that move on him! Ty's hand flashed, clamping on Danny's thin wrist and twisting hard. The boy screamed, and the knife hit the concrete with a tinny sound.

Blood seeping from the slash in his sleeve, soaking the cuff and running ruby down his wrist, Ty grabbed Danny again and shoved him backward across the drive-through lane and into the oncoming fog. The rotten fence shook its whole length as Ty slammed his brother against it. A board popped loose behind the boy's back. Danny's teeth suddenly gleamed stark in the darkness. He tried to tear into Ty's bloody wrist. Ty cracked the boy under the jaw, snapping his head up, then clutching his shirt one-handed and savagely shaking the kid. "Stop it, Danny! Fore I gotta hurt you! Game over, man!"

The boy went limp, his knees buckling, held only by Ty's grip on his shirt. His eyes shifted past Ty. Wary of a trick, and scared the boy might try biting again, Ty risked only a quick glance over his shoulder. Through the fog he caught a glimpse of the restaurant's interior, warm-lit and safe-looking, its bright decorations making it a world apart behind glass. Like life, Ty thought, all the good things locked behind glass. The high school kids had gone, but Ty saw the dark girl peering out through a window, a hand shading her eyes as she tried to pierce the fog. She clutched a mop the way Zulu warriors on TV held their spears. Ty hoped she would stay inside. Eyes flicking back to the boy, Ty saw a strange sort of desperate hope in Danny's face. Then Ty realized that Danny wasn't looking at the girl at all but to Deek, who was coming over carrying the skateboard and knife.

Danny made a sudden move, wiggling out of his shirt and darting under Ty's grab. Ty spun to catch him, but Danny only skidded to his knees on the fog-slicked pavement in front of Deek.

"Please, man!" Danny sobbed. "I wanna work for you. I got to! PLEASE!"

Deek gave the kneeling boy a one-sided smile, then reached down and patted his head. "Chill, boy. You see yourself this never fly."

Danny jerked his face around, fresh tears on his cheeks. His finger flashed to point at Ty like a blade. "HE gots no say over me! He don't give a shit bout me! It MY life, man! MINE!" He spat bright blood at Ty.

Deek folded the knife shut, then dropped it and the board in front of Danny. Ignoring the boy, Deek looked over to Ty. "Ain't this a bitch, man? Motherfuckin family shit do you every goddamn time. Word! Listen up, stupid. I *need* ya tonight!" Scowling, he glanced at his watch. "Look. We gots about a hour. Can you get this goddamn mess cleaned up by then?"

Ty was staring down at his brother. Danny was still kneeling at Deek's feet, sobbing with his head lowered. The boy's thin body glistened with fog-wet, his shoulder blades standing out stark under black velvet skin, his sides heaving as he panted steam. The soles of his Nikes were worn through. Ty's own breath came suddenly hard through a thickness in his throat, but blood still pounded hot in his veins; he could feel its pressure behind the steaming wet oozing from the slash in his arm. He saw the knobby ridge of his little brother's backbone, bent now, and so fragile he could have broken it with a kick. Rage flared in Ty. He *wanted* to kick the boy... wanted to systematically beat the shit out of him just like any other of the stupid, snot-nosed little niggers he had to handle. But there was more; he *wanted* to hurt this boy! It was like he *cared* about hurting this boy!

Why?

Ty found himself wondering over that, and his rage leaked away like what was flowing from his arm. He saw that his little brother was shivering. Ty bent down and took Danny's arm, lifting him gently to his feet. He handed the boy his shirt, though expensive black satin was no shelter from cold. He noted that the girl behind glass was still watching. "Put it on, Danny. You catch the sniffles." Ty's voice hardened before he knew it. "Don't you *never* go down on your knees for nobody, nigger! I... I fuckin *kill* ya, ever you do that again!"

Then Ty suddenly knelt. He pulled the boy tight against him. "I love you, Danny!"

Deek cocked his head and let out a snort. Ty ignored him. Danny's chin started to quiver as tears ran free down his cheeks. Ty stood, unzipping his jacket and gathering the boy beneath it. He saw the girl turn from the window and walk away slowly, dragging the mop like a mop once more.

Ty leveled his eyes at Deek over Danny's head. "Can't clean up in a hour what this motherfuckin world done to him in twelve years."

Deek's scowl deepened. "Look! We drive him home, then meet them dudes. After that you can take all rest of the fuckin night... all fuckin tomorrow too, if you gotta. But I need to know if they done the Crew..." Deek's mouth snapped shut and his eyes flicked to Danny. "If it a done deal. Anyways, I can't have them cotton suckers hangin round here when I don't need 'em no more. They stupider'n a goddamn dozen little kids put together, an that goddamn van stick out like a big black dick! They talk, best you believe! Be showtimin all over town! Prob'ly end in jail, when they broke again. You seen that little sucker Wesley. He fixin to fold any second. Hittin 'em after school today just maybe snapped his little mind. IF them cocksuckin field niggers done it right!"

Deek eyed Danny once more as if not liking what he saw. But then he smiled and leaned down, nudging the skateboard closer to the boy. He didn't seem to notice Ty stiffen when he dropped a hand on Danny's shoulder. "Yo, Furball. Wanna make yourself a *whole* half-buck tonight, dude? All you gotta do is be cool an let us motor you home. Then stay there. Word! Shit, man, that only what your big brother want for ya anyways, ain't it? An, hey, now you even gonna get paid for bein cool!"

Danny studied Deek, peeking from under Ty's jacket and shivering. Deek grinned and waved a palm toward the 'Am. "Yo, dude, bet you never ride in nuthin like that a'fore, huh?"

Ty clasped the boy tighter. "Never rode in no car his whole life, I know bout. But you best believe he ain't gonna ride in *that* one!" Ty locked eyes with Deek and hid Danny's face in his jacket. "World don't pay you for bein good, man. Or cool. Danny ain't takin no goddamn money for doin what he s'posed to do anyhow. If that stupid, then that just what it is!" Ty lowered his eyes and sighed out steam. "I get my board. Me an Danny take the bus home. Got us some talkin to do. I ride my board back. Meet you front of your place soon's I can. So what we late? Be the selfsame goddamn trick you just pull on my brother! Sides, I ain't so stupid but I can't see them dudes goin nowhere till they gots their money!"

Deek's eyes had narrowed but he seemed to consider Ty's words. A moment passed, then he shrugged. "Mmm. Maybe you right, man. Well, so how's I just cruise on over your place an pick you up when you done your little heart-to-heart?"

Ty's lips closed over his teeth. His voice came from low in his throat. "Don't you *never* come by my family's place, man! NEVER!"

Deek and Ty regarded each other over Danny's head, but Deek finally gave a short nod. "What it is, I guess. Family shit like that." He glanced at Ty's dripping arm. "Blood. My ass!" He spun on a toe and started for the car. "I get your goddamn fuckin skateboard toy, stupid!" Then he paused and looked back. "Word! You get this here shit covered, man! Total! An you make goddamn sure that little.... That your brother keep his mouth shut!" Deek snorted and walked on.

Ty waited until Deek was only a ghost in the fog, then pulled a black bandana handkerchief from his jacket pocket and handed it to his brother. "Here, Danny. Wipe your face. It, um, it cool I still call you Danny?"

The boy nodded solemnly. "Yeah. You can."

Danny dabbed at his face, then blew his nose with a comical little-kid honk. "Um, I sorry as hell I cut you, Ty. Is it bad?"

Ty flexed his arm, wincing when more blood dribbled from his sleeve. "Naw. Fact is, I hurt myself worse just fallin off my board when I was your age."

Danny studied Ty's arm, looking doubtful, but then smiled. "Yo. That 'your age' stuff sound like what daddy used to say sometimes. When he come home." He gingerly touched Ty's arm. "Done a total number on your cool jacket. Yo! Maybe Mom could sew it? She way good at fixin shit like that." He hesitated. "Or maybe you just wanna go an score yourself a new one. You can, huh? For cause you got the buck. Um, Ty? You do that, maybe you gimme that one, huh? I always want me a cool jacket like that."

Ty pressed his sleeve together to slow the bleeding. "No, Danny. This not fit for you. Look like just somebody's throwed-away shit. Tomorrow, you an me, we go shoppin right uptown at the 'spensive mall. We score you any kinda jacket you want. One what fit you proper so everybody *know* it yours only. An we get you some new clothes. Whatever you want, man. An the bestest goddamn Nikes they gots. Maybe you help me buy some stuff for the other kids too?"

Danny's eyes widened. "Word, Ty?"

"Best you hear, man. Cause... well, cause I love you."

"It sound funny you sayin that, Ty. I don't mean bad-funny, just funny, y'know?"

"Yeah. Well, maybe true stuff... stuff from your heart sometime sound uncool. But, anyways, I gonna be comin home more. You an me, we do us some movies, check us out some arcades. You oughta be kickin on games, man, fast as you was with your blade."

Danny's face broke into a sudden grin. Kids' faces were like that, thought Ty, their expressions never still, always changing. Hate or fear could vanish in a second and never leave a trace, to be replaced by wonder or hope... or love. Only when they got older did kids' faces harden to reflect the world around them.

"Aw," said Danny. "That only for 'cause you wasn't watchin when you shoulda. Deek 'stracted ya. That weren't cool at all, man." He slipped his hand into Ty's. "Um, is it okay I hungry, Ty? There weren't much for supper again, an I just barely 'forded myself that coffee so's I could sit inside an wait." Danny hesitated once more. "Um, that there Deek kinda a asshole, ain't he?"

Ty glanced toward the fog-shrouded Trans-Am. "Yeah. That a fact." Ty looked down at his brother again. "But you just forget all 'bout him, Danny man. I mean that now. Word up."

Danny giggled. "Or you kill me?"

Ty's bloody fingers tightened on Danny's hand. "I don't know what I do. An that the God's honest truth. But I love you always more in my mind if you dead than seein you livin doin shit like just now. That, um, sound kinda stupid, huh?"

Danny searched Ty's face. "I don't know. But *you* doin bad shit, Ty."

Ty shook his head and shrugged. "I don't know what the fuck I doin no more, Danny. An that the God's truth too. Seem like everthin round here all backwards. Like a picture negative."

"Huh?"

Ty shook his head again. "Yo, I just a stupid niggerboy, man. Maybe we all just picture negatives. Forget it." He smiled and brushed fog droplets from Danny's hair. "Yo. I hungry too." He wiped blood from his watch. "We gots us bout a half hour fore the next bus past home. Let's you an me get usselfs somethin to eat, man."

Danny grinned, his face childlike and eager once more. He tugged on Ty's hand, not seeing the pain it caused. "Word up, Ty! Yo! That girl in there, she give me a *free* coffee, man! Just like that! Shit! Maybe she peek you out an like what she see an give you somethin too!"

Ty glanced toward the restaurant, doubting very much if the girl had liked what she'd seen.

As they started back to the building, Deek rolled up beside them in the 'Am and shoved Ty's board out the window. Danny darted to catch it before it hit the ground.

Deek's golden eyes speculated on Ty. He muttered, "'Member, man. I had me another bodyguard." He popped the clutch and the big car snarled off into the fog.

A family of six was just gathering around a table as Ty and

Danny came in. There were four kids, boys and girls, the oldest
about eight. They were giggling and maxing the way kids do in
restaurants because they know their parents won't yell at them.
The mother was only half seriously shushing them while their
father balanced a huge tray of food in one hand like a waiter and
made a game of passing it out to the children. The man gave Ty
and Danny a careful glance as they walked to the counter, but Ty
had his arm around his brother and his bloody sleeve pressed to
his side. The man smiled at them. Ty tugged at his jacket to make
sure the .45 stayed covered.

Markita's eyes were wary as the two boys came up to the
glass. She noted the small kid's split lip, puffy eyes, and the tear
streaks on his face. She'd seen most of the fight, if it could've been
called that, including the flash of the knife. She winced now at the
sight of Ty's slashed sleeve and blood-covered hand. Keeping her
face closed, she silently took Ty's order for cheeseburgers, fries,
and drinks, not repeating it to Leroy because he was hovering just
behind the racks and heard every word. She felt Ty's gaze on her as
she scooped up fresh fries—even though there were packs already
on the rack—but pretended not to notice.

The smaller boy had gone back to the corner booth and sat
expectantly as Markita put the food on a tray and slid it into the
pickup slot. She waited while Ty pulled out his nylon wallet with his
bloody hand and dug for bills. It seemed to hurt him to move his
arm and, despite herself, Markita felt sympathy for the dark, homely
boy. And that was so stupid it brought a following flash of anger,
especially when she recalled how scared she'd been of him
minutes before. She snatched the money as he pushed it into the

slot, ignoring the blood on it, then shoved the tray through and stared full into his eyes. "Proud of yourself, nigger?"

For a moment the dark dude looked totally confused. Then he lowered his patient eyes and fumbled the tray out the other side. His arm seemed to hurt him like hell. If he'd looked up he would have seen sudden pain mirrored in Markita's face. But he didn't look up. "That my brother," he murmured, almost sadly, as he turned away.

Markita watched, bewildered now, as Ty carried the tray over to the booth. She didn't notice Leroy beside her until he touched her hand.

"Ain't life a bitch, girl?"

Still watching the boys in the booth, Markita spoke softly. "They're *brothers.*"

"Mmm," said Leroy. "I heard." He snorted and shook his head. "Ain't no wonder whitey figure we all stone-cold crazy!"

Lyon woke with Curtis' beer-scented breath in his face. The smaller boy's warm body was pressed to his own beneath the wool Army blanket. Lyon slept lightly, waking often in the night, and restless whenever the moon neared full. And tonight it was; he could sense its pull inside him as it rose beyond the ceiling of his tiny windowless room and far above the fog that chilled the air and stilled the city sounds.

He felt as if he hadn't slept for long. Sitting up in total darkness, he confirmed it from the ember-red numbers of his clock. It was just 10:13. He and Curtis had gotten back from escorting Tunk at nine. Curtis had gone right to sleep, drunk as he was, and his breathing now was slow and peaceful. He'd escaped the city until morning, and Lyon envied him that. A siren sounded in the distance, and there were some gunshots, but Curtis, like all city kids, would dream right on through it.

Lyon eased from the narrow mattress on the bare board floor, kneeling a moment to tuck the blanket tighter around his friend. Then he stood with hands on slim hips and scanned the blackness as if he could see every detail. Even with light there wasn't much to look at.

Lyon had his own room, across the hall from his mom's place. The three-story brick building had originally been built for offices, and the eleven apartments now shelled inside were all different shapes and sizes. The wiring was always overloaded and blowing fuses, and the nigger-rigged plumbing was a leaky stinking joke even when it worked. Lyon's room had probably been for maintenance, but little of that was done anymore. It was about twelve by twelve, its ceiling gridded with pipes that groaned and thunked and flaked insulation. The walls, where not covered by posters of rockers, rappers, movie monsters, and collages made of magazine pictures, showed more lath than plaster. Opposite the hallway door was a huge deep sink, revealing rusty iron where chunks of porcelain were chipped, that often did duty as a bathtub and sometimes a toilet. On a shelf to one side squatted a crusted double-burner hot plate that Lyon had tapped to a gas line himself, and where he cooked most of his meals. In cold weather a big clay flowerpot turned upside down over one burner furnished heat. A shelf above held a battered collection of dumpster-salvage pots and pans. To the other side of the sink, a 1950s GE refrigerator completed Lyon's kitchen. It was all streamlines and girlish curves with sleek chrome handles and trim like an Art Deco space capsule. It worked perfectly despite being rescued from a condemned building, skidded by the gang down four flights of stairs, pushed six blocks on skateboards, and then battled and cursed up here to the third floor. Lyon had painted it black. It was funny how nobody ever imagined a black fridge.

In the center of the room stood a table and two chairs, survivors of a chrome dinette set. The Formica was cracked and yellowing, and the seats patched with electrical tape. The plating was mostly peeled from their rusty legs. Over the table a bare bulb dangled from wires with a little rubber bat spreading its wings from the pull string. Lyon's few clothes and special things were stored in a bashed-up three-drawer filing cabinet. His many books and stacks of magazines were neatly arranged against one wall on board-and-brick shelves. To anyone breaking in—lucky enough to get past the fire ax suspended ready to swing from above—Lyon's TV would look like an ancient black-and-white model of water-warped wood, and not be worth a second glance. Actually, there was a good Sanyo color set mounted inside. Lyon was good with tools, and his toolbox was one of his proudest possessions.

For all practical purposes, Lyon had lived alone since about age seven. His mom paid the half-buck a month for his room, occasionally gave him some money to buy clothes and food, signed his report cards, and remembered him with a present on Christmas and sometimes his birthday. Since she worked independently, and often had customers in her two-room apartment, this arrangement seemed fine to both her and her son.

Lyon, when he thought about it at all, supposed his mother loved him just as much as any kids on TV were loved, and knew for a fact more than a lot of kids in the neighborhood, even though he'd been an unwelcome accident that never should have happened. But, as his mother had sometimes reminded him when he'd been bad, she *could* have just left him in the dumpster. In fact, the dumpster baby story had been told to him so much at bedtime that it was more like "Goldilocks and the Three Bears" by now.

His mom was only twice his age anyway. Lyon figured the reason she didn't know jack about kids was that she'd never been one herself.

Lyon put his hand out in the darkness, his fingers finding the little bat on the first try. But then he flicked it away. He didn't want to wake Curtis. And yet he wished he had someone to talk to. This was going to be one of those nights when sleep wouldn't come. He wished he had a lot of beer. That was the only thing that might work. He considered begging a bottle of Night Train off his mother—there was no reason *not* to drink himself to sleep, now that the day's hassles were done—but she might have a customer. With a sigh, he slipped into his clothes, shoved the Iver-Johnson in back of his jeans, picked up his board, deactivated the ax, and quietly opened the door. Finding a winehead passed out with a partly full bottle was a good possibility. Putting his head out first, Lyon checked up and down the corridor. Only one weak bulb burned in the stairwell, but it was enough to see that the shadowy hall was deserted. He stepped out, easing the door shut behind him until the locks clicked, then bent to the baseboard where he'd drilled the two tiny holes. He pulled on the piece of picture-frame wire sticking a half inch out of the left-hand hole. The ax was now on guard again. Anyone opening the door without first pulling the right-hand wire would get the ax blade in the face, neck, or chest, depending on how tall they were. A kid about Curtis' size was safe, and the other gang members always ducked anyway.

Carrying his board by its front truck, Lyon silently descended the stairs, pausing at the second-floor landing to check out the hall and the dark steps below. The only light here was the ruddy glow of an EXIT sign; any other bulbs got stolen as fast as they could be replaced, their filament wire being just the right size for reaming the #25 needles junkies liked best. The building was still except for muffled TV and radio sounds from some of the apartments, and nobody with any real business or brains would linger long in these halls after sundown.

On the ground floor, the street door had a small window of thick glass embedded with wire. It was starred and cracked from being beaten with bottles and so layered with spray paint that the streetlight outside filtered through like something from a church. Tonight the door was locked, though the latch was often jammed open with wadded-up paper for various reasons. Lyon peered out the one little section that was still mostly transparent to make sure no one lurked beyond in the entry. He'd just stepped out, his nose wrinkling at the stinks of shit, piss, and puke, when the rattle of skate wheels carried from down the block, coming fast.

Lyon hesitated, a hand darting first to his pocket to feel the door key, then touching the worn butt of the gun. Head cocked, ears erect, he listened. Whoever the skater was, he rode hard wheels, maybe Bullet or Rat Bone 97s... noisy, rapid-wearing, and expensive. Only rich kids skated that type wheel; the gang and the neighborhood dudes went with softer stuff like Powell 85s or Variflex Street Rages. Lyon's own board glided silent as cat feet on ancient 70mm Kryptonic Reds. Staying in shadow, Lyon moved closer to the steps to get a good peek-out when the skater passed by. The dude—not very many girls rode, and never at night—had a definite destination and was shredding to the max to reach it, his wheels snapping over the cracks and buckled sidewalk slabs or ripping like machine-gun fire across iron access plates and sewer covers. The dude was a good skater too, Lyon thought; hard wheels were bad news on slippery wet pavement. The space between kicks told Lyon it was an older dude with long legs.

The skater shot past in a second, but Lyon's eyes caught him like a camera: tall, long-bodied, new jeans and Nikes, and megabuck bomber jacket, sharp razored hair, and ebony face like a cold starless midnight, gleaming with sweat and fog-wet. He rode a serious Sword and Skull plank, and his panting trailed puffs of steam that drifted behind like a jet plane's trail.

It was Deek's bodyguard.

Rage flared in Lyon. He leaped the steps, landing silent on the sidewalk, gun ready in hand. By rules he should shoot the sucker on the spot, but he didn't take aim. There was logic in the rules, and to shoot the dude dead right there wasn't logical to Lyon. The rules also let you use your brain and your heart to do the right thing. Not like what the cops and the TV called laws. Maybe the rules seemed hard sometimes, like not letting Curtis and Tunk hang together. But if the rules didn't make sense, what kid would obey them?

Lyon lowered the gun, watching the dude's shadow fade into the fog. He scented the strong, older-boy sweat, curious because there was blood in it too. He knew Deek's bodyguard lived somewhere a few blocks west of Friends' ground. Since Lyon's building was on the east-border block, that meant the dude was probably shortcutting through. Gordon could decide what to do in the morning. Anyway, there were just the two bullets in the revolver, and Lyon had seen the .45 when the bodyguard's jacket lifted on a long kick. The rules gave no time to fools.

Then Lyon heard the crack of another skateboard slapping a curb down the block behind him. He whirled and scrambled up the steps, just melting into the dark entry once more when the second skater shot by. Again, Lyon's quick eyes caught all.

Except for his worn-out clothes and wild puff of hair the second dude could have been a young clone of the first. He rode a fan-tailed Rob Roskopp, first series, almost as old as Curtis' Variflex, rolling on the sort of soft no-name wheels that came on toy boards and could be scored for a dollar apiece from the poor box at most skate shops. One of his bearings ran loose and dry, and his truck bushings creaked when he kicked. The boy wore only an oversized black satin tank top, and his thin body glistened and steamed in the cold. He panted low urgent sounds like sobs in his throat, breath rasping, maybe from smoking too much, and trailing vapor behind. He seemed desperate not to lose sight of the older dude. He also looked sort of familiar. Lyon wondered if he'd seen him at school.

As soon as the boy was past, Lyon leaped back down on the sidewalk. All thoughts of drinking himself a six-hour death burned away. Something hot was up tonight, along with the blood in the air and the full moon above. If anything was worth being black and thirteen in Oaktown, what it is was this!

Besides, he told himself, decking and kicking off after the two boys, the gang needed all the data scoreable on Deek and his schemes. Lyon slipped the gun back into his jeans as he rolled. Gordon's huge tee covered it easily. Ghosting the dudes wouldn't be hard; even hidden in the fog the rattle and snap of the bigger boy's wheels came clear through the night. The main prob would be not running up on the younger dude. Lyon felt a slight stab of uncertainty as he neared the next corner: the Crew/Friends borderline. Wesley sometimes put a dude on night patrol to check who was dealing after dark. But then Lyon heard the wheel sound swing right, up the cross street into unclaimed territory. He saw the faint figure of the younger boy follow, his wheels as silent as Lyon's own. Lyon wondered if he also had a gun. Maybe he was after Deek's bodyguard to do him? But the boy was maintaining his distance, and the logical place for a kill would have been back in the darker western blocks. Lyon considered: Deek covered a lot of ground in his car; it was likely that some other gang was interested in him too, and had put out a scout. It was too goddamn bad that gangs couldn't work together on this sort of shit, but then the cops would do their damnedest to bust it up. Lyon rolled on.

There were people and traffic farther up this street, cars cruising, their headlights like pale cones in the mist, their boom music beating deep. The streetlamps were haloed, and the neon signs swam from the fog as Lyon ripped past. He dodged the figures that materialized in his path, and cut cautiously around the clusters of men and mid-teen boys, some with their ladies and most of them drunk or otherwise fucked, who hung by the bars and liquor stores. There were a few taunts, but most from dudes close to his own age; the older people didn't seem to see him as well. A bottle whistled past his head once and shattered in the street. Two bigger boys on boards tried to pace him, so drunk they kept getting in each other's way, but he lifted his shirt for a moment and they checked the gun and dropped back, laughing and howling for him to do the motherfucker. Lyon wasn't sure who they had in mind. A woman in a doorway flashed her tits when Lyon looked twice to make sure it wasn't his mom. They weren't bad for an old lady's. His wheels crunched often through broken glass, and he skidded one time in a puddle of puke, but managed to maintain his distance with the second skater, who seemed to be tiring fast, his kicks getting ragged, and just barely clearing the curbs on his ollies. Lyon wondered how much longer the boy could keep matching the older dude's pace. Whatever else Deek's bodyguard did, Lyon had to respect his skating.

Lyon's own breath was burning his throat; one of these days he'd cut down on Kools. His T-shirt was soaked now and clammy with fog-wet and sweat. His knees were beginning to ache. The Iver-Johnson's big old-fashioned front sight was chafing a spot on his butt. A bunch of small boys zoned in a doorway with crack pipes stared openmouthed as he passed. Glimpses of the dude ahead when he rolled under lights showed him to be just about dusted; he'd fallen back so far that Lyon couldn't hear the older boy's wheels anymore. It was beginning to look like Deek's bodyguard was headed all the way uptown, and Lyon considered dropping the chase. Then he saw the small boy cut into a side street.

Lyon slowed, coasting a moment, then tail-skidding to a stop beneath a dead streetlamp. A golden glow pooled on the sidewalk from a bulb behind the barred windows of a closed-up corner market. A girl's laugh echoed softly in the store's shadowed doorway. "They done gone thataway, pardner."

Lyon's smile flickered as he fought back his breath. "Yeah?" he panted. "Then maybe I head em off at the ole pass, huh?"

The girl laughed again, a good open laugh, and her tone was friendly. Must be a slow night, thought Lyon.

"It way past ten, boy," said the girl. "Your mom know where her children are?"

Lyon's smile faded, and he turned away. "I not know where she be neither."

The girl was silent a few moments, then she sighed. "Mmm. Well, sympathy spread pretty thin around here, boy."

Lyon frowned. "Don't 'member me askin for none. Special from the likes of you! Anyways, I bet you just got that outa some ole book."

The girl sighed once more. "Used to read me a lot of books, boy. An not just them they make you in school. Got no time, no more... no time for nuthin but eatin an sleepin an workin, seem like." Her voice trailed off and she seemed to study the slender boy. "Look to me like you on some kinda quest." She sniffed. "Bet you don't even know what that mean."

Lyon snorted. "Your ass I do, girl! Quest be a seekin thing... for justice an truth an that sorta shit. Nobody go on em no more. So there!"

Again, the girl was quiet a time. Finally she nodded. "Keep on seekin, little warrior."

Lyon decked. "An you take care, sister. Night." He rolled down the side street.

It was narrow, dark, and silent after the blocks of bars and noisy fucked-up people. The crumbling old buildings seemed to lean over the sidewalks. More than half looked abandoned, their windows and doorways blanked with boards and spray-painted plywood. The others, mostly small shops and garages at ground level, had their windows defended by bars or big screens. The echo of the bodyguard's wheels had been swallowed in the fog. Lyon skated carefully, his ears alert, eyes straining to pierce the mist, and nostrils flared as if to scent danger. Garbage and trash lay everywhere, and a few stoves and refrigerators had been shoved from windows above, and looked it. The curbs were lined with a zombie parade of dead cars without wheels, their hoods, doors, and trunk lids gaping open like mouths, glass all smashed and strewn in sprays of icy glitter. Most were stuffed with more garbage, all were spray-painted, and some showed bullet holes. Rats scuttled in and out of them, a few sitting up and eyeing Lyon as if it were only a matter of time. One had its doors shut even though its glass was all gone. Lyon heard a child's cough as he rolled by. It was a lonely sound. There was also an occasional big battered truck, its hood secured by a padlocked chain or cable to protect its battery. Only the city's overglow, heightened by the hidden moon above, lit the block. A sick orange flicker farther down indicated a dying streetlamp at the next intersection. A half dozen upper windows in buildings showed lights, but these only seemed to strengthen the darkness.

The trash made skating treacherous, and the glass crunching under his wheels set Lyon's teeth on edge. Fearful of the noise, he tailed and strained his ears for sounds from the other boys. Nothing. Picking up his board, he stood a moment while sweat chilled on him, shivering and trying to decide what to do. He must have lost the dudes... they could have gone into any of those buildings farther down the block. He found he wasn't disappointed; he'd had his night's adventure—quest—and even if he hadn't learned anything to help his gang, he'd be so dusted by the time he got home that he'd probably sleep like the dead. He glanced around; there were gang marks on the cars and buildings, but too many of them and all different. Still, this might be somebody's ground; at least the kids would all go to a different school, so nobody would know him. Maybe he could score a cigarette from the girl on the corner before he started back. She might be able to say if he was in somebody else's territory so he could watch his ass on the return run.

Gordon's black tee was technically colors, piss-poor maybe, but he could always strip it off. It suddenly seemed like a long way home.

He was just about to turn and deck once more when the parking lights of a car winked on toward the end of the block. They looked like the amber eyes of some huge jungle cat. Then a voice carried to his ears; an older boy's, sounding slightly drunk and pissed to the max. "C'mon, stupid! It way fuckin past get-busy time! I don't wanna *hear* no more bout your motherfuckin family shit!"

Lyon froze. The voice was Deek's.

A shiver, this one of fear, went down Lyon's spine. For sure he'd wanted to find Deek, but wanting was something like dreaming, and dreams didn't usually end the way you'd hoped. He hesitated. Still, anything he could learn about the dealer would be good for the gang, and might give them an edge over the Crew at tomorrow's meet. If nothing else, just knowing where Deek cribbed could be a major advantage. Lyon decided, since he'd come this far, he might as well check things out.

Stepping off the sidewalk, he eased between two abandoned cars and moved slowly down the line of vehicles on the street side. The panther-eyed stare of the Trans-Am's parking lights disappeared behind a big old box-bodied truck as Lyon neared, but the murmur of voices sharpened with each step closer until he could hear every word. Deek was doing most of the talking and seemed mega-pissed at his bodyguard.

"You stupid shit! It almost *eleven* now an them dudes just might be lame enough to go out cruisin an start askin everybody in sight if they seen us! Fuck that cocksuckin little brother of yours, man! Blood mean nuthin 'cept trouble! Tell me you can't handle no skinny-ass little twelve year-old! What in hell you figure you gettin paid for, stupid? Babysittin?"

Then came the bodyguard's voice, hard and sulky. "Call my brother no cocksucker, man! Danny ain't one of yours! An he ain't never gonna be! So just shut up your goddamn mouth, Deek!"

Deek's voice dropped low, and that somehow made it dangerous. "You best think long an hard fore you tell *me* to shut up again, nigger. An shit! What the fuck make you figure I even want him? Word, stupid! I seen a zillion Dannys! An he's figured out what it is, man. . . oh yes he has. An you a even bigger fool for denyin it! Buck, what it is, stupid! An not you an not nobody gonna stop him from tryin for some now, best believe! Cause he KNOW for a fact he just a rag-ass little niggerboy without none!" Deek snorted. "Blood don't mean nuthin to him no more. You deny that, then what the fuck runnin down your arm right this minute, sucker?"

Lyon edged around the burned-out hulk of a Honda Civic. The big truck loomed ahead, parked facing up the street. Deek's car was behind it, in front of what looked like a tall, narrow apartment building. Stopping beside the Honda, Lyon studied the truck: it would be no prob climbing over the cab to the flat roof of the van box. He could crawl to the rear and see and hear everything. He slipped his board onto the charred front seat of the Honda where he could snag it fast.

Then another thought hit him, so intense that he shivered again. Deek and his bodyguard caught unaware! A gun and two bullets! Lyon's hand found the Iver-Johnson and pulled it from his jeans. The law checked Deek's license and let him go on killing kids. The rules said different!

Then Lyon thought about the bodyguard. . . who had a twelve-year-old brother named Danny. Lyon knew enough about love to recognize it when he heard it in somebody's voice. His long fingers clenched tight on the gun butt. The ancient revolver was warm from his skin. If he killed Deek, would the bodyguard's duty be done? Or would his loyalty hold beyond death? Maybe there was a rule about that too?

Lyon eased along the Honda's flame-blistered fender, the gun gripped two-handed and ready. He remembered the green-crusted cartridges. Well, one had fired that morning; there was a good chance both of these would too... even better odds that at least one would go off. He recalled the bodyguard's .45. Maybe the dude loved his brother enough to see that this had to be done?

Deek's voice suddenly raged, breaking in the middle. There was a soft thunk that sounded like a fist against flesh and a short wuff of breath. "Don't fuck with me, man! NEVER!"

Lyon pictured Deek's chubby fist and the tall boy's lean washboard belly.

"NOW where the fuck you goin, stupid?"

The bodyguard's voice sounded strained, but stubbornly patient. "Got to tie somethin round this arm. Bleedin won't stop."

"Aw, SHIT! Know what? You losin it, man... lettin some little sucker slice you like that! For chrissake, nigger, shag your ass!"

Lyon heard the wet squeak of Nike soles as the bodyguard ran up the building's steps. Now Deek was alone! The lock clicked on the building's front door. There was a squeal from a spring as it opened. Lyon felt his heart thumping in his chest. Tensed, trembling, the gun gripped in hands gone suddenly cold, Lyon stepped to the front of the Honda. He'd give the bodyguard another thirty breaths to get deep inside the building or up the stairs. There'd be plenty of time to do Deek, grab his board, and roll before the dude could get back out again. Lyon poised on his toes, ready.

Lyon scented the boy before he saw him. The second skater! He was crouched on the curb side of the truck, pressed to the huge front tire, peering around it at the building. Wisps of steam curled from his thin body and bushy hair. One strap of his tank top hung at his elbow, and his shoulder blade stood out knife sharp under his skin above the ridges of his ribs. His board lay beside him, its nose aimed for the street.

Lyon froze. The apartment building's door clacked shut. Lyon tried to still his shivering. What in hell was happening? Who the fuck *was* this kid? Lyon was almost positive now he'd seen him before at school—not in any of his classes, just a face in the hall or cafeteria. Pale light flashed on in a third-floor window. It threw enough glow down onto the Street to show the notch in the boy's left ear. Furball! He had a name with his knife but belonged to nobody. Was this the same boy the bodyguard had called Danny... his brother?

Lyon's mind replayed what he'd just heard: if Danny was Furball, then he must be the kid who wanted to work for Deek. And his big brother didn't want him to. So what the fuck was he doing here? And, Lyon wondered, what was *he* going to do now?

On TV the hero would creep up behind some unsuspecting dude, press the gun to his head, and whisper something showtime like "Freeze, sucker!" Prob was, that didn't really work. In real time the dude would likely give a yell. It was a human reflex. For sure the hero might also clunk the dude over the head with the gun butt. Then he'd always stay out just long enough for the hero to do whatever heroics needed to be done. Maybe that would work *if* you had a lot of practice thunking dudes on the head, knowing how hard to hit them and exactly where. Maybe cops did, but Lyon didn't. Besides, Lyon had seen Gordon get clunked with a Night Train bottle one time in a fight. The fat boy had only cursed and proceeded to kick the sucker's ass.

Now, Lyon thought a string of curses, wishing he knew what to do. Finally, he just stepped into the space between the truck and the Honda, aimed the gun one-handed at the boy, put a finger to his lips, and softly shuffled his Nikes.

The boy's head snapped around. "Uuuuuh!" His eyes popped wide, flicking, one, two, from the gun to Lyon's face. His jaw started to drop, but then comprehension flashed over his features, and he relaxed slightly, breathing out a vapory sigh. Lyon took a step nearer, then knelt, keeping the Iver-Johnson aimed. "Furball?" he whispered.

Furball scanned Lyon's face, his own expression a mix of fear and mounting anger. "Yeah? So what, man?" he whispered back. He studied Lyon again, then his eyes narrowed. "I seen you. At school. You Lyon. You belong to the Friends. Word say you magic. I don't believe none of that shit. Yo! An you a fuckin homo!"

"Chill out an shut the fuck up!" hissed Lyon. "Else you be tellin everybody round school tomorrow how a blow boy kick your butt!" Lyon jerked his jaw in the direction of Deek's car. "Spose you know who *that* be?"

Furball's eyes turned suspicious. "Shit stink? What it by ya?" He spat near Lyon's feet. "An I ain't ascared of no pussy little faggot gun neither!"

Lyon's V smile clicked on. "Pussy little faggot gun be shootin pussy little bullets, meanin dirt-nap time for assholes what don't shut the fuck up. An here be some magic for ya, man. I know Deek not wantin you workin for him. An your brother not neither. Maybe cause he love ya, sucker." Lyon's smile faded. "Best you believe us Friends ain't too stoked over it our ownselfs."

Furball looked uncertain a second, but then his eyes hardened. "I don't live in your ground, man. You dudes got no say over me." A new thought seemed to hit him. "Yo! How you know Ty my brother?"

"Could be by magic. Could be I just know he love you, man... don't wanna see you sellin yourself to the likes of Deek. Like a blow boy."

"Fuck your magic, sucker! An Ty gots no say over me. Not no more... "

Lyon cut Furball off with a jerk of the gun as the light went out in the window above. That meant the bodyguard—Ty—would be back in less than a minute! Lyon stood, still covering Furball with the gun. Was there enough time left?

Furball stared at the upper window, then turned back to Lyon. There was fear in his eyes once more. "You come to *do* em, man? Dint ya?" He trembled like something trapped. "No!" he hissed. "Not my brother, man! PLEASE!" He jumped to his feet, a hand darting for his pocket. Lyon whipped the gun up in a two-handed aim. But Furball ignored it. He stared straight into Lyon's eyes. "No! I ain't gonna let ya!"

Desperate as the seconds ran out, Lyon tried a fake. "So I kill you too, sucker!"

Furball's own magic was the knife appearing out of nowhere in his hand. "I don't care! C'mon, nigger, do me, ya gots the balls! Ty hear. Then he kill YOU!" Furball's chest puffed as he sucked breath for a yell. The building's front door creaked open.

Lyon lowered the gun. "Okay, man. Your game. Word."

For a long moment the two boys just stood facing each other. Ty came down the steps and crossed the sidewalk. The Trans-Am's engine snarled to life. Finally, Furball let his knife hand drop to his side. "C'mon, Lyon. I don't want Ty seein me. We slide round the truck when Deek pull out. 'Kay, man?"

The Trans-Am's tires fried rubber. Its headlights slashed the fog. Furball and Lyon barely made it around the truck's front fender before the car shot past up the street, tires still smoking as it burned away. The fog flared blood red for an instant as Deek tapped the brakes at the corner but ran the stop sign. Rubber screamed again as the car slewed right and disappeared.

"Seem like Deek gots plans for somebody," murmured Lyon.

Furball was just staring after the car. His eyes were slitted and his lips pulled back from his teeth. "Motherfucker gots no right callin Ty stupid, man! Or all them other sucker names!" He swung around to Lyon. "Cocksuckin fat-ass prick HIT Ty, man!" His knuckles paled as he clenched the knife. "I should kill him for that!"

Lyon glanced once at the knife, then lowered the Iver-Johnson's hammer. "You gots no chance in hell 'gainst Deek with nuthin but a blade, man. What the fuck you figure I doin here?"

Furball looked Lyon up and down. "Yeah? Well, you was gonna kill my brother too, wasn't ya?"

Lyon let the gun hang at his side, its muzzle down in his long loose paw. His uptilted eyes beneath their soft lashes held a calculating curiosity. "Not less he make me."

Furball's knife hand whipped out. The blade was suddenly at Lyon's throat. "Cheer me up, sucker!"

Holding the other boy's eyes, Lyon spread his arms wide and slowly sank to his knees. The blade followed him down so he ended, head back, throat offered, gazing up into Furball's face. Seconds passed. Bitter smoke from the Trans-Am's tires drifted across the sidewalk. Finally, Furball sighed out steam. His lips clamped shut over his teeth. He jerked the knife away and folded it closed against his leg, then stood proud with arms crossed and chest puffed. "Get up, man. Don't never go down on your knees for nobody, nigger. My brother say that."

Lyon rose. "Your brother give it a name. That why Friends not be workin for Deek sucker, nor no others like him."

Furbail snorted as he pocketed the knife. "Yeah? So try an eat names, asshole! Know what? Way I see, the whole fuckin world tryin to keep you on your goddamn knees when you ain't gots no money!" He spat on the sidewalk and yanked his tank-top strap back up. "So give THAT a name, magic boy!"

Lyon slipped the gun into his jeans. "So world always be tryin, man. That somethin new? Don't mean you gotta eat shit, just cause it shoved in your face."

Furbail gave Lyon a long look. The shirt strap slipped off his other shoulder. "Yo! You done that a'purpose just now, huh? Shit. You ain't stupid! You never leave yourself open like that by accident! Why?"

Lyon shrugged. "Wish I had me a smoke."

"Huh? Oh. I gots a couple Kools here." Furbail dug in his pocket and pulled out a squashed pack. "Gots no fire, though."

A Bic appeared in Lyon's paw.

"See?" said Furball. "I knowed all the time you was fast!" Lyon smiled, and the two boys leaned together to fire their cigarettes. Their eyes met over the flame. Lyon asked, "You love your brother, man?"

Furball snorted smoke. "What a fuckin stupid question! COURSE I do!" Then he turned away and picked a scab of paint from the truck's fender. "But *he* work for Deek. Gots him a gun an everthing. A *real* gun, not some piss-ass little toy like yours! Dudes respect him! Want me some of that!"

Lyon let smoke trickle from his nostrils. "Respect not be the same like you scared of somebody, man."

"Shit! I know that. Like, who respect cops?"

Lyon nodded. "Mmm. So you figure your brother respect Deek?"

"Huh? Well. . . *course* not! Deek treat Ty like shit, man! You *hear* what that sucker call Ty just now? An he HIT him, man! Hard's he could! I SEEN it, man!" Furball's chest puffed again. "But know what? Ty just stand there, man! Like, hard's that motherfucker hit him weren't jack, man! Word!"

Lyon took another hit on his Kool. "So what you sayin is, Ty don't respect Deek, an Deek don't respect Ty. So what kinda shitty job that be? I askin ya, man."

Furball fingered his cigarette. "Well... well, he just doin it for cause to help my mom. Maybe that all the respect he need. I mean, I ain't sayin he don't got lotsa way cool clothes an shit. But know what, Lyon? Most all his buck come home, uh-huh! Yo! Him an me? We goin UPtown mall shoppin tomorrow! Gonna score our whole goddamn family all kinda clothes an food an shit we need, man. Word! that why Ty takin Deek's shit, man. . . doin it for cause he love us all!"

Furball's eyes suddenly slitted. "But YOU dint know none of that, did ya? Yo! All you seen was some dude to kill!" He flipped his cigarette away and clenched his fists. "Shit! Why I dint do ya just now, I don't even know!"

Lyon sat down on the truck's running board. "Cause you be knowin what is, inside like, even you smoke you ownself that you don't." He met Furball's eyes. "Word. I COULDA killed your brother, man. Just now! Listen up. Can't you be seein how total easy it happen? Give it a name, man. You ain't stupid. You figure me an who I belong to be the onliest ones waitin on a clear shot at your brother?"

Furball watched as Lyon crushed out his Kool. It made a soft hiss on the wet rusty steel. Furball stared down at his ragged Nikes and kicked a taped toe on the concrete. "Spose I never think it like that a'fore. I never belong to nobody."

Lyon shrugged. "Man, you don't *need* to belong to nobody but yourself. I say this, dude, bet your ass your HEART knowed it all along."

Furball looked down at his chest, half bared where his shirt had slid off. "My heart know my little brother an sisters hungry, man. An walkin round wearin ole raggedy-ass Salvation Army clothes what white people throwed away." He looked up at Lyon. "So maybe my heart DO know, man... what gonna happen to Ty. So what I do? My mom scared. I can tell for cause sometime she cry in the night. She scared for Ty, an I think she scared what happen not havin the money Ty bring us home. Somebody got to take up the slack, man. Why I come here tonight. I figure to talk Deek alone, out my brother bein round."

Furball frowned. "You fuck that for me, man." He shrugged. "All what you tellin me? Bout hearts an shit? Sound magic. Gotta be magic for cause I don't unnerstand. Like churchy shit. I don't believe none of that neither. Tell you this, man. Word up! There a God, he be white. Believe it! Anybody with eyes see that! Nigger kids got no God, man! He cost too fuckin much!"

Furball kicked at the concrete again. "Aw, what it is, man. Shoulda knowed none of this shit work out for me!" He touched his left ear. "Dudes think my name come from this." He snorted. "Me? I figure it come from bein borned unlucky. Or black. Shit. Maybe mean the same, huh?"

Lyon nodded. "Mmm. Sometime seem that way."

"Well, I gotta say that one way cool name you got yourself. Lion. There *power* in that, man. Somethin you can respect. Word!"

Lyon smiled. "It *be* my name. With a y. See, my mom leave me in a dumpster, night I be born. Cold as hell, she say. Then, long bout mornin time she... well, she say she hear a callin. In her mind, like. Say she be thinkin bout me all them hours. So, she goes running down. Frost all over everthing. Say she lift up that lid, figurin I be total history. But there I was, she say, smilin right up at her like shit don't stink... like I knowed all along she be comin back." Lyon looked suddenly shy. "She tell me only a lion live through that."

"Jesus," breathed Furball. "Man, that musta totally sucked! Shit! Wonder you gots a heart at all!"

Lyon shrugged. "Well, only real lions left be in cages."

"Yeah. Guess so, huh? Shit, I'd hate bein caged, man."

"Mmm. Word say it go with bein black. Mean you way past bad."

"Word fulla shit sometimes. Just for cause it black don't mean it true." Furball was quiet a time, kicking at the old truck's tire. He pulled up his shirt strap but it slid right off again. He frowned and fingered it a moment but let it hang. "Um, Lyon? Wanna get drunk with me tonight? I talkin DEAD, man! Shit. Way I feel now, 'most wish I dead for real!"

"Mmm," said Lyon. "I hear that. But best not be wishin bad shit. There enough of it floatin round already." Lyon smiled. "I be proud to die with you, man. You got somethin by?"

Furball puffed his chest once more. "Word! Gots me a whole motherfuckin quart of Jack D. That do us both till mornin, believe! It in a 'bandoned buildin on my block. Better keep your gun ready on the ride back past them bars, man. That street only get badder, night go on."

Lyon stood up and pulled his tee over the gun. "For sure, man. An this time you gots permission to be shortcuttin Friends' ground."

Furball grinned. "Oh! So's you ghosted me, huh? Shit, I shoulda knowed. That the onliest way you find this place. Nuthin magic bout that."

"Word. But followin your brother be the onliest way *you* find this place too. An I woulda ghosted him anyways. So, just maybe you being here save your brother's life tonight. Tell me there not no magic in *that,* man. Shit. What you spect, rabbits outa hats?" Lyon's face hardened a little and he pointed to the building's upper windows. "Yo. Now I know where Deek be cribbin. Mornin come, all the Friends know too. Dudes like Deek get done cause of little ole fuckups like that. Last word from me." Lyon went around the Honda and pulled out his board, then studied Furball across the car's blistered roof. "So, you gonna be tellin your brother Deek gettin schemed on?"

Furball's eyes shifted from Lyon to the window above. "Word, you ain't gonna try an kill Ty, man?"

Lyon shook his head. "You know for a fact I can't be promisin nuthin like that, man. You know it be Ty's job to cover Deek's ass. Word, we try not to hurt your brother if there be any way other. You know, by rules, it the best I can give. So?"

Furball stared down at the sidewalk. "If I say I gonna tell, mean you gotta kill me right now, huh?"

Lyon sighed. "No, man. You coulda done me with your blade, but you didn't. By rules, I owe you. But that not what it is, man. I trust you. Your heart. Forget all that good an bad an magic an churchy shit. Just listen to your heart. Black hearts be strong an good all by theyselfs, deep down." Lyon thought a moment. "You tell your brother this, word up. Say you hear Deek playin with power where he gots no right. Even the ghost of a dog gots teeth."

"So, you trust me, man?"

"So, I trust your heart, brother."

Furball nodded. "Okay. Done deal. An you owe me nuthin, man. You coulda killed me first with your gun an then gone right ahead and done Deek an Ty. So, maybe I see a little what you talkin hearts."

Lyon thought about the two bullets, wondering what he would have done if he'd had more. But that didn't matter. Now. He smiled. "Done deal, dude."

Furball grinned. "So, let's go die, brother."

"So, what it is with Furball, man?" asked Deek, steering with one hand, the other steadying the beer bottle between his legs as he slid the Trans-Am, tires crying, around a corner. "Did you go an smoke his little butt?"

"No." Ty stared straight ahead through the misted windshield into fog, his body braced as Deek recovered the fishtailing car with a twist of the wheel and a jab on the gas. "Danny home in bed. Where he belong. Put him there myself. Need his sleep for school tomorrow."

Deek gave Ty a glance, and grinned. "He get good grades, man?"

"Yeah."

"Them an seventy-five cents score him a cup of coffee anytime."

"Don't fuck with me, Deek. I ain't in no mood."

"Yo, stupid! Better GET in the motherfuckin mood! Nuther few minutes an you just might be facin a couple a Uzis! Ain't nuthin more dangerous than makin a payoff, special if it the last one!"

Deek eyed the tall boy, then sighed. "Aw, I sorry I hit ya, man. Did I hurt ya?"

Ty shook his head.

"Well then, don't pout. With your lips it just make ya look... "

"I know," said Ty.

"Mmm. Well, if them cotton suckers went an hosed down the Crew like they sposed, Wesley gonna be on his little ole niggerboy knees BEGGIN enough work for to score him some fire." Deek grinned again. "Just maybe I surprise the little sucker with a present. Show my good faith, what I sayin."

Ty shrugged. "I do my job. Leave the thinkin to you." Then he turned. "What you sayin, *present?*"

"Done me some of that thinkin, man. While you was babysittin. Listen up! I give the Crew a Uzi—now what I even need the Friends for? The Crew hold em down, best believe. Or just do em all. I could give a shit which."

Ty frowned. "Mean, you gonna hand them kids a one-grand gun, just like that?"

Deek snickered. "What I say, man? My good faith! Kids LIKE to be trusted. Shit, you of all people should oughta know that!"

Ty glanced at the back seat where the carbine lay. Deek saw him and smiled. "Naw. Not that one. It almost new. I get em another. At a discount."

Deek hunched over the wheel, peering ahead through the mist, then swung the car into a shabby old gas station. It was closed for the night, its pumps protected by plywood panels chained around them. Accordion bars were drawn across the front of the rusty steel building. A small bulb burned inside the office section, revealing bare shelves and a wide-open cash-register drawer. A sputtering fluorescent tube over the service-bay door lit an ancient RICHFIELD sign. Deek drove carefully around behind the building, threading the 'Am through piles of bald tires and junked auto parts. The headlights swept past several gutted car bodies and a mountain of dead batteries along the back fence. Deek eased the 'Am to the building's far side so that it was facing the street once more. He killed the lights but left the engine running.

"What up?" asked Ty as Deek set the parking brake.

"Nuthin. Just gotta piss."

Automatically, Ty flicked off the .45's safety and moved to get out.

"Naw," said Deek, pushing open his door. "Place a total graveyard. I'm cool." He swung the door shut and walked back around the building.

Ty watched a moment in the mirror as Deek disappeared into mist. Why was he going so far just to piss? It probably had something to do with the lame-looking little dance he did to get his zipper zipped again under his sagging sack of lard. Another six months and Deek wouldn't be cruising the designer racks anymore... just plain old fat-boy 501s like Gordon wore. But Gordon carried himself with pride.

Six months. Ty scanned the shadows. Six months seemed an eternity. Coldly, Ty considered if he'd even live that much longer, especially the way Deek was maxing things lately. Ty thought of Danny: he *had* to stay alive for the boy! What Danny needed was a man, but Ty decided he'd have to do.

Ty noticed another stack of old batteries piled against the station wall; probably saved back until the price of scrap lead went up again. Word said the major dealers sometimes did that with their shiploads of shit. He remembered how his dad had tried scrap salvaging for a while; same as he'd tried almost everything else a poor, honest black man could do to make a living for his family. Ty had helped, prowling with him through the back streets and alleyways in a rattly old '58 Ford flatbed, picking up every stray piece of rusty scrap iron, digging in dumpsters for aluminum cans, and snatching dead batteries out of empty lots and junk cars. They'd been worth about a dollar apiece. On a good day they might score a whole half dozen.

Ty gazed at the batteries now, noting the fluffy white fuzz grown thick on their terminals from oxidation. He'd been just about Danny's age then; same miserably thin body and underfed muscles, struggling to heft those heavy goddamned things the four feet up to the truck bed, but mentally counting each as one more dollar for his family. Chump change for sure, yet there'd been a proud sort of feeling at the end of the day; maybe like one rag-ass niggerboy who couldn't be beaten down.

Ty flexed his slashed arm, wincing a little. Six months of that and he'd been wiry as a cheetah he'd seen on *Wild Kingdom*. He pulled up his shirt and ran a palm over his belly. Deek's punch hadn't hurt him, but all the beer and riding in this goddamned car was starting to show. Deek could afford to get sloppy and fat. A bodyguard had to stay hard and fast, and right now Ty didn't feel much of either.

Deek used to have another bodyguard.

Ty shrugged and popped another Heineken. You gonna die, nigger, die happy. He looked at the batteries again, recalling how that fuzzy shit used to burn in the cuts on his hands. He remembered how, in the hot afternoons, after they'd sold their day's earnings at the scrap yard, he and his dad would sit dusty and sweaty and shirtless in the truck and split a quart of Colt .45 before going home. Ty used to like the malt liquor with a grape Popsicle. They'd talk about all sorts of stuff, things a dude just no way could ask his mom. And supper had always tasted so goddamn *good* with a half quart of Colt already inside him. Ty remembered his dad's strong man-smell. Danny needed something like that.

Ty's mind drifted. He could get a license. They charged now for the driver training course at school—another advantage rich kids had over poor—but coming up with the buck would be no problem now. There were lots of old flatbed trucks scoreable for under a grand. He'd put in a CD for sure; it would make the work go smoother. He suddenly realized he could make it all happen in only a month more of working for Deek. One motherfucking little month! Why in hell hadn't he thought of this before? Maybe you had to know what you wanted before you could try for a grip on it.

Deek returned and slid back into the car. Ty stayed silent as they headed out to the street. In the city you learned young to keep your dreams to yourself. It was funny, thought Ty, that now more than ever he'd have to cover Deek's ass.

The old motel was way over east, off Foothill; a two-story shoe box of cracked, scabby stucco and peeling pastel paint. Its second-floor landing was railed by rusty wrought iron. The neon sign flickered half dead, and more of the yellow bug-light bulbs by each door were burned out or broken than working. The shabby black van looked totally at home in the parking lot, among bashed-up, wanna-be-bad sixties and seventies 'Stangs, Cams, and GTOs. There was also a tricked-out Vee-dub, and a battered, big-pig station wagon that probably belonged to some homeless family who'd checked in for one night of showers, warmth, and black-- and-white TV.

Deek parked the 'Am facing out toward the street. Ty made sure his .45 was cocked, safety off, and nestled it carefully in the back of his jeans, He noted the cautious movement of curtains in several of the motel windows, and felt eyes on him for a second or two. Pale light shone from behind faded shades in the second-floor room of the Bakersfield dudes, but no one was doing a peek-out from there. Deek left the car unlocked and didn't arm the alarm.

Ty moved in front of Deek as they neared the stairs. "I go first," he murmured. "I knock, an you keep way 'hind me."

Deek grinned, puffing up the staircase at Ty's heels. "Times like this make up for all the shit you cause me, man."

Once more, Ty was aware of eyes behind curtains as he moved along the landing. Some of the peephole glasses darkened. A lot of those people were waiting for something, and it probably wasn't Domino's pizza. Most of the TVs seemed tuned to the same channel: likely this place had no cable. The low voices of happy children came from the room next to the Bakersfield boys'. It didn't take much to make kids happy, Ty thought. Food, love, and a warm place to sleep counted most.

Reaching the dudes' door, he heard TV sound in there as well, news noise, something about Iran or Iraq and sending them guns or money. Motioning for Deek to stay back, Ty stepped to the door and rapped softly with his knuckles while keeping his other hand on the .45's butt.

For a minute nothing happened. Finally, the voice of the older dude called out. He sounded drunk on his ass again, but his tone was surprised and eager. "Hang on, I comin', bra."

"Why Santa ain't got no kids," Ty muttered.

"What?" whispered Deek.

"Cause he don't come but once a year, an then it down the chimney."

Deek gave him a strange look, but Ty had relaxed, sighing out vapor. The hand that had hovered on the gun slipped to his side. "Danny tell me that."

Deek frowned. "It gettin so's I can't tell when you drunk or not no more, man."

Ty only smiled slightly as the door locks clicked open. The big boy wore just his filthy 501s, half unbuttoned and slipping so low that curls of hair showed and he walked on the cuffs. Despite all his muscle his body seemed slack, belly out from drinking and powerful arms dangling loose at his sides. A Night Train bottle hung loose in his hand. He swayed on his feet and stumbled forward so that Ty had to catch him. The big boy laughed and crushed Ty's slim body to the solid slabs of his chest. Ty felt a moment of panic, but the big dude only focused red-rimmed eyes on Ty and laughed again. "Yo, bro! I jus now sayin to Lionel here you not be leavin your bros out in the col'!" He lifted Ty off his feet and swung him into the room. "Bring your asses in here where it warm, niggers!" He set Ty down and offered him the bottle.

Ty took a gulp of warm wine laced with spit to be polite, even though he hated Night Train, then scanned the room at a glance, missing nothing. The big boys had been here for days now, with

Deek paying the rent and some extra bucks for food, which went mostly for Train. The motel maid had probably gotten disgusted a long time ago and given up trying to clean. Train bottles and empty KFC buckets lay everywhere, along with pizza boxes and empty potato-chip bags. What few clothes the dudes owned were all on the floor. The sooty Panel-Ray heater was cranked full-on, and the air was a smothering stew of wine sweat and old socks, and murky as the fog outside with Lucky Strike smoke. The sheets of the one double bed trailed gray on the dirty beige carpet even though a stack of fresh ones was dumped by the door. The other boy was sprawled on the bed, wearing just a pair of Jockey shorts so ragged that they showed as much skin as cotton. He held a Train bottle about ready to spill on his stomach, and a cigarette smoldered forgotten in his fingers. He didn't look as if he realized yet that company had come.

The old Zenith TV atop the dresser-desk was advising people to buy their Toyotas now while the dealers were eager to deal. The light in the center of the ceiling was one of those energy-saving fluorescent rings. It threw a sick bluish glow that turned the tan walls the color of puke and tinged the gunmetal skins of Ty and the big boys a cold, corpselike violet. Ty had seen too many of these goddamned rooms in the last few months. For some people they might have been a beginning; for most they meant the end was near. He remembered a thing he'd heard in history class one time: black death. It was a sickness.

One chair stood cockeyed in a corner, its plastic cushions patched with silver duct tape. Both Uzis lay on it. Ty gave Deek a short nod, signifying all was way past cool. These dudes were nothing but overgrown children trying to play a game whose rules took a lifetime to learn. As he had that morning, Ty felt sorry for them. He found himself hoping they'd have the sense to go home when their money ran out. He also hoped they hadn't killed any of those young boys, so maybe, in time, this whole thing would fade to a sad little joke.

Deek had come in and eased the door shut when the big boy had let go of Ty. Ty watched his eyes find the guns and a smile curl his lip. The second boy, Lionel, had finally figured what is and was struggling to get to his feet. He spilled the Train on the bed, and would have fallen on his face but for the first boy clapping a huge arm around him and pulling him close. Ty wondered if they were real brothers.

The first boy's face was all eagerness now as he towered over Deek and held the other dude. Ty thought of those twins when they'd scrambled for the beer.

"We done it, man!" the first boy laughed. "Done it good, best believe!" He stopped and pondered a moment. "Well, we dint get none, you was spectin that. But, maaan, we ever scare the holy shit outa them little bastards!"

Deek studied the boy for one quick second, then grinned and slapped a massive shoulder. "Way cool, bro! I knowed I could trust ya. Yo! Sit down, crew. Gots a bonus for ya. Word!"

Ty watched the big boys drop heavily back on the bed. Their faces were totally childlike now, their eyes bright with the pleasure of Deek's praise. Ty's nose wrinkled; the Train taste in his mouth was sickening. Ripping open his pouch, Deek pulled out a hundred and slapped it into the first boy's callused palm. "An that only a part what I gots for ya, bros."

Ty's eyes narrowed. He wondered what was up. Was Deek going to get these dudes to really do somebody—maybe that other gang, the Friends?

The big boys exchanged happy grins, each holding a corner of the bill. Ty suddenly wanted to kick them. It was like some ancient nigger joke; Rastus and Remus getting their woolly little heads patted by the massah. Flinching at the pain in his arm, he dug in his pocket for his Kools; anything to get that goddamn sick taste out of his mouth.

Ty saw Deek pull something else from his pouch. A motherfucking watermelon wouldn't have surprised him. His eyes narrowed again as Deek produced something small wrapped in Kleenex. Deek unfolded the tissue to reveal a pair of plastic syringes, the kind the anti-AIDS people gave away on the street to junkies. Ty saw the sudden flicker of uncertainty in the big boys' eyes.

The first dude swallowed, shying slightly back from Deek's offered palm. "Uh... we don't us do nuthin like that there, man. Don't wanna get ourselfs hooked on no heroin."

Deek chuckled. "Hey, no, brother! Yo, what it is be just coke. . . but some super major shit. No way you get hooked, man! Hell, you dudes ain't stupid. You figure I want anybody workin for me full-time what on somethin?"

Lionel was too drunk to be very doubtful of anything. And Deek's voice could *soothe.* Still, he asked. "But, um, what I sayin, don't coke get snorted up you nose?"

Deek grinned and patted his shoulder. "Not when it THIS good, my man, best believe!" Then he seemed to consider a moment, bouncing the barrels in his open hand. "Look, bros. What it is, this sorta like my blood thing. Hear what I sayin? My *test,* sorta, for dudes what I thinkin bout takin on, long-time. Shit, you tellin me you can't handle it?"

The first boy took several huge gulps from the bottle, then passed it to Lionel. "Sho! We up for some good stuff, best you believe!"

Lionel tilted the bottle back and killed it, then nodded hard. "Like he say, man, we up fo it. Uh... you gonna show us how it done, right?"

"Word," said Deek.

Ty had slipped the Kools back in his pocket. He took a step closer, his eyes slitted and his lips clamped over his teeth as Deek pulled a little cellophane packet from his pouch. Ty had seen enough of those, he packed them, but Deek's coke was no way in hell fit for shooting. Ty remembered his job, and kept himself from going any closer. But he scowled when he saw that the stuff was pure white, almost luminous under the bluish ceiling light. He dug out his Kools once more and fired one fast, sucking smoke-deep and holding it long. Some sort of new shit? he wondered. Like a test-market thing? He didn't like the idea. Some people on TV didn't want stuff tested on white rats and rabbits. Ty flicked ashes on the floor. Well, it was Deek's game. Maybe he did have some other plans for the dudes. And even if the stuff was the purest China white, the boys were way too drunk to get anything out of it. Fact was, they'd probably puke up their Night Train-soaked guts and never try anything like that again. Maybe that was Deek's plan.

Deek went into the bathroom and returned with a bottle cap of water. His voice was gentle. He could coax a bat into hell when he wanted. The big boys watched, fascinated, as Deek's Bic furnished a flame. Ty moved back by the door and quietly smoked, though his eyes missed nothing. The shit *was* pure, whatever it was. It melted instantly in the water. Deek didn't use cotton to strain it, just loading the barrels right out of the cap. Ty's gaze shifted: with all their muscles the big boys had beautiful veins.

Something scratched at the back of Ty's brain. He wished he hadn't been drinking all day. He was going to have to stop that, especially now. He tried to force some of the fuzz from his mind. Only the finest coke would have melted that way. But this shit had no sparkle. The best street smack he'd ever seen had never been that snowy white, and still needed straining.

Deek wiped the gleaming points with a flourish of the Kleenex, reminding Ty of the Burger King girl's touch of magic with the sugar packets for Danny; something to please a small child. The two big boys bent forward to cautiously take the needles from Deek. Lionel looked about ready to pass out anyway, but struggled to concentrate as Deek pointed out good veins and warned about poking all the way through. Almost together the needles went in. Both boys winced and bit on their lips. They had to be brothers, Ty thought. Work-callused thumbs pressed plungers.

Then Ty remembered. "NOOOOO!"

It was a story his dad had told on one of those hot afternoons laid-back in the truck. Ty recalled the sun slanting orange through the city haze and the grimy windshield; the taste of grape Popsicle and Colt .45, sour-sweet with an ass-kicking bite like Night Train.

Back then he'd thought Train was way past bad. It was just the cool kind of story you'd never get from your mom—no ghost stuff at bedtime to scare little kids—an old junkie revenge trick. That white fuzzy stuff that grew on junk batteries had the same look and texture as the sort of smack sold back in those days. It dissolved exactly the same in a spoonful of water.

But, shot into your body, it was pure death in a second! Ty sprang for the bed even as the two big boys crumpled forward, the needles still stuck in their arms. Deek had stepped back to give them room to hit the floor. He watched with the same sort of interest he might have shown for a school science experiment. He spun around when Ty screamed, looking more annoyed than anything else. Ty thought, if he could only catch the boys, yank out the needles, they'd somehow be good as new again. Those big black bodies could never be *that* easy to kill!

Deek grabbed one of Ty's outflung arms, the one that Danny had slashed, grabbed it with both chubby hands For all his slack muscles, Deek clamped on like a pit-bull bite, twisting viciously like little kids gave Indian burns. Ty felt his skin rip open. Pain lashed up his arm and exploded in his brain. He screamed again, in agony now, and dropped to his knees, hitting the dirty carpet in sync with the thuds of the two big bodies. Blood gushed from his sleeve.

Rage tore through Ty's mind, smashing back at the blackness that roared in like a wave to drown him. It was like being slammed in the stomach or kicked in the balls: he couldn't get air. His sight blurred and dimmed down like a dying TV screen, to a tiny point of light with darkness crushing it out. He fought the black, the tears in his eyes as hot as the blood pumping from his arm. Somehow he forced strength to his legs. He struggled up from his knees. His free hand searched for the gun.

Then Deek's voice filtered through the hurt and fury. "Game over, Ty."

Vaguely, Ty realized that Deek had let go of his arm. The pain still cut him in razor-edged ripples. He sucked a breath through clenched teeth, and again the blackness tried to smother him. He sank back to his knees. The hand that had sought the gun now clutched at his bleeding arm. He tasted puke but choked it down. Finally, head lowered, panting for breath, he managed to whisper, "Why?"

Deek's voice came fuzzy, like from far away. The words were a bad joke from a million old movies. "They knew too much."

Deek's tone went soothing. Ty felt himself being helped to his feet, then led to the chair. There was a double clunk of the Uzis hitting the floor and then he was slumped on crackly old plastic. A bottle was shoved in his blood-covered hand. More Train? Ty didn't care, he tilted it up and drank.

Slowly, his vision came back into focus. He found he was shaking. He drank again, hating the shit but needing it bad. He saw Deek wrapping both Uzis in one of the dead boys' T-shirts. His eyes found the bodies and shied away fast. He gulped the rest of the bottle like Kool-Aid, then looked back at the boys.

Wasted was another word for dead. And that's what a kid's death was. Maybe they *had* known too much, but in another way they hadn't known enough. Kids playing TV games for keeps. Was the whole motherfucking world nothing but kids playing parts? And who in hell wrote the scripts? Black kids played at being bad. And died for it. What did white kids play, keeping nigger kids in their cages?

Clutching his arm, Ty lurched to his feet, forcing his eyes from the figures on the floor. The TV was talking about someone getting sentenced to prison for shooting a sea otter. A child's laughter carried from the room next door. Black death meant nothing to nobody.

Deek's hands glistened with Ty's blood. He wiped them on the bundled T-shirt, then snagged the one-buck bill from the floor and folded it back into his pouch. "Sorry, man. Didn't know it was gonna freak ya like that. Yo. You cool now?"

Black and cool, thought Ty. I the motherfuckin iceman, the iceberg, the coolest nigger breeze you ever done seen, sucker! What in hell was wrong with being black and *warm?* He pressed his torn sleeve tight so no more blood would drip on the carpet. A month, he thought... one more motherfucking month and he'd get himself free of this trap. Fuck cool! Fuck cool forever! He'd be warm and stupid for the rest of his goddamned life! Let Deek find some other cool fool to pimp pain and death to black kids! He'd already had another bodyguard...

Ty's eyes found the dead boys again. Then he raised them to Deek's... warm obsidian facing frozen gold.

Deek's gaze was calculating. "Yeah, well, you deserve a day off, man. Tell you what. I handle things alone tomorrow. You an Danny go an have a real cool time. Yo. Danny a way cool little dude, man. I really hope nuthin ever happen to him. Seem like kids get wasted so easy, an just nobody give a good shit. Know what I sayin?" Deek nudged the bigger boy's body with his toe. "So what you figure they rate, man? Tomorrow, next day, a few stupid lines on the *Trib's* back page? Just another couple niggerboys found dead. Gang, drug killin?" Deek pointed to a ragged nylon wallet half sticking out of the boy's back pocket. "Wanna know his name, man? Maybe he gots pitchers of his family?"

Ty suddenly shivered in the hot steamy room. "No. I cool."

Deek smiled. "Yeah. You are." Bundle under one arm, he moved to the door. Glancing first out the peephole, he opened it slightly and checked up and down the landing. Finally he stepped out, puffing another Kleenex from his pocket and draping it over the inside knob. Ty wiped it carefully before following Deek, then, gripping the outside knob with the tissue, he started to ease the door shut behind him. Just before the lock clicked, he tensed. Darting back into the room, he wiped the Night Train bottle. He glanced at the other empty, then remembered that the boy had wrapped his big hand around it again. He supposed that was a cool thought. He caught sight of one more full bottle as he turned to leave, hesitated a second, then slipped it into his jacket pocket, eased out on the landing, where Deek waited, and closed the door, making sure that the lock caught.

Deek grinned at him. "Way past cool, dude. I lucky I got ya." Then he frowned slightly. "Yo. Can't you hold your arm like it ain't hurt? Case anybody watchin us leave. An careful you don't drip no more blood."

Gritting his teeth against the pain, Ty shoved his hand into his jeans so the blood would run into his pocket. He followed Deek back along the landing and descended the stairs. Their shoe soles were silent, and Ty didn't feel any eyes as they crossed the weedy parking lot to the 'Am. A breeze was stirring from the distant Bay, and the fog seemed to be thinning, but Ty doubted if anyone could have read the car's plate as they drove away. In a place like this it wasn't likely that anyone would even try.

Deek swung off Foothill onto 64th, rolling slow through a quiet neighborhood of old but well-kept houses, each with its own small yard. Trikes, Big Wheels, balls, and a few big Tonka toys lay here and there on wet lawns. Only the age of many of the cars and pickups parked in the driveways hinted at a black community. Here, Ty thought, was peace and pride... at least for now. Ty remembered this was where his mom had always talked of moving someday.

Instead of taking East 14th toward downtown, Deek cut back up to 73rd, then out to 880, where the traffic was still heavy. Once northbound, cruising casually among the rumbling semis, Deek stopped checking the mirrors so often.

"Yo, Ty? How your arm, man? Shit, I sorry I had to do ya like that, but you almost freak on me back there, y'know."

Ty's arm throbbed and felt twice its size but the bleeding had almost stopped. He shrugged, pulling out the bottle, twisting off the cap, and taking a long hit. "I live. Only the bad die young."

Deek arched an eyebrow. "Well, I woulda told you the plan, cept I didn't know myself till I sure them suckers done what they sposed." He glanced over again. "Yo. Could you handled it if I'd told ya first?"

Ty took another drink. It wasn't so bad. He could learn to live with it. "I don't know. Weren't there no way other?"

"Never trust nobody, man. Yo. You ain't pissed or nuthin?"

Ty felt only a dull aching sadness that seemed to throb through him like the pain in his arm. He swallowed more Train. It eased the hurt a lot better than Heineken. "No," he murmured. "Not no more. I just tired, Deek. I wanna go home."

"Cool, man. I drop ya."

"No. I get out down by that late-night market. Wanna pick up some stuff for breakfast."

Deek drifted the car onto an exit ramp, still studying Ty. "Now you *sure* you chilled, man? What I sayin is, this shit ain't gonna come back an freak ya later on?"

"I just too fuckin tired to be freaked by nuthin no more."

"Mmm. Well, I seen you look a lot better, man. An that arm of yours still bleedin. People in that store might see."

Ty stared straight ahead. "Nobody in that hood gonna pay no 'tention to some niggerboy bleedin, even he lay dead on the sidewalk."

Markita came out of the grocery store, moving quickly away from the bright white fluorescence and standing in shadow so her eyes could adjust to the night. She carefully scanned the small parking lot, and then the dark foggy tunnel of the three-block walk back home. It was an obstacle course she hated and feared. On nights like this with the fog drifting thick between the crumbling old buildings, some abandoned and boarded, the city seemed to close down on her like one of those funnel traps on nature shows. There was some small relief on the second block, where the weedy asphalt of a shut-down car wash offered no cover for night-lurking things. She always breathed a little easier when passing it, knowing she might be able to dodge and play a desperate game of hide-and-seek in and out of the wash bays if chased. But then the third block would close in once more and cut off her options. And it had its own special terror.

She glanced at her Kmart watch: 12:23, and sighed at the thought of having to be at work again in just five and a half hours. She shifted the small grocery bag in one arm: a quart of orange juice, another of milk, and a box of oatmeal for her son. Though she ate for free at the Burger King, and brought leftovers home for her mom. Markita had vowed she'd be damned if she raised her son up on junk food. J'row was going to need every muscle and mind cell to survive, and Markita didn't believe jack about all that fast-food "leaner and lighter" dogshit.

She stared down the gloomy blocks again, then pulled the little spray can of Mace from the pocket of her old Navy-surplus peacoat and nested it atop the groceries. Her mother had scored her the stuff. You were supposed to be eighteen and have a license or something to carry it, and Markita supposed she could be fined or go to jail if caught. Of course, when you were poor, being fined was only a joke *before* you went to jail, as if having no money was a crime in itself. It seemed like, sooner or later, if you didn't have money you ended up in a cage. And the law made protecting yourself a crime too, even though it never did a goddamn thing to help you.

Lately, Markita had been considering a gun, something small and semiautomatic. Leroy would know what was best. She decided to ask him about it in the morning. After what had happened tonight — the bodyguard boy Ty dragging the younger kid out of the restaurant right under everybody's noses — Markita no longer felt safe anywhere. The fact that the boys had been brothers didn't do much to cheer her up. Fear was like that; you went from being scared of what did happen to living in terror of what *might* happen. And from what Markita had seen of life, it seemed to get worse as you got older.

She glanced at the Mace can again. Well, like her mother often said, just as well be hung for a sheep as a lamb. They were one and the same when you were black and poor. If trying to save your own life and protect those you loved was a crime, there wasn't much hope left anyhow. She remembered reading something in a Charles Dickens book at school: "If the law says that, then the law is a ass!"

Looking once more down the street, she turned up her coat collar and started for home, putting pride in her stride. She met no one on the first block, and the only traffic was a lone pickup chugging past, missing on one cylinder and trailing oil smoke, with garbage cans rattling in back. She crossed the side street, hurrying clear of the corner lamp's light cone. They've turned us into children of the night, she thought. A little of the fear left her now: fifty percent home free. The breeze was strengthening, thinning the fog into swirls, and she could just make out the steps of her own building up near the next corner. A newspaper page fluttered past like a little ghost, making her jump. The last ordeal was an alley mouth midway up the block. For her, crossing it at night was like some ancient child's story of whistling past a graveyard. Even safe on the other side she always felt as if someone had slid out to follow her the last hundred yards home. She would hunch her shoulders and plead with herself not to run, afraid to turn and look and just as scared not to.

She deepened her breathing as she neared the black gap, storing up oxygen—she supposed—in case she did have to bail her behind. Screaming for help would be one total waste of breath. She fingered the door keys in her pocket. Then, just a few feet from the tunnel of fear, she stopped so suddenly that her Reebok soles squeaked.

Over the years, Markita had heard a lot of things going on in that alley; snatches of slurred talk from wineheads and cracked kids, screams, fighting, gunshots, and even the carefree laughter of children. She remembered playing there herself; one time sitting and giggling on the slashed front seat of an abandoned car, watching through the shattered windshield while her friends acted and danced on the hood. They'd called it their drive-in movie game. Bodies had been found: stabbed, shot, OD'd, or just with their hearts worn out at fourteen. Once there'd been a baby stuffed in a dumpster and, last summer, a little homeless boy who the cops said had been killed and half eaten by rats.

But Markita had never heard crying come from in there before... at least not like she was hearing it now. If there was such a thing as pure misery it would sound like this, she thought. And it was all the stranger for being boy-crying. She'd always thought a child's cough in night silence was the loneliest sound in the world: now she wasn't so sure. The sobbing echoed softly between the walls in the same sort of lost-soul keening she might have imagined coming out of some cemetery crypt in a Friday Frights movie.

Ain't no concern of yours, girl, she told herself. Sympathy spread too goddamn thin around here as it is. She stood a moment, recalling she'd said something close to the same to a young boy on a skateboard while she'd been on an errand for her mother a couple of hours ago. Usually she kept those kinds of things to herself, but, then, it hadn't seemed to matter. The kid probably thought she was a whore anyway. Lady of the night? How fucking poetic! He'd been a strange sort of boy, so delicate-looking yet so totally self-sufficient; like a prototype of something new or a reprogram of something very old that was better equipped to survive. Evolution in action. The shape of things to come. Shape changers. Weren't werewolves called children of the night?

Markita shoved those thoughts aside. Whoever was in the alley crying couldn't have been too far up, judging by the nearness of his sound. And he couldn't have had many options left to suffer alone in such a place. Anybody who was past caring about himself wouldn't be very concerned about others, and it took a hell of a lot more than a silver crucifix or a bunch of wolfbane leaves to ward off evil in this neighborhood. Markita glanced across the street, wondering if a short detour might not be the coolest move up next. Instead, she found herself edging closer to the alley mouth.

This ain't gettin it, girl, warned a part of her mind. You bein a goddamn fool, all you are! Somebody else's busted-up heart be no business of yours, best believe, specially when your own barely Scotch-taped together. She remembered Leroy's words; about it being a black thing and not nothing nobody could do.

Well, she thought, reaching the corner of the last building and pressing her back to cold brick. If black don't do nothing for black, who in hell will? She listened a little longer, feeling strangely cool. You didn't often hear big boys cry, and this had to be one... a kid would have blubbered, and no grown-up man would cut his own heart out like that. It was so... *uncool.* Markita frowned, her lips forming the words, "Shut up, fool!" She recalled an old thing her mother sometimes said when life seemed to go seven ways to hell: "What did I ever do, to be so black and blue?" Finally, Markita set the grocery bag down and pulled out the Mace. Finger poised ready on the little button, she sucked a breath and stepped around the corner.

Only the fog-filtered glow of a light at the alley's far end penetrated the passage. Markita realized too late she'd silhouetted herself against the openness behind her. But the lonely sobbing went on without pause. The breeze was growing stronger, twisting the mist into tortured shapes and wafting the smells of sodden garbage and wet cardboard into her face. She scented boy-sweat, and the familiar fumes of Night Train. And something else. She suddenly shivered, catching the coppery bite of fresh blood. She almost bolted then, half turning to run for home and leaving her food forgotten. The Mace seemed no more protection than a cross in the hands of a doubter. But the fog slit open above and the silver face of the moon swam out of it, casting a ghost-glow that glimmered off the weeping walls and glistening dumpster lids. The boy hadn't gone very far, as if not even trying to hide. Markita saw his huddled form, back to the wall, long legs pulled up like a little kid's, arms crossed on top, and face buried against them. Something blue-black and metallic hung loose in the fingers of one bony hand. Markita took a step closer before realizing it was a gun.

Part of her saw the picture she must be making, standing there, stupidly, with her silly can of Mace, while not ten feet away crouched a boy with a gun, his mind gone from drinking by the smell of him, and who looked long past caring about anybody's life. Yet, Markita remembered something else her mother often said... that black women always seemed to find the strength to carry on while their men were beaten down. Markita had always wondered if black women were really stronger, or was it just that the men and boys wore themselves out so fast by shaking the bars of their cages?

Without thinking, Markita let the hand holding the Mace drop to her side. She took another step toward the boy, his male sweat strong in her nostrils above the smells of wine and blood. A skateboard lay beside him, next to a fog-limp paper bag. He might have been older than her, or just tall for his age, but there was something familiar about him.

Maybe it was the expensive leather jacket with its own distinctive scent, somehow male in itself. Markita's jaw thrust forward in the way her mom always scolded as "boyscaring" and not at all ladylike. She said the first thing that came to mind:... said it loud and proud.

"Hush yourself, boy!"

The boy's head snapped up, and the moonlight fell full on his harmless, gunmetal features. Big teeth and tear streaks glittered. Recognition flashed across his face even as Markita spoke his name.

"Ty?"

Like a little kid, he almost melted back into tears once more.

But then his big loose lips stopped quivering, his lean jaw set, and sudden determination iced his eyes. Slowly, his gaze locked on Markita, he raised the heavy pistol and jammed the muzzle against his head.

Markita froze in horror. It seemed to take every bit of strength in the boy's thin body to hold the gun. His finger trembled on the trigger as if that slim piece of metal between him and death was beyond his power to pull. Then, as if the weight was just too much, his arm fell back and the gun butt clunked on the pavement. Ty's chin shook and fresh tears flooded his cheeks, ice blue in the moonlight.

"I... can't!" he sobbed, and hid his face once more.

Markita's moves were deliberate. She shoved the Mace into her coat pocket, dropped her hands to her hips, and stared down at the boy. She could have been surveying some little mess her son had made.

"Ohhh... SHIT! All that tell me is you still got some sense left in your goddamn head!"

Ty's head came up again, his mouth opening and eyes widening until he looked like Buckwheat with a flattop.

"Some," Markita went on. She found she was shaking her finger just like her mother. It was so lame yet she couldn't stop. "But not one hell of a lot, best believe!" She saw the Train bottle and kicked it spinning up the alley. "What the matter, boy? Killin yourself with that shit ain't fast enough for you? Tell you this for a fact, you just keep on sittin there, bawlin your goddamn heart out for all the world to hear, an somebody be comin right directly along happy as hell to do it for you! Yes, they will!"

Ty's mouth shut with a clop. Leaving the gun where it lay, he crossed his arms on his knees once again. Markita saw him wince. His expression grew sullen, and he stared at the alley's opposite wall. "I not that lucky," he muttered. He glanced up at Markita from the corner of his now narrowed eyes. "An what it to ya anyways, girl? Shit, you not know from nuthin what it is!"

Markita's finger jabbed the air to her right. "Oh, don't I, boy? Who in hell you figure you talkin to, nigger? All my goddamn life I livin just three door up that way! What you tellin ME I don't know from nuthin? Shit! Gots me a two-year-old at home know ten *time* more bout what it is than you!" She stamped her foot, something her mother did too. "You! With all them way cool clothes, an all your money-bucks, an your gun, an all your... all your goddamn motherfuckin BAD! So, what in hell it get you, boy? Not a goddamn friend in the world, am I right? An here you sittin on your drunk-ass black butt in the garbage an wet just like any other little ole throwed out kid got no home!"

Ty rested his chin on his arms. His long steamy sigh sounded as tired as Markita felt. "You don't know what I just gone an done, girl." He considered, glancing up at her. "Else you run screamin all the way home. Word."

Markita tensed a little, but then her arm fell to her side and her shoulders sagged under the heavy coat. "Mmm. Well, I might run but I wouldn't waste my time on screamin. Spose you went an shot somebody?"

Ty squinted his eyes shut. Fresh tears squeezed out anyhow. His lean body shook with choked-back sobs. "There a difference tween a killin an... an a murder. Killin a thing the world make you do. Somethin you *got* to do when there ain't no way other. Murder... " He shut his mouth and set his jaw, turning away from Markita to watch a rat that had scented his blood and was creeping close. "You just now tellin me you know from jack? Then you know I can't say no more."

Markita had felt ice down her spine when Ty had said the word. It was a word you didn't hear too often, strangely enough, on the streets where it happened all the time. People got "done," "smoked," "iced," "wasted"... little kids talked of "dirt naps." But it just didn't seem cool to use the M-word. Part of her did want to run home now. She realized that she didn't actually know jack about this boy, that all her feelings toward him and recent thoughts about him were mostly made up in her mind. Ty looked so basically gentle and harmless—even uncool—yet she'd watched in fear as he'd dragged his own brother into the night and hurt him just hours ago. Killing to defend himself, maybe even protecting that slimy sucker Deek, she could accept as just a part of this goddamned life. But that other word—even in this place it still sounded evil. She was being some kind of fool, she thought. If she had any goddamn sense at all she'd get the hell away from this crazy, drunken niggerboy just as fast as she could and pray God she'd never see him again. Maybe a while later, home safe and in bed, she'd hear that single gunshot.

But still she stood there, gazing down at the boy who'd treated his little brother to burgers and fries and sat talking to him with love in every look and gesture. Markita shoved her hands in her pockets and shuffled her Reeboks. "Murder a... evil word."

Ty seemed to be watching the rat edge closer. But he nodded.

"Yeah. That say it all. Mean a cold killin without no good reason. An what difference it make if you the one actual pull the trigger or just stand by with your head up your ass an let it happen?"

Markita sifted Ty's words in her mind. In a way it was like trying to get a confession out of her own son—that he'd done some way naughty thing; but maybe not quite as naughty as he thought. Ty had buried his face once more. Suddenly, Markita moved to him and knelt. She lay a gentle hand on his shoulder. "Tell me. It can't hurt."

Ty looked up. "It... it put you in a bad way, girl."

"Put *you* in a worse way keepin it all inside, look like to me. An, it Markita."

"What is?"

"My name."

"Oh." Ty wiped his face with his sleeve. "So how come you know mine?"

"I hear Deek callin you." Markita settled herself next to Ty. "Now. What it is, I ain't leavin till I get the story, an till I sure in my mind you ain't gonna go an do somethin stupid."

Ty glanced over at the rat again. It was sitting up, whiskers quivering, its little eyes black and cold. Ty sighed out wine-scented steam. "Stupid my thing, an I do it good. I tell, could put you in shit, Markita."

Could put you *in deeper shit*, thought Markita. *For all you know I go runnin to the cops.* But Ty didn't seem to have considered that. Markita shrugged. "You let it keep eatin you all by yourself, you gonna be spendin a lot of lonely nights holdin that gun to your head."

Ty spat, hitting the rat full in the face. It squealed and scuttled away.

A few minutes later, Markita's hand found Ty's bloody one and held it. "But you didn't *know,*" she said. "What that evil bastard Deek was gonna do. An by the time you read him, it was too late. Yes it was." She shook her head. "An all for a couple of goddamn guns."

Ty wiped new tears from his cheeks, flinching when he lifted his arm. He hadn't told the girl what the Bakersfield boys had been hired to do. Now he found himself wondering if he would have felt any differently over their deaths if they had killed one of the young gang kids. But what would give him any right to feel differently? After all, he did know Deek's plan for the younger boys—and he'd been ready to shoot at least one of them himself that morning. Or at least he'd thought he was. He sighed steam once more. "It funny, what it is. I mean, if I coulda got to my gun, right there in that room, I'da killed Deek. Word! But now it like I gone all cold an nuthin inside. It like a cage he make for me, an now I caught in it. Anything happen to Deek, come from that, happen to me too. Seem like life here ain't nuthin but some long line of cages. You step in the first one, all you hear from then on be them bars clankin shut 'hind your black ass. An them cages keep on gettin smaller an smaller."

Ty went silent, just staring over at the opposite wall.

Markita pressed Ty's bony hand, thinking how cold it was. "That a way cool little brother you got."

Ty's face twisted like he might cry again. "No. He a *warm* boy, right on the edge of goin cool." Ty turned to Markita. "He at the age where he standin at the door of that first cage... sniffin the sucker bait. An it smell so GOOD!" He waved his bloody hand. "So way past good 'pared to what he see all round him here. Eleven, twelve, thirteen, them's the magic ages. Don't care what they tell me in high school, bout futures an career shit. You start choosin you life bout time your own dick wake up... " Ty glanced quickly at Markita. "Um, sorry." His arm fell back and he gritted his teeth. "What I sayin is, Danny could still be saved. Cept it don't look like there gonna be nobody round to save him. Like, there ain't nobody in the whole fuckin world even figure he *worth* savin! Cept Mom, course. But what she do? World make it so she all the time bustin her butt just tryin to keep food on the table an rent money in some sucker's hand. Leave her no time for *bein* with her kids. Everthing Danny learnin bout life come from right here off these motherfuckin streets. Tell him the only shit what matter be money, an bad... an cool." Ty shrugged. "An it funny, that maybe I gotta stay in a cage to keep Danny outa one."

Markita sighed now. "I don't know. An I never knew nobody what did... not for real. Maybe, like everbody say when they can't figure somethin out logical, it just a black thing." She leaned close and gently lifted Ty's arm. "Mmm. You been cut bad."

There was a funny note of pride in Ty's voice. "Danny done that." Then he turned away. "My cool little brother." Ty made a sound that was too cold for a laugh. "Show he bout up for life in the hood, don't it?" Ty looked back at his arm. "TV say all these kids ain't nuthin but wild little animals. Well, maybe I just gotta tame Danny down. I gotta try." He glanced at the gun on the pavement. "Maybe that why I can't do my ownself. It like, when I put up the gun, this voice come to mind, whisper, 'Don't, sucker.' "Ty's forehead creased. "Young voice." He shook his head. "Shit. Only crazy-ass people sposed to hear voices! Like them old niggers what holler all day in the street."

"I don't think you hurt when you crazy," said Markita. "I think goin crazy the onliest way some folks got to make the hurtin stop." She pressed his hand again. "You got other family? I mean, sides your mom an your brother?"

"Nuther brother, eight. Two little sisters." Ty turned to Markita once more. "Say you gots a son?"

"J'row. He two."

Ty looked away. "Oh. Then that mean... "

"Mean I gots a son, what it mean."

"Oh... Sorry."

"Don't be. I ain't." Markita pulled her coat a little tighter, then pointed. "So, what's in the bag?"

Ty dropped his chin back on his arms. "Nuthin."

"Now, what you tellin me, nuthin? I see Popsicles, gonna melt, an Cocoa Puffs an stuff gettin all foggy-wet. Shoulda got plastic."

"Huh?"

"You know? Paper or plastic?"

"Oh. Well, I can't never member what best. Ain't paper sposed to save the 'vironment or somethin?"

"Shit, boy, what good all that stuff do when you can't even put food on your table fit to eat?"

"Yeah. Guess you right."

"Mmm. Ain't no normal dude gonna be thinkin bout that sorta

stuff, anyways."

Ty sighed steam once again. "Yeah. Spose it ain't cool. I was gonna take Danny uptown shoppin tomorrow. Score stuff for the other kids too, clothes an shoes an nice shit like that. Hell, I prob'ly mess it all up, same's I do everthing else."

"Oh, stop makin yourself out a fool! Ain't that just the main trouble with you dudes! Facin down guns an knives don't scare you a bit, but just the thought of pickin out little girls' clothes get you actin like Norman Bates on Mother's Day! You know their sizes?"

"Uh-uh."

"Course you don't! Listen up, boy! Get your mom to write em down for you. She *can* write, can't she?"

Ty frowned. "Course she can."

"An you can read?"

"COURSE! Well, good enough for that kinda shit."

"Mmm. I spect she know all about what them little brothers an sisters of yours be dreamin an wishin for. Ask her."

Ty nodded slowly. "Yeah... yeah, spose I could go an do that. Shit, I just now think on me an Danny lookin through little girls' clothes. Bet he like to die!"

"Well, it be a warm thing for you dudes to be doin, wouldn't it? An, yo. You really wanna help them kids, you best start by keepin to your word. Ain't nuthin cut a kid deeper'n gettin promises busted." Markita gathered up the groceries, mindful of the sodden sack. She got to her feet and gazed down at Ty, her jaw jutting once more. "You just c'mon now, boy... up outa that goddamn garbage an wet fore you catch your death. Spose you too goddamn drunk to walk?"

"No, I ain't!"

"Well, get your ass up, then. An stop lookin like you just found out you engaged to a lizard or somethin. I live right on the next corner. Got me a nice big plastic Mervyn's bag I been savin by. We put all your stuff in that." Markita hesitated, then added. "An I take me a good careful look at that arm of yours too. Bad-ass niggerboy like you gonna get himself enough hate stares in them uptown stores out lookin like you fresh from a gang fight!"

Five minutes later, Ty was following Markita into the warm dimness of her second-floor apartment. His skateboard dangled from the fingers of his bloody hand. Markita carried both grocery bags, which was cool, because Ty had fallen a few times.

Automatically, he scanned the little room as he eased the door shut behind him. It was cluttered. A streetlight's glow through the single window showed old but well-kept furniture: a comfortable-looking couch and two matching chairs, end tables with lamps, and a coffee table stacked neatly with magazines. Against the wall by the hallway door was a massive chest of drawers with a small TV and lots of framed snapshots on top. Ty saw several of Markita and a baby, and there were a couple of a smiling woman who was probably Markita's mother. Ty caught himself searching for pictures of boys her age. There were none.

On the opposite side of the doorway was a big bookshelf lined with paperbacks and what looked like a set of encyclopedias. Off to the left, beneath the window, was a single bed, still made up, with a frilly sort of spread. In the wall across from the bed was another door, closed, and beside it an old wooden baby crib. On the wall above it hung a framed picture of Martin Luther King. Scotch-taped close by were some child's drawings in crayon and a

Ninja Turtles comic book cover. The floor space remaining was mostly covered by throw rugs of every size, shape, and color. Where bare boards showed, polish gleamed. A long counter separated the kitchen area. A narrow door, standing open to darkness back beside the fridge, probably led to the bathroom.

Markita pointed to the door by the crib. "Mom," she whispered.

Ty nodded. The room's warmth was a comfort after the street's wet cold. The apartment had a background scent of cleanliness and lemony polish that was somehow defiant. It reminded him of his own home. He thought he could catch a faint trace of perfume above fresh-laundered sheets and pillowcases. There was also the warm, sleepy smell of a small child that seemed to stir some sense of protectiveness in him. The deep bass of music beat softly from another apartment, soothing like a heart. Blocks away a siren howled, but that only seemed to make the room more peaceful and secure. Ty noticed a few bright toys beneath the crib, and then coloring books given equal importance with the magazines on the coffee table. What looked like a baby version of a Speak 'N Spell computer lay beside them. Ty scanned the room once more, slower now, taking in more detail. Only the hurt in his arm remained to remind him of the world beyond these walls.

Putting a finger to her lips, Markita moved silently to the crib and motioned Ty to follow. He stood for a moment, looking down. The little boy lay on his back, pure ebony against the pale sheet. The blanket had slipped below his round tummy. The baby chub padding his chest and outspread arms promised muscle to come.

His hands were half open as if undecided between offerings or fists. The tiny fingers of children always looked so perfect. Ty reached to touch one, then saw the dried blood on his own and jerked back his hand. He turned away, murmuring, "Maybe I catchin a cold, like you say." He wiped at his nose.

Markita had been watching Ty, wondering how this could be the same boy who'd just seen two others die. "His name's J'row," she whispered.

"It a good name. Strong. It African?"

"I don't know." Markita smiled, looking back down at her son. "I kinda made it up. Sound a little African, though, don't it?"

A woman's sleepy voice called from behind the closed door. "Markita?"

"Yo, Mom. Everthing cool."

"It's so late, honey. You need your sleep."

Markita smiled at Ty. "I still gotta take me a bath yet, Mom. Good night."

"Sweet dreams, child."

Gently taking Ty's hand, Markita led him around the counter and set down the groceries. She slipped the orange juice and milk into the fridge, and Ty's pack of Popsicles into the freezer section. Then she motioned him through the bathroom door, following as he felt his unsteady way into the darkness. She shut the door behind her and pulled the light chain. The naked bulb was small, but Ty blinked as it came on. The little bathroom was so totally female that he felt like some big, clumsy, wet animal. He didn't move for fear of soiling something. He just stood, stupidly, skateboard clutched in one hand, waiting for whatever the girl had planned to do.

The walls were painted a pale peach color, and the toilet tank top and lid were fitted with fluffy lavender covers that matched the bath mat beside the big claw-footed tub. The chrome was half gone from faucets and pipes but the brass winked like gold wherever it showed. The air was scented with talcum powder and Dove. A long, flower-papered shelf above the sink was lined with all those mysterious bottles and jars that women and girls seemed to find so important. Staring around, mouth open, Ty could hardly imagine that just a few inches of ancient brick separated this fragile little world from what lay outside. Here too was a kind of defiance.

Markita's movements were casually cool; she shrugged off her coat and hung it on a hook, then took Ty's board and stood it by the door. Ty wasn't surprised that she seemed so at home here; what came to his mind was how confident she'd looked sitting beside him in the alley.

Besides her Levi's and Reeboks, Markita wore just a faded purple T-shirt. Ty saw her proud breasts strain the thin cotton as she reached high to hang her coat. It took effort for Ty to shift his eyes away. Like words in a book, her slim, supple body and graceful movements made him think of young panthers. He caught a glimpse of himself in the cabinet mirror and decided he looked like something washed from a flooded graveyard. Markita was studying him now, for the first time in light, but if she thought as he did she gave no sign. She aimed a commanding finger at the toilet lid. "Sit."

Ty's jeans were wet and slimed with garbage. He perched uneasily on the edge of the fluffy cover and kept his eyes on the floor. He suddenly noticed his big sloppy footprints on the spotless bath mat, and felt his face flush. None of Deek's paid girls, innocent or otherwise, had ever made him feel this uncool, as stupid as Deek always called him. But Markita was all flowing coolness as she bent close to examine his arm. Ty stole another glance at her: as he'd thought, she wore nothing beneath the T-shirt. With breasts like those, so firm and high, she didn't have to. Her nipples tilted up slightly, standing tight beneath the soft cloth. From the cold? he wondered. He thought first of Hershey's kisses, but those were common candies. Then he remembered the heart-shaped box he'd bought for his mother on Valentine's Day, each fine chocolate nestled within a cup of gold foil. There had been some like kisses, but larger, rounder, and made of some smooth creamy sweetness that melted in your mouth like cocoa-brown magic.

Ty felt the warmth of Markita's body so near to him now, and a heat of his own stirred restless in his loins. Her scent was honestly female from a long day of work. Ty breathed it deeply, his nostrils flaring to pull it all in. He let his eyes run down her legs: her Levi's old and shaped to her girl-muscled curves, hugged low on her hips, cuddling her behind, and snuggled to the soft swells of her thighs. He imagined the satiny feel of her skin, and the strength hidden beneath it. He dropped his gaze to the floor again, noting that one of her shoelaces had come undone. He resisted the stupid urge to reach down and tie it.

Markita frowned as her fingers lightly probed the slash in Ty's sleeve. Her lips pressed together like a pout when he winced. She hadn't missed his quick, almost shy peek-out of her, and heard him suck air through his nose. Her own eyes flicked to the tight crotch of his jeans and noted the wakening there. She glanced at his feet: the big clunky Nikes made them look huge. There was a saying about that. Was it a black thing? Of course, she'd seen some puppy-footed white boys too... but never one naked, and she doubted she ever would. And, for that matter, girl, she told herself, what's got you thinkin you ever gonna see Ty that way?

"Goddamn jacket linin all stuck to you there," Markita muttered. "Most god-awful mess I ever did see!" She clicked her tongue. "Let's try an get this thing off you, out hurtin too much."

Fussing, Markita helped Ty shed his jacket, turning the bloody sleeve inside out and peeling the clotted satin lining away from the wound. Ty clenched his teeth and tried to flow cool. It hurt like hell. The gash looked hideous when bared to the light. Danny had done a way cool job with his cheap little blade, and Deek had ripped it deeper when he'd twisted. Dried blood, black and sullen, caked around the six-inch slash. Flakes of it fell when he flexed his wrist.

Bright crimson still oozed from within, and clotted ruby caked the edges like sticky spilled wine. Ty tasted copper in his mouth through the numbness of Night Train. He chewed his lip, his eyes shifting once to Markita's and seein worry and pain. She kept hold of his arm. There was a quaver in her voice when she spoke.

"This really 'mergency-room stuff, Ty. Best you believe it oughta get stitched. You be lucky as hell not comin down with infection."

Ty looked sulky and made a halfhearted move to pull away. But Markita held on and he gave up because it hurt too damn much. "Never get me no goddamn affection in my life," he snorted.

He looked up in time to catch a smile flickering on Markita's face. "I'm sure you did," she said. "Maybe you just don't remember. Hush now, an don't you go fightin me. Let's get that shirt off too. Then we see bout cleanin this up."

There was no reason to take off Ty's skimpy tank top to tend to his arm. But Markita had her own reasons, and Ty didn't seem to consider them, letting her slip the shirt over his head and guide his arm out of the strap. He felt suddenly vulnerable, half naked and hurting in this girlish little world. But heat still flowed into his loins, and he watched Markita from beneath lowered lashes. Her gaze felt like warm water washing over him. She seemed to have trouble looking away. He scented something else in the air, half familiar, and shifted uneasily on the edge of the lid. He felt his dick harden and strain his tight jeans.

Markita scented it too, grateful that Ty was staring at the floor so she could scan his body. His long wiry frame was just as she'd imagined that morning: each muscle sculpted clean, and the squared plates of his chest sharply defined as if they'd been added after his skin was already fit. His nipples were tiny black buds, almost invisible, and sexy as hell for some reason. The slender chain around his neck and the delicate, disk-like little medallion suspended between hard-edged muscle shone stark against his gunmetal tone. It seemed to tremble on its fragile chain... to the beat of his heart? Markita wanted to touch the small silver thing, to hold it and know what it was. It would be warm. A sheen of sweat made Ty glow like polished midnight, but the scent of it told of too much beer and bad food. Markita's eyes drifted down the arch of his rib cage and the ripples of belly muscle to the softness that showed at his waist. She thought of a young panther, caged and dying slow, and not caring any longer to test the bars.

She drew back a little, letting his shirt slip from her hand to the floor by his jacket. Her voice came out husky. "Got to wash that clean with peroxide. Shoulda been done hours ago." She moved to the medicine cabinet above the sink and took down a big brown bottle. "Gonna hurt."

She thought she saw a little boy's fear flash for an instant in his eyes. But then his gentle face set hard. There were pictures of African warriors' masks in her mother's encyclopedias.

He shrugged, then looked up at her. "Markita. That a real pretty name. Sound African too."

"Sposed to be." Markita took out a box of cotton, then added, "Shit. Ain't nobody round here care bout no 'African,' cept some old doctor man my mama know who teachin her Swahili. Can't figure why, less he lonely for someone to talk to. Don't know why she troublin neither. Spose she gots a thing for the man." Markita's eyes narrowed a little, and her jaw jutted. "She only thirty. Ain't *dead,* y'know?"

Ty spread his palms. "What I done now?"

Markita's eyes softened again. "Nuthin. Sorry."

"Well," said Ty carefully. "Doctor be 'portant. Seem like to me your mom... do a lot worse?"

Markita shrugged. "He ain't 'lowed to do no real doctor stuff. Not here in the U.S.A. He from real Africa. South. Only went to nigger doctor college there or somethin. Can't help no white folks." She frowned again. "So, *there* be all the goddamn 'African' you need to know."

"Um, can you say somethin in Swahili?"

"Taka—taka."

"What that mean?"

"Polite way of sayin shit, what it mean. Yo. You figure white schools teachin Caucasian heritage or somethin? Shit, *cho-boy*, what in hell good it gonna do you knowin your umpteenth great-grandfather ran round in his birthday suit chuckin spears at lions an tigers an bears? Hey, that stuff gonna help you survive in this *here* jungle? Gimme a break, boy! You want 'African?' Go an get yourself a dose at one of them Muslim meetins or that there black social thing they got way over East. Go an listen to 'em speechin down bout how they gonna MAKE them white suckers pay US back IN spades for all the shit they done to us two hundred years ago! My ass! Yo. They even GOT some white folks there, lookin humble as hell an all shit-eatin sorry over what *their* great-grandfathers prob'ly never even done in the first place, an ready to kiss YOUR black butt cause of it! Bout like to make ME puke, best believe!"

Ty's eyes had widened as the girl spoke her mind. And that was giving it a name for sure! But she *had* a mind to speak, he realized. His loins had cooled a little, but it was somehow worth it. He nodded slowly, trying to make his own mind come up with words that made sense.

"Boy, case you ain't figured what is an what ain't yet, white folks runnin the whole goddamn world! I can't see where they doin such a cool job of it myself, an our turn gonna come one day, best you believe. But what scare the holy shit outa me is that it sure ain't lookin so far like we gonna run the zoo any goddamn better! Special if this here part of Oaktown be any example!" She sighed then, as if she'd been through this before. "Listen up, boy. How in hell you spect me to go worryin over what some dogfuckin skinheads or KKK cocksuckers or just plain greedy-ass white motherfuckers gonna do to me when I scared half to death just takin my two-year-ole son out on the sidewalk at broad-daylight noontime in my very own pure black neighborhood? Shit, boy, make bout as much sense as YOU worryin over paper or plastic while you bleedin to death. Word!" She thought a moment. *"Uhuru,* my ass! Ain't got ME no goddamn *uhuru* round here, an that a fact, jack!" She cocked her head. "Yo! Spose YOU think *uhuru* mean that soulful-eyed lady on *Star Trek?"*

Ty had, so said nothing. He sighed out a tired sound. The warmth had almost totally gone from his loins now. Thinking took energy too. And it was hard to think about love when you hurt. Still, he watched the proud profile of Markita's body show itself under her T-shirt again as she reached back to the top shelf of the medicine cabinet. The tee's purple color was perfect against her dark skin. The shirt climbed as she stretched on tiptoes, revealing the concave of her stomach which had just enough baby chub to shape and beautify her navel. Ty noted how the jeans slid low on her hips, and thought her as perfect as J'row's tiny fingers. Lieutenant Uhura had never been his idea of perfect.

He blinked to find Markita standing over him once more, the peroxide bottle in one hand and a blue box of cotton fluff in the other. He thought he heard another little quiver in her voice, so different now from just moments ago when he'd asked something stupid and got a good talking to. A smile tugged at his lips: a girl who *could* talk! About as rare in his life as a roller-skating rat.

Markita ordered him to scoot back on the toilet lid.

"Can't," he said. "This goddamn gun be pokin my butt." Markita tried to put impatience into her voice, like when some Burger King customer dawdled over the menu while people piled up behind. "Well, pull it out, boy."

Ty stood, and a little smile broke into that kind of goofy grin Markita had always imagined on his face. She flushed, thinking what a stupid thing to say. She stepped back. She could have stepped farther back. Ty laid the .45 on the side of the sink, then met Markita's eyes. Warm, he thought. Funny he'd never noticed before how hard it was for ebony eyes to look cold.

That exciting scent of two bodies and minds who wanted and needed each other flared in his nostrils once more. He felt the pull... like playing with the little magnets his mom kept on the refrigerator door. You brought them close and that mysterious force that drew them together grew stronger and stronger until they met like magic no matter how hard you tried to keep them apart. He felt power pulsing between his legs again, throbbing hot and hard. He forgot the pain in his arm, and his big bony hands clasped Markita's slim waist. He lowered his face to hers and whispered her pretty African name.

Markita felt the same magic force, even as she sensed the new heat in Ty's body and smelled his longing for her in the air. This was a time she seemed to have been dreaming of for years. It was almost funny to realize that she'd gone from a dream to the dreamed-for reality in less than a day. She set the cotton and bottle beside Ty's .45 as his hands found her body and pulled her close to him. She let her eyes run freely over him now. Her fingertips traced the squared plates of his chest and lingered a moment on one tiny nipple. That seemed to send a shiver through him, surprising her; she hadn't known boys were sensitive there. She touched the little silver medallion, curious, but that could wait. Then she lifted her gaze to a face that could only be kind. Ty bent his head and his lips brushed hers, almost shyly at first. He held her as if she was some fragile and pretty thing he was scared he might break. And that made her *feel* pretty and fragile... the way she'd always wanted to feel, except that this world tore fragile things apart. Ty's tongue quested but didn't force. She let him in a little at a time so that she would always remember this moment. It must have hurt as he gathered her tighter against him. She felt new blood soaking her shirt, but his eyes were at peace. His tongue explored, bringing the taste of him into her mouth; a sensation of sweat and blood, and the taint of too many cigarettes and too much drinking... a sad, sick taste, but that of every boy she'd ever known. It was frightening in a way, and yet she wanted him all the more because of it.

For Ty, Markita had a sweetness he'd always imagined a girl should have. Her full lips were soft, made for slow kissing, and the click of her teeth against his sounded some how fierce and clean. Their first kiss lasted long, and then Ty released her to slip the shirt over her head. He stepped back to see her, smiling, maybe stupidly, but he no longer cared. A powerful backbone she had, he thought, to carry those beautiful breasts so proudly like that above a waist so slim. He thought of candies again, velvety smooth and the darkest chocolaty brown this side of midnight. He lowered his head and kissed each nipple and heard her breath quicken. Then her hands were at his jeans, her fingers fast and sure as she undid the buttons. Once more he kissed her nipples, teasing their tips this time with his tongue so they stood tight and hard. His hands slipped down her body to the buttons of her Levi's as she slid his off his own narrow hips. Her hands found and cradled his maleness, making him moan in his throat and shiver again. She, like himself, wore nothing beneath her jeans. He pressed his lips to hers, sliding his hands to her smooth-muscled behind and pulling their bodies together.

They stayed like that, minutes passing, their eyes closed, exploring each other by touch, taste, and smell so they seemed to melt into one. Outside in the street a siren screamed past and gunshots sounded a few blocks away. But nothing could hurt them here. Ty's arm was bleeding again, and Markita was soon streaked with crimson. The room seemed to warm with the heat of their bodies. Ty glistened now, and his breath came hard, but he didn't try to enter her. Markita had seen his ebony shaft before taking it into her hands. This part of him too was all she'd imagined, throbbing with power to the beat of his heart, unsheathed and *bad.* She wanted to feel him surging inside her. . . wanted this drunk and bleeding and dying niggerboy more than anything else in the world.

And yet, close to the edge, he still held himself back.

Markita took hold of him, to guide him into her or thrust her own body onto him. Why didn't he take her? she wondered. Had she been so totally right in her dream... that this gentle, savage boy had yet to learn the physical moves of love? Then she saw his eyes, desperate for her even as he pulled away, and she suddenly knew the reason.

The room seemed to chill. A coldness washed over her. Was this time she'd dreamed of, like so many of her dreams, ended before it had really begun? Nigger dreams; grab what you can while you can, *now,* because the good things went around but never came around again. Selfish thoughts flashed through her mind, hateful and cruel: he would die, just as all the other boys like him would die. He'd be shot or stabbed in the heart, OD'd, or just drink himself to death before another time came around like this. It wasn't fair!

Yet, as she saw the love for her in his eyes, Markita's feeling of loss faded a little. Ty *did* love her! Yes, he did! His denying her now when it would be the cool thing to do, even expected of him to go on, surely proved that.

Didn't it?

Markita's eyes narrowed. Ty had backed away, panting, gleaming, his lean chest heaving. He still stood straight and solid, clutching himself with one hand as if to ease the weight of his throbbing power. Had she been a fool one more time? Markita wondered. Was the end of the dream really: *down on your knees and suck, bitch, lotta bad shit goin round?*

Then she saw him clearly through her doubt, and knew for a fact that he loved her. She cursed herself for not preparing on the chance that a dream would ever come by. Since J'row, she'd been living on dreams a lot. What cool dude wanted anything but a fuck from a bitch with a kid? What cool dude even *liked* kids? Maybe that was a black thing too—God help all niggers if it was. And Markita had been fucked over too much to care about that kind of fucking. Even stupid dreams were better than that, and besides, she could always dream up the happy endings. Of course, there was Leroy, but lame as it sounded, Leroy was *a friend;* he could make her laugh, probably even in bed, calling it something like "jumping her bones." He *would!* She *could* love Leroy, and be happy with him... and he had a future. Maybe the trouble with dreaming was that you began to believe you really had choices.

Frantic thoughts ran around in her head: the market would be closed, the nearest liquor store was blocks away. Ask a neighbor? At this hour? *Don't be a fool!* And in spite of herself, Markita could see the funny part of it... so motherfuckin STUPID!

Markita saw Ty's eyes widen with a surprised look. Good Jesus Christ, had she said that out loud? But he suddenly looked shamefaced, his cheeks way too dark to show much of a blush, though Markita could see it. Then came that wonderful goofy grin once more—did he ever do that when he wasn't drunk?—and he dug in his jeans for his wallet. "I, um, I forgot I got one," he murmured.

Savage and gentle, loving and dangerous, jeans off his butt and his shaft thrust out fierce like a weapon, he made such a picture that Markita broke up. She moved to him quickly before he could misunderstand, hugging him tight while tears of laughter ran down her cheeks. "Ty, you just so way past cool, you FLOWIN cool!"

He grinned again and blushed again, fumbling out the little foil packet with big bony fingers. "It, um... actually it Theodore."

"Theodore! But how you get Ty outa that?"

"Well, um, like I sayin, I the oldest. An you know how little kids' shoelaces forever comin undone? Seem like most my life I followed round gettin called to like that."

Markita busted into laughter once more and kissed him long. "I like the sound of it, now that I know." She looked down at both their blood-smeared bodies. "Christ, what a mess we make of everything!" She turned from him and opened the bathtub faucets, full-on. Ty grinned again. Markita popped the stopper into place as Ty sat back on the fluffy lid cover to take off his shoes and jeans. Markita sat on the mat, beside the splashing water, to take off her own.

The ancient tub was huge and deep, its bright whiteness a fierce contrast to the glistening ebony bodies of Ty and Markita as they faced one another, entwined within. Ty was big, but that was a fact he seemed to know in the same way he'd be careful of his feet. He entered her slowly, gently, and that made it all the more pleasurable for her as she parted to him. She locked her strong legs around his lean hips and pulled herself even tighter onto him. His power was the surging, loving savagery inside her that she'd dreamed it would be, so stone hard and straight it was almost like the intense, tearing pleasure-pain of the first time. She bit her lip to keep from crying out. Steam rose around them like wispy little ghosts. The warm water was soon pink-tinted with Ty's blood, ebbing and flowing to the rhythm and pulse of their movements. Markita nuzzled Ty's face, tasting again the desperate sadness of his life and maybe the foreshadow of his death. But he shared all his love with her freely, every sensation and pleasure... patient and caring and making his search her own. She could feel when he held back for her, waiting until she climbed with him. And when they found that place at last, it was together, and he held her there so the dream-moment lasted a long, long time.

So *this* was love, Ty thought at that instant... a thing of two parts. There was this one intense and beautiful moment, and then there was knowing you could never be happy yourself when those you loved were not. Even a stupid nigger could figure that out.

A time later, Ty and Markita stood naked, hand in hand, gazing down at the small sleeping child. They nibbled grape Popsicles. No words were needed. Markita bent to tuck the blanket up around J'row's chin and then kissed his forehead. Ty reached down a long gunmetal finger to touch a tiny perfect one. The little hand curled over it, tightly. Ty leaned close and kissed the child where Markita had.

A clock on the TV showed almost 3 a.m. Markita's hand pressed Ty's, and she looked over toward her bed. "You could stay," she whispered.

But Ty was thinking of Danny; how the boy would look peacefully sleeping beside his smaller brother on the big old mattress with room enough for three. Ty thought how Danny had looked a few hours ago, naked and climbing sulkily into bed. Ty wanted to be home, to ease himself under the blankets between the two younger boys and feel their warmth against him as he had for so many years. He and Danny could talk about stuff before school, any sort of shit, just like they used to do. They'd scheme out the day ahead, the years ahead. Ty would tell him about the truck. Maybe it would sound lame to Danny at first—chump change and uncool—but they'd split a quart of Colt .45 after the shopping was done, sitting together someplace quiet in the sun with their shirts off, and somehow Ty would make him see it was right.

"No," said Ty. "But, um, thanks." He smiled. "Maybe tomorrow. I gotta get them groceries home so's the kids got somethin sides mush for breakfast. But you keep the other Popsicles for J'row." He glanced at his arm, bandaged now with gauze and hospital tape. "An thanks, Markita. For everthin."

Their arms went around each other, and they kissed again. Then Markita sat on the edge of the coffee table and watched while Ty began putting on his clothes.

"I could get off early," she said. "That is, if you figure you an Danny might want some help with them little-girl things."

Ty hesitated, shirtless on the floor, his hands on his shoelaces. This too was love, he realized, making choices and praying to a God who never seemed to listen that they were the right ones. Danny was just twelve, and though he already knew a lot about life, the idea of sharing his brother with this girl might be more than his heart could handle, especially since Ty had been out of his life for so long. *Long?* Ty wondered. Yeah. At twelve a few months seemed years. It might be a hard fight to win Danny back. Ty felt a chill in Markita's warm apartment, wondering if he'd have to give up his love for this girl for the love of his brother.

Markita saw Ty's hesitation, and knew the reason. Ty had told her more about Danny while she was bandaging his arm. He'd also told her of the truck he hoped to buy, and how he'd have to suffer with Deek at least another month to do it. Markita had been around enough younger kids to know how fierce and jealous Danny would feel toward his brother's attention and time. A twelve-year-old in this place might even kill to keep love. But Markita didn't think about that. What frightened her was the thought of losing Ty to save a young boy she didn't even know... a boy who might already be way past saving.

Markita knelt down in front of Ty, putting on a smile and leaning close. "I understand. It just boy stuff you two gotta do together."

"Yeah. That what it is. But, yo. We come by the Burger King soon's Danny get out of school, fore we go uptown." Ty smiled. "Danny tell me tonight, sorta, that he figure you cool. Spose it mostly cause of that free coffee you give him. But he smart. Smarter'n me, best believe. I think he be gettin to like you soon."

Ty stood, and the little medallion glinted in the streetlight glow from the window. Markita touched it, warm from his body as she'd known it would be. She bent close to study it in the dimness, but the detail looked half worn away.

Ty smiled again. "Oh, that just a silly ole thing my mom give me way back a long time ago. Don't signify nuthin cept her givin it me, course. Don't even know why I still wearin it." He shrugged. "Hell, who know, maybe it lucky. Sposed to be St. Christopher."

Markita let go of the little silver disk. Its warmth seemed to linger a moment on her palm. "I seen em in cars sometimes. St. Christopher sposed to be lucky for travelers, I guess."

Ty's smile widened to a grin. He reached for his jacket and shirt. "That case, can't see it doin me no good. I sure as hell goin nowhere."

Markita helped Ty put his shirt on over his stiff bandaged arm, and then held his jacket while he slipped into it. "I read bout him one time, sorta by accident when I was lookin through my mom's cyclopedias over there. I think he sposed to be lucky for somebody sides travelers too. He carryin somethin on his shoulder."

Ty nodded as Markita zipped his jacket and tucked its tail

carefully over the .45. "Yeah. Cept you can't see what it is cause it too wore out."

"You Catholic, Ty?"

"Nuh-uh. I a nuthin. Mom try to raise us up some kinda churchy stuff, but it never rub off on me." Ty's smile faded. "Nor Danny neither, look like. Guess it come down tween money an God round here, an God lose. Ain't no wonder He don't give a shit." Ty chewed his lip a moment. "How bout you, Markita?"

She shrugged. "Guess you could say the same. My mom a regular churchgoer, but I don't bother much more bout what God gonna or not gonna do than them bad whites an skinheads we was talkin before."

Ty nodded again. "Mmm. Spect that right." He snagged his board and took the plastic bag of groceries from the counter. Markita opened the hallway door. Ty automatically checked the hail before stepping out, then turned and gave Markita a last long kiss.

She stood watching until his shadow faded down the stairwell, then whispered, "Please don't let him die."

"Yo, Lyon!"

Lyon spun around. He was still wearing Gordon's old T-shirt that looked like a tent on his slender body and totally concealed the Iver-Johnson in the back of his jeans. One pawlike hand darted for the gun while the other brought his skateboard up to shield off a knife. Beside him, Curtis' books thudded on the floor as the smaller boy also whipped his board into defense position. Around them, the laughter and shouting and rowdy roar of kids in the school hallway died down. The tinny slam of locker doors and the rattle of cheap combo locks cut off. Kids nearby slipped quickly out of the line of fire.

Then Lyon saw it was Furball with his binder and board under one arm. The boy had frozen, looking surprised at the reaction he'd caused, his free hand hovering automatically near his knife pocket. Not far behind Furball, Lyon noted the twins at their shared locker. Their eyes were still red-rimmed and puffy from last night's drinking, but they'd come instantly alert and were measuring the distance to Furball in case Lyon needed backup.

Lyon and Furball broke into grins. Both wore black shades to cover the aftermath of a quart of JD and talking together all night until they'd watched the sun rise from a mud flat down by the ship channel. Tenseness faded from the air. There were some snorts and muttering among the other kids, a few who'd been hoping to see some sort of fight, but most relieved they wouldn't be dodging bullets or blades. The casual savagery of another school day's end echoed through the hall once more, mixed with the smells of kid sweat, hair sheen, girls' powder and perfume, and hundreds of pairs of well-worn sport shoes. Furball came up to Lyon, and Lyon lowered his board and tucked his tee back over the gun. Curtis and the twins relaxed, but still watched both boys with suspicion.

Furball's grin vanished as he faced Lyon. He shed his shades, narrowing his eyes with a message and shifting them briefly to Curtis, who had bent to pick up his books. "Um, can we talk, man? I mean, some more?"

Lyon took his own glasses off and glanced at Curtis. Curtis nodded and moved away, but brushed the dreads from his eyes and kept close watch on Furball. Lyon flashed his V smile at the twins, who'd been slowly advancing down the hall. They stopped, exchanged tawny-eyed looks of speculation, then shrugged in stereo and returned to their locker, where they usually did a good business selling Kools on credit. Curtis checked Lyon a final time, then started walking down the hall to the front doors.

Lyon looked back at Furball and raised an eyebrow.

"Bout last night,"said Furball. "What it is, I done me some thinkin all day. Bout bein 'bad,' what I sayin... an how you tellin me dudes like Deek go down from little fuck ups sometimes. I been thinkin bout my brother too, man. Like, how he might could get done right longside that dog-sucker Deek." Furball searched Lyon's face. "What I sayin here, Ty a *good* dude, Lyon. Word. Know what? Yo, he come home this mornin with all kinda cool food an shit. Flintstones vitamins too! Make everbody do one. Even Mom. Tell us we gotta, ever day from here on, for cause to stay strong. You hearin this, Lyon?"

Lyon nodded and smiled, but looked past Furball to where Gordon was coming out of the boys' room struggling to button his jeans at least halfway. As usual, the T-shirt he wore didn't near cover his belly but he had a shiny black nylon jacket, its tail long enough to hide the .22.

Lyon's eyes came back to Furball, and his smile warmed. "It cool to be hearin you say them things, man." His forehead creased a little. "But I don't gots much time to be talkin right now. There somethin by."

Furball looked uncertain and scanned the fast-emptying hail. The twins had stopped Gordon; all three boys murmured together and flicked occasional glances at Lyon. Curtis stood by the open front doors as the last of the other kids poured through, also keeping watch on Lyon. Furball looked down at his Nikes and kicked a toe on the faded tile floor. "Yeah. Word up, you an the Crew gonna meet."

Lyon's eyes cooled slightly. "Mmm. Word say, huh? Well, you tell me yourself lotsa word go round don't signify dogshit."

Furbali shrugged, still staring at his shoes. "Yeah, I know, but..." He seemed to choose his words carefully. "Listen, man. I gonna meet my brother soon. At Burger King. For cause of that shoppin thing I was tellin you last night."

Lyon could see impatience on Gordon's face. "Yo. Better cut to the chase," he told Furball gently. "What it is, you be tellin me you thinkin on changin your mind bout givin your brother word we find Deek's crib."

Furball's mouth opened. "Shit! You really *can* read minds like magic, Lyon!"

Slyness flickered at the edges of Lyon's uptilted eyes. He smiled his V and touched a delicate finger to Furball's chest. "What it is, readin hearts be easier. They most never lie."

Furball shifted uncertainly under Lyon's soft touch. His face hardened. "What I sayin is, I ain't gonna let nuthin happen to my brother, man. What it takes!"

"Mmm." Lyon's fingertip gently traced muscle as if measuring something. "That ain't hard to hear at all, man." He lowered his hand, palm open. "But you know inside yourself Deek's shit gotta be chilled. Maybe below zero. What it take be what it is."

Furball squeezed his eyes tight shut and sucked a breath. "Tap your Nikes together three time," said Lyon. "Who know, might even work."

Furball's eyes snapped open. "Huh? Oh." Then his gaze leveled cold. "Oh, shut up an listen to me, sucker!" He flicked a glance toward Gordon and the twins, then dropped his voice to almost a whisper. "Yo! Last night, fore you show, I hear some shit Deek tellin my brother. It bout you an the Crew. I not unnerstand a'zactly meanin all, but he talkin drive-bys an—"

Gordon's voice cut him off. "Yo, Lyon! C'mon, man. It gettin way past get-busy time."

Furball ignored the fat boy, who had come quietly close, the twins following. Furball gripped Lyon's arm. "Word, man! This crucial!"

"Gordon..." Lyon began.

But Gordon shook his head. "No! Gots no TIME now! What up too goddamn 'portant for dickin round with!" He eyed Furball. "Who this dude anyways?"

"A friend," said Lyon. "Listen up..."

Gordon clenched big fists. "NO! Goddamnit, Lyon, *I* talkin now. An what I sayin is we gots no time for dudes what don't count. Not today. Maybe I listen to your magic shit too much anyways. What it gettin us? I say one time more, man, c'mon."

Lyon sighed, but nodded, then touched Furball's shoulder. "Seem Gordon be right, man. But you was too, bout the word. Gangs meetin an talkin be major 'portant shit special bout THIS sorta shit. But you know where I live now. You come over tonight. We talk more. Word." He turned to Gordon. "Yo. Give him a pass. Total an forever."

"*What?* Goddamnit, Lyon, you don't tell ME bout rules!"

Lyon's voice changed, turned strange and menacing. "Just do it!"

Gordon blinked, staring at the slender boy as if just seeing him for the first time, but the twins only watched in curiosity. Gordon's eyes shied away. His big body sagged loose. He nodded to Furball. "Okay, dude. Whoever the fuck you are, Lyon trust ya. You pass. Anytime."

"Yo! How come?" demanded Ric.

"Yeah!" piped Rac. "What this shit?"

"Shut up!" roared Gordon. He grabbed Furball's shoulders and spun the thin boy around to face the twins. Surprised, Furball's hand darted for his knife, but Lyon touched his arm and he didn't pull.

"You see him?" demanded Gordon. "You hear me?"

The twins nodded sulkily.

"Word." Gordon snorted and let go of Furball, then moved for the hallway doors. "Let's bail!"

Lyon followed the other boys, but looked back once.

Furball still stood by the lockers. He'd slipped his shades on once more, way too big and half hiding his face, but looked fierce and determined just the same.

"Yo! Lyon-o! What by?" asked Rac, close behind the slender boy as they ran down the steps and out the school gates.

"Yeah," puffed Ric. "We gots Furball in Crabzilla's class. He pretty cool. Gots a name with his blade. Yo, he wantin to be a Friend?"

Lyon slammed down his board, decking and kicking away after Gordon, who was already ripping up the sidewalk. "He be already a friend," said Lyon. "A friend alone."

"Must be more magic shit, he meanin," muttered Ric to his brother as they decked and rolled after Lyon.

"Yeah," agreed Rac. "Or what. Don't unnerstand none of it!"

Curtis caught up and spat between their boards. "Yo! COURSE it a magic thing, suckers! Magic by the heart. Ain't no wonder in hell YOU two can't unnerstand. Shit! Prob'ly gots only one pussy little heart tween ya both. So THERE!" He kicked hard, shooting between the twins, dreads flying, to roll beside Lyon.

Ric and Rac made a few kissy noises but shrugged to each other.

"Yo, Lyon," Curtis panted as they rounded a corner. "I seen you *change* back there in the hall! Sometimes, when I stayin with you an it's late an you figure I sleepin, I swear I see you do it then, in the dark. But *this* was daytime!"

Lyon grinned, cutting around a sewer cover. "What kinda crazy talkin that be, homey? You seen too many movies. An you been readin my spooky books too."

"Don't mean jack, Lyon! Gordon seen you, an he like to shit! An Gordy ain't scared of nuthin! So there."

"Prob'ly cause Gordon gots more 'portant shit to be scared over than what he *think* he see. An same by you. Or oughta be."

Curtis frowned. "Well... you was out last night. ALL night. Yes, you was! I woke up alone. There was a moon just comin clear out the fog. I went to the hall window an looked. You went somewheres to do magic shit, huh, Lyon? Know what? I bet you gonna magic that Deek motherfucker to death."

Lyon grinned again, his big teeth gleaming. "Yo, home-boy. Why for you be askin me all this silly-ass shit?"

"Cause. Hey, I know you a lot better'n you think I do, man. Cept, times I don't unnerstand you at all. I known you all my goddamn life, but sometimes it seem like you somethin else."

Lyon smiled. "*Somebody* else, man."

"Nuh-uh! SomeTHING else! Shit, I know what I wanna say!"

Lyon and Curtis separated to pass a cluster of people in front of a funeral parlor. All the boys studied the coffin with interest as the bearers carried it down the steps. It wasn't a full-sized one. Curtis cut back beside Lyon again, and the slender boy said, "Well, homey, that maybe make two of us what don't always unnerstand." Lyon's jaw set and he skated on in silence. Gordon was keeping up a killer pace for all his extra weight, and the old car wash was only a few blocks away now. Curtis was about to drop to his usual place in the rear of the file when Lyon spoke again.

"Times I get thinkin my life ain't my own, man. Like really I die that first night in the dumpster. But then somethin come along... "

Curtis kicked close once more, his eyes widening. "No! SomeBODY, man. Don't say someTHING!"

Lyon stared ahead at Gordon's back. "What it is, man. Somethin. There's times in my dreams when I can almost see him. There musta been a moon that night. Funny, though, I can't never 'member nuthin bout him cept he look so goddamn sad."

"Nuh-uh!" cried Curtis. "No way in hell you 'member shit like that, man! You was a goddamn little baby!"

Lyon didn't seem to hear. "He had this big sack, all shiny black like Gordon's jacket there. Only, it was sorta all rainbowy too... like a puddle on the street."

"No. No! NO! You motherfucker! It was just some ole winehead trollin for cans, what it was! Now shut the fuck up, sucker! I don't wanna hear no more of this shit!"

Lyon smiled. "Yo. You figure everthin out on them streets at night be just wineheads or junkies, man? Or *people?*"

"Not funny, Lyon! Look, I ain't even listenin to you!" Curtis clapped his hands over his ears, almost losing his balance for a second.

"They be *collectors,*" said Lyon.

"What?" Curtis dropped his hands. "Well, *course!* What I just say."

"But not *them* kind. See, these here collectors I talkin bout been round a long, long time. Like, before there was even a Oaktown. Or America."

"Um... Did they come from Africa? All chained up in ships?"

"Ain't nobody chain up *these* dudes, man. For sure, once, in ever long while, people might catch one, but then they try an kill it. The collectors be all over the world, man. But mostly where kids die a lot. See, they go round at night, collectin up all the spirits of dead kids."

Curtis stubbornly shook his head. "Nuh-uh! No way! Dead kids go to heaven! Like the one in that box back there."

"Shit, I thought they be goin to Jamaica, mon."

"Not funny, asshole!"

"Well, anyways, this collector had himself a whole sackful of kid spirits, an he stuck em all in me."

"No, he didn't! Why would he do that for? Goddamnit, there ain't no motherfuckin thing as collectors! Same's Draculas an werewoofs!" Curtis considered a second. "Well, I think they do got some werewoofs in Pennsylvania... but that clear cross the goddamn ocean! Stop tryin to freak me with your spooky talk, Lyon. Not even in daytime."

Lyon grinned once more. "Dint your mom never tell you that nuthin be there at night what ain't in the day?"

"She weren't talkin no collectors an werewoofs!"

Lyon shrugged and kicked harder to keep pace with Gordon. "Then don't be askin me questions if you can't handle the answers, man. Maybe all dogs go to heaven, but kids sposed to get REAL lives first. That why there be collectors."

"Oh, yeah, right, man! An them collectors is what ole people call werewoofs! Uh-huh, uh-huh, I'm sure!"

Lyon shrugged again. "So, you tell me who be better for the job? They black an scary an nobody fuck with em much."

"So, what happen to all the kids get collected?"

"Don't know. Maybe they get new hearts an another chance to be kids somewheres. Hell, GOT to be a place where kids wanted." Then Lyon smiled and reached out to touch Curtis' arm. "Yo. We almost there, homey. Story time over. Best be savin back your breath case we end up gotten to fight. Heart magic be good strong stuff, but there just ain't enough of it goin round yet."

"Um, you figure there ever gonna be, Lyon?"

"Believe, homey. But it gotta START with kids. Most people lose the good part of their hearts when they get older."

The twins had been skating close behind, both shirtless now, and gleaming. Ric murmured to his brother, "Yo. Figure Lyon a good dude, or just a crazy niggerboy?"

"Don't know," said Rac. "Shit, you prob'ly be crazy too, spendin your first-borned night in a motherfuckin dumpster, man."

"Shit. Spendin MY first-borned night with YOU prob'ly done me!"

Rac only held a palm to his chest for a moment, then to his

brother's. "Well, say this, we still gots ours."

Ric did the same. "Yeah. Hey, figure we oughta make Curtis get his butt back behind us where he belong?"

"Mmm. Maybe we should let him cruise with Lyon from now on. They sorta just like you an me, even if they ain't. You can watch our ass."

"No, you. I the first, 'member?"

"Shit! How I forget, you 'mindin me ever goddamn day of my life! Flip ya for it?"

Ric flashed a finger. "Flip THIS, niggerboy!" He glanced over his shoulder. "Anyways, who in hell be followin us, doofus?"

"Yeah? Well, if a werewoof sneak up an do ya, an you get your ass collected, don't come cryin to me, sucker!"

Deek was right, God damn his soul to hell! Ty shoved the *Tribune* away and smashed out his Kool in a little foil ashtray already brimming with butts. Elbows on the table-top, he dropped his face to his hands and squeezed his eyes tight shut until points of light danced in the darkness. There was a single short paragraph on the paper's back page: two youths found dead in an East Oakland motel room of an apparent drug overdose. Details were being withheld pending further investigation. Ty wondered how much "investigation" would really be done. They were young, they were black, and they were dead: end of story.

A story he'd helped write.

His slashed arm was stiff and hurt to move but he deliberately used it so it hurt all the more, digging in his jacket pocket for cigarettes. He fired one, sucking smoke deep, then hissing it out in sadness and disgust; sadness for the boys—he *would* have stopped Deek if he'd known—and disgust for himself and the world he had to live in. The paper's front pages were filled with details of some hump-back whales that had beached themselves in the Bay. A massive rescue operation was underway to save them. Ty took a swallow of cold coffee, not tasting that it was, then looked at his watch. Danny was late; really late. He should have been out of school over an hour ago. Maybe he'd gotten detention? His grades were good but he didn't take shit from other kids or his teachers, so it would probably be for fighting one or speaking his mind to the other. The boy was proud. Was there such a thing as being too goddamn proud... or just proud about the wrong sort of things? Was this what black pride had—Ty searched for the word, Markita had used it once when they'd been talking last night: *evolved.* Was this what black pride had evolved into? There was another word; Ty couldn't bring it to mind, *de-*something.

He glanced over at the girl; she was busy behind bulletproof glass but still managed to give him a smile whenever she caught his eye. Ty found himself wishing he knew more about life, stuff the street couldn't teach. Did black kids hold life so cheap because they couldn't see any future in it? Was the whole fucking world evil, or just this city? Ty remembered a Bible story his mom had told him a long time ago: about how God had destroyed an evil city. Ty had never liked the story: hadn't there been any children in that place? Some God! Ty fingered his medallion and watched Markita boxing burgers. He recalled her joke about the Muslim center: they said God was black, or Jesus was; something like that. Well, so fucking what! Black, white, or every goddamn color of a motherfucking rainbow, *He* didn't seem to give a shit about kids either! So, what in hell was there left for them to believe in? Whatever color Christ had been, he'd got his fool self nailed to a cross for nothing!

Ty studied Leroy, who was busy at the broiler. His shirt sleeves were shoved high up his wiry arms and he'd squashed and shaped his stupid little hat so it looked like something Bobby Brown might wear. In a world of cool Leroy was a loser: working days in a Burger King, finishing high school at night, and taking a computer course on top of it all. Ty knew a lot of bad dudes who would say that Leroy had sold out, gone Oreo... *incognegro.* But who in hell was the joke really on? Ty wondered again what Danny would think of busting his butt hauling scrap iron when dudes years younger than him could fill up a goddamn truck with money. Maybe *that* was the color of God: black on one side and green on the other! How much was love worth in a place where money bought life and death?

Ty glanced at his watch again, flicking away more dried blood. Where in hell *was* the boy? Ty decided he'd wait another fifteen minutes, then skate over to the school. Time was running out. Deek would want him back on the job tonight, and he *had* to go. Ty crushed his half-smoked Kool and dropped his face back into his hands.

There was a soft touch on his shoulder. Ty looked up to find Markita beside him with a fresh cup of coffee. He noticed that Leroy was now at the counter, taking orders. The customers all seemed to be kids just out of school, most toting binders or wearing backpacks stuffed with books and homework. Ty met Leroy's eyes for a second, and the dude nodded. It was funny; Ty had expected him to be pissed; it was plain he had a thing for Markita. But there was only a sad sort of understanding in Leroy's eyes, like he'd been to hell and burned his wings but was satisfied to have come back alive. There was something cool in that. In a way, Leroy was badder than Deek would ever be. He'd chosen a life that didn't hurt anybody. That took real balls. You could dress up a lion in a clown suit and make it jump through hoops, but it would still be a lion. Ty shrugged as if it didn't bother him, but added, "Hurt some. Inside-like."

"Always gotta hurt some to get better."

Then the room seemed to darken as if the gunmetal uniforms of the two cops just entering had sucked up the light. Ty tensed, and felt Markita's grip tighten on his shoulder as the big men neared. It was the pair who helped hold up the pyramid. Ty scented leather and gun oil and aftershave. A coldness flowed through him, but he felt no fear. If the cops had come for him because of the two boys, then somebody else was going to die. There was no way Ty would let himself be locked in just another kind of cage.

"Move away slow," he murmured to Markita. "Get clear of me. Back inside the kitchen."

Markita hesitated.

"Do it, girl!" Ty hissed.

She obeyed, coolly, walking casual toward the steel door. Ty shifted on the slick plastic seat so he could get at his .45. The cops wore bulletproof vests but were carrying their helmets like the football players they'd probably been in high school. Ty wished he'd had more practice with his gun. And now his arm was stiff and clumsy... and the motherfucking room was full of kids!

When he'd been about Danny's age, Ty had seen a seventeen-year-old cornered in a parking lot and surrounded by twenty cops. The boy had only a cheap little revolver. Yet he'd brought the gun up and aimed, knowing full well what would happen. He'd smiled... Ty was sure of it! The paper said he'd been hit by seventeen bullets and a shotgun blast. And his own gun had been empty all the time! Ty suddenly knew why the boy had died smiling: he'd finally escaped from the cage.

Ty's hand found the .45. But there was no sign of interest or even recognition as the cops' eyes passed through him. All Ty could sense was the mutual hate that somehow bound him and the two men together. The white one yawned, saying to the other, "Christ, I hate these fucking rotations!"

Rotate on *this,* sucker! Ty thought, flipping the finger under the table.

"Hey, girl," called the black one to Markita as she passed by. "What's the chance of getting breakfast?"

Markita snorted. "Bout the same's a Popsicle in hell. An I damn sure ain't your girl!"

The cop flushed slightly, but strode to the order window in silence. A few kids snickered and flashed signs to Markita. The white cop squeezed his creaking bulk into a booth with his back to Ty.

Ty wanted to leave then, to get out fast and onto his skateboard and be a kid again for just a few minutes. But he stayed. To leave now wouldn't be cool.

Wesley, the Crew leader, was one of those beautiful boys who were usually displayed in commercials or movies as the one cool black who hung with a bunch of uptown whiteys. Girls of any color would want to cuddle him, and dudes of any race would at least envy his build. He wasn't muscled to the point of awkwardness; just perfectly proportioned like some sort of coffee-colored model of God's ideal thirteen-year-old boy. No one blamed him much that he knew it; dressing in short cutoffs even when it rained, and wearing only skintight tank tops or mesh tees when he wore a shirt at all. Word said that a perv-shop owner had once paid him a bill to pose in black leather for a magazine, holding a whip over some old white sucker in a KKK suit.

His hair was a natural bush—why fuck with perfection?—and the massive gold-plated chain with its heavy medallion slapping his solid, square-stabbed chest looked like something he'd won in a war. He never just stood but he posed, but he was so way past cool to look at that you could forgive him for it. If he'd been a sculpture in a park, nobody would have spray-painted him.

He was posing now atop the rusty tin roof of the pressure-pump shed behind the peeling, sheet-metal bays of the closed-up car wash. He watched, coolly, as the Friends rolled across the weedy, trash-strewn asphalt. His feet in big megabuck Cons were spread wide apart, and his hands rested half-curled on his narrow hips. The fingers of one held a smoldering Marlboro, the other the stick of a strawberry Popsicle.

Three other boys sat on the roof: two, a tall, thin ebony dude and a chocolate-brown boy of average build, on one side of Wesley, and skinny little Tunk on the other. All were shirtless in the hot afternoon sun, and dangled their faded-jeaned legs over the edge, swinging Nikes and Reeboks in the air. All had cigarettes and half-eaten Popsicles. Each had his skateboard beside him: Wesley's lay between his feet. Tunk was the only one smiling, as if you couldn't be bad and suck on a Popsicle at the same time. A fourth boy, round-faced and roly-poly with a chest like a pair of water balloons, sat on a battered vacuum unit at the back of the car-wash lot, munching his Popsicle and eyeing the Friends. His shirt lay beside him, wadded up and covering his other hand. Gordon gave him a long glance as he tailed about thirty feet from the wash-bay structure. "Bet Game-Boy there gots the gun," he murmured to Lyon. "He look like some kinda chocolate marshmallow, but he badder'n hell when he don't gotta move much. Ain't nobody never smoke his ass on Nintendo."

"Mmm," said Lyon. "Sound like my kinda dude. I watch him." He gazed around. Behind the vacuum box, a six-foot chain-link fence ran along the back of the lot. It was the saggy kind without a pipe rail on top, and hard to climb.

Beyond was a narrow strip of dry weeds and then a concrete-lined ditch about four feet deep and twenty wide. Its bottom was covered with what looked like black Jell-O pudding that stank like everything slimy and rotten. The blank back sides of buildings lined the ditch's opposite shore. There were no hiding places.

"Wesley gots him *five* dudes," said Lyon. "Seem he be down one today."

"Um," whispered Curtis. "Maybe one got shot or somethin yesterday?"

"Tunk woulda told us a major thing like that," said Gordon.

"Well, then maybe he home sick? Happen to bad dudes too, y'know?"

Lyon smiled a little, but shook his head. "Yo. Wesley gots him a brain in that way cool bod. He be holdin back a reserve, best believe." Lyon scanned the lot again: all four of the wash bays were empty, except for a junked Ford Pinto in one. The metal door to the pump shed was chained and padlocked shut. "Well, there be Tunker, Brett, an Ajay up on the roof side Wesley, an Game-Boy on the vac. Even money say Turbo be coverin us from somewheres."

Ric and Rac moved close. "Thought Gordon say Game-Boy gots the gun?" whispered Rac.

"Yeah," said Ric. "Yo. Anybody see there somethin under his shirt there."

Lyon frowned. "An it might just be nuthin but his fist, sucker."

Gordon wiped sweat from his face and scowled. His T-shirt was soaked from the warp-seven ride and stuck to him like a coat of paint under his jacket. "Yeah. An if the Crew already done score that Uzi from Deek, an Turbo gots it, we all dogmeat right now! Spread the fuck out! You goddamn know better'n to be bunchin all up like one easy target!"

The boys moved apart. Gordon looked at Lyon again. "Well, Game-Boy major hot shootin Space 'Vaders, but I don't know how he handle a real gun. Ask me, he ain't the one gots it. Keep a good watch for Turbo. I seen *him* shoot. You figure Tunk tell Wes bout our chrome gun?"

Lyon glanced up to the small skinny boy on the roof. "Mmm. Don't know. But best we be keepin it iced long's we can. Don't be showin yours neither, less you gotta."

"Yo! Gordy!" Wesley called. "You look hotter'n hell with that there jacket on, man. G'wan, take it off, you want. Shit, I know you packin the fire." He grinned. "An you late, man. We save by some Popsicles for ya, but they start in meltin, so's we hadda eat 'em. Oh well." He bit off the last chunk and flipped the stick away.

Gordon glanced at Game-Boy again, then shifted slightly so the .22 in the back of his jeans wouldn't be seen as he peeled off his jacket. Facing Wesley, he stripped his shirt off too and wiped under his arms with it. "So, where Turbo?"

Wesley shrugged. "His mom take him to the dentist after school."

"Uh-huh." Gordon yanked up his jeans, squinting because Wesley had the sun at his back. "This meet sposed to be by rules, Wes. Everbody need to be here."

Wesley took a last hit off his cigarette and flicked it away. He spread his hands. "Yo. Dude gots a Popsicle habit. Don't brush his goddamn teeth or somethin. Can I help that?"

"Mmm." Gordon planted his feet wide apart and crossed his arms over his chest. "Say we let that slide, man. I still gots a prob with you dudes bein up on that roof while we on the ground. Wanna be cool, best you come down with us." He pointed to the wash bays. "An we all be cooler kicked back in the shade, man." He jerked a thumb sideways. "Shit. Check out poor Game-Boy, there. He lookin like to melt. Yo, don't you give a shit over your dudes, Wes?"

Wesley frowned. "My ass! Why you figure I ain't got em all packed together so's some motherfuckin ole black van come by an spray em dead?!"

Gordon pointed. "Street gate chained up, man. An I *know* you smart enough to check out it locked." He scowled. "Or maybe it ain't really locked, huh? Maybe you gots Turbo standin by ready to drop it an let that cocksuckin van in on US?"

Wesley considered a minute, then his face softened a little. "Chain locked, Gordon. Word, man. You wanna, send one of your dudes to check it out." He waited, and when Gordon did nothing, looked down at Tunk. "Yo, Gordy, my 'bassador tell me y'all get yourselfs sprayed too. Least that what he say YOU say. My prob is, how I for sure know that?"

Gordon nodded to Curtis, who pulled off his shirt and turned around to show the bandage on his back. "You come down," said Gordon, "You see we both gots the same prob, man."

Wesley exchanged quiet words with Tunk before facing Gordon again. "Yo! Let's see your gun, Gordy."

Gordon recrossed his arms, and snorted. "You first! An don't call me Gordy, man! I hate that!"

"Goddamnit, Gordon, stop fuckin around! Yo! I let you copy my goddamn English homework last week!"

"BFD! An I told Coach you was in the fuckin nurse's office when you went an cut PE!"

Up on the roof, Brett and Ajay snickered. Wesley shot them a look, then stabbed a finger toward the back of the lot. "Game-Boy gots it! Never figure you was that blind, Gor-DEN!"

Gordon turned. The fat kid on the vacuum box slipped a little black snub-nosed revolver from under his shirt and held it pointed to the sky.

"So there!" sniffed Wesley. "Now you!"

Gordon's eyes went to Lyon, who nodded. Slowly, Gordon pulled the pistol from his jeans and held it muzzle-down.

Wesley nodded. "That thing still jam up, man?"

"Naw. We got it fixed a way long time ago."

"Uh-huh. Well, why not ya give it to one of them clones an he slide on over an shoot shit with the Gamer. Then we come down. Okay?"

Gordon exchanged glances with Lyon, who nodded again, then held the gun out to one of the twins. "Yo, Ric."

"I'm Rac."

"Whatever. Just do it."

Rac took the gun and strutted over to Game-Boy, who had put his revolver back under the shirt again. Ric's eyes carefully tracked his brother. Wesley snagged his board and leaped from the roof with the other boys close behind. All landed lightly, then spread wide and advanced warily to within ten feet of the Friends. Curtis stood patiently as Wesley came forward to study his back. The

Crew leader nibbled his lip for a moment, then faced Gordon. "Mmm. Gotta say, man, all I see's some Big Bird Band-Aids an gauze stuff. Hell, that red shit be ketchup, all I know."

"Yeah?" said Ric. "So put some on your wienie, dude."

"Shut up, asshole!" hissed Gordon.

Curtis clenched his teeth. "Take it off, man."

Gordon looked at the small boy, then smiled. "Yo, Wes, go for it. Don't faint or nuthin."

For a few seconds Wesley looked uncertain. Then he gingerly took hold of the top of the bandage.

"Um," said Tunk, moving close. "Do it fast, man. So's it don't hurt him so much."

"Shut up! I know bout goddamn Band-Aids!" Wesley ripped the bandage loose. Curtis sucked air but stayed silent. Tunk, Brett, and Ajay crowded close to check out the gash, which had started to bleed.

"Um, sorry, man," murmured Wesley.

"S'cool," muttered Curtis.

"Black van," said Gordon. "Shitty paint job. Ole Dodge with a two-piece windshield. Yesterday mornin, fore school. Deuce Uzis."

"An the second motherfuckin time!" added Curtis.

Wesley dropped the sticky bandage to the ground, and nodded. "Okay. So's we gots the same prob. But who it is, an why they wanna do us? Deek say... "

"Shit!" said Gordon. "Lemme guess, man. Deek tellin ya it some big dudes wanna move our grounds. An he wantin to front a Uzi to work for him."

"Word," said Wesley. "Or give him a dealin pass."

"Dint know you sold em, man."

Wesley scowled. "We don't! Dint know you did, man!"

"We don't! Gots enough motherfuckin probs in the hood without that shit!"

Wesley met Gordon's eyes a moment, then sighed. "Mmm. Maybe we do too."

Gordon thought for a second, glanced at Lyon, then said. "Well, just maybe we gots us a handle on somethin, man. Leastways over Deek sucker."

Wesley scanned Gordon's face. "Yeah?" He fingered his jaw, then waved toward the wash bays. *"Yo.* Maybe you right bout the shade bein the place, man. Let's us all slide in an be cool while we talk some. Maybe we let Game-Boy an Ric catch theyselfs a tan a while?"

"I'm Ric," piped Ric.

Tunk and Curtis snickered. Wesley smiled. "Whatever."

The boys were just turning toward the wash structure when suddenly there were yells and fighting sounds from around one side. "Wes-LEEEE!" screamed a voice. "LYON!" bawled another.

"Turbo!" yelled Wesley, spinning toward the sounds.

"Furball!" shouted Lyon.

Wesley whirled back to face Gordon. "You lyin motherfucker!"

"YOU the liar, cocksucker!" Gordon roared back. Ajay and Brett whipped out their knives. Tunk hesitated a few seconds, then unhappily pulled his. Ric and Curtis snatched up their boards and clutched them like clubs. Gordon and Wesley both spun toward the back of the lot. Rac had the .22's muzzle buried in Game-Boy's chest. Game-Boy was staring down at it. Wesley's hand went for his pocket. Brett and Ajay circled their blades in the air and took steps toward Curtis and Ric. Tunk was holding back, looking miserable. Gordon jerked up his own board. Then the bright little gun flashed like magic in Lyon's dark paw, aimed square at Wesley's heart. There was a loud click as he thumbed back the hammer: ancient as it was, the little gun had a solid steel sound. All the boys froze.

Wesley's face twisted in rage. "You SHIT!" he screamed at Gordon. "You fucked over the rules!"

Gordon glared back. "YOU fucked em first, cocksucker! You lie bout Turbo!"

"You lie bout your gun, motherfucker! What Rac got there? A toy?" Wesley whirled to point at the wash structure. "An who you gots tryin to do Turbo, you lyin sucker?"

"Both you shut up!" Lyon bawled. He jabbed the gun at the Crew boys. "Ajay! Brett! Tunk! Bail them blades! Nice an far! NOW!"

The three boys shifted their eyes to Wesley as the fighting sounds got louder from around the wash bay: struggling bodies slamming loose tin, yells and panted curses.

Wesley gritted his teeth. "Just do it!"

Three knives glittered bright arcs through the air, hitting the asphalt about thirty feet away.

"Rac!" shouted Lyon. "Get Game-Boy over here! Then watch all these dudes!" he jabbed the silver gun again. "Gordon! Wes! C'mon! We all gots enough probs now, out we doin each other, goddamnit!" He darted for the wash structure, not looking back.

Wesley and Gordon stared at one another for a few seconds,

then followed on the run. The other gang boys regarded each other uneasily, their eyes shifting to Game-Boy as he came slowly across the lot with Rac holding the pistol to his head, then all turned to gaze in wonder after their leaders and Lyon.

Turbo was a dark, wiry dude. Furball had him flat on his back on the gravelly pavement, crouching on the boy's chest, knife point at his throat. Turbo clutched a snub-nosed revolver jammed to Furball's cheek. Both boys gleamed and panted hard, their bodies scratched and dirt-streaked, and little chunks of gravel sticking to their skin. Close by lay their boards, wheels in the air like dead things. Lyon rounded the corner and skidded to a stop. Gordon and Wesley almost crashed into him.

"Furball! Chill!" yelled Lyon.

Furball's eyes were wild. "He do me, I back off! He do me, Lyon!"

Lyon spun to Wesley. "Call your man! Fast! Or we lose em both!"

Wesley just stood for a second, fists clenched, chest heaving, looking like a kid about to explode. His eyes seemed to seek escape but couldn't find any. Finally he sucked a breath. "Game over, Turbo."

Turbo's eyes were huge and scared, showing white all around, and rolling. He swallowed and a thread of crimson appeared on his throat beneath the knife point. "Wh... what you tellin me, man? How I know he not...?"

Wesley shot Lyon a glare, but growled, "Cause *I* tellin ya, man! So just do it!"

Turbo choked back a sob, then cautiously lowered the gun, letting his arm fall back on the ground. Furball's eyes flicked to Lyon.

"Heart," Lyon murmured.

Furball drew back the knife and got to his feet. His thin body started shaking. Lyon nodded, then turned to face the gang leaders. Both were looking more confused than anything else. Raising an eyebrow, Lyon let down the Iver-Johnson's hammer. Then he tucked the gun back into his jeans and moved to Furball. The skinny boy's tank top had slipped from both shoulders and hung at his waist. Lyon began brushing gravel off Furball's back. His touch seemed to calm the boy.

Wesley had been watching all Lyon's moves, alert for some trick. His eyes now shifted to Gordon, unarmed except for his board, and seemed to consider if he could take the fat boy. Then he looked down to Turbo, who still had the revolver in his hand. He seemed to feel Lyon's eyes on him, and raised them to the slender boy. Finally, he muttered, "Get up, Turbo. Chill out. Be cool, man. You done good." Then he faced Gordon. "Yo! This here suck somethin way total, man! What IS this shit... gots yourself another dude hid by an he go an jump my man! Yo, not fair! Word!"

Gordon was just staring at Furball. "But he ain't... "

Lyon coughed.

Gordon read. "Well... shit, Wes! You keepin Turbo hid by! Not fair neither, man!"

Wesley puffed a chest that didn't need it. "Yo! Just 'tectin my dudes, what it is, man. I gots a right! If that ain't a rule, then it for sure the fuck oughta be!"

Furball was watching Turbo get up, one finger restless on the knife handle. Turbo kept the gun muzzle pointed down. Furball suddenly snorted, puffing his own little chest. "Yo! I not jump nobody, man! This here sucker come round an try an grab me from a'hind!"

"Call ME no sucker, you skinny-ass motherfucker!" Turbo spat.

Wesley slammed a fist into Turbo's chest. "Yo! You tellin me you jump him with a gun, an he only gots a piddly-ass knife, an HE get YOU grounded like that? SHIT!"

Turbo sputtered, but Lyon smiled and touched his arm. "Yo! Furball be way past bad with his blade. Hell, everbody know. Ain't Turbo's fault."

Turbo nodded sulkily. "Goddamn right it ain't!"

Gordon searched Lyon's face, then gave Wesley a nudge. "Yo. I rent him to ya for givin your dudes lessons, man. Twenty bucks a hour."

"My dick!" Wesley clenched his fists again, but finally relaxed and shrugged. "Oh, too funny, man." He glared at Turbo. "Put that goddamn gun by fore you go an hurt yourself!" He turned back to Gordon. "Yo! Not fair you gots yourself two guns an not say!"

"Get out my face, Wesley! YOU gots two guns an not say neither!"

"I tole you, goddamnit, gotta 'tect my dudes, man! Whole motherfuckin world gone total apeshit!"

"Well, you got that right anyways. Word up now, Wes, no more shit tween us. Okay? We talk real-time. Straight."

"Mmm. Okay." Then Wesley grinned. "Sides, it a squirt gun painted black. Gotcha, Gordy."

"Huh?" Gordon stared at the revolver Turbo was slipping into his jeans.

"WHAT THIS SHIT?" squalled Furball. "Mean I almost do a dude over a goddamn motherfuckin squirty gun?!"

Lyon grinned with Wesley and gripped Furball's shoulders with both hands. "Maybe that be why white folks on TV don't want their kids playin with war toys."

Turbo brushed gravel from his arms, and puffed. "Yo, sucker. MINE for real, believe! It Game-Boy gots the water gun!"

"Oh," said Furball. "Well, I guess you'da done me after all."

Turbo touched his throat, then looked at his bloody fingertip. "Shit. Prob'ly been my last game, man. Your reflexes stick the blade in even after you dead."

Furball cocked his head. "Word up? Jeez, I never knew that. Yo, man, I sorry over your neck. It bout stop bleedin now."

Turbo shrugged. "Hell, I live, man. S'cool."

Wesley scowled. "Fuck no, it ain't cool, goddamnit!" He spun to Gordon. "Yo! Rules! Check it out, your man draw blood!"

"Aw, shit, Wes!" Gordon groaned. "You callin rules on a fuckin little ole pussy scratch like that?"

"What it is, man." Wesley crossed his arms. "You just now say we gonna follow the rules. Yo. That mean only rules fit you?"

Lyon's grip tightened on Furball's shoulders. "Give Turbo your blade, man."

"What?"

"Trust me. Rules gotta be followed. What else we got?"

Furball shifted the knife in his hand. Turbo started to step toward him, then saw his eyes and hesitated.

"Well?" said Wesley. "We ain't gots all fuckin day, y'know?"

"Do the heart thing," whispered Lyon.

Carefully, Furball reversed the knife and offered it handle-first to Turbo. Turbo cautiously slipped it from Furball's fingers, then slowly brought the blade tip up against Furball's throat.

"Well?" Wesley demanded. "S'matter, Turbo? Blood puss ya out or somethin?"

Locking eyes with Furball, Turbo flicked the knife point, drawing a thin line of blood. Furball didn't flinch. All the boys relaxed. Turbo gave back the knife. Furball folded and pocketed the blade, then reached out a tentative hand and wiped a streak of dust and gravel bits off Turbo's back as the boy turned away. Turbo grinned and let himself be cleaned. "Ahhhh, little mo to the lef, bro."

Gordon gave Wesley another nudge. "Cool?"

Wesley looked thoughtful. "Mmm. Game-Boy's squirt gun be full of battery acid, Gordon. That for free."

"Jesus, Wes!"

Wesley shrugged. "What I say, man? World get shittier, mean you gotta do shittier things to live. Word. C'mon, man, best we get our dudes chilled down for somethin really nasty happen."

Gordon nodded and moved with Wesley around the corner. "Y'know, Wes, word we meet seem like all over at school today, fuck if I know how. Prob'ly be up an down the hoods, come mornin."

"Or what," agreed Wesley. "An if Deek sucker true talkin bout some big dudes schemin round, might just make em put the moves on us, speed of light. Know what I sayin?"

"Yeah. We best get busy, man."

Wesley signaled for Turbo to follow as he and Gordon walked away. Lyon kept a hand on Furball's shoulder and stayed where he was. Gordon glanced back at them, his forehead furrowing once more. Lyon crooked a finger at him.

"Um... Yo, Wes," said Gordon. "Gimme a minute, huh, man?"

"Mmm. Well, no more tricks. Word?"

"Up."

"'Kay. I get everbody together inside. Set a watch. Who for you?"

"Use Curtis."

Wesley nodded and moved on, Turbo following.

Gordon stalked back to the other boys. "All right. What the fuck IS this shit anyways? Lyon, you gone total crazy, bringin some strange sucker to a meet? You coulda got dudes killed!"

Furball twisted free of Lyon's hand. "Sucker yourself, man! An Lyon dint bring me! I follow ya!"

Gordon spat on the ground. "Then YOU the crazy one! What in hell you thinkin... wanna try an join up or somethin? So you way bad with that blade, for sure you go an choose the world's shittiest time for showin it!"

Furball puffed his little chest. "Fuck that! Don't need ME no gangs an pussy rules! Know what? I only wanna tell you somethin... a thing maybe save YOUR ass! But, oh no, big, bad, 'PORTANT gang man got no time for me what don't count!" Furball's outthrust jaw began to quiver. "Nobody gots no goddamn time for me!" His shoulders sagged and a tear squeezed from one eye. "Fuck you, man! You don't even know what I give up for cause just to come here!" More tears ran down his cheeks. He wiped at them savagely, then spun to Lyon. "YOU done this, fucker!" Furball began beating with both fists on Lyon's slim chest. Lyon just stood, his slender body taking it.

"Homo!" Furball blubbered. "Motherfuckin dumpster baby! I wish you woulda died!"

Suddenly, Lyon caught both of Furball's fists and just held them.

Furball struggled for a moment, then slumped against the slender boy, crying like a little kid. "I wanna go *home!*"

Gordon had stood silent, watching first with anger, then uncertainty as Furball cried. Now he moved to the smaller boy and turned him around. "Stop it, man! Just... oh, STOP cryin, goddamnit! Listen up! You CAN'T go home! Case you not figure, you in deep shit now. Hell, even if I let you go, Wesley won't." Gordon grabbed Furball's shoulders and shook him gently. *"Think,* dude! What happen if Wesley find out you ain't one of us? Bad blade or no, you one dead sucker! Be cool now, cry all you wanna when you out of this shit."

Understanding suddenly flooded Furball's face. Then fear. He turned to Lyon, who laid a hand on his shoulder once more. "Listen, brother," Lyon said. "You gotta trust us now. There be no runnin home to Mom no more when the game get scary an you don't wanna play."

Lyon gathered the smaller boy to him as his crying faded to sobs, then looked at Gordon. "Last night, when I tole you I find Deek's crib? Furball was there fore me. He hear things Deek be sayin bout us an the Crew."

Gordon's eyes hardened. "What things?"

Footsteps sounded from around the corner, crunching gravel. Wesley's voice called. "Yo, Gordon! We ready up."

Gordon glanced quickly over his shoulder, then pressed close to Furball. "Listen, dude!" he whispered. "You hang right by Lyon, an you do a'zactly what he say, when he say it! Keep your mouth shut, an hope to hell my dudes gots enough cool to cover ya! Just maybe you come outa this with your ass!"

A few minutes later, both gangs were sitting in a ragged ring on the cool concrete floor of a wash bay. Cigarette smoke swirled like fragile blue ghosts over their heads as the breeze sighed through. A loose strip of roofing tin creaked softly above, occasionally lifting to let a sunbeam stab into the center of the circle, where it spotlighted a dance of dust motes. The air was thick with kid sweat and concentration. Curtis stood at one end of the bay holding the little .22, and Tunk kept watch at the other with the Crew's .38. Gordon and Wesley sat together, their backs to the sheet-metal wall below a control box that had been beaten with a sledgehammer until its empty coin tray stuck out like a mangled tin tongue. Lyon sat to Gordon's right, legs drawn up, arms crossed atop, and chin resting on them. His uptilted eyes under his soft puff of hair seemed to take in everything without looking long at anything. Furball crouched close to him like a lean little cat, his eyes scanning brightly and small muscles tight. Ric and Rac were next, pressed shoulder to shoulder as if charging each other's batteries by contact. Their tawny eyes stole cool, curious glances at Furball's tear-streaked face, not missing the thread of blood at his throat or the matching one on Turbo's. Wesley's dudes completed the circle; Game-Boy beside Rac, kicked back in the soft, sagging pose of a fat kid who knew he was and didn't give a shit. Then came Ajay, Turbo, and Brett. Wesley had called the meet, so was obligated by rules to lay out the reason; the details of the drive-by shooting and Deek's offers and threats were no major news to anybody. Gordon's story followed; basically the same, with Curtis called into the sunbeam spotlight to show his wound once more.

Then came the discussion. Rules were simple; raised hands signaled questions, speakers recognized by mutual consent of the gang leaders. If an adult had been listening he would have probably figured the boys were just following a form learned in school. But the ritual was ages older than Oaktown, Lyon would say, older than America. If the circle of boys had been gathered in darkness around a fire, and if the setting had been a jungle glade or forest grove, and the boys clad in lion skin or chain mail, the rules would have been the same.

Wesley flipped away his Marlboro and blew out smoke. "Deek know too much."

Nobody snickered.

"He come an curb us yesterday mornin," Wesley went on. "Bout a block from the school. He talkin same ole dogshit bout how we just rag-ass little niggerboys, gots no hope in hell without bucks. Then he start in bout some big dudes schemin on the hood. An then he come sorta sideways—like bout somethin mighta happened to you dudes, Gordon, over the same sorta shit. Well, course we hear some auto-fire over your way, but hell, you hear *that* all the goddamn time an get so's you don't pay it no mind no more."

"Less it aimed at you," added Turbo.

"Go without sayin, man," Wesley murmured.

Gordon's face was thoughtful. "Mmm. That when Deek make you a offer for a Uzi?"

"Yeah. Course, he done that a'fore. Only, this time, he sound in my ear more... um... "

"Sincere?" murmured Lyon.

"Uh-huh. You good with them big words, man. An you ain't no puss bout it... make em come cool. Anyways, Deek talkin us up way you do by cops... sayin what you figure they wanna hear... tellin us all bout how word say you dudes movin up your hood, wantin more ground."

Gordon snorted Kool smoke out of his nose. "Shit, man. Why we wantin more ground? Gots enough probs hangin on to what we hold now."

"Yeah. My own mind tellin me that too, all the time Deek talkin. But he talk so motherfuckin *cool*, man... like Lyon might could if he want. Say how *you* might just be doin a deal with him..."

"My ass!"

Wesley held up palms. "I know, man, but you wasn't *there.* Know what I sayin? Deek come on with how you score yourself some major fire, you get to believin you somebody, man... stead of just another little Buckwheat gang. All of a sudden you way past baaaad. Gotta take more ground. Get some respect."

"Shit," said Gordon. "An just tell me what that really get you, man? You gots more ground, mean you gotta cover it. An that take more dudes... dudes what you dint grow up with an don't know.

Then, more dudes an ground you got, more deals an shit you gotta do to keep em. Pretty soon you gots no fuckin time for doin nuthin but gang stuff." His eyes drifted past Lyon's. "An tell me how you go to a dance with a girl, tryin to come cool, when there a goddamn gun stickin out your ass?" He snorted again. "Sides, a Uzi shoot bout five hundred fifty goddamn 'spensive bullets a minute, man. Know what that cost?"

Wesley smiled. "Ain't Popsicle money, for sure. Hell, man, here we just tryin to save by for scorin usselfs a CD boomer. Yo. What I sayin is, *we* been figurin the same shit too, man. And sound like to me, we come to the same, um... " He looked expectantly at Lyon.

"Conclusions, man."

"Yeah! But then here come Deek sucker motorin by like shit don't stink, tryin to tell us, if you dudes gettin drive-byed, you just might start in thinkin it were us settin it up. That when I say myself, this here shit gone far as it goin, I sendin 'bassador Tunk over cross the line for some realtime talk." Wesley considered a moment. "Seem like to me Deek goin round shit-disturbin, what it is. An he too puss to go messin with the big dogs, so he schemin on us. Shit, man, I take that motherfucker down myself, cept he ain't never out that bodyguard of his, an word say that dude one way bad sucker."

Furball stiffened at that but only Lyon noticed. Then Lyon's pawlike hand went up. The other boys stared at him for a second like he'd just materialized from the *Enterprise's* transporter deck.

"Man," said Wesley. "How in hell you do that? It like you only get seen when you wanna! That a thing come in handy for sure!"

Lyon smiled. "Mostly it a quiet thing, I guess. Anyways, rewind a little, Wes man. You just now tellin us that when Deek curb you yesterday mornin he seem to already know we been drive-byed. That a little passin strange, ain't it? Our hood mostly quiet mornin times. An for sure we'd marked *his* car cruisin three blocks away, so he wasn't there, so he couldn't seen nuthin, yet you tellin us that he know."

"Mmm," said Wesley. "Well, I not sayin he actually come out an word up. But, one to ten, I give him a eight for knowin shit he shouldn't."

"I give him a ten for *bein* in places he shouldn't!" growled Gordon. "An I just like you, Wes. Gots enough goddamn probs comin round without no motherfuckin dealer movin in full-time."

The twins shot their hands up together. "Too bad Deek sucker don't live round here," said Ric.

"Word!" added Rac. "Then we could just do him an his bad-ass bodyguard an everthin be way past cool again!"

Game-Boy grinned. "Leastways, close enough for Oaktown, huh?"

"Raise your goddamn hand next time, man," muttered Wesley.

Furball had stiffened again at the mention of Deek's body-guard. Lyon laid a hand on his shoulder and leaned close, whispering, "Be almost time for you, man. See the words in your heart fore you let your mouth make em."

Lyon put up an open palm. "I know where Deek be cribbin out."

Murmurs buzzed among the boys until Gordon glared around the circle and Wesley snapped his fingers. Wesley cocked his head, gave Lyon an uncertain look, then shifted suspicious eyes to Gordon. "So, how long you dudes know this, man?"

"Chill out, Wes," said Gordon. "Not till just this mornin when I see Lyon at school. He ghost Deek's bodyguard last night."

Wesley studied the slender boy. "Mmm. Ghost be the word when you talkin bout *him,* for sure! I see that with my eyes, man! Big words, big balls, an spooky like somethin sittin on a tombstone!" He smiled. "Bet cops come round messin with you, they end up not knowin if to shit or go blind, man." Then his smile faded. "So, where this place of Deek's?"

Lyon told. Nobody seemed to notice that he kept a hand on Furball's shoulder, just as no one seemed to notice Furball was shaking. When Lyon finished, Gordon turned to Wesley. "That anybody's ground over there? Deek could be payin for 'tection."

Wesley shrugged. "Nobody's I hear bout. Course, wanna get technical, all this here part of Oaktown sposed to belong either Gorillas or some other major-time gang. But that sorta like sayin cops there to 'tect ya. None of them big-dude gangs give a shit bout no little rag-ass niggerboys like us, or what we do to each other over a few dogshit blocks. Long's we don't get in their way. Even Deek ain't nuthin but chump change to them, an he keep a pretty low pro, considerin." Wesley thought a moment, then added, "Maybe... if we all knowed totally an for sure that it Deek sucker puttin schemes on us, we hang together an take the motherfucker down."

Gordon glanced at Lyon. "Spose we try warnin him off first. Like to let him know we know what it is. We could trash his 'partment."

242 Way Past Cool

"An leave a dead rat in his bed," added Tunk from the end of the bay.

Curtis giggled at the other end. "Leave him a rat-meat pizza with a note!"

"Naw," said Turbo. "Just tie a note to the rat's tail."

"Shut up," said Wesley. "All you! Got no time for little-kid shit! Yo, Gordon! You always sayin second warnin's for good cops an bad movies. Well, way I see it, we both been givin Deek all kinda warnin's to keep off our hoods, man, an then we turn right round an let him buy off little chunks of our asses with beer. What I sayin is, we settle this shit right now, man. If Deek really puttin drive-bys on us, then we do the sucker cold, NOW, fore we start losin dudes!"

Silence followed. The boys all stared at one another. Cigarettes were fired. Wesley looked around, his nostrils flaring, then spat into the sunbeam. "Well? Ain't nobody gots nuthin to say all a sudden? Seem like, second ago, y'all was chippin your goddamn teeth bout dead rats an pizzas like a bunch a third-graders at recess time!"

"But we still not know for sure if it Deek puttin the moves," said Tunk.

No one saw Lyon gently nudge Furball, but all the boys turned when Furball's hand went slowly up like it took all his strength to lift. Silence settled once more around the circle. The loose tin creaked softly overhead, strobing the sunbeam. Gordon and Wesley both nodded to the small boy. Furball sucked a breath, then got to his feet so the dusty sun spotlight played over him. One of the shirt straps slid off his shoulder but he just let it hang. He looked like a kid on his first day at a new school who'd been forced by the teacher to introduce himself to the class. Eleven pairs of eyes scanned him; those of the Friends more curious than the Crew's, except for Lyon. For a few seconds Furball seemed to be judging his chances of escape, of getting past Curtis or Tunk even though both boys had guns. Furball's knife hand hovered near his pocket, but he pulled it away and picked up his skateboard instead. Finally, he locked eyes with Lyon and spoke as if only to him.

"I was there, last night, front of Deek's buildin, fore Lyon come. I hear things Deek tellin my... his bodyguard."

Wesley's gaze could have cut glass, and his voice slashed like it. "You ghost him too, man? Why?"

Gordon tapped Wesley's knee. "Chill, man. Wait. Furball recognized now, let him talk."

Furball's eyes shifted to Gordon. He took another breath. "Deek know all bout you Friends gettin drive-byed yesterday mornin. Word, man. Just like Wesley say, only a lot more. Words an music, man. He even knowed you shoot back an put a bullet in the van."

"I *did?*" said Gordon.

"Shut... shush!" hissed Wesley.

Furball turned to the Crew leader. "An Deek know all bout how you dudes get sprayed after school yesterday, man. Time an place."

Wesley's eyes went to slits. "Yo, Tunk! You tell Gordon the place when you see him last night?"

"Um... don't think so."

"He didn't," said Gordon.

Wesley nodded. "Mmm. An I never did, just now." He looked

back at Furball. "What place, dude?"

Furball swallowed. "Backside the truck shops."

Wesley nodded again. "That where it happen. Word. So, what else Deek say bout us, man?"

Furball swallowed once more and took another breath. "He say... say you gonna meet him here, tonight... for cause to do a deal on a Uzi."

Gordon jerked around to face Wesley. "Well, ain't that a goddamn bitch, man!"

Wesley shrugged and looked sulky. "Oh, chill, Gordon. Ain't nuthin been cut. Yo. Why the fuck you figure I call for this here meet anyways? Hey, you figure I WANNA deal with that sucker? Shit, I gotta keep all my options open, man. Just like you. Everybody gots to have options. What it is." He shrugged again and looked back at Furball. "What else, man?"

Furball hesitated. His eyes drifted down to Lyon's. "Deek was raggin on my... his bodyguard... "

"Yo!" said Gordon. "What all this 'my' shit?"

"Chill," said Lyon. "You all be makin him feel like Buckwheat at a skinhead concert."

"Yeah," agreed Turbo. "What it is. Let the man breathe."

Furball's fists clenched, and he got out the rest with a cracked voice. "Deek was raggin on his bodyguard bout them late for some kinda payoff clear cross town. It was to some dudes sposed to done a drive-by!"

Furball's knees seemed to give. He sank down close to Lyon and stared at the greasy concrete. "That... all what I know."

"Shit!" yelled Turbo. "That plenty enough for ME, best believe!"

Both gangs exploded into voice, cursing Deek, until their leaders shouted them down. Wesley twisted around to Gordon and demanded, "Yo! You not even know this shit till right this minute, huh? Don't lie to me, man, I can read faces most good as Lyon!"

Gordon glanced at Lyon, then shrugged. His voice came out careful. "I know bout Lyon... an my new dude, Furball findin Deek's crib. But not what Furball just now say. Word, Wes."

Wesley looked doubtful. "Your 'new dude, Furball,' huh? Tell me, man, just how long Furball been a Friend?"

Gordon's face turned stubborn. "That my own goddamn business, sucker!"

Wesley puffed a moment, then relaxed and let out air.

"Uh-huh." He snagged a Marlboro pack from the floor and shook up a cigarette. Ajay fired it with a Bic. Wesley pulled in smoke and blew it carefully away from Gordon's face. It smogged the sunbeam now slanting orange in the late afternoon. "Somethin ain't gettin total told here," he muttered. "Like my mom always sayin, I can feel it in my bones. But, like Turbo just now say, we gots more'n enough reason for takin Deek down." Wesley sucked more smoke, then pointed his cigarette. "An Furball was right over what he say he hear. We sposed to be meetin Deek here at nine to do a deal for a Uzi." He turned back to Gordon. "My option, case this meet with you went dogshit, man. Know what I sayin?"

Gordon nodded. "Seem like we cut it fine, brother."

"Mmm. Got that right, homey." Wesley's eyes roamed the circle. "Well, guess that mean we into makin a plan together for doin Deek sucker, huh? Best time to my mind be when he show here tonight."

Gordon was also searching the faces around him. "Word. Spect that gonna mean takin down his bodyguard too."

"NOOOO!" Furball's cry beat between the tin walls, so sudden that all the boys froze for a second. Furball leaped to his feet and whirled to run. He might have made it.

Curtis and Tunk were just staring at him open-mouthed, their guns hanging loose in their hands. But Furball took extra seconds to whip out his knife and throw it in fury at Lyon's chest before trying to get away.

Days later the word would go around how Lyon had caught the glittering blur out of the air, and no one would doubt he'd used magic. But now the other boys scrambled, yelling for Furball, piling onto the small skinny boy and dragging him down.

Furball fought like a panther cub as both gangs tried to pin him to the floor. He kicked and clawed and bit, small fists flailing. Ajay screamed, kicked in the balls, and staggered back to double over and puke. Ric stumbled out of the fight, his nose gushing blood, then Brett backed away with a hand torn open by Furball's teeth. Tunk and Curtis still stood, guns at their sides, not knowing whether to leave their positions. Once, Furball almost escaped, his shirt ripped off and left dangling in Game-Boy's hands. But Gordon grabbed his Nike and yanked him back down again. Even then Furball almost got free by kicking off the shoe, but Wesley leaped in front of him and smashed a fist into his face. Furball wavered a moment on his elbows and knees, shaking his head, trying to clear it, bloody mist spraying from his mouth and nose as he panted for breath. Then Rac darted forward and kicked him in the stomach. Furball collapsed on the greasy concrete, and the other boys massed in to grab arms and legs.

A minute later Furball lay gasping for air, half choking on his own blood, his nose streaming it and his battered face a mask of it. His jeans were torn half off, and his thin body was streaked with dirt and scratches. He'd been dumped back against the tin wall beneath the bashed-up control box. Rac and Game-Boy each held an arm while Lyon and Turbo pinned his legs. For a little while the only sounds were Furball's strangled gasps, the panting of the other boys, and Ajay's moans as he lay curled on the floor with both hands clasping his crotch. Gordon and Wesley stood shoulder to shoulder staring down at Furball. Gordon's own jeans were about to slide off, and his lip was split and puffing. Wesley's wrist oozed blood where Furball had bitten him.

Wesley shifted his eyes from the small boy to Gordon, his nostrils flaring and his voice low and dangerous as he demanded. "Okay, man. Game over! Now who the fuck is he?"

But it was Lyon who spoke, holding Furball's leg and not looking up. "Deek's bodyguard be his brother."

Furball struggled weakly, then spat in Lyon's face. "I gonna kill you!" he sobbed. "Word!"

The day was dead. Only a faint ruddy glow lingered in the sky across the Bay as Ty tailed his skateboard by a corner phone booth. He thought of San Francisco somewhere over in that direction, of the Golden Gate Bridge and the cable cars he'd only seen in movies or on TV. The news always made San Francisco sound so clean... and Oakland so dirty. But then the TV lied about a lot of things. Maybe, he thought, he'd take Danny over on a BART train someday and they could ride a cable car; maybe check out China-town, where everybody always said you could score firecrackers no prob. Danny liked them, but they were hard for kids to get. Ty wondered if Markita might want to go too.

Ty stepped into the booth, then scowled. There was no phone, though there had been one just a few days ago. Now there was only a blank metal mounting where the phone had been, with a few colored wires dangling down like veins from a chopped-off arm in those gross little Garbage Pail Kid cards he used to collect when he was Danny's age. A sticker was slapped on the mount, already half covered by graffiti, gang marks, and anger. What little of it Ty could read said something about public nuisances and how the phone company in cooperation with law enforcement was concerned with serving and protecting the community.

What it translated to was drug dealing.

For a minute Ty just stood and stared stupidly at the stark steel plate the way a person whose home had been robbed might stare at the empty places where belongings had been. Ty was tired; bone-weary as never before in his life. The evening air was cool, but sweat sheened his face. His arm was swollen, and the knife slash burned beneath Markita's bandage. Rage flickered inside him as he stared at the useless phone booth; rage trying to spark off a flame like the tiny flash of a cigarette lighter's flint. Images drifted through his mind of somebody hurt, or sick, or lost. He thought of Markita again; of how she had to walk these blocks alone at night because the bus had been routed away from danger, and now even the last chance of a phone call for help had been denied her. He thought too of Danny: being chased, or stabbed, or shot, and dragging himself to this booth only to find a nightmare of nothing inside. Ty's knuckles paled as he clenched his fists and thought about a race of people, and a whole generation within that race, being punished for the sins of a few. The rage kept sparking inside him, trying to fire off something bigger. Ty recalled Danny trying to make a hand grenade by taping a firecracker to a Bic lighter.

And who were that few... *really?* Were they the hungry or unwanted kids who'd never had anything good in their lives and saw no future ahead? Or were they the unseen white tip of the pyramid who sucked up the profit from it all?

Ty remembered things from the TV news: of people shot and

killed for nothing but looking at somebody the wrong way, or flipping a finger, or cutting into someone's parking space. The safe, clean, well-fed world behind the TV's glass always acted so shocked and disgusted that people could kill for such tiny insults. But Ty knew why it happened: it was all those little sparks of anger, constantly firing day by day, week on week, month on month, and building to years of held-back rage that finally exploded.

Ty dug out his Kools, wincing at the fire in his arm. He remembered a sixth-grade health book that showed a cartoon picture of antibodies dressed up like cops and battling an infection gang clad in chains and black leather jackets with skulls and crossbones on the backs. It was funny to imagine there was a war going on right here inside him. He slipped a cigarette between his lips and fired his lighter, having to spark it several times because the fuel was getting low. The butane in the lighter was a liquid under pressure. It could only be held captive and kept under control by constant pressure. Take off the pressure and it would escape... become a free vapor. Danny's Bic hand-grenades hadn't worked. Maybe because, once the little plastic prison was shattered, the butane would rather be free than explode?

Ty recalled an antidrug commercial: some famous black basketball player telling kids that if they used drugs they were garbage and *he* didn't want garbage in his neighborhood. *Yo, boys and girls, you're garbage! Nothing to do with garbage except bury it—no hope for you at all!* How way past fucking cool, thought Ty, like offering a drowning man a glass of water. Hell, why not just come right out and tell the kids to go ahead and kill themselves and each other because they were just garbage anyway and nobody gave a shit!

Ty sighed out smoke. Even garbage could be recycled, if somebody gave a shit.

His rage sparked again but nothing exploded. His fuel was too low. He turned from the booth and gazed up the darkening street. It was that quiet time between day and night. Traffic was light. Day people were home, and the night prowlers and concrete cannibals were just waking up, arming and armoring themselves for the jungle hours ahead. Streetlights were coming on: sodiums flaring sulphur yellow, mercury-vapors glowing dull, sullen purple until they warmed. Traffic signals winked like pirate-movie jewels along the blocks, and the headlights of passing cars seemed to leave the sidewalk a little darker each time they swept by. The afternoon breeze had died, and there was no scent of fog in the burned-out air. The night would be clear with a big full moon.

Carrying his board, Ty walked a little ways, wondering for probably the thousandth time why Danny hadn't come. The boy hadn't been kept late at school: Ty had managed to slip past the security guard and checked at the office. Danny hadn't gone home; Ty had checked that out too. Ty had considered going back to the Burger King to ask Markita if Danny had finally shown up, but didn't want to risk getting her in trouble with the manager by hanging around. Instead, Ty had skated a weary grid of blocks in the hope of finding his brother. Maybe, he thought, that was why he seemed so tired now. He stopped in the middle of the sidewalk: goddamnit, Danny had been way past stoked about going uptown for new clothes; what in hell could have happened to make him change his mind? It hurt to think that something else in Danny's young life could be more important than hanging a while with his big brother. Maybe it *was* too late for the boy.

It was for Ty: his time was up. Deek wanted him, and like a lost soul who'd been bitten by a vampire or a zombie under a spell, Ty had to serve his master. Just ahead, an old neon sign struggled to light above a cafe doorway, sputtering and buzzing as it flickered to life. Ty knew the place: a rib shop run by a Vietnamese family where Deek often sent him for takeout orders. There was a pay phone inside.

Ty stepped to the door. Pain jabbed dull needles through his arm as he reached for the handle. A small sound of hurt escaped from his throat. His vision blurred. Blackness hovered at the edges. He swayed a little, his hand clutching the cold brass handle for support. Its ornate old design made him think of coffins. The cigarette slipped from his lips and hit the sidewalk with a burst of bloody sparks. He blinked his eyes and looked into the face of a corpse.

A scream tried to tear out of his throat, but in the next instant he realized that it was his own reflection in the door glass. The fitful blue neon above had eaten his face, cutting stark hollows under his cheekbones, shadowing his eyes into empty sockets, and tinging his dark skin a sick rotting violet. The scream came out as a sigh of relief—like a little kid waking up from a nightmare to find he was home safe in bed. Still, icy sweat chilled Ty's body. He forced himself to study his living-dead image, deciding he was just tired as hell, and that he was going to let his hair grow out naturally into an Afro or a Buckwheat or whatever the fuck anybody "cool" wanted to call it. Fuck being cool! Who in hell needed the latest look for digging through dumpsters and loading scrap iron? Just being black and somehow fighting free of the trap was all the identity he needed. Let the suckers decorate their cages; chains were still chains even if solid gold! Ty waited until the chill and dizziness had passed, then pushed open the door and went in.

The tunnel-like room stretched back into smoky dimness, higher than it was wide. A narrow counter with a row of chrome-pillared stools, their worn red leatherette seats patched with silver crosses of duct tape, ran along one side. Behind the counter were the grill, sinks, and barbecue pit. A line of tall, old-fashioned booths, their backs at least six feet high and their padding the same sort of cross-patched plastic as the stools, took up the opposite side of the room. The ceiling was black as midnight with soot, and lost in shadow. Three bare little bulbs dangled from ten-foot wires, but most of the useful light came from a pinkish fluorescent tube hanging from grease-caked chains over the grill. A few beer signs, one showing a pretty mountain waterfall, shone bright colors along the wall above the booths.

For all its ancient shabbiness the little cafe was still somehow friendly. The air was thick and steamy with food smells and people like a big family's kitchen on a Sunday dinner night. The solid old wood of the counter and booths, the massive Art Deco Hamilton shake machine beside the grill, the chrome-smothered Seeburg jukebox by the door— "high-fidelity," whatever the hell that meant—and the neat little clusters of sauce bottles, ketchup squeezers, sugar jars, and nickel-plated napkin holders on the counter and tables gave the place a homey kind of kicked-back atmosphere that all of McDonald's or Burger King's showtime plastic and high-tech Formica could never match. Markita would like it here, he was sure. He could almost picture himself and the girl together in one of those dim-lit old booths. Even Danny might think this cafe was cool in a funky sort of way, even if there were no games.

The space behind the counter couldn't have been much more than three feet wide, yet the whole Vietnamese family seemed to work happily together the way Ty had always imagined a family should. The father tended the pit, the mother polished and stacked the silverware, and a small slim boy about Danny's age with silky black hair flowing midway down his back, dressed in jeans and a sleeveless half-tee, scrubbed dishes in the sink while a wrinkled old woman who could have been his grandmother or great-grandmother sat by the new IBM cash register and carefully read some kind of Vietnamese newspaper. Did they lie in that language too? Ty wondered. The boy had Walkman headphones clamped over his ears and moved to what might have been rap. The old woman had a beat-up little AM pocket radio near her elbow that was tuned low and wailed what was probably a song but sounded more to Ty like cats being swung by their tails. Ty supposed the only reason he heard it was that he always listened whenever he came in, and it always seemed to be the same song. He'd sometimes wondered what real African music sounded like... probably as alien to him as that tortured-cat stuff was to that boy.

There were only two customers at the counter, both older men, who could have been garbage-truck drivers and appreciated kickin' barbecue. Both glanced once at Ty, marked him as trouble to be carefully ignored, and went back to eating. Ty paid no attention to the people in the booths, though he heard the cheerful squabbling of kids and a mother half trying to get them chilled down. The Vietnamese man was watching the news on a greasy little six-inch Sony that sat on a shelf above the pit as he tended a rack of ribs. He turned and, recognizing Ty as a steady, gave him a smile and a nod. The boy, either noticing his father or feeling the chill from the door, glanced around too. He had the faintest smudge starting on his upper lip. His expression showed he knew who Ty was but didn't live in the same world, so wasn't impressed. That was way past cool as far as Ty was concerned.

The phone was on the back wall by the dark little hallway that led to the bathrooms and the alley door beyond. Above it, Scotch-taped over the scratched and scribbled numbers, messages, and doodles, was a small square of cardboard with NO DEALING neatly printed in blood-red Magic Marker. Somehow Ty knew that the young boy had put it there. Why didn't Danny have that same sort of pride? Ty felt the eyes of the Vietnamese boy bore into his back as he dropped a quarter in the slot and punched up the number of Deek's service... carefully because his fingers seemed stiff and clumsy. Behind him, Ty heard money clunk into the Seeburg and then an old M. C. Hammer song, "Pray," begin. He gave the Vietnamese boy a quick glance: the dude was washing dishes once more but had the headphones hanging around his neck while he listened to the jukebox. Ty noticed what looked like a school book propped open on a shelf above the sink.

The answering-service girl sounded cheerful and white. Hell, thought Ty, for all she knew Deek was a doctor. Maybe he was. The kind who made megabucks treating the symptoms and not the disease, the sort whose operations were always successful even though the patients died. Ty gave the girl Deek's code, then hung up and leaned against the wall, waiting for the phone to ring. The room seemed to have gone hot and hazy. Ty wiped sweat from his forehead and unzipped his jacket. Maybe it was all the barbecue smoke. He gazed over at the beer sign showing a cool mountain waterfall splashing down between snow-covered rocks. Were there really places like that? The jukebox beat seemed to throb in time to the ache in his arm. "We got to pray just to make it today..." You tell it, Hammer, Ty thought. Maybe you was voted Oaktown's prime booster or something like that, but you made your bucks and got your ass out! He closed his eyes, feeling dizzy again. Maybe it was the food smells? He remembered he hadn't eaten anything all day except a bowl of Cocoa Puffs with his family that morning, and yet he wasn't really hungry.

"Yo, dude! What kinda fire you gots?"

Ty opened his eyes and saw nobody. For an instant a chill hit him again. Then he blinked and looked down. There was a fat little boy, maybe eight, who had probably played the jukebox. He had a flattop and wore a Bart Simpson T-shirt with a black Bart saying, "Yo, don't have a cow, man." It seemed painted on the kid, and a roll of chocolate-brown chub hung out underneath. His hands and face were smeared with sauce.

Ty tugged at his jacket, but the gun was well-covered. The little sucker had spotted it anyway. Evolution in action?

"A .45," sighed Ty.

"Yeah. Them's way kickin, but I want me a .357," said the kid.

Why? Ty wanted to ask. The little boy's clothes were clean and new, he was stuffed to the max and obviously loved. But Ty only shrugged. "Yeah," he murmured.

The kid flashed a sign from one of the major gangs and waddled on back to the bathrooms. At eight, that was still funny, even cute, but in a couple more years the kid could get shot for something like that. Ty recalled a passage from his mother's Bible reading... something about when I was a child I thought as a child and spoke as a child but when I became a man I put away childish things. So when did that happen? When they'd been talking in the tub last night, mostly about Danny, Markita had mentioned that in primitive societies a boy became a man when he could father other children. That made Danny a man. But "father" seemed too responsible a word somehow... Our Father who art in heaven... our father who deserted his children! No wonder some whites call us *boys!*

The phone rang. Ty almost jumped. He picked it up, aware again of the Vietnamese boy's hostile eyes. "Yo!" said Deek's voice when Ty answered. "It bout way past motherfuckin *time,* stupid! Where the fuck are ya? We gotta cover us some street fore we meet with the Crew."

Ty closed his eyes again. His throat felt hot and dry. He wished he had a Popsicle. "Don't have a cow, man," he murmured.

"What?" Hey, you drunk again?"

"On life," said Ty. He told Deek where he was.

"Kay, man. I there'n less'n five. Be out front." Deek hung up.

Automatically, Ty checked the coin return, found nothing, which was what he had expected, then walked back out to the street. A mercury-vapor was burninig bright now in front of the cafe, but Ty slipped into the shadows of a boarded-up storefront next door. It seemed only a minute before the arrogant thunder of the Trans-Am's engine echoed down the block... or maybe the reverb was only in Ty's head; he wasn't sure. The streetlight's glare hurt his eyes, and the bluish-white globe seemed to have a fog halo around it. Only there wasn't any fog tonight. Ty moved to the curb as the big car cut close. He noticed the fat little boy watching wistfully from the window as he slid into the seat. Wrong movie, Ty thought. It's the dude washing dishes that's going somewhere. "Don't pay no 'tention to the man 'hind the curtain," Ty mumbled.

Deek studied him. "Shit! You look like warmed-over death, man! Yo! You sick or somethin?"

Ty wiped more sweat from his face, then tossed his board in back. "Maybe the vampire what bit me gots rabies."

"What the fuck's THAT sposed to mean, asshole? You talkin like some kinda crazy ole street nigger!" Deek swung the car away with a squeak of rubber.

"Just tired," said Ty.

"Mmm." Deek studied Ty once more, then groped on the floor and handed Ty a bottle. "Here, man, you *need* this."

Ty took the bottle of Train. It was cold. Sighing, he twisted off the cap and drank. It soothed his throat.

"Just take it slow, man," said Deek. "I need you full-up tonight."

"Yeah. After that I go back in my box again."

Deek gulped Heineken and burped. "Oh, shut up, stupid!"

Deek had an old Too Short disk in the deck: the "raw and uncut" album that white boys played loud while mall cruising in their jacked-up Japanese four-by-fours. Maybe raps like that were supposed to tell the world how bad black dudes were, but after you'd told everybody to go fuck themselves, their mother, their dog, and their hamster about ten million times, it just sounded stupid... like a little kid who'd just learned a naughty word and was running it by everybody in sight to check out what sort of reactions he got. As far as Too Short's sex life, Ty sometimes wondered if the dude was trying to cover with words what his name might really signify. If the message was supposed to be that blacks were big and loud and knew how to fight and fuck, then maybe they should take a lesson from the Vietnamese, who were small and quiet but had won a war and, judging from the size of their families, were way past kickin cool at fucking. More, they seemed to know how to love each other—besides serving up some bad-ass barbecue.

"You been bit girl, what it is."

"Huh? Oh." Markita turned to find Leroy beside her. She was on the sidewalk behind the Burger King, just outside the steel-plated back door. Over to the east a huge full moon was rising, ivory like the top of an old skull, and shining through the skeleton of a distant water tower so it seemed to be beaming from behind bars. Markita found herself holding the handles of a big black plastic garbage can she'd been going to empty in the dumpster. She wondered how long she'd been standing there staring at the moon like some sort of loony lizard.

She smiled. Leroy was a friend. You could say off-the-wall things to a friend. "Could be. I spose you gonna go an run me a line from some ole movie now?"

Leroy looked like he was working up one of his goofy giggles. Instead, he pulled the stupid little hat from his head and mashed it as if he'd considered dropping it into the garbage atop some leftover burgers and fries from the hot racks. Company rules said, politely, that all such unsold food should be disposed of in a proper and hygienic manner. That translated to churning it into a sickening mess with paper and coffee grounds and floor sweepings until it would gag a maggot, and keeping the dumpster padlocked. Markita had forgotten that disgusting ritual tonight. She saw Leroy's eyes shift across the drive-through lane to where a pair of small shadows were hovering near the dumpster: a boy and girl, maybe six or seven. They had to be new to the street not to know the word on company policy.

Leroy looked away and sighed. "You talkin some ole Western... bout good women always goin for gunfighters?"

"Somethin like that, I guess."

"Mmm." Leroy shaped his hat into something else he wasn't satisfied with, but put it back on anyway. "Look like to me a lot of you girls go wastin half your lives tryin to make somethin outa dudes what ain't. Can't figure why in hell you call that love. Ask me, it more like takin in some sorta sick wild animal and then cryin your fool heart out cause it bite your hand an run right away again soon's it get well."

Leroy sighed once more and fiddled with his hat, while watching the two small figures by the dumpster and looking unhappy. "But since you askin, girl, sideways like girls do, I don't figure you wastin your time on that dude." Leroy squared his hat and turned back to the door, then stopped and added, "Just don't never let him get to thinkin he in some kinda cage. Even a nice one." Leroy giggled. "Shit, he a lot like me... just ain't figured it out yet."

Markita turned and gave the lanky boy a sudden kiss on the mouth. He blushed, and Markita smiled and touched his arm. "That a way cool thing to say, Leroy. An you right. He is just like you."

Leroy giggled again. "Mmm. World's chump-change champeen. Well, girl, you tell him, he don't 'preciate the prize, I gon smoke his butt!"

Markita's eyes drifted back to the rising moon. "Y'all figure the manager get pissed off if I go on home early? I like to tuck J'row in my ownself for a change. Seem like I never got no time to be with him."

Leroy grinned. "Hell, girl, hours you been workin, I tell the sucker he can put his pissed-off in one hand, shit in the other, an check which one fill up first! You get your ass on home to that son of yours now. I dump that ole trash."

"That's okay, Leroy. I'll do it. An thanks." Markita hefted the heavy can and lugged it over to the dumpster. The two small shadows shied from her but watched with big sad eyes as she keyed the padlock. She hesitated, then snapped it shut again and walked away, leaving the can behind and not looking back as the little kids scrambled for it.

Headlights swept around the building as Markita reached the door. She turned, seeing the children's eyes glitter as they looked up from eating. It was a cop car, and the kids were frozen between fear and hunger as it stopped. Markita faced the car, her feet apart and her hands dropping to her hips. She recognized the cops as the pair who'd wanted breakfast served in the middle of the goddamn afternoon. The manager might have obliged, figuring it might be good for business to have cops as regular customers, but in this neighborhood it would probably have the opposite effect. What cop talk she'd overheard in the past seemed to class people into three categories... cops, civilians, and garbage. These two didn't act like they thought any "civilians" lived around here.

The black one leaned from the window and jerked a thumb at the kids. "You shouldn't be doin that, girl."

Markita felt like spitting. She wished she wasn't wearing that goddamn stupid hat. And, for a moment, she was also afraid that if she spoke her mind these cops would check up on the hours she worked. They always had *ways,* she thought, another dusty old movie line. But hadn't Ty said something last night about going down on your knees?

Her voice came out cold. "Why not? It the exact selfsame sorta garbage you gonna get served up hot out the window. Stuff outlast the box it come in!" She sniffed. "Or you gonna be big brothers an buy them kids a meal?"

The men exchanged glances. Finally, the black one shrugged. "Try raisin up a family of your own on *my* salary, girl, an see how much sympathy you got left over."

Markita snorted. "I sure as hell like to give it a try!" Spinning on her heel, she stalked back into the restaurant and slammed the steel door behind her.

Again the cops exchanged glances. Then the white one looked over at the little kids who were grabbing food as fast as they could and stuffing their shirtfronts full in case they had to run.

"Jesus!" said the white cop. "What in hell's it gonna be like around here when *they* get to be her age?"

The black one dropped the car into gear and squeaked off for the drive-through window. "You best believe I ain't stayin that long to find out!"

Lyon stood alone on the pump-shed roof, a slender silhouette against the golden globe of the rising moon, somehow too fragile and fine to survive the world that surrounded him. From a wash bay below came the quiet murmur of kid voices, subdued and serious, their scents edgy and tense, and the smell of Marlboro and Kool smoke. At the front of the lot, invisible in shadow except for his cigarette ember, Turbo stood watch for Deek's car. Wesley hadn't lied to Gordon about the entrance chain being locked; he'd just not mentioned at the time that the iron pipe post at one end could be pulled out of the ground.

Wesley had said that the Crew had met with Deek in this place before, around back of the wash structure so as not to be seen from the street. One of the gang always stayed at the entrance, replacing the pipe once Deek's car was in so the dropped chain wouldn't be noticed by any cruising cops, but ready to pull the post again to let Deek out. But plans were being made, and there was a chance that Deek wouldn't be leaving this place tonight—or ever. But what about Ty? And then, what about Furball? Ty was good at his job—way too good—Lyon had seen that on the street yesterday morning. If Deek could be done, shot dead with no doubt, then the bodyguard's job would be over. He'd be free, and might be spared. But the talk in the bay below still went around and around without figuring a way to get past Ty to the dealer except to kill him first.

Lyon gazed at the moon. Its light was turning silver as it climbed. Lyon looked past it to the few stars strong enough to pierce the city's glow. But no answers came from out there. They never did. On cold concrete, other young minds struggled with the problem like high-powered computers fed insufficient data. Furball was tied up and gagged with strips of his shirt. It was done every day on TV. Of course, detailed instructions never came with the model... like, exactly how tight? The reality for Furball was probably too tight. Lyon decided he'd check the boy soon to make sure there was still circulation in his hands.

Or would that even matter in a little while?

Lyon was tired; getting old, he supposed, all the drinking and smoking and nights without sleep finally wearing him down until he felt like something that *should* be sitting on a tombstone. It would be a peaceful job, he imagined, like a hall monitor for dead kids: check their passes and point them in the right direction. He'd left the council a few minutes ago to be alone and to think. He felt the moon's pull but, for the first time he could remember, there seemed little power in it. It was just a cold, dead ball of rock that didn't even shine with a light of its own but only reflected the unseen sun. If Furball's brother was killed tonight, the dude wouldn't run to the cops; that wasn't the way. Even if, gasping for breath and spitting blood a couple of hours ago, he hadn't already vowed it before both gangs, Lyon had seen in his eyes that the boy would hunt them down and kill them one by one, or until he was killed himself. *That* was the way, and it went by the rules.

Lyon sighed. The trouble with rules or laws seemed to be that once they became a system they stopped being justice. Lyon recalled the old *Moby Dick* movie, and Captain Ahab's little black cabin boy, Pip. The Great White Whale hadn't given a shit that Pip was innocent; just one woolly little head smashed down beneath the waves because some raging white monster had a harpoon up its ass.

There were scrabbling sounds, and Lyon turned to see Curtis' baby face peering at him over the eaves. "Um, can you help me, Lyon?"

Lyon came silently across the loose tin, took the smaller boy's hand, and pulled him up.

"Um," said Curtis. "I dint mean to corrupt ya or nuthin I mean, if you was doin magic or somethin?"

Lyon smiled. "That cool. You never corrupt me, homey. I just be tryin to think. The reg'lar kind."

"Oh. Um, wanna smoke, man? Nobody down there can figure out nuthin."

"Yeah. I was kinda 'fraid of that."

Curtis pulled a couple of slightly bent Kools from his pocket and fired his Bic. The two boys sat together and gazed silently at the moon for a while. Finally, Curtis blew smoke. "Wes an Gordon wanna talk to you in a minute, man. Bout the plan... an I guess over Furball too."

Lyon breathed out a moon-silvered sigh. "Yeah. I figure they would. Mostly bout Furball. It be my own fuckin fault the little dude follow us." Lyon stared at the stupid, smiling moon face. "Seem like listenin to your goddamn heart be way past hazardous to your health round here."

A tear glistened like a drop of chrome in Curtis' eye. "Yo! How can we just go an kill him, man? Ain't nobody down there WANT to! They don't even wanna think bout it, I can tell."

Lyon nodded. "Yeah, I know, homey. Spect that what Gordon an Wes be wantin me to handle."

Curtis' eyes went wide. The tear left a glittering trail as it rolled down his cheek. *"You?"* he whispered.

Lyon stared at the stars, so clean and pure and forever out of reach. "By rules it be my 'sponsibility, man." His long hands clenched into fragile-looking fists, and he spat at the moon. "Hearts an magic! Motherfuckin dogshit, man!" He suddenly faced Curtis, his lips pulled back from big teeth. "What fuckin good a heart do ya here, man? This goddamn world twist love all round so even *it* kill ya!"

Curtis shrank away, but then reached out a hand to touch Lyon's arm. "Don't talk like that, man. Please. I mean, if you wanna go an grow fur an claws an stuff, it ain't gonna scare me. But don't change inside, okay?"

Lyon shook off the smaller boy's hand. "Oh, get real, you little puss! I ain't no different from any other stupid niggerboy! All I done was jack myself off in my mind. Like everthin was gonna be all way past cool just cause I believe in somethin I figure was good. But it don't work once you been down with what real, man!" He stabbed a finger skyward. "There be no goddamn power up there, man!

Nuthin what give a motherfuckin shit! Onliest power be HERE!" He waved a hand around. "An it evil!"

Lyon swung back to face Curtis, his uptilted eyes narrowed to ebony slits. "Yo, sucker! Can't you *feel* it, man? It comin right up outa the goddamn ground... from the stinkin dirt what been shit on an tore open an shoved round till when some of it show through a crack in the concrete it don't even look like no real dirt no more! I'm sick of this place, man! I wanna go home!"

Curtis took the slender boy's arm again. "Um, maybe you can come to Jamaica with me? I can ask my mom an dad."

Lyon grabbed Curtis' shoulders and shook him hard. "Yo! Grow the fuck up, you stupid little sucker! You ain't never goin nowhere! It be all fuckin lies, man! The TV lies, the school lies, the cops lie, an the worst lies of all be them what you tell your ownself!"

Tears ran down Curtis' cheeks to spatter silver spots on the rusty tin roof. He lowered his head, grabbing handfuls of hair and yanking them over his face. "I am so goin to Jamaica, man!" he sobbed. "Someday! Just long's I keep wearin dreads an believe it!" He jerked up his head and shoved his locks aside. "So THERE, sucker! That heart shit an magic too, man! My own! An it don't make no fuckin difference to me if YOU stop believin or not! THAT what it is, man! Get your ass down there an check out Furball! HE still tryin to fight! An know what else, sucker? You CAN'T go home till you done your job! So just do it, Lyon! Shit, if you can't save Furball, ain't nobody can, an I ain't gonna be your goddamn homey no more, pussy clot!"

For a long time Lyon just stared at the smaller boy. Then he finally flipped away his Kool and looked back at the moon. It was still pretty, even if it wasn't good for anything. "Mmm. Maybe I see you in Jamaica someday, homey."

Curtis wiped his face and sniffled. "It a island, y'know? We gonna fly there on a airplane."

Lyon nodded. "That be way past cool, mon." He glanced at the moon once more. "Wonder what it look like there."

Curtis smiled a little. "Same moon, mon. Shit, even I know that."

Lyon fingered his jaw. "Mmm. Deek gonna be here at nine. Don't leave us a lotta time for much more figurin. Let's get busy, dude." Lyon rose and leaped from the roof, landing lightly on the weed-buckled asphalt below. Somewhere, he thought, down in that dead-looking dirt, the seeds of young growing things were still fighting through no matter how much shit got dumped on them.

Eyes glittered from the dark wash bay, and the ruby points of cigarettes glowed. The two gangs were gathered by the back entrance, leaving Rac with the .22 watching Furball, whose small shape was huddled on the floor beneath the control box. Game-Boy giggled as Lyon appeared to drop from the sky. "He's baaa-aaak!"

Even in the soft moon shadow Wesley seemed all muscle and hard angles, making Gordon beside him just a tired-looking fat kid, Game-Boy a shapeless mass of lard, and the other dudes skinny and frail. Wesley was standing in his usual pose, hands on hips, while the other gang members were scattered around on the floor. Some sat on their boards. Wesley had tensed when Lyon landed close, but covered with a short cough of Marlboro smoke. "Shut up, man," he muttered automatically to Game-Boy. He gave Lyon a glance, then faced the other dudes again.

"So," said Wesley, as if summing up a school report. "We ain't nuthin but goddamn fools if we try an take Deek down with just the pussy little pops we got us now. Sides, there just six bullets in the .38, seven in the .22, an," he jerked a thumb at Lyon. "Only two in that there ivy-whatsis. We know Deek's bodyguard gots a .45, and that Deek pack least one full-auto Uzi in his car, sides the one he sposed to deal us tonight. So," Wesley spread his palms. "What I sayin is, we be cool to wait till we gots that Uzi in our hands. Then we hose both them suckers down. Game over!"

Under the control box, hands tied behind his back, Furball made savage sounds through his gag and struggled until Rac stuck the .22's muzzle in his ear. The other boys darted glances at Furball, but none tried to meet his eyes.

"What it is, be a piss-poor plan, man," Lyon said quietly.

Wesley puffed. "Yeah? So, you gots a better one, magic boy?"

"Bet your ass!" called Curtis, climbing down from the roof and moving close to Lyon.

Wesley flipped away his cigarette, then turned to glare at Gordon.

Gordon shrugged. "Lyon talk, mostly cool to listen."

Lyon stepped into the shadows of the bay. All eyes shifted to him. Furball's felt like laser beams focused to burn through steel. "Wesley here be a doin kinda dude," said Lyon. "Take things head-on. Kickin bad."

Wesley relaxed a little.

"But that be like tryin to take on the law, man," added Lyon.

"Yo. You just can't fight it that way. Got to dodge an twist an lie to it same's it be all the time doin to you. Word. You ain't no fool, Wes. But you don't figure Deek gonna be one neither? You think he gonna hand you a loaded Uzi? Uh-uh! Yo. Maybe he deal you that gun tonight, but you best be believin he hold by the clip another day."

Murmurs started among the other boys. There were nods in the shadows. Furball had gone totally still, his head cocked, listening. Wesley didn't look too happy but finally nodded. "Yeah. Got to say you right, man. Shit! What the fuck we gonna do now?"

Tunk nudged Ric. "Yo, Rac," he whispered. "That Lyon chill you out fast, huh?"

"I'm Ric. Word, man! Lyon always like that. Even when we was little an playin some make-believe game, like *Star Trek* or somethin. Then here come Lyon along an shoot it all fulla holes... like you can't breathe the air on Venus or somethin like that. Who knew?"

"Well," added Rac, taking the gun out of Furball's ear. "Been lotsa times Lyon-o keep US from gettin shot fulla holes with the stuff he know."

"Shush!" said Gordon. He looked up at Wesley. "Well, there go one *more* motherfuckin idea down the toilet."

Wesley frowned. "Yo! You hear me arguin, man? I say he right, know I say it cause I feel my lips move when I say it!" He turned to Lyon. "So, what we gots to work with now? Shit, we all been curbed by Deek enough to know his moves... bodyguard come out the car first with his .45 ready-up. Hell, that chill everthin from first level on! Deek only spectin us Crew here tonight. Mean you Friends gotta stay hid by. Deek careful. Word. He gonna park his car way out in the open, best believe. Then he wanna see our .38 all the time. An him or his guard gonna keep on countin heads so's to make sure nobody come or go while we dealin."

Gordon nodded, then looked up at Lyon. "So, us gonna stay cool in here, man. We wait our chance... maybe when the guard gots his gun down helpin Deek or somethin. Then we hit them suckers full-on with the .22 and the chrome gun. You an me the best shots, man. Tween us, we oughta be able to take out the guard. Meantime, Wes do Deek with the .38. The other dudes gonna keep screamin an yellin and throwin shit to keep Deek an his man all confused. We even use the squirt gun for a... a... "

"Decoy," said Lyon. He considered. "Mmm. Could work. But there be a good chance some of us gonna get hit. An what if the guard come out the car with a Uzi stead of his .45?"

Wesley shrugged. "Goddamnit, Lyon, we already thought bout that. But, hey, what the fuck ELSE can we do, man? They bigger'n us, an maybe smarter, an gots more firepower for sure."

"Get the bodyguard out the way first."

Gordon snorted. "Yeah? How, man? You gonna magic him to sleep, or throw some kinda spell so he just drop down his gun an walk away?"

"I need to talk to Furball. Alone."

Wesley's eyes turned suspicious. The other boys all swung around to stare at the small figure tied up on the floor. Finally, Gordon shrugged. "Go for it."

"Chill out!" Wesley barred Lyon's way, then glared down at Gordon. "What's this shit, man? There too much fuckin smoke in the air tonight."

Gordon got to his feet and faced the other leader. Muscles showed under their padding of chub. "No. YOU chill, sucker!" He jabbed a finger at Furball. "Yo! You figure I let one of my own dudes get the shit kicked out him like that over some sorta stupid trick?" He spat at Wesley's feet. "Hey! You think that, then we best just call down this whole goddamn donkey show right here an now, man! Hell, you go for it, score yourselfs that motherfuckin Uzi! Sell yourselfs to Deek like cheap little blow boys! Yo! Maybe we get a Uzi too. Maybe a Mac or a AK, or somethin else BETTER than an Uzi! Maybe then we take YOU on! Listen up, man! That what you want? What it is, we don't take Deek down together; here an tonight, we just end up fightin each other while Deek an any other suckers like him keep right on shittin all over us an killin our little hood kids!"

Wesley took a deep breath and let it out slow. His own massive muscles seemed to sag. "Okay," he sighed. "Go for it, Lyon. I just hate to die a fool, that all."

"Dead be dead," said Lyon. "Cool death be just the same as fool death. Your mom cry. Maybe your homeys run you a rap that be forgot in a week, but nobody else give a shit if you was cool or a fool."

Furball was quiet as Lyon moved to him and knelt at his feet. Black-ice eyes bored into Lyon's with suspicion, but a little uncertainty too. Lyon took Furball's knife from Rac. He cut the strip of satin that bound the boy's ankles, then slipped Furball's Nike back on and tied it. Furball's face was a mask of caked blood, his lips split and swollen, and one eye half shut, though no less wary than the other. Lyon helped the smaller boy to his feet and held his tied hands while he struggled for balance. Both gangs watched in silence as Lyon led Furball away. Rounding the corner of the pump shed, the two boys walked down to the last wash bay. Inside lay the gutted corpse of a Ford Pinto wagon, its shattered glass, small parts, and puffs of slashed upholstery scattered all over. Lyon pointed, and Furball sat stiffly down on the front fender. Lyon gazed into the other boy's eyes as he flicked open the blade.

"I still trust your heart, man," said Lyon. "Could be you don't trust mine no more, but I gots to know."

Furball didn't flinch when the knife flashed, slicing first the gag then the strip of shirt that bound his hands. He said nothing, just sitting and rubbing his wrists.

Lyon went on, "You already hear what been decided, man. You know for a fact that Deek gonna die tonight. An, less you an me get back trustin each other again an do us some figurin, fast, your brother an some other good dudes prob'ly gonna die too."

Lyon gave Furball the knife and stepped close, his hands at his sides. "Course, there be another way you might save your brother, man. Spect you know. Do me now an run. You be half up the block fore Turbo know what is. You can spot Deek's car an stop him fore he get here."

Furball fingered his knife. His voice came out husky. "You weird sucker! How come you always gotta make easy shit hard?" He jerked up the blade so the point poised against Lyon's chest. "Know what? I *know* you let me do ya, man! It like you *like* puttin your stupid life in somebody's hands... like you checkin to see if they know what it worth." He shrugged. "Christ, man, cool as you are, ain't you figured a life like yours ain't worth shit? Hell, for all I know, you just plain crazy stead of good. Sometimes it hard to tell... make you 'spicious why somebody treat you nice, know what I sayin? Shit, man, now you go an do it again! Put it on ME! Like a magic curse! Here you say, go to Deek, save my brother, when all the time I knowin what Deek gonna do to you dudes later on. An it worse for cause he makin my own brother be part of it, man! You make me know that killin Deek the onliest way I get my brother back!"

Furball coughed and spat blood on the floor. He held the knife so its point poked through Lyon's shirt but hadn't cut him yet. "Shit," Furball rasped, "somethin busted inside me. I can feel it."

"You heart?" Lyon asked softly.

"Get real, sucker!" Furball coughed again. "That got busted a long, long time ago!" Then he sighed and wiped his mouth with the back of his free hand. "Okay, magic boy. I play this game with you. But if Ty get killed tonight, you gonna stand to me just like you doin right now an I gonna cut YOUR fuckin heart out forever so's it don't go givin nobody else no stupid ideas. Deal, man?"

"Word," said Lyon. He smiled his V. "An it be on the left side, man."

"What is?"

"The heart."

"I know."

"*My* left, not yours."

"Oh." Furball shifted the knife momentarily, then lowered and folded it. "Funny, huh? Seem somehow like it oughta be on the right."

The kid was cornered, cracked to the max, and lying like a dog. Ty had him backed into the deep, dark doorway of a dusty-windowed junk shop, cowering against rusty accordion bars which weren't even locked because there was nothing behind them worth stealing. The small, lean-muscled boy, maybe eleven or twelve, was so wasted from smoking his own profits he could barely stand. Mostly he pleaded, but threw in a threat now and then. His begging bought no sympathy from Ty's tired heart, and his threats were as empty as the blackness at his back where not even a night light burned. Ty felt the way he had in the phone booth; weak and sick yet with something inside that sparked feebly without finding fuel to catch flame. Images kept drifting through his mind, blurring what should have been solid and hard; like the time last year when he'd had the flu and a fever so bad that for two days he hadn't known if the comings and goings of his family around him were real or just in his head. He remembered having a serious talk with Danny about sex... while all the time the boy had been in school. Now he thought of those piles of old batteries, their cells dead and empty, and the plates that had once produced power all warped and dry and falling apart.

The small boy's lying and babble seemed to filter through a dirty fog. It didn't matter: Ty had heard it all before, too many times for it to touch him anymore. In a way it was like *being* a battery... a jumper battery that had had its juice sucked down so often trying to start worn-out engines that it would never hold a full charge again. It was funny, though, with the world all hazy around him, that smells could stand out so sharp: the small boy stank with a sourness that reminded Ty of a motor struggling to burn the rotten old gas his dad had siphoned out of abandoned cars. Their truck would barely run on the stuff, smoking and spitting and sometimes stalling dead with its filter clogged with rust and varnish. Even a big old truck engine needed clean fuel. His dad had joked that the siphoned shit from the wrecks would be pure poison to the new little motors made today.

Not long ago, maybe a month, this kid had been one of the showtimes: designer jeans, moon-boot Reeboks, three-bill bomber jacket bought to match Ty's, and a do so sharp it needed biweekly tuning. That kind of kid burned out fast but brought in big bucks while he lasted. Ty tried to remember what the boy had looked like when he'd first started; ragged, underfed, and hungry as hell for all those good things locked behind bars and glass. Danny's face drifted through Ty's mind, but he made it go away. Besides, this boy looked nothing like Danny, and had gotten everything a way cool little black dude would want. And now the ride on Santa's magic sleigh was over.

"Straight up, Ty! Word, man! I got jumped! Just now! Big

suckers... bigger'n you, even! Rousted all my buck! Swear to God, man!"

Ty wiped a hand over his forehead. It came away wet. He forced his eyes to focus on the kid, not even sure if he'd heard his exact words. It didn't matter; whatever the boy was saying would sound something like that. What it translated to was... *taka-taka:* a thousand dollars' worth of shitty fuel burned up by a fine-tuned little engine that had finally stalled in rush-hour traffic.

"Swear to God," Ty repeated in a murmur. "What make you figure He give a shit?"

The boy gave him a strange look. "Huh?"

Ty shook his head slowly. "I give you a jump start just last week. A warnin, an one more chance. What it is, my own battery almost dead. Cars pilin up behind you. Onliest thing left to do is shove you out the way."

"Huh?" The kid was staring now, his eyes red and wild but suddenly scared despite all the shit in his brain.

Ty went on, listening to his own voice as if it were somebody else's. "Deek want you stripped for parts. Left in the gutter on blocks to show others what happen to burned-out junk."

The little boy tried to look fierce and bad. "Shut up, sucker! I ain't ascared of you!" He stabbed a finger at the Train bottle half sticking from Ty's jacket pocket. "You drunk! I can take you, man!"

Ty sighed. He pulled out the bottle, drank the rest, and tossed it over his shoulder, hearing it smash on the sidewalk behind him. The shatter of glass made the little boy wince. Ty studied him through the fog in his mind: at least Danny's old Nikes, 501s, and castoff tank top had a dignity of sorts, never having been much to begin with. But nothing looked worse than expensive, cool clothes turning into dirty rags.

There was still a gold chain, and an earring glinted half the price, thought Ty, of a ton-and-a-half truck. The boy would have cash in his pockets, or probably stashed somewhere on him in what he figured was an original hiding place. And there was the little .32 Colt pistol in the back of his jeans, worth an easy two bills, and which the kid would try to do him with very soon now. Crack was intense, but cruelly quick. On top, where the boy had been a minute ago, you were pumped to the max, and it wouldn't have surprised Ty if the little kid had gone for him with only his fists. The kid's eyes still glittered with danger, but snot glistened on his lip. His fingers, small and perfect, twitched, and one hand was already inching toward the gun. The fall from grace was fast; into pure hell and paranoia where everyone was THE ENEMY and wanted you dead or worse. It was funny how, for these kids, that was often the real truth.

Seconds passed as Ty tried to make his tired mind work. Through the fog that wasn't real he could scent the dank mustiness of the junk-shop merchandise piled behind cracked windows that were held together by bolted plywood patches. The small boy's breathing was shallow and fast. Ty could swear he heard the kid's heartbeat above the low rumble of the Trans-Am idling at the curb. They were on a shadowy side street just around the corner from a block of bars and nightclubs where the boy did most of his business, and the deep bass boom of rap seemed to vibrate the concrete underfoot. Then, from light-years away, Ty heard the faint, sweet singing of angels. For a second, Ty forgot the dangerous little boy and his gun. He was suddenly six again, and sitting beside his mother in church.

Then he remembered the shabby storefront up near the next corner with its childish painting of a dark-skinned Jesus in one dirty window. He should have known there would be no miracles in Oakland; that nobody was going to die for his sins except himself.

The little kid went for his gun.

He wasn't Danny, and Ty was up for the move. The Colt was almost new, nickel-plated and ivory-gripped, a bright shiny toy for a cool niggerboy. It flashed in the shadows as Ty grabbed the kid's wrist and twisted. The gun clattered on the pavement just like Danny's knife. But this boy wasn't Danny, and he didn't scream as Ty twisted harder. He had his own dirty fog to muffle his mind. This boy wasn't Danny, and Ty wrenched his wrist until there was a soft snap of bone. Then the boy screamed, but only for a second until Ty's fist smashed into his mouth.

Ty didn't pull his own gun; the kid was beyond threats. If he had to use the .45 there would be only one reason. A broken wrist would have stopped any normal twelve-year-old, but this boy hardly realized he was hurt. For the first few seconds Ty felt fear as punches that would have put older dudes on their knees just rocked the kid around like one of those rolly-bottomed toys that always bounced back for more. The boy beat and kicked savagely back at Ty, even using his slack-wristed hand. Old horror movies played in Ty's mind; of fighting the living dead who couldn't feel pain. It was almost a surprise to see and smell bright fresh blood instead of something rotten and green gushing from the boy's mouth and nose. And tears on his cheeks.

Corpses couldn't cry.

The kid choked on blood. It sprayed dark and glistening as Ty hit him in the stomach once, twice, and again with all the strength in his own body. He felt the knife slash rip open beneath the bandage. He remembered a scrap-yard crane, its throttle jammed wide open and engine running wild, screaming in iron agony until the operator had ripped off his shirt and smothered its air intake. Even a heartless machine needed air. Ty stepped warily back and let the kid fall to his knees, where he doubled and puked something that didn't seem much like food.

Behind the diamond pattern of bars, Ty saw Deek's reflection in the door glass. He was sitting in the car, arms crossed on the windowsill, chin resting on top, and that same science-class expression on his face as when watching the two big boys die.

"Kick him," Deek advised.

But Ty only gazed down at the kid while his own chest heaved for breath and his heart struggled like a water pump sucking air. The pain in his arm seemed to lash him like fire when he saw the way the boy's hand was hanging. Ty shook his head hard to clear the fog, then bent and snagged the Colt, automatically snapping on the safety before slipping it into his jacket. He leaned down again and pulled the gold chain over the boy's lowered head.

"Yo! The earring too!" Deek called. "Was my motherfuckin buck bought it. Just tear it out, man."

But Ty undid the tiny catch, almost gently even though his fingers felt numb, and eased the ring from the boy's earlobe. Then he straightened and waited a few moments more, but the boy's brain had finally got word that the body it lived in had been badly hurt. No fight was left as Ty took the kid under the arms and hauled him to his feet, then propped him like a dead thing back against the bars. A tiger-striped nylon wallet Ty pulled from the boy's pocket held two bucks and some ones. There was also a Boys' and Girls' Club card, a school picture of a pretty girl, and an old faded one that was probably his mom and little sister. And a Trojan. Ty closed his eyes, wondering why the beautiful memory of last night's lovemaking with Markita was playing in his mind. The boy was still bent over, clutching at his stomach with his good hand while the other hung useless at his side. He whimpered, dry-heaving and spitting more blood, thick little bubbles of it frothing from his nostrils. Slowly, he slid down again, his shirt riding up so the rusty bars raked his back, to sit in the stinking puddle he'd made. The babyish smell of piss-wet jeans drifted in the air.

Kneeling, Ty pulled off one of the kid's Reeboks and checked it and the sock for money. Nothing. He did the same with the other, not much surprised when the result was the same... the boy was too smart for that. Ty sighed once more, and rocked back on his heels. Faintly from up the Street, above the booming of rap and the soft sullen purr of the 'Am's idling engine, the choir singing carried.

Then came Deek's voice cutting through. "Little shit owe me a grand, man! Get your ass busy, stupid!"

The boy's retching had stopped, and he just sobbed and moaned while his nose bubbled blood. His body was still numbed by the crack, but that little mercy would be gone all too soon, leaving him alone on the dark street with a broken bone and maybe, as hard as Ty had hit him, something else smashed up inside. There were things in the night who would prey on even what little was left. Ty felt rage sparking, throwing off fire like a Chinatown pinwheel. "Maybe," he murmured, "I leave you your soul."

He reached to the kid's crotch and pulled open the zipper. The boy wore shorts, a luxury denied Ty and his brothers. The rage kept sparking as Ty felt in the warm and wet where only a few sparse curls had sprouted. He found the wad of bills. The boy's earthly debt was paid. Jamming the money into his jacket atop the gun and the gold, Ty stood. Suddenly, he cocked back his foot for a kick.

Then he saw Deek grinning in the glass. "Do it, nigger!"

The choir voices soared up out of the city on the wings of a note as pure and sweet as a young child's laughter. Dark angels, thought Ty, as the sparking pinwheel spun. He whirled around and stalked to the car, where he wordlessly yanked the two hundreds from the kid's wallet, added them to the mass of cold metal and warm wet money, and flung the whole handful past Deek and onto the floor.

"Hey!" yelled Deek.

But Ty had turned away. He went back to the junk-shop door and jerked the boy to his feet by his good hand. The kid whimpered but didn't resist. Ty stuck the wallet into his jeans.

"What's this shit, man?" Deek demanded.

Ty only shook his head. "Collectin his soul ain't my motherfuckin job."

Ty pulled the boy a few paces up the sidewalk. The kid stumbled on his bare feet through the glass of Ty's bottle, crying,

"No!" in a voice without hope. Then his legs gave and he fell to his knees. Ty gathered him up and slung him over one shoulder. Deek's curses echoed in the empty street as Ty walked on. Through the fog, Ty heard the car pull away and pace him. Deek's shouts of rage were muffled. Only the angel song carried clear.

The storefront church was a pitiful parody of God's house on earth. The angels had heard of Ty's coming, and fled. Ty blinked in the glare of one big naked bulb as he kicked the door open. Its glass pane shattered with a jagged kind of music. There was one small room, high-ceilinged and narrow like the rib shop. The walls were bare Sheet-rock with a few African Bible pictures Scotch-taped to them like the torn-out magazine images of rock and rap groups that kids always worshipped. The floor was cracked and curling linoleum, and a long way from clean. The altar was a kitchen table draped in cheap crimson velvet, and the sweaty-faced preacher behind it looked like a fat-assed Uncle Remus from the Disney cartoon. On the wall at his back hung a picture of what could have been a black Jesus or a nigger faggot. There were a few rows of battered folding chairs. Besides the preacher and the six choir members, there were maybe a dozen other people: mostly old women, a few old men, and two wide-eyed little girls about four and five.

The sweet singing had shattered to jagged pieces like the door glass when Ty busted in with his bloody stinking burden. Metal chairs creaked like old bones as people turned to stare. Outside, Ty heard Deek's car pull up and stop.

Ty glared around the now silent, shabby room. The .45 was in his hand before he knew it. He jabbed the gun toward the fat preacher, and the man paled and slumped against the wall beneath the black Jesus.

"LIAR!" bawled Ty. He desperately searched faces but found only fear. "How much?" he demanded of the people. "How much you payin him to lie to you?"

There was no answer, and Ty had expected none. The ceiling above didn't split open. No lightning bolt struck him down. The little girls began to cry. Ty was sorry for that. "Suffer, little children," he softly said.

Staggering under the boy's weight, Ty stumbled up what passed for an aisle. Blood, the young boy's and his own, dripped a trail behind. Reaching the velvet-draped table, he knocked the preacher's big Bible to the floor with a sweep of the gun barrel and laid the boy gently down. The people were watching but nobody moved. In no face did Ty find compassion, least of all the preacher's... except, strangely enough, in the little girls'. Only their eyes seemed to see the bleeding boy and not the gun. The preacher cowered back against the wall. Ty spat at his feet, and the man flinched. The boy on the altar had curled into a sobbing ball of pain. Ty faced the people once more, and pointed with the gun. "HE the one dyin for your sin, suckers!"

Spinning around, Ty straight-armed the pistol above the preacher's head. The .45's blast beat from the walls and echoed loud in the little room as Ty emptied its clip into the heart of the picture. The preacher sank down to a quivering mass on the floor below it. He hid his face in his hands.

Ty jammed the smoking gun into his jacket, then stabbed a

bloody finger at the boy. His rage was draining away, leaving him cold and empty. His voice, when it came, was quiet and sad. "Save *him,* niggers. That the onliest way you save yourselfs."

Ty walked back out on the street and got into Deek's car.

Deek smoked rubber, peeling away fast, and eyeing Ty all the while with real amazement. "Hell, man!" he muttered, awe in his tone. "I never knowed you had *that* kinda power in ya!"

"Jesus," snickered Deek as he eased the 'Am around a corner. "I mean, whatever possessed ya, man?"

Ty said nothing. Deek had produced another bottle of Train, and Ty was just holding it in his hands. Now he twisted off the cap and drank.

"Stuff make ya chase your mother," said Deek.

Ty recapped the bottle, then concentrated on reloading the .45's clip from a box of bullets in the glove compartment.

"Well. Check. It. Out. My man," said Deek, pointing with his Sherman. "Tell me that ain't Miss Rwanda 1992! Hell, she so totally African she still cook with flies!"

Ty hardly heard Deek. He shook his head to thin the fog. Maybe he'd been listening inside his mind for angels—*real* angels—coming after him and pissed as hell. In a way that would be a relief. Then Ty saw Markita across the street, trudging home, her hands buried in the pockets of her old Navy coat, its high, upturned collar hiding her face.

Ty slipped the pistol back into his jeans. "Leave her be, man," he said as Deek started cranking down his window to yell something.

Deek swung around with a scowl as they passed the girl. She didn't look up, though Ty knew she'd marked the car and probably guessed he was in it.

"Yo! What in hell's wrong with you tonight?" Deek demanded. "You sick or somethin, stupid?"

Ty drained the bottle in a few guips and dropped it on the floor. "Somethin stupid," he repeated in a murmur while gazing at the outside mirror. He watched the girl melt into the darkness and wished he'd seen her face.

Deek snorted. "Yo, sucker! What the fuck's THAT sposed to mean? Hey, check yourself, man... all sweaty an smelly. An for Christ sake DO somethin bout that goddamn blood fore it get all over my motherfuckin car!" He punched Ty in the shoulder, his scowl deepening when Ty hissed and clenched his teeth. "Yo. It your fuckin arm, ain't it, man? That stupid sucker brother of yours give you affection!"

Ty nodded slowly. "Yeah... yeah, got to be what it is. First time in my goddamn life I get some an it got to come from him. Funny."

"Ain't nuthin funny bout it, stupid." Then Deek's face softened slightly. "Mmm. Sorry, Ty. I didn't know." He peered ahead to where the car-wash lot made an empty gap in the next block of buildings like missing teeth in an old dog's snarl. "But this one fuck of a time to go an get sick on me, man. I ain't spectin no shit from Wesley an his little rag-asses, but it for sure gonna make me look like a goddamn fool if you go an pass out or somethin." He turned to study Ty. "Yo. Can you hang together another hour, man?"

"Hell," Ty mumbled. "I hold together another month."

"Huh?" Deek gave him a strange look, then dug a tiny bottle from his jacket pocket. "Here, dude. Take a snort. It fly your ass through."

Ty glanced at the white powder and suddenly shivered. "No. I... cool, Deek. Let's just get it done, okay?"

Deek nodded, and slipped the bottle back into his pocket, then pulled out a Hershey bar. He snapped it in two, handed half to Ty, then gently patted Ty's shoulder. "Yo, homeboy, soon's this deal done I takin you uptown to one of them duty-doctor places. They make you all better again, believe."

Ty met Deek's eyes, remembering even Lucifer had once been a handsome young prince. If God were really all-loving and all-merciful, did it mean that even the Prince of Darkness had only to go down on his knees to Him and beg forgiveness to be saved?

But then who would run hell?

Deek popped the last of the candy bar into his mouth and licked his fingers. "Better pack the Uzi tonight, man. Show em where we comin from. Sides, way you look, you prob'ly couldn't hit jack with that .45 if them little suckers try some shit."

Ty took Deek's carbine from the back seat, leaving the pair Deek was going to deal Wesley, both minus their magazines. Up the street, Ty saw a lanky boy standing at the car-wash entrance. The boy flashed a hand signal to others unseen, then pulled the chain post from the ground. Ty caught a flicker in the mirror; a car was rounding a corner a couple blocks behind. Its headlights silhouetted Markita's slim figure, still back on the last block. Deek noticed the lights too. His eyes shifted between the mirrors and the lot. The lanky boy had dropped the chain and stood waiting.

Ty knew that Deek was debating whether the cool move would be to cruise on past and circle around once more so as not to be seen pulling into the lot.

"Shit!" muttered Deek. "Yo. Figure that car back there a cop, man?"

Ty turned and squinted through the rear window. "No way to tell from here. But it ain't movin very fast. Cops cruise like that."

"Mmm. Yeah. But so do any car fulla dudes lookin for action or trouble." Deek checked the mirrors again. "Naw. Can't be no cops, man. Car slowin down back by your African queen." He grinned. "Hope they don't give her no shit."

Ty remembered the night before, Markita coming up the alley alone with just her silly little can of Mace. "She be cool," he said, hoping it was true.

"Mmm. Look like you been bit, my man. You two make a way cool couple, like prom night in the Congo or somethin." Then Deek grinned. "Shit, who am I to stand in the way of true love, man." He cut the car into the lot, killing the lights as they passed the watcher boy, who moved quickly to replace the post.

Ty put the last bite of candy into his mouth, tasting blood from his fingers on the chocolate. He scanned the wash bays as Deek motored along the front of the structure before swinging around to the rear. The moon was high, and its light didn't penetrate far into the four short tunnels. From what he could see they seemed empty except for the corpse of a car in the last one. He checked the Uzi, making sure the stock was locked open, the clip fully seated, and the select-fire switch all the way forward to A. He cocked the bolt, and caught himself whispering a prayer that he wouldn't have to shoot any kids. That thought was funny, sad, and frightening all at the same time. Who in hell did he figure could be listening anyhow?

The wash structure's shadow stretched halfway across the back of the lot. Beyond the moonlit strip of weedy asphalt that glittered here and there with broken bottle glass was a six-foot chain-link fence and then a big storm-drain channel. There was water in it tonight, glinting like gunmetal under the moon. Ty supposed it had something to do with tides in the Bay. Anyhow, the water left no place outside the fence for anyone to hide. Ty turned his attention back to the wash bays. It took effort to keep his mind clear and concentrate on his job, but everything—his own escape from the cage, Danny's future, and maybe even Danny's life—depended on protecting Deek. Ty glanced toward the fence again, noting the low square shape of a battered vacuum box. One small kid might conceal himself behind it, but why? Even these young boys wouldn't be stupid enough to try an ambush with just one kid hidden there. Besides, the only fire the Crew had was an old snub-nosed .38 like TV detectives carried. A short-barreled revolver like that was only good at close range, and then only in the hands of an expert shot. A kid would hardly be able to hit anybody with it over thirty feet away, except by stupid blind luck. And Ty saw that all the gang were gathered in plain sight at the edge of the moon shadow, strictly by rules.

Except for Wesley, Ty didn't know their names but there were five boys here, which left the sixth watching the gate, just like the other times when Deek had met them in this place. Wesley was

even holding the .38 up by its barrel. Ty relaxed as much as he
dared without letting the fog flood back into his mind, but scanned
the wash bays once more as the Trans-Am growled to a stop and
its engine settled into a silky-smooth idle. From this side of the
structure there was a clear view through to the moonlit street
beyond. The junk car's roof was mostly caved in, so there wasn't
much chance of anybody hiding inside. And yet Ty couldn't shake
the feeling that there were other eyes watching him besides those
of the five boys standing in the moonlight. It had to be in his head,
he decided. He studied the kids, thinking how they looked like
ebony sculptures... somehow pure and fine in the cold silver glow.
It was sad to know that some would be dead in just a few years,
crushed beneath the pyramid, a structure that stood only by
keeping the best and strongest bricks on the bottom to hold up the
old rotten ones on top. What would happen if those bottom bricks
just slipped out from under? That thought made a funny cartoon
picture in Ty's mind.

Deek slapped the stick into neutral, pulled the parking brake,
and then snagged one of the empty Uzis from the back seat. "Yo,
Wes man!" he called, holding the gun up sideways. "Check out
your future, dude!"

Ty popped his door and slid from the car. He saw the kids'
eyes widen a little when they checked that he carried the carbine.
They would know from the clips that his was loaded while the one
Deek would deal them wasn't. Ty noted that they were careful to
keep from bunching together, but at this range, with a full-auto,
they would also know that it wouldn't much matter.

Deek opened his door and got out. "Yo, Wes. What it is, why

don't you just go an put that there little toy of yours on my hood, an let's all be ground-floor cool." He snickered. "Careful bout my paint, man."

Wesley stepped forward and laid the .38 on the 'Am's hood, where it vibrated lightly to the engine's idle. Ty hardly glanced at the gun, except to note how cheap and toylike it looked... like a Taiwanese copy of a Colt. But, mostly, he scanned the boys' faces: even street-hardened kids like these hadn't yet learned to completely cover their quick-changing emotions. Still, their expressions stayed guarded and cool, eyes watching Deek with wild-animal wariness and shifting sometimes to Ty's Uzi to check where it pointed. That was normal enough, yet something *was* different tonight: Ty could feel it; almost like walking into a room where some other dudes had been talking you down or telling a joke that you missed. The kids were avoiding his eyes instead of flashing occasional glares of challenge to show they were bad and not scared of him. If he were in school, Ty would have checked for a tack on his seat or a sign Scotch-taped to his back saying: KICK ME.

But he wasn't in school. This was real-time, where missing the joke could mean death. His voice came out rusty, and he coughed to clear his tight throat. "Maybe I better search em, Deek? This here neutral ground, we gots the right."

Wesley snorted contempt. He wore no shirt anyway, but nodded to his dudes, who stripped off theirs and turned around slow, arms out, while Ty watched. Tight jeans showed worn spots on pockets, and bulges that were probably blades, but Ty wasn't worried about knives. The kids didn't look like fine little sculptures anymore, just dirty, snot-nosed, rag-ass niggerboys. Ty expected more contempt to flash on Wesley's face, but seemed to get speculation instead. Whatever the joke was, he'd missed it again. He scanned the roly fat boy, whose apron of loose lard hung even lower than Deek's. Stepping to the kid, he felt below his belly where there was plenty of room to hide a small gun.

The boy giggled. "Yo! Tickles, man."

Deek grinned as Ty moved away and the boys slipped back into their shirts. "Ty here take good care of me, huh, dudes?"

Ty's finger curled tense on the Uzi's trigger as Deek handed the empty carbine to Wesley. One of the other kids, a skinny little boy whose huge Army Desert Storm shirt made him look like a camouflaged bat, suddenly let go a loud and childish germ-spraying sneeze. Ty's finger jerked tight at the sound. He wanted to slap the little sucker the way his own mom would have whacked him at Danny's age for something like that. Newspaper words floated through his mind: TWELVE-YEAR-OLD SHOT FOR SNEEZING.

"Ty! Help!" screamed a voice. It was Danny!

The gang boys froze, but their eyes flicked to the vacuum box. Ty couldn't tell if their faces showed rage or fear. He clutched the Uzi, covering the kids, ready to fire, and feeling the trigger spring tighten behind his finger. Nobody moved. Danny's voice called again, sounding hurt. "Ty! Hurry!"

Deek's head whipped back and forth between Ty and Wesley. "What's this shit?" he bawled.

Ty was staring toward the fence: Danny had to be behind the vac box. Rage blasted the fog from Ty's brain so things stood out sharp-edged and stark the way they had in the church. He jabbed the Uzi one-handed at the gang while jerking the .45 from his jeans. "Nobody move!" he shouted. "You God DAMN little animals! You hurt my brother, I fuckin kill you all!" Snapping off the .45's safety, he skidded the Uzi across the car's hood to Deek.

Deek snagged the gun and covered the kids. He flashed Ty a furious glare. "That motherfuckin little BASTARD! I tell you an tell you blood mean nuthin but trouble, but you too goddamn stupid to listen!" He stepped forward and jammed the gun muzzle to Wesley's chest. "All you suckers! Move close together! Way slow!"

Ty dashed for the vac box, his .45 up and ready. Wesley's scared voice quavered in his ears as he ran, pleading with Deek now, all cool gone. "It that cocksucker Furball, man! What make all this shit! He come here to do ya, Deek! Swear to God, man!"

But Ty didn't hear any more. His Nikes skidded on the rotten asphalt as he rounded the box and stopped, dizzy, sweating and panting even though the distance was less than fifty feet. Danny lay on his back in the narrow, shadowed space between the box and the fence. He was half naked, hands behind him, his knees drawn up, and his ankles tied together with what looked like strips of his shirt. Another satin strip hung loose at his neck like a gag he'd managed to work free. Even in the soft moonlight Ty could see that his brother had been badly beaten: his face puffy and caked with dried blood, lips swollen and split, and scratches all over his body. Fury flamed inside Ty. He *would* kill them! *All* of them! Slamming the pistol down on top of the box, he dropped to his knees at his brother's feet. From over at the car, Wesley's pleas carried to his ears. "Yo, Deek! *Listen,* man! He *follow* us, man! We *catch* him! Tie his ass up. Word! He say he come to *kill* you, man! I swear it!"

Lies! thought Ty, as he bent over his brother. Lies as stupid and childish as those of the snot-nosed dealer boy he'd dumped in the church. All these goddamned kids were lost! Save them? What a motherfuckin joke! They should be exterminated like the dirty, garbage-eating little black rats they were! Yet, though raging inside, Ty's voice came out a sob. "Danny!" He reached to gather the boy against him.

Something silver flashed in the moonlight. Suddenly Danny was sitting up, his arms free, and kicking the loose strip of satin off his legs while he pressed the muzzle of a shiny little revolver to Ty's heart. Ty froze. A cry choked off in his throat. Tears burned his eyes like battery acid. "No!" he whispered. "Not you, Danny. Jesus, not you too!"

Danny's eyes locked on his brother's, desperate and pleading. "Don't move, Ty! PLEASE! I love you, man! I swear it! But don't move!"

The fire in Ty flickered and died. Cold seemed to cover him, and he shivered, no longer sure what in the world was real anymore. Deek's voice could have come from the moon, calling, "Ty! What the fuck's goin on?"

Ty's mind wandered, lost in his own skull. His gaze drifted to the little gun in his brother's hands: it looked somehow familiar. The words came out stupid, like most of his words seemed to do. "What you swear it on, Danny?"

Ty saw tears glisten in Danny's eyes too. The boy's chin quivered and his ragged lips moved as if in prayer. "You, Ty. I swear it on you. I gots nuthin else, man."

Ty's hands were still outstretched and open. Slowly, he turned his head, looking past the pistol which lay just a foot from his face. At the car, the gang was still bunched together under Deek's gun. Deek's face and stance showed uncertainty. Wesley was still talking fast, pleading like a little kid caught doing something naughty, trying to explain what Danny was doing here and tied up. It sounded all too true in Ty's ears. He realized suddenly that Danny had come to save him. What a joke! But why was Danny holding a gun to his heart?

"Please, Ty," Danny whispered. "You gotta trust me, man! Listen! Last night, you say you love me so much you could kill me. I *know* what that mean now! An I love YOU that much, man! Believe. *Please!*"

Deek's voice cut through Danny's whisper. "TY! Goddamnit, what's up?"

Ty looked at the tears running down Danny's cheeks. He closed his eyes, but the fog flooded in and tried to smother him. He blinked and shook his head in confusion, and shivered once more, scenting his brother's fear over the smells of sweat and blood and sour saltwater from the storm channel. "Danny," he murmured. "I got to get you out of here." He turned toward Deek. "It... true. Danny been beat an tied up."

The Uzi wavered in Deek's chubby hands. He eyed Wesley a few moments more, then lowered the gun. "Mmm. Sorry, my man. Look like you done me a favor." His eyes flicked over to Ty, and he spat on the ground. "Just too motherfuckin bad you dudes didn't go all the way with that little sucker. Maybe we talk more bout it another day." Letting the gun hang one-handed, he faced Ty and called, "Yo, stupid! Get that little shitball out here so's we get this deal done! You an me, man, we gots some major talkin to do later on!"

Wesley grinned as he fingered the unloaded carbine. "Yo, Deek! We come a cunt hair close to doin that dude already. Word! Hey, you oughta go on over an check him out, man. Major street pizza or what!"

"Yeah?" Deek looked back toward the box. A smile spread slow over his face. "Mmm. Yo, Ty! Just chill there a minute, man!" Deek gestured casually to the gang with the gun muzzle. "Yo, Wes. Just you leave your little ole toy there on my hood an you an your way cool dudes come with me, huh?"

Deek was all moves, Ty thought: he kept the kids in front of him as they came across the lot. The gang boys were snickering and grinning now, puffed and proud of what they'd done to Danny, practically pissing themselves like puppies under Deek's praise. Heartless little animals, all of them... lost. And the Bible said, "A little child shall lead them!"

Ty tensed then: what would happen when they saw that Danny had a gun? Ty noted Wesley's .38 left lying on the Trans-Am's hood. The vibration of the engine was inching it forward. In a moment it would slide off and hit the ground. It was such a cheap-looking thing it might even fall apart. But what would that matter? These little animals would leave here tonight with an Uzi. One day, maybe they'd turn on Deek. "I got to get you out of here, Danny," Ty whispered again.

It was almost a surprise when Ty felt the gun still pressed to his chest. He looked down at it, and suddenly knew why it seemed familiar: he'd seen it last in the pawlike hand of that strange-eyed slender boy. Ty's mind began running around in his skull like something trapped. How had Danny gotten it? Why? Deek and the smaller boys were nearing. "No, Danny!" Ty hissed. "Don't do it, man! You gots no chance alone... an we *need* Deek!"

Tears still flowed down Danny's face, silver in the moonlight. "No, we don't!" he whispered back. "That a lie, man! We all dyin for cause we believe that lie! You an me, man, we DON'T need his kind!"

Ty looked up again. The .45 atop the box was so close! But what could he do with it now? Then he caught a movement at one end of the wash structure: it was the lanky boy from the gate. He was easing carefully through the shadows, and he had a gun... *another* snub-nose revolver! He crossed a patch of moonlight. The gun's blue steel glinted cold. Ty stared back at the .38 on the hood. It had no metallic shine, and now it slipped off and fell, and the sound of it hitting the asphalt was so small that Ty heard it only because he was listening... a hollow, *plastic* clatter! The gang's snickering and boasting around Deek drowned the tiny noise. *There* was the joke, stupid! These little suckers had fooled him with a toy!

Danny was watching his brother's face. He seemed to read Ty's thoughts, and saw him suck breath for a warning yell to Deek.

Ty felt the gun muzzle rake across his chest, heard Danny's words, "I love you, man." Then Danny pulled the trigger.

Being killed was like nothing Ty had ever imagined. On TV it looked heroic and cool: in real-time fast and final. But it always happened to somebody else. The sound, with the gun jammed tight to his skin, hardly seemed more than a grunt. He saw orange fire spit back from the loose-fitting cylinder. Its flash lit Danny's face, but Ty couldn't read his brother's expression. There was no pain, only a slam to his side that knocked him over backward. It seemed almost funny being killed by such a pussy little gun. Danny had killed him because he loved him: child logic, but the same thing he'd said to the boy only last night. It made about as much sense as anything else in this twisted-up world. Ty knew he was dead before the pavement rushed up to crash against his back; knew it because he saw angels at last. They were small, dark angels, like bare-chested boys. And they glistened like ebony sheathed in crystal-clear fire. Beads of ice-flame, like molten chrome drops, scattered from their bodies as they came for him. All wore expressions of vengeance. It was funny that they had no wings, that they had to climb the fence like ordinary kids. But maybe God didn't give wings to little black angels.

A half block away, Markita heard the shots through a red fog of fury. The two cops, the black and the white who would rather see kids starve than let them eat garbage, were just getting back in their car, laughing. They'd searched her, alone there on the deserted street, searched her body with warm loving care. It wasn't rape, but rape would have left her feeling this same way. She was sure. They'd taken her Mace: she too could legally be turned out to die under the law's loving protection. They'd told her she was lucky she wasn't spending the night in jail. Maybe she imagined it, but she wondered now if they would have taken it if she'd been more cooperative. Translate: a good, submissive little niggergirl while they were feeling her up.

"Thing about Oakland," the black one was telling the white, "it's a real *cop's* town, know what I sayin?"

"I hear that, brother," chuckled the white, tossing Markita's Mace can onto the dash.

Then the shots had crackled up the street, the first one faint and muffled, then more: one, two, three, small-caliber and raggedly spaced, and finally the short stuttering burst of full-auto.

She watched, momentarily frozen, and forgotten by the cops as they piled into their cruiser. The white grabbed the microphone but the black caught his hand. "Wait, man! I'm sure that was junior-bad's car pulled into that lot up there! Best we check it out fore callin backup!" He dropped the car in gear and burned away, letting the door slam shut by itself.

Markita had seen Deek's Trans-Am motoring by, heard Too Short's old raunchy rap about cool Oaktown and all the bad bad niggers—and white people on TV worried about heavy metal turning *their* kids into twisted little suckers!—and noted Ty's tall profile in the car. She was sure he'd noticed her too. But then the cops had curbed her, smirking like dogs eating shit when they recognized her as the Burger King girl with the attitude, and she'd forgotten about Ty in her anger. But now she didn't hesitate. She bolted up the sidewalk for the car-wash lot. A hundred yards ahead she saw the cruiser slew sideways, tires whimpering, lurch nose-down for an instant as if undecided, then hit the chain head-on with its heavy push bars, snapping it like a cheap necklace.

Ty discovered he wasn't dead, and that the glistening ebony angels swarming over the fence were only wet kids. Danny had shot him in the shoulder... in that stupid showtime spot where every TV hero always took his lead. Ty lay on his back for a minute, dazed, with all hell busting loose on every side, and the only thing he could think was that Danny had even managed to miss bone. Ty felt his sleeve soaking with fresh blood, but the wound wouldn't kill him. Maybe that was luck. His arm didn't even hurt anymore; in fact, he could hardly feel it at all. He concentrated on getting his breath back. The shot seemed to have cleared the fog from his mind, as if something inside him had decided to throw all its remaining resources into survival. Still, for those first few seconds of ass-kicked reality, it was like being totally drunk and trying to follow some fast-action kid's game or skate moves from the sidelines.

The strange-eyed slender boy was the first over the fence which was stupid because he wasn't even armed. But *he* at least still looked like some sort of small avenging angel. He actually seemed to fly for a second as he leaped from the mesh, which was bent almost double under the weight of Gordon, the fat boy, and the twins scrambling over. He landed lightly on the vac box. Gordon hung by his elbows long enough to aim his .22 pistol and fire three orange flashing pops in Deek's direction. The bullets must have cut past just inches from the slender boy's ear but he never flinched.

Ty's hearing, dulled after he'd hit the ground, now came back with a crash. He heard all the kids screaming and yelling on every side while their leaders bawled commands and curses. It sounded like a major schoolyard fight. Danny's voice called, "Lion," and Ty saw him toss the nickel revolver to the slender boy. It took Ty a second to realize what that meant.

"YOU!" he yelled to the fragile-looking kid. *"You* set this up!"

The slender boy turned and met Ty's eyes for an instant. Maybe there weren't little black werewolves any more than there were ebony angels, but the name, Lion, came close enough. Then the boy was gone, not vanished exactly but blurring away as if only half real. Danny snatched the .45 from the top of the box and aimed double-handed for Deek.

"Danny! No!" Ty found he could move. He lunged for his brother. Deek's Uzi blasted a short burst of fire, yellow-orange flame licking out from its muzzle. Bullets thunked the vac box, spraying paint flakes and rust before the gun's recoil bucked its barrel skyward in Deek's hands and sent shots slicing the air over Ty's head. One bullet twanged off the fence mesh. From the edge of sight, Ty saw Deek spin in a frantic circle as the gang boys tried to move on him from all sides, some wielding knives. The Uzi spit another burst of flame and noise.

"Bail!" Wesley bawled to his dudes. He swung the unloaded carbine butt-first at Deek's head, but Deek dodged away and the boys scattered like windblown trash. Deek fired a few more rounds, trying to target one of the running kids. The small boy in the huge Army shirt yelped and pitched forward on the pavement, but scrambled up fast and darted away, one hand clutching his side.

Deek was no fool, Ty thought, even as he grabbed for Danny. Deek knew how fast his clip would empty on full auto and wasn't wasting shots until he marked the odds. Danny managed to fire the .45 once before Ty got a grip on his arm and pulled him down. The bullet went wild over Deek's head to rake paint chips from the wash structure's roof.

Danny screamed curses, tears still streaming down his face as he fought and bit at his brother. But Ty twisted the gun from his hands. A heavy bulk crashed onto the top of the box, buckling the thin sheet metal: Gordon. Ty slapped Danny aside and tried to grab Gordon's leg as the fat kid fired another .22 pop at Deek. But Gordon, seeing the shot miss, leaped down and pounded away after the Lion, his wet jeans slipping low while his shoes squished and spurted water.

Danny's small fist smashed into Ty's cheek, striking sparks in his brain. Ty backhanded his brother out of the way, then saw with horror that the Lion kid had dived into Deek's car and snagged the other Uzi off the back seat. He threw it to one of the twins. Now he'd found the two loaded magazines and bailed out with one in each paw. Ty tried to get a shot at him, but then Danny was clawing for the gun before he could aim. Ty jerked the trigger anyway, and the bullet starred the 'Am's windshield, sputting glass shards that glittered ice-blue as they scattered. The Lion hit the ground and rolled, yet managed to fling one clip to a twin and the other to Wesley, who leaped up and caught it one-handed from the air. The twins dropped to a crouch, frantically trying to figure out how to get their gun loaded.

Deek saw them, and whipped his Uzi around to cut them down. Wesley had his magazine in, but was struggling with the bolt, forgetting to hold in the safety lever so the gun would cock.

Gordon roared something at him, and Wesley found the problem. The bolt snicked back, ready. Ty tried to target Wesley, barely feeling Danny battering at him or hearing his pleading screams. The boy didn't understand! Deek *couldn't* die now!

Deek shouldered his gun to shoot down the twins, who had managed to get their Uzi loaded and cocked but were now, unbelievably, fighting over which one would fire it! All around, the unarmed boys of Wesley's gang were scooping up rocks and bottles and anything else throwable and hurling them at Deek. The small camouflaged kid had a bloodstain on his shirt but darted in to fling a rock. Most of the stuff missed Deek, and he didn't seem to notice when something did hit him, but the jiggly-fat boy heaved a Bud bottle that clunked the Uzi aside so the burst of bullets ripped up asphalt a foot from the twins instead of tearing into them. They stopped arguing. One let the other have the gun.

Then Ty saw the lanky boy break from the wash structure and dash toward Deek from behind, the .38 clutched ready in both hands. Desperately, Ty drove an elbow into Danny's stomach and broke free of his grip. He swung the .45, steadying it on top of the box for a straight shot at the kid. Something small and wet and savage crashed down on Ty's back. He glimpsed dripping dreadlocks framing a furious little-boy face and bared teeth. Then there were four small hands clamped on his gun arm and twisting it sideways.

Suddenly a shotgun blast roared out over the shouting and yelling of the kids. The lanky boy seemed to leap into the air. Bloody spray, black as oil in the moonlight, exploded from his chest. The shotgun blasted again, knocking the kid another yard before he hit the ground. He smashed face-down on the pavement, the .38 skidding away from his outflung hand. The boy's body quivered and twitched for a few seconds before going totally still.

Ty's ears were ringing from the gun roar, but there might have been silence for a moment or two. Danny and the Rasta kid had frozen and were no longer fighting him. Then Danny's cry cut the quiet, sounding as if it were ripped from his heart: "Turbo!"

Ty glanced at the body; dead kids always looked so small. Then he saw the crouching bulks of the two cops in the wash-bay shadows. The white one whipped the smoking shotgun around to target Gordon, who had his .22 aimed at Deek. The man pumped another shell into the chamber and sighted, while the black cop aimed his pistol at Wesley. Ty expected them to yell "Freeze!" but they didn't. A dark blur flashed at the edge of Ty's vision. He saw the slender little Lion, silver revolver in hand, leap to the Trans-Am's hood. Big teeth gleamed in a stark white snarl. The boy's voice was a pure animal scream, seeming too huge to come from his fragile frame at all. "THEY ON DEEK'S SIDE!"

It was true! Ty saw Deek bring the Uzi to his shoulder, aiming for the Lion. Then both cops swung their guns at him too. A voice echoed in Ty's mind, like the voice that had kept him from pulling the trigger last night. *"You be sellin ALL your little brothers, fool!"*

All three guns fired.

Markita had come running into the front of the lot just in time to see the two cops melt into the shadows of a wash bay. Their dark uniforms were perfect camouflage, except for the helmets, which looked like pale skulls floating. One carried a shotgun.

Markita skidded to a stop on the gravelly asphalt, panting back her breath, and not sure why she'd come or what she expected to do now. Nearby, halfway between the wash structure and the street, the cruiser idled quietly. From beyond the flimsy tin building came the screams and the shouting of what could have been a wild kid's game except for the gunshots. Markita had heard many gang fights before, but no one she cared about had ever been involved.

The cruiser's radio spat code words and static, tuned low. It took Markita a moment to realize what was wrong with the picture. The cops hadn't called in at the first sounds of shooting; they hadn't used their siren or strobes, and now both. doors stood open and all the lights were off. Only a tiny green eye that was probably the radio's pilot lamp glowed from the dark interior.

Moving warily, moon shadow going before her, Markita came up to the car. The cop had called him "junior-bad," but Markita had known he'd meant Deek. For sure there was always word about cops who took money from dealers, mostly to turn their backs but sometimes to protect them. But then there was word about everything in the city, and if it didn't touch you, you let it slide by. There was plenty of trouble going around without borrowing any.

Reaching the driver's door, scenting the cop smells she'd hated and feared half her life, Markita saw her Mace can still lying on the dash. Suddenly she wanted to run for home, like last night with Ty in the alley, and have her mother hold and comfort her even as she comforted J'row. Her mother would murmur the old words, promising that someday everything would be all right. And in another year, when her son would be old enough to discover the street and run crying home from its terrors, she would whisper those same goddamned old promises to him. And nothing cut a kid deeper than getting promises broken.

And *nothing* was all right! Day by day the cage seemed to close in tighter around her, crowded with things that clawed and tore at each other in a blind fight for a freedom they *knew* existed but saw only as second-hand shadows behind a TV screen. It was like the ancient cartoon where a starving wolf tried to eat a picture of a Thanksgiving turkey.

She trembled at the car door. She could feel her heart pounding as the alien smells and the radio's unknown language warned her away. Then her nostrils flared: "serve and protect"! The law had just helped itself to a serving of *her,* and then stolen her only protection! More shots sounded from the rear of the lot. She scented gunpowder smoke in the air. Stay clear, girl, her instincts warned, be cool; steal back what's yours by right, and then run home. She thought of what Leroy had said; maybe she did just have a thing for bad-acting dudes. But that's all Ty was doing... acting a part that the world wrote for black kids. Bad. Cool. The only protection, pitiful as it was, that couldn't be stolen; like children not allowed to play in the real game so they made up one of their own and pretended they didn't give a shit.

Two shotgun blasts roared out. An instant later came a warning scream. It hardly seemed human, more like something Markita had heard at the zoo or maybe in an old horror movie. But the words were plain, and so was their meaning: she'd known who *they* were for a long, long time. Snatching the Mace from the dashboard, she ran for the wash structure.

Danny and the Rasta boy had stopped fighting Ty when Turbo had died. Now they were both clinging to Ty as if he alone could save them from the same. The words still echoed in Ty's head: not the warning scream, but the other words, the ones meant only for him. Maybe they'd come from God, or maybe they'd been inside him all the time and it took the little Lion's magic to set them free. It didn't matter: what is, *is,* and what ain't, ain't worth nothing. And no magic could save the little Lion.

Ty fired his .45 just as the three other guns blasted at the slender boy. Ty caught only an eye-corner glimpse of the Trans-Am's windshield exploding inward and spraying slivers of glittering glass. But the fragile little Lion was gone!

Ty had no time for miracles. His first three bullets took Deek in the chest, where his heart would have been a long time ago. Whatever had replaced it was probably cool as hell, but it wasn't black. Deek spun half around, staggering backward, two of the bullets tearing on through him. His mouth opened but no sound came out. His eyes found Ty's an instant before he fell. Ty swore they looked disappointed. The Uzi's fire cut off, its empty brass still spinning across the pavement as Deek's dead hand unclenched from the safety. But Ty didn't wait to see him go down: he emptied the rest of the .45's clip at the cops, then yelled at the small boys beside him to run. Amazingly, both obeyed, darting in opposite directions along the fence line. Ty couldn't tell if he'd hit the cops, and they were armored anyway. Again the shotgun roared. The fence mesh twanged and a strand blew out just behind Danny, but the boy kept going.

The other kids of both gangs were dashing for shelter behind Deek's car. The black cop's pistol boomed again and again. The jiggly-fat boy screamed and went down, clutching one side of the chub roll at his waist. Gordon and Wesley both grabbed him and dragged him to safety. Another shotgun blast channeled asphalt inches from the Rasta kid's feet as he doubled back to snatch up Turbo's .38 before joining the other boys behind the Trans-Am. Were these kids really that brave, Ty wondered, or just too stupid to know any better? Then he remembered the Lion. He jerked his head around, expecting to see him blown apart like Turbo. Instead, the slender boy was just leaping down from the roof of the car... or the sky? No miracles in Oaktown; maybe just a way past cool skate move.

The cops were still firing, bullets and shotgun loads spewing gravel and pavement chunks, some slashing the water beyond the fence. Another blast from the shotgun crashed into the vac box, slamming the sheet-metal cover against Ty's chest. The big buckshot pellets clanged something solid inside, but one ripped through and tore into Ty's leg above the knee. Ty clutched at the place, blood running hot between his fingers. He fought back the pain and stared toward the car. Would those kids let him come?

Yes! Danny and the Lion were both signaling him to run. Gordon stood, bawling orders. One twin and another of Wesley's dudes had the roly-poly kid's shirt off and were crouching beside him as he sat against the car door. Wesley and the other twin were scrambling up along the 'Am's front fender with their Uzis. Both stood and opened fire across the hood at the cops. Gordon aimed the .22 around the shattered windshield and tugged on the trigger but it seemed to be jammed. "Ty!" screamed Danny. "C'mon!"

Ty shoved the crumpled cover away, but agony lashed up his leg when he tried to put weight on it. Another bullet banged the box. Wesley and the twin must have fired half their clips, the big carbines bucking upward in their small hands, their bullets raking the wash structure's sheet metal, ricochets clanging and whining away off the heavier trusses and brace beams. The shotgun roared in return. The Trans-Am rocked on its springs as the blast blew a huge hole in the left front fender and a headlight exploded in a spray of shards. Blood spurted from Ty's leg as he tried to get up. No way!

"Bail!" he shouted to the other boys. "Run, you stupid little suckers!" He sank down, crying, and whispered, "You poor little niggers!" He looked back toward the car. The boys were all watching him, waiting for him. Why? *What is.*

Using his good leg, gripping the box cover with one hand, Ty stood, exposed to fire from the waist up, his empty gun hot in bloody fingers. The gang kids were staring at him, wide-eyed now. Tears gleamed on Danny's face. Ty stabbed the gun at Deek's body. "Game over!" He aimed at the cops.

Markita saw Ty through the wash bay's short tunnel, over the crouching cops' shoulders. She stood at the front entrance, Mace can in hand, flinching back as full-auto fire raked the wall above the cops' heads. Moonbeams stabbed through the holes like light-show lasers while ricochets rattled and screamed all around. She'd seen Ty shoot Deek down, and then the muzzle flame from his .45 spurt out at the cops. One had grunted when a bullet hit his armor. Other bullets had hissed past her toward the street. One had thunked into the cruiser. She thought she could smell hot antifreeze. A quick glance over her shoulder showed steam ghosting up from the front of the car. Then the white cop snarled, "It's over! Bastard's own bodyguard took him out! *Animals!* Get that backup now!" Then he'd fired at Ty's little brother.

The black cop shot at the other running boys as they dashed for cover behind the dealer's car. "Got one!" he'd muttered when a fat kid went down, then cursed as he'd had to reload, and two other boys dragged the wounded kid away. He jerked the walkie-talkie from his belt, thumbed a button, and called some words, then cursed again. "Goddamn steel all around! Like a motherfuckin cage in here!"

More Uzi fire blasted from over the Trans-Am's hood.

"Get back to the car!" yelled the white cop. "Those little shitheads ain't gonna run!"

The black cop started to scuttle away. "Move yourself, man! We out-gunned an a half!"

The white cop backed deeper into the bay, but suddenly stood and shouldered his shotgun. Markita gasped, seeing Ty stand unprotected.

"*He* knows!" the white cop snarled. "Nobody'll listen to those little suckers, but *he* can shit all over us!"

"So take him! Who's gonna care?" The black cop turned to bolt for the cruiser.

Markita leaped in front of the man, Mace can out in both hands, and sprayed him full in the face.

The big man screamed, dropping his gun and clawing at his eyes. Markita flung the can at the white cop, then tore the black cop's club from his belt and ran at the white one. His head had whipped around when the Mace can bounced off his back, and now he ducked in time to take Markita's wild swing on his helmet.

"Nigger BITCH!" The man jammed the shotgun butt into Markita's stomach, slamming her back, then jerked up the shotgun to blow Ty away.

"Ty! DOWN!"

It was the little Lion. Ty saw him break from behind the car and race for the cop. The stupid little sucker was going try taking out a shotgun with that pussy piece of shit! To save *him!*

The other boys saw it too. Gordon roared a warning. Wesley and the twin aimed their Uzis at the cop but couldn't shoot now without hitting the Lion. The Rasta kid dashed after him with the .38. Ty saw the shotgun swing from him to the Lion. The slender boy's shape was strangely blurred, like some sort of double image of something bigger around him. The kid would vanish, Ty thought, believe!

The little nickel-plated revolver spat one flash of fire just as the shotgun blasted. Above the roar, Ty heard the Rasta boy scream the Lion's name, and Danny's voice echo it. The shotgun load blew the Lion's slim chest apart and flung his body backward against the Trans-Am's grille.

Sudden silence switched on. The shotgun slipped from the white cop's hands and hit the concrete. The man groped at his throat where the one little bullet had buried itself. Blood pumped in gushes through his fingers. He made wet, strangled sounds as he crumpled face-down beside his gun.

Ty saw the other kids gathering around the little Lion's body.

From beyond the wash structure came a man's cries and curses and the sounds of puking. Then Ty saw Markita come running to him from the shadows.

Ty tried to move to her, but his leg buckled under him. He grabbed the box to keep from falling. Pain shot up his arm like he'd dipped it in fire. His sight blurred. Blackness rushed in from the edges, almost familiar now. The fog was coming back.

Dimly, Ty felt Markita take hold of him. Then a small figure appeared from nowhere to help: Danny. Ty took a few stumbling steps, one arm over Markita's shoulders, the other around his brother. Maybe this fog *was* real, he thought, the kind that drifted in off the Bay. Real or not, it was getting hard to see. Small forms surrounded him: not little angels, only kids. There were Wesley and Gordon, standing together, the other gang boys all around—except for the little Rasta, who stayed crying at the Lion's side. Scents of gunpowder and blood and kid sweat filled Ty's nostrils. Wesley was pointing. "You want we do him, man?"

It took Ty a second to realize what Wesley meant. The black cop was staggering in blind circles, trying to find the cruiser. Ty noticed two things in Markita's hand: a cop's belt radio and a microphone with a broken cord, little colored wires sticking out. That reminded him of something, but the fog was thickening, closing in, and he couldn't think very good. "No," he heard himself say. "He can't hurt us no more."

Ty tried to focus his eyes on all the young faces. For the moment there was no need to be cool or bad and they were just kids again.

"Game over," said Ty. "Go home."

The blackness took him away.

Ty woke to the sound of a young child's laughter. It wasn't an angel but it was close enough for Oaktown, and probably the closest he'd ever get to the real thing. He opened his eyes, blinking in the soft golden sunlight streaming through the window. It had that pure, clean sparkle of early morning. A square of it fell on the floor nearby, and J'row sat in the center, laughing. The little boy was naked except for baby-blue Huggies, and the sunlight shone warm and beautiful on his ebony velvet skin.

Ty blinked again as his vision came into focus like the opening scene of a movie. Danny was on the floor with J'row, his legs in a V around the child. He was beautiful too. It took Ty a second before he noticed Danny's new clothes... nothing showtime, just 501s that fit him right, the big Nikes he'd always wanted, and a black satin tank top his own size. His hair was still a wild bush, but it glistened now in the sun. He was sharing bites of a grape Popsicle with J'row, and both were bent over the little Speak 'N Spell computer. Ty tried to make words, but his throat and lips were swollen and dry and his tongue felt thick and clumsy. He gave it up and looked around.

He was in Markita's apartment... in her bed. The scent of her lingered on the pillow and sheets, waking a warmth in his loins that surprised him. The frilly spread was folded neatly at his feet, and he was naked beneath the single blanket. His body felt clean, as if he'd just been bathed. There were stiff new bandages on his forearm and around his biceps and leg. They smelled and felt professional. There was a tightness to the skin of his forearm that had to be stitches... at least he supposed that's what stitches would feel like. There wasn't much pain but he felt weak all over, like when he'd had the flu and the fever had finally broken. His eyes roamed the room; even by daylight it looked warm and safe. Against the wall by the hallway door two skateboards stood together, his and Danny's.

Then he heard Markita laugh. "Oh, Danny, you can't program it to *say* them kinda words."

Danny giggled... not a smart-ass snicker, but a sound as innocent as J'row's, who joined in too.

Ty turned his head, squinting at the computer's little screen. "Danny!" he croaked. "Jesus Christ, that ain't no kinda word to be teachin a baby!"

"TY!" Danny hurled himself at the bed, all arms and legs and elbows, landing flat on top of his brother and hugging him in the awkward, brutal way that boys hug other boys they love. Maybe it hurt, but Ty didn't notice. He locked his arms around the boy and pulled him even tighter. Danny winced a little, though he tried to hide it, and Ty felt the bandages under his shirt. "You been shot!"

Danny smiled. "Naw. Just a cracked rib when they kick me. Ain't nuthin."

Ty scowled. "When WHO kick you, man?" be demanded.

Danny only smiled again. "Don't matter. My heart ain't busted."

Ty studied his brother carefully, then kissed his cheek. "Yeah. Your heart be warm an strong an black, man." He added a kiss to Danny's notched ear. It was good to see the boy blush. Then he noticed that Danny's lips were almost healed and that the bruises on his face had faded.

Markita came over with J'row in her arms. She was smiling happily, but looked tired, like she hadn't slept much. "So how you feelin... boy?"

Ty tried to wet his lips with a dry tongue, feeling them crack when he smiled in return. "Okay... girl." His voice sounded like sandpaper. "Thirsty," he added.

Markita's smile brightened even more. "Just like the doctor say you be. I get you some orange juice." She turned, about to set J'row back on the floor.

"Put him here," said Ty, pushing the covers off his chest as Danny stood up.

Markita gave him the little boy. Tiny fingers, warm, sticky, and perfect, grasped Ty's, then found the little silver medallion and jingled it on its chain.

Danny slipped the Popsicle between Ty's lips. It tasted way past good. "Gots any beer?" Ty called to Markita.

Danny snickered. "Yo! Now we know he okay for sure. Word!"

Markita turned, frowning slightly. "You... ain't gonna keep on drinkin, Ty?"

Ty smiled, getting his lips used to it again. "Not like I done."

"Mmm." Markita opened the fridge and took out a can of Bud. "Doctor prob'ly have a cow, but it likely do you more good than orange juice right now."

Danny laughed. "He give you a testicle shot, Ty. In the butt!"

"You mean tetanus."

"Yeah. For cause why?"

"For cause rabies."

Markita came back with the beer. "Ty gots no probs with his balls."

Ty felt his face flush, but there was pride in Danny's eyes.

"Yo, *memsaab,* I have me a *pombe* too," said Danny.

"Huh?" said Ty.

"That Swahili for a beer an a lady you spect. Doctor dude talk like that all the time."

"Oh." Ty didn't insult the boy's dignity by saying okay.

Markita handed him the beer and went back for another.

Ty studied Danny's face once more. "How long it been? Almost seem like a kinda bad dream."

"Three days," said Markita, returning. "It Sunday mornin." She gave Danny the Bud and glanced out the window. "Even this goddamn city look a little better on Sunday mornins. It my day off. Mom in church."

Ty sipped beer. It opened his throat and tasted as good as the Popsicle.

"Got some soup ready for you too," Markita added. "Make it up myself."

Ty smiled. "Chicken, right?"

"Course. Everbody know chicken soup be the thing when you

sick."

Danny snorted, sipping his Bud slow, like Ty. "Shit! Somebody oughta cook up bout a zillion gallons an feed it to the world!"

Ty gave Markita an uneasy glance. "Um, what church your mom go to?"

"That big ole churchy-lookin one with the steeple, bout six blocks over. Why?"

"Oh," said Ty, feeling relieved. "Nuthin." He considered, watching J'row play with the medallion. "Guess if God ain't everwhere, He ain't nowhere. But you still gotta look for Him."

Markita gave Ty a look of speculation. "Mmm. Spose that sound right enough. Now, for sure you feelin proper, Ty? I mean, you been talkin out your head for most three days... angels an stuff."

"Lions an werewoofs too, man," added Danny.

Markita nodded. "Course, doctor say you likely gonna do that, what with all the blood you lose an the infection fever."

"Um, I sorry, Ty," said Danny. "I give you that affection."

"It cool, man," said Ty. "Gonna get some, best it come from my own brother." Ty glanced at his arm. "Ain't there a law say doctors gotta report all gunshot wounds?"

Markita shrugged. She sat down on the bed. One hand went to Danny's shoulder, the other stroked J'row's curls. "Used to be a law sayin we gotta ride the ass end of buses too. My mom always say they get more laws everday, an less justice. Sides, I told you bout this doctor bein from South Africa. Best believe he know the difference tween a law an the right thing to do!"

"But how I pay for all this fancy-ass bandage shit an shots? Man gotta live, don't he? He live round here, for sure he can't be rich."

Danny grinned, digging in his pocket and pulling out a wad of bills. "Yo! Curtis come over next mornin. Give us five bucks, man!"

"Curtis?"

"The little dude with the dreads."

Markita looked sad. "Poor kid. He been comin here everday. Stay a while. Seem like he crazy or something always talkin bout lions in Jamaica."

"Lyon was his homey," said Danny. "Lyon, with a y. He the dude what help me. Make the plan to save your ass when it woulda been a lot easier just to do us both fore takin out Deek."

"Yeah," said Ty. "That woulda been the coolest way."

"Curtis one grade down from me, but I gots him in PE. I used to figure him an Lyon was homos, for cause Lyon was always so... I don't know, gentle, I spose I mean. Course, for sure he weren't that night! Maybe he was on somethin? He was drunk most of the time, but only Curtis knew."

"Maybe it was love?"

Danny thought a moment. "Yeah, I guess that could do it. Anyhow, Curtis always talkin up how him an his folks gonna move to Jamaica someday, when they save emselfs back enough bucks. Now Curtis tellin everbody that Lyon already gone there. That a island somewheres, ain't it?"

"Yeah," said Ty. He looked up at Markita. "What bout them other kids? What happen, after?"

"Well, they help me bring you here. It seem best, bein only a block away." She snagged a paper off the coffee table. "Made page four next day. Same ole shit bout gang violence, an how all gangs should be busted up."

Ty snorted. "Be like tryin to bust up them Little Rascals."

Markita shrugged. "Seem like nobody out there see it that way. Or know what happenin in places like this. Everbody blamin it on the drugs an guns... like the doctor say, treatin the symptoms stead the disease. Anyways, that black cop sucker never know he owe his life to *you*... for what it worth. He been s'pended till some sorta 'vestigation done... somethin bout unproper procedures. But mostly the paper people screamin over that white cop gettin killed. Gonna be a big ole funeral. With honors." She offered the paper. "Wanna read it?"

Ty shook his head. "Wonder what kinda funeral they gonna give Turbo. Or Lyon. An what happen to them other two dudes, the fat boy and the little one?"

"Game-Boy an Tunk?" said Danny. "Weren't nuthin major bad. Doctor fix em right here. After you. Take the bullet out Game-Boy's chub. Shit, man, he even shake their hands! Say, where he from, kids younger than they be fightin! Say *'Uhuru!'*" Danny reached under the mattress and pulled out Ty's .45. "I take it all apart, Ty. Clean it total. Better'n new. Word! Score you new bullets too."

"He bought himself a gun book," said Markita.

Ty took the gun, but only because Danny seemed so proud. J'row dropped the medallion and reached for it. Ty frowned and laid it aside. "Mmm. Spose it words in a row. Maybe kids read more if it bout stuff relate to real-time." Then Ty smiled and gave Danny the gun. "Ain't sure now just what I gonna do with it. Maybe you get good at fixin our ole truck too."

Danny turned the big gun over in his small hands. "You ain't gonna stop fightin, Ty?"

Ty touched the medallion J'row had picked up again. "No, Danny. Word. But there other ways to fight this shit, man. You can't just go round shootin down every hungry kid dealin on the corners. Most of em wouldn't be if they had some kinda... a... "

"Option," said Markita.

Ty nodded. "Um, you figure Leroy talk to me bout that night school he goin to?"

"Course he would. Fact is, he just bout to graduate with his high school diploma. Gonna be quittin the King pretty soon to take a computer job." Markita hesitated. "Danny here been tellin me you a way past cool cook... if you call Burger King cookin."

"Ty ain't gonna wear him no goddamn lame little uniform!" said Danny. "We gonna score us that truck! Do us some real work!" He turned to Ty. "Huh, man? Markita tell me all bout it. Yo, Ty, me an her, we talk over all kinda shit these last days. We even went an did that uptown shoppin. Markita come an talk to Mom, tell her enough what it is so's not to worry. We even score stuff for the little kids too. Yo! We score us that truck, man. Believe! I help you after school." He flexed his thin arm. "Yo. Check it, Ty, I *need* me some buildin up! Course, you wanna go night school, that make me proud too."

Ty smiled. "Yeah? So what happen to chump change not bein cool?"

Danny shrugged. "Well, there cool, and there way past cool, Ty. So, fuck cool."

"Fuck coo," laughed J'row.

"Jesus, Danny!" said Ty.

Markita smiled. "Maybe I can get Leroy to program that into his Speak 'N Spell."

"Mmm," said Ty. "So how much of that five bucks we got us left, Danny?"

Danny's smile faded. "Only bout two. Spose that ain't enough for a truck, huh?"

"You needed them clothes, man. Same's all our brothers an sisters deserve nice stuff." Clumsily with his bandaged arm, Ty slipped off the medallion and put it on his brother.

"Here, man. This yours now. Might be some magic in it, who in hell know?"

There was a knock on the door.

Danny gripped the .45. "Motherfuckin cops been goin apeshit all over the hood!"

Finger to her lips, Markita rose and crossed quietly to the door. She peered through the peephole. Ty watched her face, but she only looked surprised. Shooting back the bolts, she pulled the door open. The Friends filed into the room, carrying their boards, Gordon leading, his eyes casually wary. There were four boys behind him, Ty saw. One was the small camouflaged kid. He wore his huge shirt open to show the white bandage, already grimy, around his ribs. Ignoring Markita—she was only a girl—they came over to the bed. Markita smiled and went to the fridge, returning with Buds for all. The kids accepted them by right, with murmured thanks.

Gordon yanked up his sagging jeans. "Yo, Ty. You cool now, man?"

Ty smiled and nodded. "I flash your sign if I knowed what it was."

Gordon shuffled his feet a moment. "Um, we ain't figured one out yet, man. It like, there only so much you can do with five fingers, y'know?" He took a gulp of beer. "Anyways, we come to, um, tell you thanks for savin our asses, man. Word! An Wesley, he say the same." He pointed out the window. "This, um, our ground now. Wesley trade us a block so's we get Tunk." He glanced at Markita. "We be watchin for dealers an shit." He turned back to Ty. "Yo, an Furball can join us, he want."

Danny looked at his brother. "Maybe part-time?"

Ty smiled. "That be cool. The right kind."

Curtis stood at Gordon's side. Gordon nudged him forward.

"Um," said the small boy. "We 'cide to give you this, man."

Ty stiffened slightly, seeing Deek's pouch. There were dark, rusty-colored stains on it.

"We took some," added Gordon. "Spenses. But there still most five grand." He shrugged and drained his beer can. "Yo! I mean, what the fuck *we* gonna do with all that buck? Stay drunk a year? Shit, then what good we be? Only scare hell out our parents, we give it to them. An just a lotta trouble, man, if word go round we gots mega-money!"

Ty accepted the pouch from Curtis. "Thanks, man." Then he met the small boy's eyes. "I sorry over Lyon."

Curtis only shrugged. "He in Jamaica now. I see him when I get there."

Ty nodded.

Gordon set his beer can on the coffee table. The other boys chugged theirs and did the same. One of the twins burped.

"Rac, you fucker!" bawled Gordon. "Say 'scuse me, asshole!"

"I'm Ric. 'Scuse me, asshole."

Gordon sighed. "Well, see you round, Ty. Um... maybe, sometime we need big-dude a'vice bout somethin, we ask ya, okay?"

"Believe, Gordon. Take care now, all you dudes."

The boys turned to go. Ty saw the little nickel revolver just showing under Curtis' shirt. "Yo. What happen to the Uzis?"

The small boy faced Ty once more and shoved the dreads out of his face. "We keep one. The Crew get the other. Number three hid by for 'mergencies in neutral ground. We make a rule over it."

Ty took the .45 from Danny. "I still might be needin me a gun sometime, but maybe this one be better for you. Danny here go all through it. Trade me, man?"

Slowly, Curtis pulled out the little revolver and fingered it. "Um... well, it hard to score bullets for this... an it pretty old."

"Aw, go for it, man," advised Rac. "Heart magic's cool, but there ain't very much of it goin round."

"Or comin round neither," added Ric. "Lyon-o woulda said you need a good gun."

Curtis turned to Danny. "You figure he woulda, man?"

Danny smiled. "Believe, homey. Just cause that's what it is."

"Okay, Ty." Curtis traded guns and stuffed the big pistol in the back of his jeans. Tunk helped him cover it. "Um, see you round, Ty," said Curtis. "An, thanks, brother."

The boys filed out.

"Maybe I'm a fool," said Markita as she closed and bolted the door. "But I think I gonna feel a little bit safer walkin home nights."

"You ain't no fool," said Ty. "Believe." He studied the bloodstained pouch in his hand. "Yo, Danny. You talk to Curtis. You find out how much more money his folks need for movin to Jamaica. I think he really find his Lion-brother there."

Danny considered that. "Naw. Prob'ly just some cool dude *like* Lyon. Hell, maybe there a lot of em in Jamaica. Or somewheres. I mean, he never really belong *here,* know what I sayin? Maybe he just finally got to go home?"

Ty glanced out the window. He heard skate wheels clicking sidewalk cracks. He looked over at his own board by the door. "Mmm. Maybe you right, Danny. But I wish there was more of em here... whatever they are."

Danny nodded, then took a last bite of Popsicle and a gulp of beer. "Yo, Ty! Know what? Grape Popsicle an beer sound like shit but taste way past cool!" He stared at his brother, then moved close. "Yo! Why you cryin now, man? Game over."

Ty took his brother's hand and smiled up at Markita. "Maybe it really just startin."

Jess Mowry was born in Mississippi in 1960 and raised in Oakland, California, by his father. Jess has been a drug-dealer's bodyguard, made his living collecting scrap metal, and worked in a center for street kids.

In 1988 he bought an Underwood typewriter for $8 and began writing. He is the author of more than eight books, several of which have been published or are forthcoming from Blue Works.

Bonus Features

It's not your favorite premium DVD. It's a Blue Works novel for young adults. We pack every Blue Works novel with "extras" because our books are created at premium quality — no wasteful mass-production, no newspaper print pages, no formula stories. With every purchase of a Blue Works novel you'll receive some or all of these incredible features:

Downloadable from our webcenter:

- A full-color poster.
- An extensive study guide written by the author.
- Deleted or extra scenes not found in the novel.
- A limited edition, official trading card for the book.
- A full-color bookmark, door-hanger and more.

By sending us your purchase receipt:

- An autographed Blue Card™. An archival-quality, deep blue, luminescent card hand-signed by the author.

www.windstormcreative.com/blueworks/

Blue Works
Attn: Bonus Features
c/o Windstorm Creative
7419 Ebbert Dr SE
Port Orchard WA 98367

For a partial listing of other great Blue Works novels, turn the page.

Blue Works Novels

Take 20% off every book at our webcenter. And while you're there download or request the first chapter of any book, and much more.

FICTION

And Featuring Bailey Wellcom as the Biscuit (Peggy Durbin)
Awakening Curry Buckle (Michael Donnelly)
The Brute (Mike Klaassen)
Makoona (John Morano)
Mrs. Estronsky and the UFO (Pat Schmatz)
Out There, Somewhere (John Morano)
The Pirate Queen (Christina Bauer)
Present from the Past (Janet & Mike Golio)
Puzzle from the Past (Janet & Mike Golio)
A Wing and a Prayer (John Morano)

SCIENCE FICTION & FANASTY

Menace Beyond the Moon (Ted Butler)
The Rune of Zachary Zimbalist,
The Connedim: Book One (Pamela Keyes)
The Legend of Zamiel Zimbalist,
The Connedim: Book Two (Pamela Keyes)
The Mythfits (Gary Goldstein)
On a Distant World (Joseph Yenkavitch)
Merlin's Door: Book One, Outside of Time series
(Wim Coleman & Pat Perrin)

See our webcenter for a complete list!